CAT SUMMER

The Cat Seasons Tetralogy: Book 1

by Mollie Hunt

Cat Summer
Copyright 2019 © Mollie Hunt
Cover Design Livia Reasoner
Fire Star Press
www.firestarpress.com

All rights reserved.
ISBN: 9781686753244

This is a work of fiction. The characters, incidents, and dialogues are products of the author's imagination and are not to be construed as real.

No part of this book may be used or reproduced in any manner whatsoever without written permission of the publisher, except in the case of brief quotations embodied in critical articles and reviews.

CAT SUMMER

Part 1

1. Tom

The room was dark when Lise awoke. For a moment, she was still in her dreams, the swirling not-quite-there impressions seeping over from the other side. Their content was with her, just out of reach behind a wind-blown blanket of night.

Rolling fields with a stage-prop sky. No dimensions, flat, matte, like a backdrop for a play. A wind passing through dry grass with the sound of insect wings. A soft black presence, oozing across the scene like oil, leaving adoration and terror in its wake. But it was nothing.

Sitting up in bed, Lise shook off her sleep-filled wanderings. Her mind was clear now, completely cognizant. She felt strong and alive, free from daytime distraction and acutely aware of things she would ordinarily have let pass by.

She sighed, inhaling the clear summer breeze that floated in through the open window. Sleep was out of the question. Tossing off the quilt, she rose. Her feet touched the silky carpet. Her slippers lay nearby but she ignored them. The night was warm, her body comfortable just the way it was.

For some reason, she didn't find it strange to walk naked from the room. She was alone in the big house—no one to see—but the thought never entered her mind. Her bathrobe remained at the foot of the bed, forgotten.

Lise paused by the open window, feeling the air brush across her body, smelling it as if it held clues, hints, and secrets of the hidden universe outside. She breathed deeply, allowing the delicious life-giving vapor fill her lungs. Things were going on out there in the wide night world. Like energy, it sizzled on the tip of her tongue.

Didn't snakes smell with their tongues? she considered briefly. And cats and dogs had a special gland for scent. People got the short end of the stick when it came to the senses.

The passing contemplation slipped away unresolved, leaving Lise staring, quiet-minded, down at the garden below. In the moonlight, she could pick out the luminescent spikes of Oriental lilies against the dark of the garage and the tiny pinpoints of daisies in the edging. It was one of those rare and glorious nights when everything was perfect. Temperature, texture, even the silent sky with its occasional sparkling planet throve with cosmic symmetry. It called to her secret soul; she must go out in it.

Down the narrow staircase she skipped, feeling lean and light as a thistle seed. This seemed totally natural though somewhere in the back of her mind lurked the vague remembrance of heaviness and discomfort, anxiety and tension, all the misery standard in the human machine. But that was another place and time; this was the real girl, the life force inside the trap of humanity, strong, quick, and blissfully unafraid.

The living room was veiled in darkness as she opened the hall doorway but in spite of the murk, she could see. Of course, it was her house—she designed it, arranged it, maintained it. No surprise she could navigate its twists and turns with eyes closed but there was no need. Whether it was the moonlight falling in shimmering shafts from the high windows or something more elusive, objects stood out bright as crystal. This was not light as Lise knew it—those clear harsh rays that blaze down from outside—but something subtler. An inner glow, as if each article had a luminescence of its own.

Without giving this phenomenon a second thought, Lise

started toward the back door but paused when she realized she wasn't alone. On the overstuffed couch, wedged in between a hillock of throw pillows, lounged Percy, a round-bodied kink-tailed tuxedo cat whose ice-green eyes and luxuriant fur spoke of his roots in the forests of Norway. The elderly feline liked that place and often slept there when he was not on the prowl. Finding him like that was nothing new.

On the carpet nearby, however, stood someone else—a great orange tabby Lise had never seen before. The tabby stalked toward her, halting at her feet. His eyes, like yellow lamp globes, seemed to quiz her innermost being.

"Who are you?" Lise asked as she bent down to pet the stranger.

"I am Evermore Artair Eckx," the tabby replied, rubbing his blunt head against Lise's proffered hand, then retreating to arm's length, just out of reach as cats do. "But you can call me Tom."

Lise was taken aback. She had heard him speak as clearly as anyone, but how could that be? Cats didn't talk!

At least, they had never talked to her before.

"What did you say?" she gasped in amazement. Tom chased an itch on his flank and blinked innocently.

Lise turned her questions to her own companion, Percy, but he was napping. Both animals were thoroughly cat-like now; she must have been mistaken. *That's what I get for wandering around in the middle of the night when I should be safe in bed,* she mused.

"Okay, kitties," she said for her own satisfaction. "If you're going to ignore me, I'm leaving." The chirp of crickets was irresistible, calling her outside. Once again, she started for the back door, then turned. "And I think you should come, too," she told the tabby stranger. "You don't live here, you know."

"In time. In time," the orange cat purred back, and she could swear she saw one of the golden eyes wink.

There was no doubt in her mind he had spoken. Both felines

were staring at Lise with an intensity that stopped her in her tracks.

"What's with you two?" she asked, rather too loudly, as if the sound of her own voice could exorcize whatever demons were creating this hallucinatory chat. It must have worked, because again, the cats were silent as space.

Finally, Tom rose and stretched, first his front legs, then his back, one at a time. Lise recognized the familiar cat-aerobic. It was what cats did before they went away.

Suddenly, Lise felt a terrible sense of loss, as if she were letting something very important pass her by.

"Wait, kitty!" she called, running to the kitchen for the little tin of treats. She shook the can, rattling the hard bits inside, and instantly both cats were at her feet. Lise tipped the can onto the linoleum and received purrs of appreciation. She knelt and stroked them as they ate. The warmth of their fur was comforting and the strange feeling of sorrow began to ebb.

"Is that good?" she cooed.

"Yes, very," and "Thank you so much," came the polite responses.

"You're welcome," she began, then caught herself. "Hey, wait a minute."

But the cats' attentions were elsewhere. They spoke to each other now, sometimes in throaty mews and murmurs, and sometimes, Lise could swear they used human words. Either way, she seemed able to understand all they said.

"So what do you think?" Percy posed.

"Good eats," Tom answered, chowing down a few more morsels.

"About her, I mean," Percy insisted. "I have come to believe she is She Who."

"Of course you'd feel that way— she's your person. We of the Higher Order often develop strong ties with our cohabitors. To treat them without a modicum of loyalty would be rude. But She Who? You don't think you might be just a bit biased?"

"I do not think so," Percy declared. "I have been watching her for some time now. She is perfect."

"Too big." Tom shook his furry head like a lion. "And too clumsy. She could never make her way in our World. Why, I bet she can't even catch a mouse." Having confirmed that the food was gone, he stalked away, tail lashing.

"She will learn," Percy argued. "She is smart. And if her resolve is strong, the size can adjust."

"What if her resolve isn't strong enough? We have only a single chance. What if she quits, or fails halfway through? We need to know she can complete the task."

Percy moved to join the tabby. Sitting like mirrored statues, they scrutinized the girl.

Lise's mind was flying. The pair had spoken like people, but even though she was looking right at them, she couldn't see their sly cat lips move, couldn't detect any sign that they used their mouths to create the sounds she heard. Was it telepathy? Intuition? Her own personal insanity?

And what were they talking about? Size and strength and tasks to be fulfilled? It sounded like something out of a fairy tale. What could it mean?

"Unless we're sure, we should wait," Tom declared. "Wait till the next Tri-Night. We can't risk gambling on this furless hulk."

"Hey!" Lise protested but her objection was ignored.

"If we wait, we will remain bonded to Seh. How many of us will suffer, even die the final death and cross Beyond at the hands of its minions? I do not know about you, but I would rather not see what will happen if we do not move the plan forward. Besides," Percy went on, "what if Seh fulfills the prophecy? Then we will be trapped forever."

Tom frowned. "But can she do it?" he asked with quiet

challenge.

"She is here," Percy replied cryptically. "Is that not enough?"

Lise stood rigid as a redwood. Her mind was clicking off reasons why this couldn't be happening, but in her heart, she knew better. Her sanity told her to flee, but her feet refused to move; she was already too invested. As much as she might like to run back to bed and pretend it was all a dream, she wanted answers even more. Was it curiosity—the feline addiction—or something darker? Something non-human was surely at work.

"Who's Seh?" she put to the pair.

Percy turned his head toward Evermore Tom and squeezed his eyes in a cat smile. "See? She is already taking interest."

Tom didn't commit on the matter, instead, swiveling his soft marmalade ears like radarscopes. From outside came the far-off whistle of a train.

"We don't have much time, Parsifal. This is the Commencement of Tri-Night and the hours are short."

"Yes, we must go." Percy rose and padded over to Lise. "You must be brave, Cohabitor. We depend upon you."

That said, he sauntered to the cat door under the sink with his usual swagger, giving only a momentary glance toward his food bowl on the rug by the stove. Tom followed, tail like a banner. As he was about to nose his way through the flap, he turned and skewered Lise with his golden gaze.

"Are you coming, person?" he asked.

"Coming? Coming where?"

The cat pranced on ballerina feet. "The way has been cleared, and all is in order."

"But..." Lise sputtered, "how?"

The big cat disappeared through the door. "Listen," she heard him call back, "and follow."

Listen? she mused. *Listen to what?* But in spite of her doubts and a pang of better judgment, she tuned her ears to the great hum of the world.

At first, all she heard was the buzz of the city—the distant crash of garbage trucks; the passing of an occasional car—but suddenly, she picked out other sounds. The flutter of a moth's wings; the rasp of a wood-boring beetle in the old stump by the gate; the yowl of a cat.

Then another.

And another.

The chorus of meows crescendoed into a wild wail that called to her pagan soul. Taking a deep breath, Lise dropped to all fours as effortlessly as if she were born to it. She gave a guttural inhuman cry, and dove whiskers-first into the open, living night.

2. A Journey Begins

The three stood on the back porch, scoping out the periphery. Lise was aware of a million things happening around her. Nocturnal insects filled the air with the drone of gossamer wings. A family of raccoons was feeding in the garage. Mice scurried here and there throughout the garden. That last sound sent an odd shiver of craving down her supple spine. But most importantly, she sensed cats—hundreds of cats, all over town, silently making their way through the shadows.

She glanced at her companions and an odd sensation came over her, a brief flicker of prescience, as if the dimensions were shifting, but in a moment, it was gone. Percy and Tom were off in their own worlds as only cats can be while in another's company.

They sniffed the pungent breeze, shining their X-ray eyes through the black-on-black nightscape.

"We must go," Tom charged, his voice deep and rumbling, bespeaking authority. Percy hopped lithely off the porch to the ground below, but Lise hesitated, lost in myriad sensual stimuli.

"Where are we going?" she asked, batting at a mayfly.

Percy glanced back at her. "Never mind that, Cohabitor. It is not a matter of where."

"Don't you hear it beckon?" Tom called to Lise, halfway across the garden now.

"Do not you hear it?" Percy echoed.

"It's time! It's time!" came their twin decree as they sunk

under the boxwood hedge and disappeared from sight.

Lise felt instantly lost. She had balked, and her companions had left her all alone in this strange new night. Even if she'd wanted to go with them, now it was too late. Should she go by herself? There were dangers in the dark.

A little voice nagged that the prudent thing would be to go back inside where it was safe, but when she turned toward the looming shadow of the house, the stuffy, lifeless structure depressed her. She realized how much she didn't want to be indoors. There, in the garden, were countless marvels, adventures just waiting to begin. No, whatever she did, she wasn't going to turn back now.

Bounding down the steps into the cool grass, she began to pick up an unusual perception. Where her cat friends crossed the yard, they had left tracks; not footprints but something subtler. A diaphanous mist seemed to hang in the air where they had passed, ghostly pink and phosphorescent green. The colors drifted in and out, over the lawn and into the hedge where Percy and Tom had vanished. Lise could trace this trail as easily as Dorothy's yellow brick road. She leapt into the hedge without a thought of flying monkeys.

Instantly, Lise found herself in another world. Hidden by leafy filigree, the ground was cool and alive beneath her unshod feet. Everywhere was movement—the buzzing, breathing, calling song of nature. It was all around her, from the trees above to the worlds within worlds that dwelt in the earth below. She was connected to it all like a link in a living chain. Some were to hunt, some were to fear, and some were to balance, but each species had their place, and she had her place among them. She had never felt less lonely.

And there ahead of her, sheltered in the garden jungle, were Percy and Evermore Tom, quietly waiting.

"At last," Tom commented, sniffing the wind.

"Have you decided?" Percy inquired, his ice-green eyes narrowing with concern. "Will you commit yourself to our quest?"

"Yes, please!" cried Lise. "Take me with you."

"Then come, but be careful," Tom warned. "Our World is a very large place for tiny life-forms like you."

• • •

Tom, Percy, and Lise moved through the bushes and out across the open grass. Their steps were silent, displacing a minimum of dew from the cool soft blades. Tom, a natural leader, wound in and out with no apparent reasoning except for it being how it was done. Lise could see by the luminous trails that cats had passed that way for ages. *Where were they going?* In another moment, she was distracted by a sound, a scent, and her worries vanished. All that mattered was the ever-present, pulsing here-and-now.

The three passed beyond her garden line and moved out into the quiet residential lane. A ribbon of asphalt shimmered in the darkness as it wove up toward the hill park. How different on Lise's feet was the feeling of concrete, still warm from the summer day.

Lise didn't like the openness of the naked street. It made her nervous, as if a thousand hidden eyes were watching her every move, but before she could complain, Tom slipped off to the side. For the next while, they paralleled the road, slinking from bush to bush and darting across moonlit deserts of lawn. They traveled together but each in their own way, since no cat will yield to another except in the most dire of circumstances. Percy played it safe, rounding the gardens in the shadow of the shrubbery and only crossing bare ground when absolutely necessary. Tom was bolder, taking a straight track, dashing in and out of cover as it came. Lise hung behind the two, diverted by each new sound and sensation, but she kept their paths in sight so when they suddenly took a turn through a clematis thicket, she wasn't left behind.

Racing down the leafy tunnel, she managed to catch up with them, but it didn't take long for her to become distracted again. Life was overwhelming. She felt as if she were alive for the very first time.

Lise paused to sniff at a dried-up pond in someone's ornamental garden. The scent of fishy things clung to the mud like perfume.

"Come on, Cohabitor," Percy called, already almost two plots ahead. "There'll be time for that later," he added in a softer tone.

Reluctantly, Lise tore herself from the wonders of the creepy-crawly slime and continued on her way.

Every so often, they would pass through the territory of another cat. The markings were as clear as road signs, even though they would have been invisible to a human eye. It was as if a barrier of scent had been set around the perimeter, and woe be to those who would cross with malice in mind. Tom tried to skirt these bastions when possible—whether out of respect or fear, Lise didn't know—but every so often there was no way around. Then, Tom would commiserate with the master of the tract and hopefully come to an understanding. They were harmless pilgrims just passing by, after all. Most accepted Tom's white flag with little more than a sniff and a growl. But not all.

Lise sensed it as soon as she crossed the hidden line into the animal's domain; suddenly, she felt like the moth in the spider's web. The hefty black and white short-hair was perched on the porch step like the spider, his eyes glowing with polyhedron malice. Lise shrank into the shrubbery, but it was too late.

With the ferocity and single-mindedness of a tornado, the tomcat hurled his sturdy bulk toward Lise. She froze in terror, watching the rip-saw claws and the saber teeth closing fast. Jamming her eyes shut, she braced for impact. When it didn't come—the collision, the inevitable rending of flesh—she opened them again, just in time to see a fire-colored flash hit the big cat like lightning. As he crashed to the ground, Lise realized that the flash had been Tom.

The adversaries writhed, a two-headed eight-pawed monster rolling in the dirt and screeching like ripped metal. Lise was aghast. If she'd been her normal self, she would have doused the two with water to break up the contest—but she was far from normal, and had no idea how to end their battle.

"Go! Go! Go!" Tom called as he fleetingly emerged on top, only to be thrown back down by the bulk force of the black-and-white.

"Come, Cohabitor!" Percy cried when Lise didn't move.

She tore her eyes from the fray and looked at Percy with horror. "We can't just leave him."

"This is his fight," the old cat said. "It is the feline way. Now, come, or his pains will be for nothing." With that, Percy turned and was gone.

Lise knew he was right. Tom was fighting for their protection. With one swift backward glance, she made a dash across the yard and over the fence to safety. From behind a screen of rusty chicken wire, she and Percy watched for the outcome.

The opponents were locked in a deadly embrace. Tom clutched the black-and-white's back with his claws and mercilessly pummeled his stomach with strong back feet; the other was doing much the same. Every so often, fangs would sink through fur, and a fresh howl would assault the quiet neighborhood.

Suddenly, the back door of the house crashed open and a man clothed in only a dowdy undershirt and boxers appeared. He stomped onto the porch, as angry as either of the brawling cats. Grabbing a two-by-four from a pile of firewood, he lurched toward the fighters, bringing his cudgel to bear.

"Git, you durn critters! Git outta here!" he shouted.

Down came the crushing blow, only inches from the small bodies. Tom and the black-and-white sprang apart like seeds from a milkweed pod. Scampering at high velocity, the black-

and-white dashed into the house and Tom leapt for the fence.

The man shook the board menacingly. "Don't come back, y'hear!" he roared at Tom. Clearing his throat noisily, he tramped back inside, slamming the door behind him.

"Are you alright?" Lise asked the panting Tom who had collapsed on the grass once he'd made it to safety. There was a bloody gash above his right eye, and his fur was matted with spittle where the black-and-white had chewed into his neck.

Rising stiffly to a sitting position, he licked his paw and ran it over the cut on his face. He repeated this action until he was satisfied the wound was clean. He smoothed a few of the nastier spots on his marmalade coat with his sandpaper tongue and then looked at his cohorts.

"That was a bad one," he sighed. "Remind me not to come this way again—at least, not unless I'm better prepared," he added darkly, staring with unveiled hostility at the fateful yard. "Now we must hurry, or we'll be late." With that, he stood as if nothing had happened, and trotted off across the grass, Percy in tow.

"Late for what?" Lise asked, but Tom and Percy gave no answer. Resigned to her ignorance, she followed.

After crossing another few yards, the trio came to an old wood-frame garage. Tom ducked beneath a foundation beam and up into the dark musty space inside, Percy and Lise behind him.

Lise was glad they were safe from the attack-cat, but she sensed that this place held a different kind of threat—the hidden enemy that pounced from the eves; the needle teeth of gutter rats. This time, though, instead of being afraid, the thought excited her. There was magnificent danger everywhere.

Turning a corner, she heard a shuffling sound accompanied by an appalling stench.

"Pew!" Lise blinked her sensitive eyes at the palpable smell.

"Possum," Percy told her. "Stay away from them."

"Why?"

"Because they're stupid, short-sighted, and vicious," Tom huffed. "They smell bad, defecate anywhere they like, and over-breed until half die of starvation. They have no brains. No brains at all."

"And they bite," Percy added with a knowing nod. Lise got the picture.

Crossing the dirt floor, they came to a second room, walled off from the rest of the garage by ancient, moldering planks. The sound of rushing water rose from somewhere beneath the floor. Lise spied the round metal plate of a long-forgotten manhole and realized they must be in old Mr. McDorgal's shed, a few blocks from her home. A run-off creek had flowed there before the city built up around it and encapsulated its sprightly gush in subterranean ducts.

Another surge of prescience came over Lise when she stepped into the tomb-like chamber. It was similar to her experience in the garden but more defined and undoubtedly more distasteful, as if watching predators gnawing at a corpse. She looked at the others, but they seemed oblivious. Tom had completed the perimeter of the small room and now sat on the damp dirt, arranging his tail around him. Percy did the same except for the tail because his had a natural kink that went only one way.

"Why are we stopping?" Lise asked, nervously pacing back and forth. She didn't like that place, and sought to get out as soon as possible.

Once again, she got no answer. She was tiring of this shrouded silence and thought indignantly about going on alone, but she gave in and waited, listening to the echo of the unseen stream and trying to quell her fear.

Aside from themselves, this room seemed devoid of life, and that bothered Lise. There should be something—a mouse or a few brown wood spiders. She could no longer smell the possum, and although she had been repulsed its closeness, now she craved its reassuring presence. A feeling of complete desolation surrounded them, unholy and unnatural.

Then, at the very fringe of Lise's hearing came a sound, at first nothing more than a heartbeat, then breathing and soft footfalls. Around the wall slipped another cat, a long-haired silver male with piercing blue eyes. Slate colored stripes and whorls crisscrossed his powerful body, making him seem to disappear and reappear as he slunk in and out of the shadows.

Tom rose slowly, muscles tense. The two began to circle, heads down, ears back. Lise was afraid there was going to be another fight, but suddenly the silver male plopped onto his haunches and began biting furiously at his fur.

"Darned fleas," he exclaimed. "I almost look forward to the cold season just to be rid of them."

"It's that long fur," replied Tom, reseating himself nonchalantly. "Makes you a pleasant place to roost."

"Says the cat with the crewcut," the silver sassed back. "I wouldn't be seen in public if I looked like you.

"How are you doing, Evermore, you old furball?"

"Fine, Master. Fine. Pleased you could make it."

Briefly, they touched noses and the tension in the room evaporated. Percy edged out of the corner and joined the group.

"Parsifal! The old mouser, himself. I should have known you would be here, too."

The silver raised his head and sniffed the air. "But there is something else... Someone else..." He skewered Tom with his weird-colored eyes. "Is it...? Has she...?"

"She has come." It was Percy who answered, and as he did, he brought Lise from the shadows. "Master, may I present Aliselotte Humankind, Homo sapiens," he announced formally. "Cohabitor, this is Aragdu dela Dominic, Felis domestica, and a very important one."

"Yes, very important!" Dominic blustered jovially. "If I do say so, myself." Like a lion, his booming roar resonated between the wooden walls.

Lise had thought Tom was big, but this cat dwarfed him. She was, at once, drawn to and afraid of this massive feline presence, but he seemed friendly—at least for now.

"Pleased to meet you," she said politely, but didn't waste any time retreating back to the wall a little behind Percy, whom she trusted implicitly.

After all, he was her cat.

And she was his human. She had never really thought of it that way before.

She felt a soft tap and realized she had been wool-gathering. Tom and the master cat were bent deep in conversation, again discussing this mysterious Seh.

"Seh's evil is growing stronger by the day," Dominic was saying. "We must be very careful."

"Then it's agreed?" queried Tom.

Dominic nodded. "We shall do as you recommend. I'll inform the others." He came around to Lise and stepped forward with an unexpected bow. "Thank you, Aliselotte."

"For what?" she asked doubtfully.

"Our World needs you badly," was all he said before he was gone.

"What's he talking about? What does he mean?" She eyed her companions, first Percy, then Tom. In their round gaze, she could see respect, concern, and more than a little fear.

Finally, Tom spoke. "Soon, human, you will know things you never cared to. But now it's time to travel. Much must still be arranged tonight."

Lise stood her ground. "What must be arranged? And why won't I like it?" she asked. "I'm not going anywhere until I get some answers."

Tom and Percy exchanged helpless glances.

"She's yours— you deal with her," Tom charged. "I have other things to do."

With a movement only a cat could execute, he slipped in

between the rotting boards of the wall and vanished.

Percy looked so despondent Lise almost felt sorry for him. Her nagging questions had embarrassed him in front of his peers. But even so, she was not about to acquiesce, not until she knew what was making her feel so strange.

Percy sensed her mind and sighed. "You see, Cohabitor, it is like this..."

He was interrupted by a sound, a strange rumble that grew louder and more tumultuous by the second. Percy stopped midsentence while they both turned to the utility hole where a violent spout of steam hissed up through the cracks. Before they could react, the whole thing blew, sending the thick metal lid flying into the eaves only to crash back down very near to where Percy crouched in terror. The heavy disk bounced as easily as a tin plate, sending the old cat scrambling.

"Let's get out of here!" he yelled to Lise, who stood rooted. "Come on! Before it is too late!"

But Lise had other plans. She waited, letting the tempestuous steam vent around her. Something told her this would be the answer to her queries, or at least, to some of them. Although she was afraid, her greater fear was not knowing what she was up against.

By now, white flames had begun to belch from the open hole, carrying with them the stench of burning flesh. Something was emerging. A shape, indistinct through the cold flames, but large—very large. It heaved its bulk like a sausage through a grinder until its bulbous head touched the low beams. Lise watched in the ghost-light, trying to make sense of what she saw, but it was impossible; she had no reference point. The closest she could come was pure evil.

Slowly, the monstrosity revolved its luminescent mass until its eye, great and seeping, was fixed upon Lise. She could see a flicker of consciousness as it registered her presence. Then recognition was replaced by raw fuming hatred as it burst from its hollow with a barbarous scream.

"Cohabitor!" It was Percy. He hadn't run out on her after all. "Come! Now!" he ordered, and this time, she complied.

Bounding across the room and leaping through a gap in the plank wall, they tumbled over the foundation into the dew-covered weeds outside. They didn't stop there, but streaked through the unkempt yard and up the footpath that led to the hill park. Without slowing, Lise shot a glance back at Mr. McDorgal's shed. From inside, a sickly greenish light oozed between the boards.

What was that thing? But in her mind, Lise knew. It was corruption—blatant and deadly. And it had to be stopped before it swallowed the earth and everything on it. She knew also, no matter how much she tried to deny, that it would be up to her. That was the reason she had been brought into this wild new World.

3. The Saga of Seh

"That was close!" Percy gasped between breaths.

He and Lise had hightailed it to the hill park and collapsed at the edge of the soft lawn where the Hydrangea branches lent cover. Although they had put a running kilometer between themselves and the incubus, they both took solace in knowing they couldn't be readily seen.

"My God," Lise panted to her companion. "What was that? Wait— let me guess. That's your enemy, Seh, or whoever it is that we're supposed to be fighting."

"That was only a servant of the beast, but yes, Cohabitor, you have just encountered the enemy. I hope it encourages you to appreciate our problem."

"Please, Percy, I wish you'd call me Lise. It's my name, you know," she added softly.

Beneath the tuxedo fur, the old cat blushed. "I know it is, but names are personal. It is not proper to speak them without invitation."

"Well, I'm inviting you."

Percy gave a quick but formal blink. "Then, I am honored."

Lise flopped over onto her back to gaze at the stars. An errant birdcall split the night, but otherwise the park was quiet. For a while, the two lay lost in their musings.

"Don't you think it's about time you tell me what's going on?" Lise finally asked.

At first, Percy was silent, then he skewered her with his ice-green gaze. "Do you believe in evil?"

The question caught her off guard. "I suppose so. Bad things happen, that's for sure. I try not to think about it."

"Some things that happen are beyond bad—they are pure malevolence. To understand what I am about to tell you, you must first accept that this dark power exists."

Lise wavered, then nodded.

With a sigh, Percy began his tale.

"There once was a time," he said, his soft voice rolling like ocean swells on the cool air, "when our World was small and safe—when all living things cohabited peacefully, sharing the abundance of the earth. The Equilibrium, history calls it. It is remembered as a remarkable age."

"Sounds nice," Lise pondered.

"Do not misunderstand," he snorted. "The lion never lay down with the lamb as some would have you believe. Those two are natural enemies and their conflict is part of the balance. But each species took only what it needed and no one dominated another. There was no hatred or genocide in those days. We thought such a World would last forever."

Percy rose on his haunches and peered off into the night, his eyes narrowing to crescents as he glimpsed another, father place.

"Then, something happened. No one knows exactly what, because there are no chronicles of that time, only of the periods before and after. It was as if all living things fell into a deep trance-like sleep. When they awoke, there were weapons, disease, and unwholesomeness they had never known. That was when the servants had begun to appear." A shudder ran down his spine, lifting his fur into a ridge of fear.

"No one knew where these abominations originated until they began to encounter an amalgam of evil that called itself Seh.

As time went by, Seh's infamy grew, and so did its following. Thus began a chain of mutations in the Equilibrium. Beings started to deviate from nature. The newcomers were a violent breed, with no respect for the symmetry of life. With the onset of Seh's presence, the quality of our World began to alter before our eyes."

Lise could tell this was hard for her old friend. At seventy-six seasons, he must have seen his share of change.

"What did you do?" she asked with concern.

"Felis is strong. We adapted without losing our integrity. We used our wits to become what we are today, but others didn't fare as well. Those who fought the change were condemned to die in their bowers—honorable deaths, but dead all the same, and extinction is a high price to pay for pride. Those who embraced the new age thrived, but at great sacrifice. In trade for prosperity, they lost the ability to evolve beyond what they had become— the demon emissaries of Seh." He sank into a sphinx position, tucking his front paws tightly underneath the white of his chest. "I cannot imagine giving up my dignity to be a witless breeding machine whose stink permeates all creation," he hissed.

"You mean like the possum?"

"Yes, like them and others. The cockroach; the urban squirrel..." At that last, the old cat hunched nervously, watching the new moon arc across the southwestern sky. Lise followed his gaze, but sensed no malice. Whatever his issue, it was of another world.

Lise had never heard a history like this one, but she sensed its inner truths, her mind always coming back to the demons of Seh. "Where do we—human beings, I mean—fit in?"

Percy broke his dark reflections. "Where humanity goes, so follows our World. Seh influences humanity; humanity influences all other species. This should be humanity's war."

"Is that why I'm here?" Lise asked in a flash of cold insight.

"Yes. Only a member of the human species can defuse Seh's hold and reinstate the balance of nature."

"You keep talking about Seh. Who exactly is he?"

Percy gave her an ambiguous stare. His eyes squeezed shut, as if to summon a force from within.

"Not a who," the old cat told her slowly. "A what. The beast, Seh, is not a single being but many facets of one thing—evil. Seh has the power to unite our baser natures into servants of its own cruel whim. Its vicious influence causes immeasurable harm."

Lise turned over and looked at her companion. "I'm not sure I understand."

"I will give you an example. Say a being may kill to survive, and even enjoy the killing if it satisfies his needs—that is instinct. But evil perverts natural instinct until the killing urge is no longer about survival, but about power, gain—sometimes even pleasure. Do you recognize this inclination in your species?"

Lise thought about it. The warm night and the vast star-speckled sky made it hard to contemplate cold-blooded murder, but she knew what Percy said was true.

"Why was I selected?" she asked after a bit. "I have no special gift."

"You will do what is needed when the time comes."

"But why me? And why now? It sounds like this evil influence has been around for a while."

"Oh, yes, since your story began. Actually, we cats have not done badly for ourselves. Caffre, the First One, taught us: Endear yourselves to humans and you will survive—because they will. Humans are the most ruthless of the higher forms, and the most glorious, even though you tend also to be the most susceptible to the hypnotic will of Seh."

"You paint a bleak picture of my kind," Lise protested.

"I do not mean to," the old cat faltered. "Humans achieve great things. We would all be like you if given the choice."

Lise was surprised. "Really? Why?"

Percy shot her a look of incredulity. "Because human beings are different from all other life," he explained. "You survive not only through sustenance, but also through self-interest. You consume, yet create. Art, music, literature—no other species honors our Originator in such a unique and gracious way."

A dark look crossed Percy's face and his whiskers twitched as if they sensed something drawing near. "But now, humanity grows less respectful of our World and more charmed by Seh's false promises. We are afraid that, in time, you will turn your creativity to the darkness. That would mean the end of life as we know it."

Lise contemplated the ruthlessness of her people. The way they consumed the world around them like locusts on wheat; the way they spread like a virus, breeding as wantonly as the possums; the way they, for no reason but spite of nature, poisoned the very things that nourished them the most. She had never understood that penchant for destruction. Even the most humble of animals knew better than to foul their own nest.

But humans lived in proud oblivion. In this, Lise had always been different. She was never able to shake the feeling that things needed to change.

She caught Percy eyeing her intently. "I see you have answered your first question."

Lise looked at him without comprehension.

"Why it must be you," he prompted softly.

"Oh...yes," she mused. "I suppose I've known all along." Suddenly, she sighed with relief, finally recognizing that her difference held purpose.

"As to why we have not yet taken a stand against Seh," the old cat went on, "the time was not yet right."

"And now it is?"

"Yes. This is a special phase we call Tri-Night."

"I remember you and Tom talking about Tri-Night when we first met in my house. I mean, met like this." She gestured to her feline form.

"Tri-Night comes only at odd intervals and will not occur again for many seasons. We must seize the opportunity while it is at hand. But Tri-Night is short, only the three turns of the moon as the name implies. There is no time to waste."

"I guess I'm as ready as I'll ever be. So what do we do next?"

"I cannot tell you that."

"Why? Because it's a secret?"

"No," he purred, "because I do not know. But you possess that knowledge."

The dawning awareness that this might be the case gave Lise chills. She had long wished for change, but she had never imagined she might be the instrument of it, one small girl against billions.

"Come, let me show you something." Without waiting for a reply, Percy uncurled his graceful body and set off toward the far side of the hill park. Lise followed, though her mind was elsewhere.

As they moved toward the perimeter of the park, the underbrush grew denser. There were no cement trails here, no benches or marked viewpoints. The telltale sign of humanity—scattered garbage and cigarette butts—dwindled the farther in they went. It was as if this sector was off limits to the picnicking families and cursing cruising teens.

Stands of tall Douglas fir and jack pine reached their gray-green branches skyward, weaving a thick canopy high above. In their sanctuary, blue currant grew in profusion. Lise and Percy made their way along a needle-cushioned path no wider than a raccoon's breadth until they came to a high cedar fence.

Percy stopped and stared. "What do you suppose is on the other side of this boundary?"

Lise considered a minute. "I guess it would be the Fairfield district. Some nice little houses, but a bit too contemporary for my taste."

"And why the wall?" he went on.

"Well, if I remember correctly, it was put up to stop the local kids from sneaking in at night to vandalize the park. Now the only way is the front gate, and it's closed and locked at dark."

"So the fence is here to protect the park from what is outside."

"That's right— a few kids at that rebellious age."

"But aside from these hoodlums, it is a residential district? A nice residential district I think you said."

"Yes." Lise couldn't guess what he was leading up to.

Percy moved close to the cedar planks and cocked a tufted ear. "But listen, listen carefully. Then tell me what you think about the world beyond."

Lise stalked up to the fence and leaned near the rough and pungent boards. At first, she heard only the hum of the city punctuated with normal night sounds, but as she concentrated, she began to pick out something beyond the mechanical buzz.

Animal calls. Calls she should never have heard in Fairfield.

The shriek of a night hawk; the coo of a dove; the pulsing screech of cicadas in the trees; the howls of a wolf pack. Coyotes laughing in the distance.

Scents of wilderness drifted through on the night breeze as well. Musk and moon flower, evening primrose and creosote bush. Perfumes that had no business being there. Lise was dizzy with unformed desires.

"I don't understand," she stammered, pulling away from the untamed fury.

"Would you like to see?"

Lise nodded, breathless. Percy smiled at her courage and began to slink down the hill, staying near the strange metamorphic fence. The unexplainable sounds continued to drift through from the other side.

How could it be? Lise questioned her own senses. A cat call maybe, or even a misguided owl—but a cougar's cry?

They came to a half-broken board. Lise thought Percy was going to slip on through, but instead, he seated himself comfortably on a cushion of pine needles, his green eyes locked on Lise. Evidently, this show was meant for her. She took a careful step up to the rift and timidly peeked in.

Lise couldn't believe her eyes as she stared into the magnificent wilderness. The night was alive with nocturnal species— not mice, rats, and possum as should have been in this locale but something else completely.

A rattlesnake slithered across a patch of cool glassy sand. A pack rat awaited its prey. A wasp and a tarantula fought a grizzly battle, the outcome of which would mean either death for the wasp or an even grimmer fate for the spider as its conqueror buried her eggs in the paralyzed but still-living body. It was a savage world, and it had no place here. Lise turned back to Percy for explanation.

"Does it scare you?" he asked instead.

"Of course," she replied. "All those wild and brutal creatures? I'd have to be dead not to sense the danger."

"But is it really any more treacherous than the world you thought you would see?"

"What, you mean Fairfield?"

He nodded. "Think about it."

"But I—" she began.

"Think with your heart," he told her, his voice resonant with solemnity.

She didn't understand, but she closed her eyes just the same, trying to picture the two disparate worlds simultaneously. In her mind, she conjured up the suburban neighborhood. Rows of cardboard houses with shiny new gas-guzzling fume-belching

SUV's parked in the driveways. Castrated petunia gardens drenched with pesticides and poison that ran unchecked into the water system. Concrete and asphalt entombing the natural land. And of course, children whose favorite pastime was befouling the small woodlands of the park. Glancing again at the strange but organic beauty of the desert scene, she was unsure which of the two seemed more threatening.

"In the world you know," Percy said, "this fence is here to keep intruders out of the park. But what you are seeing with your new eyes..." Percy gestured toward the missing plank, "...is a different World, one of wild creatures who still follow the rules of nature, untainted by Seh. For them, the fence is here to keep you out. You and your Fairfield District are more deadly to them than they could ever be to you."

Percy's statement pierced Lise's mind like a splinter — uncomfortable, painful even, yet no matter what she did, she couldn't get it out.

"Do not look so glum, Cohabitor. Because of you," Percy said confidently, "all that is about to change."

The old cat seemed so sure things would be alright. Lise wished she could share his faith but she was overrun with doubts. "How am I supposed to fight something strong enough to have created all this chaos?"

"Ah, but there is the key!" Percy countered. "Seh cannot create, nor can it control free will. The power of the beast only works to influence living beings. Once you have expelled that influence, the balance will be restored. At least, we hope it will," he added, though softly as if speaking to himself.

"I don't know..."

"Yes, you do," Percy challenged, back to smiling his enigmatic smile. Somehow, that made her feel better.

The slightly off-tune warble of a robin cut through the cool air, not from the savage wilds on the other side of the fence but from above them in the dark green pines. Lise looked back across the park and realized that a slim band of fire had topped the eastern horizon, carving the earth from the heavens with its golden scythe. A scattering of ominous gilt-edged storm clouds heaved along the skyline, foretelling rough weather, but they were very far away.

Morning? Already? she thought in disbelief.

"We must move on," Percy said.

He rose and stretched, first his front legs and then his back and his lopsided tail. When he was sufficiently limber, he began to amble in a downwardly direction. Lise followed, her questions evaporating with the morning mist as she fell into step beside him.

4. A Dangerous Breakfast

The sky was magnificent. Lise couldn't remember ever seeing such hues. From softest apricot to brilliant mauve, the splendid radiance cast first light upon the sleeping town. Of course, she reminded herself, she was not often up at this wee hour. Still, she did know what a sunrise looked like; this calliope of color was all that and more.

Lise and Percy sauntered leisurely through the purple shadows as if they had no cares in the world; as if they hadn't been stalked by a monster from the abyss the night before; as if the balance of their World did not rest on their furry shoulders. But that was the feline nature, to take things in stride. The sun was sending tentacles of warmth across the city and the long cold night was over. For now.

Winding through deserted morning streets, across fences and through dew-sprinkled yards, they finally returned home. Resting on the porch where their adventures had so recently begun, they gazed out over their own little corner of the globe.

"Well," Lise commented. "What now?"

Percy was silent. His ice-green eyes traveled back and forth across the garden but he wasn't worried. His charge had gone into the perilous night, had met the enemy, and had lived. That wasn't bad for a start.

"What now, kitty?" Lise repeated, thinking he might not have heard.

The old cat gave her a disapproving scowl. "You are my

cohabitor and my friend, but I would prefer you use a more respectful appellation than 'kitty'."

"I'm sorry, Percy, I didn't realize that offended you. But it's not easy, you know—one minute, you're my kitty cat, then the next, we're co-conspirators in a world war."

"The feline psyche adapts," the old cat pronounced.

"I'm beginning to realize just how much."

Lise wasn't exactly sure what had happened to her in the past six hours, but she didn't feel the least bit afraid. An unusual confidence had come over her, infusing itself into every fiber of her being. She felt keen and strong, smart and able. She felt like she could deal with anything that came her way.

And if what the cats had told her was true, she might soon have to tap into that power. The prospect gave her pin-pricks of dread, but also a thrill. Never before had she felt so alive.

"Where's Tom?" she asked, suddenly curious about their third companion.

"Oh, he is nearby. You see that big chestnut tree at the end of the lane? The red roof line? That is his residence, but he does not spend much time there. He is somewhat of a statesman, always on the go."

"A statesman?"

"That is the best I can describe what Evermore does for our World. His is a service, an obligation that pledges his soul." Percy smiled. "You did not know cats could be so honorable, did you?"

"I always thought more of cats as independent," Lise admitted.

"Selfish, you mean."

"Maybe self-centered," she defined. "Not overly interested in the business of others."

"That is true, to a point. There are many rules to the grand scheme of feline things. Rules of territory and ownership. Rules of strength. Rules of breeding. For the most part, we are very singular, but there is a basic precept that, above all else, our World must survive."

"And now that World is threatened."

"Yes," Percy said. "These are exceptional times."

The morning sun lapped at the brick-red paint of the porch. It was full day now and the sky had traded its dawn rainbow for a deep and brilliant blue. With a sweep of his crooked tail, Percy rose and marched into the old house through the cat door. After a moment, Lise came, too.

She still wondered what would happen next. The strange night was over and it was morning; shouldn't she be doing something other than playing with Percy and watching the sun glaze lacy patterns across the garden? But she couldn't remember. And somehow, she didn't really care.

Percy was at his food bowl on the mat by the stove crunching away at what was left of his dry food. She came up behind him and gazed at the brown chunks of kibble, realizing she was hungry, too.

Percy turned his head and hissed a solemn warning.

"Sorry," she said, stepping back. "It doesn't look very appetizing, anyway," she added, though her stomach was grumbling.

Percy lapped at his water and finished off with a quick face wash, licking his paw and passing it across his elegant whiskers. When done, he smoothed his chops one last time and smiled contentedly. Then he saw Lise.

She was crouching dejectedly in the corner, looking very unlike the hero he needed her to be. Realizing how unprepared she was for life in the cat-lane, he went to her and touched her nose with his.

"Hungry?" he asked.

"Yes," she said dismally.

"Okay, come on. Let's see if we can find you something to eat."

The two exited the house and resumed their place on the porch. Once outside, Percy began to sniff the air pensively. Soon enough he caught a scent and was off like a streak across the lawn.

"Come on," he called back at Lise. "I cannot do it for you."

She jumped off the porch after him, wondering dubiously what he had in mind.

He was sniffing at a tangle of honeysuckle vines. Suddenly he pounced. Out from the thicket burst a tiny gray shape. The creature was running for its life, straight toward Lise.

"Get it, get it!" he called, but he need not have bothered. Something in Lise's being took over and she was on that mouse in a heartbeat.

It was unlike anything she had experienced, an almost tangible lust for food. Certainly sitting down to the dinner table had never been like this. She could feel the prey squirm in her grasp. Visions of rending, biting, chewing flesh and bone burst through her mind. Eating! That was what she lived for. That was what her soul cried out to do.

But something was wrong. She just couldn't bring herself to kill the tiny animal. The mouse wriggled, and she loosed her hold, just for a second. Like lightning, the rodent bolted into the flower bed. Percy groaned with disappointment and frustrated desire.

"What did you do that for?" he asked gruffly. "I thought you were hungry."

"I was—I *am*, but not for that. It was too...alive."

"You did not want it? I would have gladly taken the little morsel if you had let me know."

"Percy, please," she begged. "Isn't there something else I can eat that isn't quite so...raw?"

"I left a few bites of kibble in my bowl. Ordinarily, I would guard them with my life, but under the circumstances, I suppose I could make an allowance. Yes," he added graciously, "You may have them,"

"Thanks," she reacted, touched by his generosity, "but I don't think so."

"Then what? You have to keep up your strength. We have big work ahead of us."

Lise tried to visualize something that sounded good to her but she came up at a loss. Her usual diet of vegetables, rice, and sweets from the bakery held no interest at all.

"Wait!" Percy cried, jumping up. "I think I know just the thing. Follow me, but be careful."

He sprung to the top of the fence and walked tightrope-style until he came to a cat path, made obvious by the multi-colored essences that drifted above it like rainbow fog. He hopped down lithely, turning to make sure Lise was behind him, then took off along the trail through the garden next door and on down the block.

Skirting a dilapidated tool shed, they came upon an ancient wire fence surrounding a vast unkempt yard, tall with weeds and grass tassels.

"Where are we?" asked Lise.

"An old person lives here," said Percy. "She puts food out every morning for her cohabitor, Woodrow. She does not realize that Woodrow has crossed Beyond."

"Her cat is dead?"

"Yes. His time came during the cold season. He went on his final journey and never returned. I suppose she still hopes."

Percy and Lise ducked through a hole in the netting and began their way across the jungle at a cautious pace.

"I'm starved. Let's hurry," Lise said, quickening her gate.

Percy swung around hissing. "Be quiet, Cohabitor. This is a dangerous place."

Lise shrunk flat into the grass. "You mean, more of those servants of Seh?" she whispered.

"No, not this time, but nearly as perilous. Come on, but silently."

They had cleared a small rise and could see the decrepit hulk of the house through the pigweed and teasels. The back steps had fallen down years ago, but a small portion of railing still jutted from the framework like a broken fang. Upon this precarious perch sat a gleaming saucer of fresh cream. On the porch below lay a huge black dog.

Lise gasped and Percy pulled her back into the cover of the tangled weeds. Her heart was racing. She felt a deep fundamental fear, more intense even than when she had met Seh's servant. Instinct, she told herself sternly. The racial memories of an eon of enmity between species. But logic was no help. All she could do was lie paralyzed, helpless, and panting on the stubbled knoll.

"You see the problem," said Percy. "But it can be done."

"I'm not going in there, no matter what," Lise was saying when her stomach gave out a very unladylike rumble. It seemed to be face the dog or starve, but still she couldn't choose.

"We can do this together," Percy told her firmly. "I will divert him while you sneak in behind and feed."

"Percy, you can't! It's too risky."

"I will be alright," the old cat assured her. "Blackie is even older than I am. He is nearly blind and has pains in his joints. But be fast, Lise," Percy cautioned. "Blackie is predictable. He will chase me for a ways but he tires quickly and then he will head back for a nap. When that happens, you must be ready to flee. Now, watch my lead—you will know what to do."

With breath deep and eyes wide, Percy lifted his kinked tail in the air and stalked directly toward the sleeping mongrel. It didn't take long for the dog to sense his presence. A wrinkled black eyelid began to rise, an onyx pupil focusing as awareness oozed across the animal's brain.

Like an aged firebolt, he was up and after the cat, heedless of his decrepitude. With a blood-howl that sent a shockwave down Lise's spine, he bounded across the dead grass after Percy, strings of saliva splattering from his leather lips.

Lise stood dazed until she heard Percy call, "Run, Lise, run!" Her companion was risking his life, and in spite of her fear she had to make the most of his bravery.

Within seconds, she reached the disheveled porch and hopped up to get at the cream. It was wonderful, cool and rich. She would have liked to linger over it, curling her tongue around its silky satisfying texture, then cat-like, leaving just a drop for later, but that was out of the question. The dog was coming back now, panting and limping with fatigue. She slurped up the last of her stolen breakfast, ran a quick tongue around the bowl just to be sure, and took off into the meadow before old Blackie could catch a second wind. As she fled across the ground, she felt renewed.

Following Percy's trail, she rounded a bend and came to an abrupt stop. The old cat was lying on his side in the open grass. He wasn't moving.

"Percy!" Lise cried, running to him. "Are you alright? What has that monster done to you?"

Percy raised his head heavily. Lise could see his sides heave. "I am well, Cohabitor," he panted. "Just a little spent. None of us are as young as we used to be." With that, he closed his eyes and shrugged onto his back, letting the sun warm his white satin belly.

Lise watched him, realizing with a shock just how elderly her beloved friend had become. She remembered him as a kitten—impetuous, curious, and utterly tireless. It seemed like only last week, but that was many years ago now, many seasons. The cycles of kittenhood were long gone, as were the cycles of youth and even middle age.

Percy was old. He passed most of his days in the cozy solitude of sleep. Someday his nine lives would be spent, but she didn't want to think about that. It was more than she could bear.

• • •

Lise was drowsy after her meal and her hundred-yard dash from the dog. Once she was convinced Percy was alright, her concern evaporated into a sun-warmed lethargy and a nap seemed as good a notion as any.

She glanced around to see exactly where she was. They had left the overgrown lot behind and were now at the edge of someone's fertile garden. Briefly, Lise wondered if other cats lived there, but she already knew the answer. The cat trail skirted the tidy tract but didn't extend toward the house. The only feline scent in the air was their own.

Percy was already sleeping peacefully, half in and half out of the shade of a Japanese maple. Lise found herself a nice spot underneath a peony bush, and after circling three times for good measure, curled up and closed her eyes. Moss grew thick as carpet on the cool rich soil, and the last vestiges of her tension evaporated, giving way to a euphoric ease.

In her mind, she began to travel with the sun. Up into other realms she floated, bodiless, light as the air itself. Below her like islands she could see all that was: cities, countries, continents, teeming with life. In places, there was so much life that the earth's natural face had been changed by it.

Suddenly, she was no longer enjoying her flight. As she watched, large brown and gray patches began to slither into the blue-green ones. Those zones of corruption expanded, consuming everything in their path, ugly as mold on an orange.

In the real world, her foot began to twitch.

Now, she was somewhere else, a place of great beauty and significance. A waterfall coursed through a natural valley and ferns were hung with rainbows of condensation. Tiny white flowers grew in the mossy crevices of the rock. The air was crystalline.

Lise danced to the edge of the brook and dipped into a pool for water. It was fresh and sweet, unlike anything she had tasted before. A moon-colored fish swam to the surface and gazed at her. As she gazed back at him, she felt a connection. With a flick of its fins, the fish was gone, leaving not even a ripple to show its passing. As she stared at the place it had been, wondering what had frightened it, she saw something happen.

The water was beginning to change. Darkness swirled into the limpid eddies, obscuring the rocky depths that had been visible only a moment ago. The cloudy liquid put off a faint metallic smell. At first, Lise didn't recognize what was defiling the pristine stream, but as the deep red coil began to unfurl, she knew.

The water was infused with blood!

As she slept under the peony bush, her other foot began to spasm.

She and Percy were lazing on the front steps. A white butterfly danced on the breeze above. Finally! she thought. Finally, I'm back where I belong. But even as she sighed with relief, the butterfly dropped to the ground in a daze. Before she could respond, it was joined by another, then another.

Not just butterflies but honey bees, moths, and dragonflies were hailing to earth as if poisoned. Then came the birds— tiny kinglets, a dearth of sparrows, even the hardy blue jays and a woodpecker or two were felled by whatever profane power was at work. Lise peered at the little bodies and realized to her horror that their feathers were singed and strange red knobs had sprung from their heads.

She looked closer. With revulsion, she pulled back but not in time to purge what she'd seen from her mind. The redness was all that was left of their eyes.

"Run!" she cried to Percy as she shot to her feet, but the old cat didn't move.

"Percy, quick! Don't you see? Everything is dying! We have to get out of here or we'll die too!"

Still Percy lingered, tail wrapped around his haunches and nose in the air as if he had not a care in the world.

"Percy, we have to escape!"

The old cat turned his knowing gaze on her and said in a voice grave with portent, "Do not bother, Cohabitor. Soon enough, there will be no place to go." As he spoke, his long fur started to smolder.

In the real world, Lise's body jerked uncontrollably. Waking with a start, she labored to slow her racing heart.

A nightmare—nothing more, she told herself sternly, though she had a nagging feeling it hadn't sprung totally from her own imagination. But there was neither slime-mold nor rivers of blood in this quiet summer garden. That, at least, was a good sign.

Lise rolled into a sunny spot on the grass and turned onto her back. The warmth of the rays began to draw the dread from her bones. With the buzz of insects and the bird-song in the trees assuring her that no plague had come, she allowed herself to pass back into a restful and unworried sleep.

5. Call to Arms

Lise napped away the rest of the afternoon, only rousing toward consciousness to shift position or chase off a wayward bug and then sink back down into the smooth comfortable womb of dreamless sleep. When she finally came aware again, the sun was dropping like a fireball beyond the sinister string of storm clouds she had noticed that morning. *We're in for wild weather*, Lise thought to herself, *but probably not tonight.* Higher up in the sky hung a fingernail moon, a single star twinkling brightly nearby.

Despite it being high summer, a breeze had come up and there was the hint of chill in the air. Wind ruffled the leaves of the surrounding bushes with a sound like beetle wings. Percy had disappeared, and only the slightest wisp of pale magenta essence remained to show his track. With a spike of apprehension, Lise realized he had been gone for some time.

Picking herself up, she dusted away a few blades of dry grass and started back to the house. She had no doubt she would find her companion there; she knew him well, knew he liked a little supper this time of day.

Then, she remembered Percy all but polishing off his kibbles earlier on, and an alarming thought hit her: Who would feed him once those were gone?

Where would he go?

How would he survive?

Would he leave her in search of a better provider? She was

barely capable of taking care of herself in this strange new World.

Suddenly, she was running like the wind, bolting down paths and across fences toward home. Would he be waiting on the back porch with a welcoming meow? Or would he be gone forever?

As she rounded the rhododendron, her body slackened with relief. Percy sat in his usual place on the woven doormat, his ice-green eyes tuned to hers as if he had known she would appear. A little way away, giving her a conspiratorial cat-blink, reclined her other partner in crime, Evermore Tom.

After touching noses, affectionately with Percy and more formally with Tom, she flopped onto the still-warm boards of the porch and sighed contentedly. She was so happy she began to purr.

Two unfamiliar cats were sitting on the grass in the gathering night shadows. They looked to be siblings—same small size and shape, same curious emerald eyes—but one's short mane of velveteen fur was milk-white and the other's was black as the void of space. They were quiet, expectant, but their forced restraint didn't hide their youthful exuberance. It seemed to Lise that the slightest provocation would set them off like firecrackers.

The small black and his sister white were not the only newcomers, Lise realized as she gazed around the darkening garden. Everywhere she looked, she caught glimpses of mirror eyes peering out from the trees and bushes. She glanced at Tom and Percy but they seemed untroubled by the hidden clowder.

Tom yawned widely, then rose to his tallest measure. The dusk was beginning to gather in inky pools of night.

"My friends, thank you for suspending your inherent solitude to be with us tonight." His deep voice commanded attention, bringing many of the cats out of hiding to listen. The kittens' ears swiveled as they hung on his every word.

"War! Starvation! Overpopulation! Ignorance!" proclaimed the great marmalade tabby. "And the list goes on. A terrible evil has infected our World, bringing with it horrors our ancestors of the Equilibrium could never have imagined—horrors we live with every day." He paused. "For a very long time, we have stood back and watched, hoping the state would resolve itself, hoping another stronger species would take up the call, but that has not come about." He gave Lise an ireful look that left no doubt to whom he was referring. "Now, the sword has been passed to us. It is our small but stalwart brotherhood who must save our World. Save it, or die trying."

Tom let the solemnity of the pronouncement sink in. No one moved. Not a breath was drawn.

"Tonight is the Mid-Eve of Tri-Night, yesterday being Commencement, and tomorrow being Culmination of this vital phase. If we are to break our bondage with the promoter of evil, Seh, we must disassemble it before Culmination's end."

A round of low guttural growls broke from the onlookers along with comradely braggadocio and feline declarations of war.

"We will defeat it!" someone cried.

"Defeat the beast? We have tried before," Tom scoffed. "Twice we have failed and were forced to wait many seasons for the next Tri-Night. The hell of enslavement has always been balanced by the hope of liberty. Until now. This time it's not as simple as win or wait," he warned. "This is the Centenium, the unique Tri-Night that falls on the virgin moon, prophesied as the pivot-point for this momentous conflict. The Centenium is a time of great power and will aid us in our cause. But the door flaps both ways. If we do not terminate Seh's influence this cycle, it is foretold that the beast will become strong beyond termination. Seh will be indestructible." Tom hesitated, his tail lashing violently although the rest of him stood rigid as stone. "This is our last and only chance!"

The bold chatter fell away, leaving a numb silence as the ultimatum daunted even the bravest fighters.

Changing the tone, Tom announced, "All is not lost. We have

found our human defender." He looked again at Lise, this time with admiration. "Yet, she cannot stand alone. We must be ready to help her in any way we can."

The small audience nodded gravely, and Lise realized why Percy had referred to Tom as a statesman. The dignified orator made sure he caught each eye and that each, in turn, returned his gaze.

"It is impossible to know what the future holds. If we succeed, things may return to the glory of the Equilibrium. If we do not..." Tom let the sentence drop, leaving them to draw their own conclusions. For a few seconds, the somberness lay like the storm clouds that gathered on the horizon. Then with an unexpected blink, he added merrily, "...but tonight, we party!"

Lise was astonished by the decree. Percy hadn't moved a muscle, but he was smiling. The two youngsters jumped up from their places and cavorted on the lawn, cheering at the good news.

"Kittens," Tom sighed, but Lise could see he was as excited as they.

"Malovar, Ferrin," he called to the pair. "Control yourselves. There will be time for revelry soon enough. Right now, we must send the call to meet at the Stones. Malovar, will you do the honors?"

The panther-furred youngster was thrilled to be chosen. He bowed respectfully to the massive leader, then hopped into the boughs of the fig tree and climbed the leafy branches as high as he could go. When he reached the top, he braced himself. Raising his head into the winds, he let go a wail that might have been heard in the far county.

The summoning went on and on, subtly shifting in pitch and tenor. Lise's heightened senses easily caught the significance of each part. The song— for that was what it was— had a haunted lilting beauty to it. Nothing like the back-alley discord she had come to associate with cat-calls.

As the last, searching note died away and Malovar bounded

down, responses began to come back from all around. Yowls and cries rose from every side, along with some angry human noises, Lise noted.

Tom cocked an ear. Seeming satisfied with the results, he jumped from the porch. "Time to go," he pronounced, and the band, including Lise, fell into step behind him.

• • •

"We're going to a party?" Lise whispered to Percy as they trotted their winding way through the neighborhood streets. "What sort of party?"

Percy looked over at her. "It is a very old tradition, as old as our race." His eyes sparkled with mischief.

"I don't understand," Lise pressed.

"To understand, you must know the nature of cats."

"Well, I think I know cats reasonably well," Lise shot back defensively. "After all, I've had cats most of my life."

"But see? You betray your ignorance already. No one can 'have' a cat. A feline cannot be possessed. Our spirit withers when enslaved."

"That's something you have in common with humans."

"Yes, but with cats, it is even more extreme. Humans are known to enslave themselves of their own will—to work, to beliefs, even to other humans. A cat would rather be dead," he avowed. "And many are."

"Dead? Why? What do you mean?"

"If a cat is not content, it will run, and running can be lethal. The servants of Seh are drawn to the homeless ones."

Lise felt a sudden pang as she thought of all the animals with no family to defend and care for them.

"Do not worry. That will not happen to us," Percy reassured, reading her mind again. "And tonight will be fun."

She smiled gratefully. She really wouldn't mind putting aside all the death and danger for a while.

As the band traveled toward their destination, cats of all kinds joined the procession. Silent as shadows, they slipped along, each at their own pace, wandering the yards and the edges of the deserted lanes. Although an outsider would never have noticed their seemingly random migration, they moved as one toward a single goal. Back and forth across lawn and terrace, through wild patches of vacant lots they worked their way uphill. No matter how many turns or twists their leader took, they kept climbing.

Although Lise didn't know where they were on a map, she thought she recognized the old quarter, a neighborhood once rich with grand homes and well-trimmed grounds, now regrettably run-down. The gardens frothed with wild clematis and morning glory, their white trumpet blossoms glowing like luminescent polka-dots against broken shingles, dirty windows, and peeling lead-based paint. The proud centurions stood abused or abandoned, their glory days long gone.

At the top of a dead-end street, the clowder mounted a final rise and vanished behind one of the behemoths. Lise, who had trailed a little behind, entranced by the wriggling of a night-crawler, sprinted to catch up, ducking into the jungle of vines behind them. The narrow path ran adjacent to the huge stone house, a cat-sized tunnel through the tangled blackberry. It was dark in the thicket, and the hard clay ground was slick with leftover wet from the ruined gutters above. The place imparted the kind of cold that chilled to the bone. Lise hastened for the other side.

Percy was waiting on the top of a rise. A shallow valley stretched away from the weed-choked box bushes and the skeletons of dead roses to become smooth and green with meadow grass. Below, an ancient orchard curled its knotted branches against the star-filled sky. The ground was sprinkled with wild flowers. In the center stood a ring of stones.

Huge white sphinx moths skimmed the apple and pear trees, resting on the immature fruit. Crickets sang with unrestrained joy. There was something about this enchanted place that embodied transcendence, as if the creatures here were not limited by the common rules of being. There was no way this magic heath could have existed in the city Lise knew, and yet, there it was.

A thousand cat paths of every imaginable hue glimmered in the long grass, entering the field from all sides, and as Lise peered among the trees, she began to pick out the cats themselves. The valley was alive with them—sitting, standing, slinking from place to place. There were more felines than Lise had seen in her lifetime, and not one of them made a single sound.

Ferrin and Malovar raced down the hill to join the throng. Though it was obvious the two youngsters wanted to sing with glee, once they entered the circle, they were mute as all the rest.

"Is this it?" Lise whispered.

"Yes." The old cat's voice was tight with anticipation.

"They don't seem very festive," Lise observed.

"Wait and see," Percy told her, bounding toward the others. "Come, Lise," he called back. "Time to play!"

• • •

Lise followed, hesitantly stepping across the threshold of the stone circle as if she were entering a chapel—she felt the same mixture of reverence and fear. The interwoven boughs of the old fruit trees heightened the transcendent mood, but it was the stones that held her attention.

The ring of huge boulders was ancient and covered with great mats of velvet moss and gray-green lichen. Some were so deeply mired in the earth they were nothing more than knolls; others stood well above, exposing flat slabs of rough granite surface. Long before the orchard was planted, some unknown hand had set them in a perfect ring. In the center grew a tree as old as the world itself.

The giant stave oak was a hundred feet tall, reaching for the stars. Lise wondered that she hadn't spied it peeking over the rooftops on her treks through town. Its sturdy trunk was four feet thick at the base, and its gnarled roots broke the ground like ocean swells. Its tangle of stout far-reaching limbs stretched sky-ward in a broad twisted crown. No grass grew beneath it and the powder-soft dirt was scattered with last year's acorns.

Tom had met up with Dominic, the master cat Lise had encountered the night before, and the two were making their way through the throng, greeting and touching noses with others of their clan. In a vast spiral, they closed on the primeval tree until they finally stood at its massive foundation. With a forceful leap, Tom catapulted himself onto the trunk, Dominic behind him. Spread-eagled, their claws firmly anchored in the grainy bark, they shinnied their way into the shadowy branches. Once high enough to see across the countryside, they settled.

All movement in the orchard had ceased now and all eyes were upon the two in the tree. Excitement and expectancy hung in the air like champagne ready to pop.

Tom sized up his congregation, then slowly he began. It was no more than a low growl, a drone on the bottom edge of the auditory scale, but as it continued, rising in pitch, the one voice was joined and joined again until the sound was great as rolling thunder. All those present took part. Individual notes began to rise out of the cacophony—trumpet roars and soprano cries—until the air erupted with sound.

Through the pandemonium, a lilting strain began to weave into song. Lise realized this celestial melody originated with her two young friends, Malovar and Ferrin. Perched on one of the standing stones, their falsetto call danced both with and against the chorus like a concerto.

Lise would have been hypnotized by the profound beauty of the goings-on around her if she hadn't been so compelled to sing, herself. Hesitant at first, she lifted her voice and was instantly transported. For a moment, she felt she could glimpse the perfect world.

In time, the volume began to subside as voices dropped from the ensemble. One by one, the singers finished, and even Ferrin's and Malovar's angel hymn descended the scale into silence. The roar became a yowl, and the yowl, a murmur. As the last of the song ebbed into the night, the stillness was complete. Not a cricket or a moth's wing, not a sound from the city outside disturbed the consummate peace.

Breaking the spell with a raucous scamper, Tom and Dominic scrambled out of the tree. The noise rose again, but this time with greetings and communications.

Suddenly alive with movement, every square inch of grass became a by-way for the shifting masses. The reverent adoration had transmuted into festive hilarity. *This truly is a party to beat all parties,* Lise thought to herself as she watched.

Out of the corner of her eye, she caught a white blur and felt a soft paw hit against her leg. When she turned, she found Ferrin lying on her back, feet in the air, ready to play. Unsure what to do, she touched the young cat lightly on her bared belly. Ferrin responded by clasping her tightly though she was careful to keep her claws safely sheathed.

"I gotcha!" Ferrin cried with glee. "Now you!" When Lise just stood staring, the kitten added, "I won't hurt you. It's fun!"

Letting go of her inhibitions, Lise flopped down onto her back as she had seen the younger cat do. Before she knew it, Ferrin was on top of her. She grabbed the sleek little bundle, and together they rolled on the soft grass, laughing at each other's antics.

Ferrin was right—it was fun! How long had it been since Lise had played—really played? She was a grown-up, and human grown-ups did not play. Cats on the other hand were never too old to play. Cats had people beat cold!

The excitement spread throughout the gathering. Some chased and some hid while others had fun with games of toss and catch. Some preferred to engage in mock fights or sports of war. The cat-cries rose to such a pitch that Lise was sure the families in the surrounding houses would waken and start to complain, but no one did. It was as if the delighted mob had left the human world behind and, for a brief moment, were allowed to dance in their own separate universe.

Lise was having the time of her life. Ferrin had worn her out with her youthful effervescence and gone off to cavort with Malovar, leaving Lise to recuperate under a pear tree. As she relaxed and caught her breath, she found she was filled with a sense of well-being she had never known before. For the first time in her life, she could see some real meaning to this lonely disjointed cosmic ball of dust.

Then, Lise saw something strange in the trees above her and her well-being faltered. At first, she thought it was a small cat, although the glint of red in its eyes seemed out of place among the green, blue, and gold of the others. Suddenly, she noticed there were more than one. The trees were full of them in fact and so was the long grass, a thousand pinpoints of deep red rage glaring through the dark.

Can this be right? Lise wondered, but before she could voice her fears, a great surge of tiny squirming bodies swarmed down upon her. Squirrels, masses of them, began flowing like a torrent onto the unsuspecting revelers. Up from great holes in the ground they came, their pelts mangy and sludge-gray, their beady eyes soulless as zombies.

These were no ordinary squirrels—no cute, daylight nut eaters. Lise could see plainly that this scurry was deranged.

As they launched into the crowd of felines, all hell broke loose. Cats were running every which way, foul gray beings clinging to their fur like leeches. Tiny needle claws raked sensitive skin while poison teeth sank into any flank or back or leg unlucky enough to pass. Yowls of pain pierced the air, mingled with shrieks of squirrelish glee.

Through the tumult, a streak of silver was heading straight for her—Dominic.

"Run, Lise!" he called as he fended off the stunted hordes that were intent on bringing him down.

"What's happening?" Lise cried.

"It's Seh! It has sent its creatures. It must know our plans."

Dominic narrowly dodged a swarm of the heinous minions of Seh.

"Look out!" Lise shrieked, but as she moved to help the master, a second mass cut in from the side. The dead red eyes glared for an instant, and then were upon her. She screamed as she felt rows of thorn-like teeth clamp into her flesh.

Lise knew if she went down, it would be all over. She struggled to keep her stance and actually managed to shake off a few of the smaller ones, kicking them away and taking a private joy in the fatal crunch of their puny carcasses as they hit the ground. Dominic was with her now, and the two were gaining hold. Between his lethal bites and her strong kicks, they managed to repel the second wave.

Dropping to the ground in exhaustion, Lise reached out to her savior. Touching his ruffled fur, she felt a sticky dampness on his chest.

"You're hurt!" she exclaimed. "We need to get help." But even as she uttered the words, she knew there would be no help for him there. The valley was a war zone. Battles were being waged on every side. Screeches and wails filled the air with torment. Fur flew. The sickly-sweet stench of blood rose nauseatingly from the once-peaceful meadow. Crumpled bodies of both friends and foe lay strewn across the flowered field.

"You must go now," Dominic whispered hoarsely.

"But I can't leave you," Lise began, touching the silver fur, now wet with red.

"You must," the master cat pressed. "You are the only one who can change all of this. If you are lost in one small battle, who will save our World?" He grimaced with pain, then with his last ounce of strength he hissed, "Go!"

Lise studied the mayhem, then looked back at Dominic. A third siege of blood-thirsty rodents was already teeming up the hill toward them. She knew if she were going to get away, it had to be now, but Dominic would be doomed if she left. How could she run away and leave him with no way of fighting off the mob?

Lise peered sadly into his clear blue eyes. He squeezed them together in a loving blink. "Go, Lise," he mouthed soundlessly.

With another tortured look, she fled for her life.

6. Lost and Found

It broke Lise's heart to leave Dominic and the others behind in that horrific place, but she knew the master cat was right. This was only one battle; if she were struck down before she could do whatever it was she was supposed to do to stop Seh, there would be a thousand more.

So she ran and ran, for them, her friends in the blood-soaked meadow, and for everyone else who suffered under the beast's sadistic hand. As she pressed on, panting, revenge pulsed in her mind like a mantra.

Lise had no idea where she was going, just away from the awful killing field. She had lost all sense of direction, but that didn't matter as long as she escaped the enemy. When next she glanced behind her, the roadway was clear.

The fine old homes had given way to apartments and duplexes, then to businesses, mini-marts, and gas stations. Without knowing how, she'd returned to the city maze, its alleyways and cavernous main streets.

Lise's lungs were about to burst. It seemed as if she'd been running for hours. She was a good runner but she was reaching her limit. Slowing, first to a trot and then to a dragging shuffle, she crumpled to the curb. As she stared down the gloomy lane, she expected to see the mud-gray tide streaming toward her, but thankfully all was quiet. A horn sounded in the distance, a beer can rolled across the pavement at the whim of the wind, rats scampered in the sewer below her, but nothing more.

She pulled herself into the shadow of a scrub ailanthus that had grown up through a crack in the sidewalk and peered around. The cobblestones poking through the thin skin of blacktop and the railroad tracks bisecting the lane told her she was in the old industrial part of town. She had come a long way from that idyllic meadow atop the hill.

This was a section of the city she didn't usually frequent. In the daytime, it was a bustling hub for trucks delivering goods to be redistributed throughout the municipality, but in the dead of night, only drunks and lost ones persisted, looking for a place to sleep or winding their way home after last call. And the ghosts—a place so old and hard held its share of unsettled spirits. Lise could see them, flickering penumbras at the edge of her perception.

What next? She was far from home, or anywhere else familiar for that matter. She thought she could find her way back to her neighborhood by heading toward the hill park which crouched like a black lump on the horizon, but she was hesitant. She had no way of knowing what hazards might lurk in between there and here.

"Well, you can't hang around all night," came a gravelly voice from behind her. At first, Lise thought it was an echo of her own unsettled thoughts, then she stiffened, realizing the voice was real.

"Well? Well?" it insisted. "You're in my place."

Lise turned and saw a huge tomcat sitting atop the brick wall. He was solid as the wall itself, and as big as a raccoon, black from head to claw, with sharp copper eyes that looked at her with a curious mixture of lust and savoir-faire.

"You are in my place," he repeated. "And I want it back. Unless you'd like to share it with me, that is," he added with a leer.

Quickly, she jumped to her feet and moved aside. She was in no mood for amorous advances, especially from the local street tom. "I'm sorry," she blustered. "I didn't realize."

"Horace."

"Pardon?"

"Horace," the tom repeated, coiling his sleek tail into a question mark. "That's me. I'm Horace. Pleased to meet you, whomever you might be."

He sniffed the air keenly, as if he could pick up her designation with his profound sense of smell. It crossed Lise's mind to run again but she was all run out. Instead, she stared at him blankly.

"Well, you're a piece of work!" the black tom exclaimed. "First you invade my place, then you ignore me right to my face. Rude, very rude." He sprang lightly down from the wall and insinuated his bulk into the little cubby hole Lise had vacated, making himself comfortable after circling the correct amount of times.

"I'm sorry," Lise offered once more.

"Is that all you can say? Sorry, sorry, sorry." Horace peered closer at Lise, beginning to notice her dishevelment. "What have you been doing?" he demanded. "You have blood on you."

"I'm..." Lise stopped herself before she apologized again. "My name is Lise," she said instead.

"So you can articulate after all." The tomcat let go a huge guffaw.

His sudden humor was contagious, and Lise found herself smiling too. "I must look pretty bad," she chuckled.

"That you do, little one," Horace replied. "You couldn't look worse if you'd tangled with Seh himself," he joked, laughing even harder.

Lise froze, her mirth flushed away by an icy rush of fear. To her, the cat's jest was far too close to the truth.

Horace caught her change and frowned, his hilarity dying into a few last hiccups. "What's wrong? Was it something I said?"

Lise sighed as she sunk to the ground beside him. "It's not you. You couldn't have known. It's just that..." She paused. "You were very near right."

"Oh? Oh," he repeated. "Maybe you should tell me about it."

Lise hesitated, but something in his soft liquid eyes let her know she was safe. Her voice breaking, she began the saga. When she finished, they both were silent.

"So I guess that means you are She," Horace finally said.

"She?"

"She Who... The human from the prophecy," he told her casually, as if he met prophetic figures every day. "Here, let me help you clean yourself up."

Not waiting for an answer, he started licking the blood and dirt from her with his rough tongue. The rhythmic action was soothing, and Lise found herself relaxing for the first time since the awful event.

It must have been nearing the blackest part of night, that nowhere hour when most humans were locked inside and somnolent. Nothing moved in the city labyrinth save the wind through the scrawny trees and the gypsy moths that swarmed the street lamp's glow. A satellite crossed the ebony sky like a pinhead of star-dust. A siren wailed somewhere far away.

Then without warning, pandemonium. With a screech and a roar, a monolith of metal rounded the corner and lumbered toward Lise and Horace like a manic brontosaurs, a ton of steel with a tiny glass head and round bristle brushes that drove a cyclone of debris before it. For a split second, Lise stared into the giant spinning maw, then she was on her feet, ready to bolt.

Horace stopped her. "Street sweeper," he shouted over the machine's earsplitting thunder. "Comes by this time of night. It won't hurt you. The man's pretty nice. Brings me fish from the docks sometimes. Just stay clear of the broom."

"I don't like it!" Lise cried, too shell-shocked by the events of the evening to cope with this metallic monster

"Okay, okay," Horace soothed. It didn't take great insight for him to see she was on the edge. "This way, then, little one. I know where we can go." He leapt to the top of the wall with an agility that belied his size and substance. "Just follow me."

As the sweeper neared, lurching along with the inevitability of death, Horace bounded down the narrow causeway toward a chink in the brickwork. Lise was after him in a heartbeat. Together they scrambled through the tight scraping hole and away from the clamorous lane.

Once she knew there was a barrier between herself and the invader, Lise felt relieved. She would have been content to stay right there crouched next to the protective terra cotta, but Horace had other plans. Stopping only briefly to sniff the air, he moved off between the buildings. She considered letting him go on alone, but there might be more dangers in the unfamiliar zone, and the tomcat seemed pretty savvy. Best let things unfold as they would, she decided as she jogged to catch up with him.

The huge black shadow slunk steadily along the corridor, mossy warehouse walls looming four stories above. The narrow path of packed clay was damp and slimy, as if sunlight never touched it. The reek of urine and mold assaulted their senses as the pair padded by old cans, food wrappers, and other litter too disgusting for Lise to dwell upon. Only the smallest strip of sky was visible from the passageway, but as they neared the open road, Lise noted that the stars had disappeared. Those menacing storm clouds were finally rolling in, staining the heavens black. A cutting wind funneled down the narrow pass, and Lise found herself shivering.

Her companion was pensive but seemed to have no inclination to leave her. Together they navigated the deserted boulevards and blocks of empty buildings in silence. They crossed several streets and a main thoroughfare. The asphalt lanes spread wide as a field but fortunately it was abandoned by all but a few meandering cars.

The four-lane road marked the end of the industrial district and the beginning of residential. Within a few blocks, the last of the grocery stores and cafés had disappeared. Lise's heart lightened. She knew she was headed home.

Horace led her by an indirect route of back yards and tangled gardens to a street lined with sycamore trees. Rows of tiny cottage bungalows built at the turn of the nineteenth century lifted ornate faces. Some of them had been refurbished in bright Victorian colors and others remained buffed and seasoned by time. It was a peaceful haven, the owners all inside, safe and sleeping.

Horace pulled up beside a white picket fence that had seen better days. The little house was in similar disrepair, but the narrow strip of garden between the fence and the gray-flecked front porch was lovely. In that small oasis, anemones and tall plumes of cosmos exploded in pink profusion. Trailing nasturtiums in a spectrum of earthy oranges wound their way up the pickets and across the sagging gate.

"This is where I must leave you, little one," Horace told Lise, plopping himself down full length on the sidewalk and nonchalantly licking between his razor claws. "I have other... obligations. You understand."

Lise noted the blue almond eyes of a female cat peering out from behind the wisteria bower. "Yes, of course," she said, smiling. "Thank you for bringing me this far. I would have been lost without your help."

"You're very welcome. Anything I can do for our World, you know. Good luck with, well, that thing." His tone lowered to a bare whisper. "That thing you had the trouble with back there."

"Thanks. With friends like you, we can't help but win."

Horace rose and stepped very close to Lise, his black nose nearly touching hers. In that same cautious, almost fearful tone, he asked hesitantly, "Can I give you a piece of advice?" Without waiting for an answer, he continued. "Not everybody thinks as we do, little one. I'm not talking about those who have joined the evil plague—we know they're beyond help. I mean ones like us but not us, if you know what I mean." His voice wavered and Lise saw him glance lasciviously toward the pretty cat in her leafy hiding place. A deep rumbling in his throat confirmed that his attention was wavering.

"Like us but not?" Lise began but Horace was already moving toward his paramour. "I don't understand. How will I know?"

He glanced back at her small figure and frowned. "Watch for fire in the eyes," he called before he pounced into the web of wisteria branches, his midnight silhouette disappearing from sight.

"Horace, wait. I don't..." Lise sighed. She knew she would get no more from him. But he had told her enough to make her realize she had to be careful, even when she thought she was safe.

Be careful, and watch for eyes of fire.

7. Nine Lives

Lise had no more adventures, either interesting or disagreeable, on the remainder of her journey home. She soon found she knew the way though she was constantly being distracted by strange compelling scents and secret leafy paths that led between the houses and through the garden shadows. It was near dawn when she jumped the ivy-covered fence and fell exhausted into the safe warm quiet of her own back porch.

When she woke a few hours later, the sun was just touching the grass near her feet. Most of last night's clouds had been swept away, leaving only a handful of dark lurkers to sulk on the horizon, but they didn't intrude on the beauty of the new day. She yawned and stretched. The movement brought a twinge of pain to her shoulder and another deep in her thigh. Like a swift dive into arctic water, the memories poured back.

Quickly, she looked around for Percy, Tom, or one of the others. Last time she had seen them, they were fighting for their lives. With a heart full of trepidation, she began to admit the possibility that they had been less than victorious.

Search as she might, Lise could discover no trace of them. She was completely alone and unsure of what to do. Should she hunt for her friends? Try to find her way back to last night's battlefield? The thought of returning to that doomed place made her skin crawl. Besides, there was no reason to think they would still be there after all this time. She was better off remaining where she was, somewhere they would look if they were trying to find her.

She reseated herself on the steps and stared into the bushes. She was sick with concern. Had they had been hurt by the squirrel-horde and were now holed up somewhere, licking their festering wounds? Were they dead? Or worse? Who knew what such an evil strength might inflict upon its conquered foe? To Lise, the power of Seh seemed boundless.

Suddenly, she could no longer contain her sorrow. She lifted her head toward the clear azure sky and sent forth a wail of despair. As her cry finally faltered into silence, she heard others take up the call. The air was suddenly ringing with yowls that diminished into the distance as her message was passed along.

Then she heard an imminently closer voice, not loud but thoroughly recognizable as that of her own old friend, Percy. She leapt to her feet and bounded through the rhododendrons to where he was just rounding the edge of the rose bed. He looked tired and his long fur was tousled, but otherwise he seemed unhurt. When he saw her, he stopped and sat back on his haunches. A smile played across his black and white mask.

"Cohabitor," he intoned lovingly. "You survived. Thank the Originator. I was afraid."

"And you!" Lise exclaimed, flopping down beside him, close enough to feel the warmth of his body. She smelled the sour scent of the fight still on him. "Are you really alright?"

"Not so bad," he replied matter-of-factly. "Although I would not want to do that every night."

Amazed by his fortitude, she breathed with relief. Her solace was short-lived however. Her apprehension resurged as she asked the crucial question.

"What about...?" was all she could manage before her throat constricted with dread.

"We took many losses," Percy said slowly.

"Tell me."

The old cat shifted position, easing what might have been a sore leg. Quietly, he gathered his thoughts.

"First, I must say that, all in all, we prevailed. After you were away, we managed to send those evil creatures scurrying for the holes from which they spawned. Tom and Dominic mustered the clowder into squadrons, and once we were banded, the fiends couldn't get a hold. But the victory did not come without a struggle."

"I never knew squirrels could be so vicious," Lise remarked.

"In the wild, that breed will go to exceptional lengths to protect its family, but what we met last night were no ordinary animals. Those were minions of Seh, city-bred and raised on filth. They are a dead-souled bunch who possess neither allegiance nor camaraderie. Seh programs them like zombies to do his bidding, but there is next to no brain in those tiny, flea-bitten heads. When faced with a force, they run. They can only harm us if we are divided...or if they get one of us alone."

Lise sensed something ominous in Percy's tone. "You seem to know a lot about them."

He gave her a look that conveyed absolute hatred. "Yes," was all he said.

Lise felt she shouldn't press so instead she asked, "What about Tom? And Dominic? Little Ferrin and the others? Are they okay?"

"They came through with their lives, if that is what you mean."

"Thank God—" she began.

"Do not be quite so swift to rejoice, Lise," the old cat warned. "The greatest danger from the demon squirrels is not death but disease. Their bite is infectious and their claws exude a poison that necrotizes flesh and cannot be checked. If the wound is superficial, the body can usually fight off the infection, but if the damage is extensive..." His voice trailed, leaving Lise to imagine for herself. "Some are fortunate. Their cohabitors take them to a special human who possesses the ability to help in such matters."

"A vet," Lise commented.

Percy gave her a questioning look.

"A doctor—someone who has the knowledge and resources to cure sickness and injury."

"Yes, that is the one. Ah, humanity," Percy sighed. "Such intelligence! Such ingenuity!"

Lise smiled, agreeing that the human species did have its moments.

"You took me to such a one when I had a damaged leg," he continued. "But many of the injured have no such friend. These, I am afraid, are fated to suffer and die." His usually serene countenance was grim with anger.

"I'm sorry some people don't take good care of their..." She was about to say 'pets' but stopped herself. "...their companions," she inserted. "But tell me, Percy. What about the others?"

"Tom is well, a few scratches that will heal with good cleansing and time. Ferrin, the same. Malovar fared slightly worse. He was raked badly before he could gain the upper hand, but he is young and the young recover well. It is Dominic's wounds that concern us."

"Dominic?" Lise echoed apprehensively. "What happened to the master?"

"Dominic is not the youngest of cats," Percy replied. "Younger than myself, of course, but not by as much as he would have you believe. He has lived a long life and he takes far too many chances—for his time."

"For his age? You mean for his age?"

"No, not exactly." Percy hesitated. He was worn out and had no desire to discuss feline mysticism, but Lise skewered him with unrelenting eyes.

"Explain it to me," she charged. She was tired, too—tired of riddles and half-baked replies.

"It is difficult. There is nothing that correlates to humans but I will try," he sighed. "You are familiar with the common human belief that cats have nine lives?"

"Of course. But isn't that just a fable?"

"Not entirely. The idea that we are miraculously resurrected from eight deaths and then cross Beyond on the ninth is simplistic, but as with most lore, the story is rooted in fact. You see our spirits reside on a different tier than man."

"Tier?" Lise asked, uncertain of the word.

"You could call it a plane of existence, a level of consciousness."

Lise gave the old cat a baffled look. "I don't understand."

"You cannot think that all life is like you, human," Percy flared. "With a perception as limited as yours, Felis catus would never have survived."

Lise felt a heated flash of embarrassment and Percy immediately regretted his harsh words. After all, how could she know the enigma of cats unless he enlightened her?

"Alright, think of perception as a rainbow," Percy illustrated in a much-softened tone. "Humans see the colors that run between red and purple, but that is by no means where the rainbow ends. There are ultra-violet, infra-red, and infinite hues beyond. It is the same with what you consider to be reality. You detect the obvious but our species sees so much more."

This made sense to Lise who always believed cats were extra-sensory. "So what about the nine lives?" she asked without hesitation, her moment of shame forgotten.

"The nine lives," he mused. "An idealistic notion. Leaping out of the jaws of death—but only eight times, mind you. Come the ninth, it is all over— Poof!" Percy smiled. "If only it were that simple."

He stood stiffly and began to meander the perimeter of the garden. "You do not mind a little exercise while we talk?"

"No, of course not," she said, jumping after him. She was concerned by his slow painful pace but she wanted answers.

"The fact is," he said, "felines move through time and space in much the same way as your kind embarks on a journey. Most people do it at least once, but some find they like to travel and go many times. Others—those of a special disposition—become compelled to the roving life and spend their days as drifters, sailors, wanderers, always moving, never settling down.

"We are very similar, but instead of traveling across distance, our destination lies beyond space and time. We call the action space-shifting. I cannot tell you how this is done, just that it is something we cats do naturally."

Lise was totally enthralled with the idea. "Where do you go?"

"Our physical forms go nowhere; only our essences travel."

"Your essence travels? What do you see?"

"We perceive by symbolic projection. The details are not always up to us."

"Symbolic projection?"

"Yes, rather like a metaphor come to life. If we are feeling brave, for example, we may see ourselves as tigers or bears, or even humans sometimes. If we are at peace, we may shift to somewhere pleasant, a beautiful hillside or a field abundant with mice—yes, the mice are real," he threw out to Lise though she hadn't asked. "We are speaking of another plane of perception, not merely a glorified dream. We can transport, transcend, and generally defy your corporeality as it suits our needs."

"So let me get this straight. You—cats, I mean—can leap around through space and time, changing your form at will?"

"Not necessarily at will. It takes significant training to control the shifting ability. The key is to recognize the metaphor and manipulate it to your own ends."

"So how does your space-shifting fit in with the nine lives theory?"

"We space-shift to the Alter-tier for many reasons, from holy pilgrimages to recreation. But when we are in peril, shifting is most valuable. If we can draw our consciousness away from the danger, we may keep from crossing Beyond."

"You can escape death?" Lise asked, amazed.

"In certain circumstances."

"What about your bodies? I should think they'd be vulnerable, left behind like that?"

"Yes, they are, but not so much as you might think. First of all, we always try to shift from a secluded place. That is why a sick cat will wander off when deathly ill. He is actually seeking a safe haven so he can shift and save himself. Though it does not always work that way.

"And secondly, when the essence departs, all that is left is meat—inert and insensitive. Without the brain functions constantly stimulating the senses, meat is very difficult to destroy."

"It sounds like shifting could come in handy. One minute, you're in trouble and the next, you're lying on a beach in Florida. I can imagine the advantages."

"It is not always so pleasant. We do not command the Artier. Many entities share its existence with us, and not all of them are friendly."

Lise suddenly had a flash of prescience. "Ghosts?" she asked in a hushed whisper, remembering the cold flickers she perceived in the alley.

"Yes, those." He inadvertently shivered. "But you wanted to hear about Dominic, did you not?"

"Oh, right," Lise stuttered, chiding herself for her thoughtlessness. Her mind should be on the injured master, although the subject of ghosts did seem a fascinating distraction.

"Dominic is one whose life is devoted to shifting in space. He will not pass up an opportunity to visit distant shores. He has shifted many times, much more than the feline average of nine. But there is a terrible risk. One day, he will not return."

"His lives will be up?"

"Exactly. Sooner or later, we all cross."

"You mean, die," she said soberly.

"For want of a better word, yes."

"I see." She looked up at the sunny summer sky, but for a moment, frost blossomed inside her.

"Last night," Percy resumed, "in the thick of battle, Dominic was brought down. He was trying to herd a unit of squirrels back into their hell hole when a new colony emerged right underneath him. They were on him before he could even call for help. When he realized he had no chance, he left his body and shifted to another tier."

"Then he's alright? He saved himself from death?"

"He is still drawing breath, but it was a rough journey, made even more hazardous by the proximity of Seh and his minions. The soul is vulnerable when it travels, and though Seh does not have the power to destroy, it can hold a spirit captive. This is what has happened with Dominic, and now he lingers at the brink of the abyss."

"That's awful!" Lise exclaimed. "Is there anything I can do?"

Percy looked at Lise with a strange glint in his eye. "Maybe there is."

"Anything. Just tell me..." she began, but her words strangled in her throat.

Suddenly, Lise's concerns imploded inward. Something blasphemous was rising like poison in her gut, an invading entity far too huge and horrible for her small fragile body to bear. It bloated up until she thought she would burst from the pressure, then it coiled its icy tendrils around her heart and squeezed.

You will never defeat us! it disgorged into her psyche with the dispassionate and androgynous voice of a machine. *We will break you with your own weakness and burn your flesh to cinders in our infinite fire!*

Lise froze, but only for an instant. With a reflex as quick and subconscious as a heartbeat, she reached out with her mind and crushed the spectral vision into a cube of pure hatred, then cast it aside. The cube hit the wall of Lise's intellect and shattered into a million pieces. Each piece exploded into phosphorescent flame and was consumed completely. A vengeful scream rose and died within her.

Percy was staring at Lise as if she had turned green. He was unsure of what he had witnessed but when he sensed the triumphant outcome, his eyes went round with pride.

Lise smiled, too, realizing that she had done something important. With her own inherent energy, she had vanquished one of the foe. No one had told her how to do it; she just knew. And, she realized with a sweet adrenaline rush, that wasn't all she knew.

"Maybe I really can help Dominic," she said with newborn confidence.

Percy nodded in absolute acceptance and began to lead the way.

• • •

Dominic lay in the orchard beneath an apple tree within the circle of stones. He had the cold unmoving appearance of death, but as Lise neared, she could see tiny tremors as he drew the shallowest of breaths. His eyes were closed and his head lolled. All four legs were stretched straight to his side. His silver fur was matted with blood and a ragged scabrous tear zig-zagged across his gray flesh from torso to tail.

He wasn't alone on the battlefield. Lise glimpsed several of her cats hiding in the fruit-hung branches and lurking among the purple shadows beyond. They watched her every move, though none confronted her. Instead, they waited, quiet and expectant, as if they knew her mission. She prayed she wouldn't let them down.

"Dominic?" Percy whispered as he touched his nose to the near-lifeless one. Dominic made no response and none was expected. With eyes full of sorrow, the old cat turned back to Lise.

The moment she had seen the stricken figure, her previous bravado had fled. How could she have imagined she had the power to save this poor soul? True, she had vanquished Seh's servant in her mind, but this was completely different. This was life or death. Where could she even begin?

She looked at Percy. He nodded to the unmoving patient at their feet.

"Go on, Lise," he whispered solemnly. "Try."

Try! Alright, I will try. But what happens if I fail? She couldn't let herself dwell on that possibility.

Lise took a step closer, then crouched so she could touch the long, tangled fur. It was like touching a corpse, and her instinct was to pull away, but she reminded herself that inside the ravaged body was the living spirit of the master cat, and that without her help, he might very well slip away.

Alright, she thought sternly. *I'm here. Now what?*

Suddenly, she began to feel something odd, like a distant, earthbound thunder—and it was headed their way. In milliseconds, the sky had darkened and the ground had begun to shake. The presumption that she could rescue the master was obviously not sitting well with Seh.

The coal-black storm clouds that had been lurking on the foothills were now rolling in fast. They writhed as if possessed, shards of lightning impacting within their murky cores. Suddenly the earth heaved like an animal in pain. Lise could smell ozone as well as something else, sharp and nauseating like burning bone. The cataclysm was descending like a pyroclastic flow, and all she could do was stare in dismay.

Cats were vaulting from the trees and scrambling out of the

bushes to escape. Before she knew it, she, Percy and Dominic were the only ones left in the wind-whipped field. She craved nothing more than to bolt as well, but she knew she must stay. Everything depended on what she did right now.

"Percy!" Lise yelled over the roar of the gale. "You go. I'll take care of him."

"Are you sure?" The old cat shouted, not wanting to leave her even though every atom of his being urged him to flee before it was too late.

"Yes. We'll be alright..." She hoped. "This is something I have to do, alone."

Percy's gaze moved between her and the encroaching wall of dark. "If you really think..."

Lise nodded solemnly.

With one anguished backward look, he was gone. The black void closed over Lise and her ward as they hung in the heart of the storm.

8. The Alter-Tier

At first, Lise could see nothing through the tumult, but she found that if she squinted the grit from her eyes, she was able to pick out shadows black on black in the haze. The shapes themselves were unidentifiable but she sensed they bore ill will. Like putrid oil, they swirled and eddied, trying to suck her into their emptiness. Lise clung to Dominic's near-lifeless form, knowing that if she let go, even for a second, they would both be lost.

Suddenly and unexpectedly, her mind began to clear. She was still aware of the chaos around her, but within, a healing warmth flowed. Three words echoed through her consciousness as if spoken: I AM HERE. Then, they were gone, but a small point of serenity remained.

Lise hunkered in that calm place, watching the storm rage beyond her. She must re-establish contact with whomever had sent her the message; it was the only way out of this horror. Unsure how to start, she searched within. Reaching her will, she focused. As before, when she stood against the servant of Seh, she suddenly knew.

The change was slow, but then she sensed it: the sky, a little lighter; a minute diminishing of the strafing gale. These effects, though tiny, proved she was on the right track. In her mind, the tender voice returned.

"I am here," it repeated gently. "Don't be afraid. Together, we can prevail."

"Who are you?" Lise called through the still-driving wind.

"I am..." it began. "But wait. We have more work to do, Lise. Concentrate."

Pushing her limits farther than ever, she fixed on the beautiful voice, purging all else from her mind. She was new to this, and it took all her focus, but she kept on pressing until her blood beat like a drum.

Nothing happened.

She had failed.

In anguish, she let it all go, and that was when the shift came about.

Lise felt herself lift up, leaving her world-bound body behind. With the ease of light, her spirit raced unconfined toward a shimmering curtain that veiled the distance with rainbow-play. She braced for impact as the barrier loomed closer, but with a champagne-cork pop, she was through and out the other side, safe. Where, though, she had not a clue.

The vengeful storm was gone. The air was still and clear in this very private place, like a dream—or a dream of a dream. Images grew up around her: a wooden bench, an orange tree, a flowered vine that curled its scented stem round the edges of her perception. All was serene, as if someone had created the perfect place. But a place for what?

...for a rendezvous? she finished with dismay. A rendezvous with whom?

A splinter of fear jabbed her. Maybe this was another of Seh's diabolical tricks. Maybe the beast was charming her into letting her guard down so it could jump in for the kill. Maybe trusting the strange voice was the stupidest decision of her life. And now that she was here, she had no idea how to go back again.

As if reading her alarm, the soft hail came to her once more. "Sit," it said. The tone was warm and caring, but Lise was far from convinced.

"Sit," the voice repeated patiently. "Please." The old bench suddenly blossomed with lily of the valley, Lise's favorite flower.

"There. Does that prove that I am a friend?"

Lise inhaled deeply, and the pure honeyed scent washed away every trace of earthly decay. She felt instantly cleansed. Whatever had the power to erase the cloying smell of mortality couldn't be evil, could it?

She moved to the bench and sat down as asked. From behind the tree came a man in a long robe. Although of mature years, he was handsome and magnetically virile. His flowing silver hair shone softly and his blue eyes twinkled with wisdom, honesty, and mirth. He seemed familiar though Lise couldn't place from where. Still, she knew him and trusted him completely.

"I am here," he said in the same sweet voice she had heard in her mind, "and now you know me."

Lise was uncertain, then the attractive man smiled and she understood.

"Dominic!" she exclaimed. "But how—"

"Do not ask, dear Lise. The question is unanswerable. All you need to know is that I am here for you, as you are for me."

Lise suddenly remembered what Percy had told her about the feline space-shifting ability and realized she must be seeing the master cat on another tier of consciousness. She thought of the ravaged body she'd so recently clutched in her arms, but that was another place, another time.

Wordlessly, she rose and went to him. He took her in his arms and held her gently. Warmth enveloped her, and she felt safe. She knew he felt the same.

They stood like that for unending moments. Butterflies flicked around them; honey bees droned in the soft air; rainbows grew across the heavens; worlds rose and died in splendor of their peace.

Finally, they moved apart and Lise reseated herself on the bench. She didn't understand what was happening, but she knew she must accept it. She was happy in a way she had never believed possible. Her prescience told her to enjoy it while she could; it wouldn't come again for a very long time.

Dominic nodded, sensing her thoughts. He had called her for a purpose. Now it was time to see it through.

"Lise, I need your help."

"I suppose that's why I'm here," she replied, watching the milky orange blossoms float like snowflakes through the air.

"Yes, you are my champion." He smiled, his love transparent in the sky-colored eyes.

She turned and stared into those eyes. "But I'm afraid I don't know what to do."

"That's alright, Lise. I do."

A faint breeze picked up around them, playing gently with their hair. Swallows swooped in golden arcs above. Dominic sat beside her and took her hand. "Open your mind," he said, "and you will know, too."

Lise met his gaze with naked trust. His eyes were so blue, like the ocean on a perfect day, each ripple, a dazzling mirror of the sun.

The intensity was overwhelming, blinding.

She had to close her eyes, if only for an instant.

When she opened them again, everything changed.

• • •

Like a flood, sensation poured back into Lise's body: pain, anger, anxiety, all the mortal feelings she had left behind for that brief and beautiful flash. It felt as if she were being crushed by her own sensitivity. She couldn't hold back an agonized moan.

"Lise?" came a tenuous voice.

"Dominic! I thought I'd lost you."

There was a pause. "It is me, Cohabitor," Percy said softly.

He touched his nose to hers. As his shadow eclipsed the brilliant blue, she realized they weren't the eyes of the master cat at all but the clear unsullied sky.

She was back in the apple orchard, or had she ever left? At

least the wild storm was gone. The clouds had withdrawn, though they still hung threateningly in the eastern heavens. With a shiver, she turned away from them.

Lise got up stiffly and shook off a few early-fallen leaves. Dominic still lay nearby. A quick inspection told her he hadn't moved. Her brave attempt to help him had failed.

"Oh, no," she sobbed, sinking back to the ground. "None of it was real."

"None of what?" asked Percy.

"You were knocked out in the tempest," popped in Ferrin, who along with her inky brother fidgeted by the old cat's side. "It's all over with now, but boy, that was a doozy."

"Yes," Malovar exclaimed. "We thought you were a goner for a while." Percy gave him a black look. "Glad to have you back, Miss Lise," he added formally, sending his mentor a sheepish sidelong glance.

"Really glad," Ferrin added, beaming so broadly Lise couldn't help but smile.

"You have been dead to the world for quite some time now," Percy said, dealing the kittens a stern look that told them he would be asking the questions from now on. "What happened?"

"I'm not sure," said Lise, noticing that her memories were fading like dreams do in the wakening moments. "I was in a beautiful garden," she mused, then her tone soured. "But obviously I never left this place."

The three cats exchanged significant looks.

"What?" Lise asked. "Is there something I don't know?"

"No," Percy answered hesitantly. "Not really. Once you lost consciousness, your body was still as death, but—"

"But what?"

"Did you see anyone else...in this garden?"

"Well, yes. As a matter of fact, it seemed like I saw Dominic. But he was a man." She stopped, realizing how crazy she must sound, but instead of laughing, the cats whispered among themselves.

"I do not think it was a dream, Lise," Percy finally volunteered. "I think you really did see the master, in another form. When you were threatened by the storm, you must have instinctively space-shifted to the Alter-tier. You are truly extraordinary to do what you have done." Percy squeezed his eyes in a respectful cat-blink.

"Wow!" whooped Malovar, who seemed much recovered from his injuries. "Astounding!"

"I knew she could do it," Ferrin gloated until a swift look from Percy sent her back into mannerly silence.

Lise sighed. "But if I really did see him, why couldn't I help him? He was just beginning to tell me what to do when I woke up."

Percy looked dismayed. "You do not remember?"

"No, I'm afraid I don't." She hung her head. "And poor Dominic—I mean our Dominic here..." She gazed helplessly at the still form. "I guess I'm pretty useless."

"Wait a minute," exclaimed Malovar. "Look!"

As one, they turned their eyes to the master cat. With gasps of disbelief and joy, they watched the impossible.

His wounds were regenerating all by themselves, the ragged slash across his body healing before them. In moments, the tissue had regrown, the skin had melded together, and even tufts of long silvery fur were springing up over the scar. The rigid legs relaxed and the death's-head grin slackened into a normal quiet countenance. The tormented breathing became regular and he even twitched a few times as he slept.

"Dominic!" Lise cried. The bond they had formed on the Alter-tier hadn't diminished, and her heart leapt to see him rally. "Dominic, wake up. Please."

Dominic didn't move. Although he seemed at peace now, he was obviously not all the way back.

Lise groaned with disappointment and looked pleadingly at Percy. "What can we do?"

"You have done well—he is halfway home. But I am afraid Seh may still hold his spirit on the Alter-tier. At least his body has been renewed. Now, he can gather strength. He has a chance to recover, because of you."

"He's in a nice place," Lise mused, thinking of the lovely garden and the wooden bench under the orange tree. For an instant, she caught the sweet scent of lily of the valley wafting across the dimensions.

Suddenly, she felt completely drained. She could use a good coma herself, she thought wryly. Looking around, she saw the sun was beginning to set.

So late? Last she knew, it was morning. She definitely was in need of a nap.

"What do we do with him now?" she asked.

"He will be safe. This is a special place, and there are many watchers to make sure." Percy glanced toward the trees where row after row of cat eyes tracked their movements like radar.

"You mean we can go home, then?"

Before she got an answer, a loud yowl of greeting erupted from behind her. She turned to find Tom approaching, his proud tabby tail sailing high in the air.

"Tom," she called, going him. "I'm so glad to see you. We were just on our way home."

Tom stopped and sat down. He gave the group an ambiguous stare, then he unloaded the bad news.

"I think not," was all he said.

9. No Turning Back

A sigh of frustration rose from the little band at Evermore Tom's pronouncement, especially from Lise who was exhausted from her journey to the Alter-tier, but Tom couldn't let that bother him. There was too much at stake. For a little while, he listened to their complaints. *Let them gripe,* he thought to himself. *Soon enough, there will be no turning back.*

"My steadfast friends," he began somberly when the protests finally wound down. "I'm sorry to push your limits, but it's already Culmination, the final night of the Honored Three. The sun is fading, and very soon it will be time to act. I've spent the day spreading the word so everyone knows what will be expected of them. Now you must learn your part as well."

Tom surveyed his audience. Four pairs of eyes were glued to his, four faces tight with anticipation.

"Tonight will be the reckoning—the time when we will force Seh to confront his nemesis. If we fail, it will be many seasons before the cycle comes around again. Of course, if we fail..." His voice faltered and he hissed in a whisper, "If we fail, there will be few of us left to try."

After a thoughtful pause, he leapt to the top of a moss-covered stone, his attitude brightening. "But I think we shall win!"

"Yes!" Percy agreed, his crooked tail whipping back and forth. "We have Lise. She will do what none of us can."

"Everything's ready," Tom announced. "We'll go to the river, but we must hurry—there's so little time."

He sprang from the stone and began to slip quickly through the orchard toward the city streets and the wide river beyond. The others began to follow.

"Wait," called Lise, hanging behind. "Please, Tom. I... I'm still not sure what you expect of me."

Tom stopped and turned back. He looked at her with softness in his golden eyes. "I don't know what else I can tell you, Lise. It's unfortunate that Dominic isn't with us. He's much more knowledgeable when it comes to prophecy."

"There must be something," she persisted. "I know I had a little luck against Seh's servants, but I'm sure that's nothing like facing Seh, itself. Besides, whatever powers I have, I can't begin to control them. I'm totally unprepared."

Percy came to her side, Ferrin and Malovar trotting behind.

"You can do it, Lise," Ferrin encouraged with kittenish simplicity.

"I appreciate your confidence. Do what, though?"

"Whatever needs to be done," Malovar assured.

"Please, just come," Percy appealed. "Everything will unravel as it should."

Lise gave in with a sigh—she couldn't say no to her old friend—and began to walk with the rest of them. What she didn't see was the look that passed between Percy and Tom. The old cat's glare was iron-hard, as if to say: You had better have this right, my compatriot, because if anything happens to Lise, the wrath of Seh will be nothing compared to mine.

The storm clouds had furtively begun to reclaim the sky, eating what was left of the day as they advanced. Steadily they capped the heavens like a lid on a jar, closing everything inside. One by one, the stars winked out; electric lights came on in the streets and houses. In the distance, over the river, an explosion broke the night.

The unexpected blast shattered the air with a deafening peal, and an outburst of blazing sparks reaching its bony fingers across the firmament. On its tail was another burst, then another, cascading in hellish harmony to a crescendo of smoke and flame. Ferrin and Malovar catapulted into a roadside forsythia bush. Percy and Tom stood their ground but crouched with heads low, staring. Lise wasn't sure what to do. This phenomenon seemed familiar, and the feeling wasn't one of fear. Quite the opposite, more like jubilation. She didn't know why, but this was a good sign, like a force that was with them, not against.

"What is that?" she asked. "Do you know?"

"It is the cyclic freedom party," replied Percy without taking his eyes off the optical pageant. "The humans celebrate it in the hot season. It is always a great shock to us, and very hard on our ears, but we have learned that it is not meant to hurt us."

The kittens were poking their heads out of the bush, still wary of the ongoing clamor. They couldn't quite trust Percy's words over their own quickly-beating hearts.

"This year, it was no surprise," Tom told them, "and no coincidence that Tri-Night Culmination and the human independence gathering have come at the same time. Humans have fought their share of battles, as we'll soon be doing ourselves. Their spirit will help strengthen our cause. After all, we're fighting for them, too, though they don't know it."

Now, Lise understood. Today was July fourth, Independence Day for the American people. She knew that, of course; it had just slipped her mind. As she turned her gaze toward the resplendent fireworks, she felt a new rush of conviction. Freedom was inherent in the living soul. The display reminded her this wouldn't be the first time lives had been laid down for liberty.

The earsplitting reports were coming from all sides now, though only the ones on the river were accompanied by the dazzling waterfall of fire. Most were just noise, and some were very close. Small groups of people hovered in the darkness, then BANG! Each time, Ferrin and Malovar would jump straight up in the air as if electrocuted. It might have been funny had it not been so obvious they were scared to death. Lise thought of the ordeal ahead and gave a short prayer that this would be the worst fear they would face that night.

Eventually, the noise abated, leaving only the random crack here and there. Tom gathered his group and they moved out once more. From the higher ground, they could see the river, a shimmering ribbon of onyx edged by the neon town. That was where they were headed.

The scenery began to shift. Trees and homes gave way to store fronts, warehouses, and bars. The tidy residential lanes became cobblestone alleyways, painted with graffiti and choked with filth. It reminded Lise of Horace's haunt, only creepier. Offhandedly she wondered what the huge tomcat would be doing tonight.

The alleys were alive with reverie but not the innocent sort the companions had encountered earlier. This crowd was harsher and their joy held the hard edge of despondency. Perhaps they didn't share the same boons of liberty as those more affluent, Lise reflected. Independence was a state of mind, as well as body. These unfortunates were trapped in prisons beyond their own design.

Lise began to see things that she would rather have missed: a man in an apartment yelling obscenities at some dirty wailing kids; an old woman sitting alone coughing up blood; a businessman lying in the gutter, throwing up on the lapels of his expensive suit; a scared young girl hiding behind a dumpster while a gang of ruffians shouted and banged the garbage cans with pipes, searching her out. Lise knew it was only a matter of time.

"Where are we?" she whispered to Percy. "I don't like this place."

"No one does. We are at the fringe of the realm of Seh."

"Why are we here?" Lise asked in trepidation.

Percy confirmed her worst fears. "This time, we cannot wait for the beast to come to us. Tonight, we go to it."

"Keep your head down and stay out of sight," Tom warned. "There are bad things here, both seen and unseen."

Lise didn't need to be told twice. She slunk further into the shadows and raced along, a silent streak.

Ugliness and obscenity abounded. Piles of rotting garbage marred the land. There were vast open spaces where nothing grew—nothing could grow because the ground itself was poisoned. Oil drum fires blazed like lanterns; cardboard camps squatted amongst mattresses, tires, plastic bags, fouled diapers, wine bottles, and the mass of other human debris. Shards of glass ground in the ooze beneath their feet. Everything smelled of decay.

As the group rounded a slimy heap of wet sheeting, they sensed a change. The olfactory markings of another cat's territory hung in the air. Tom stopped and sniffed but before he could decide whether to retreat or continue, the decision was made for him. Out of a maze of wooden crates came a mangy long-haired tomcat. His dirty yellow fur was matted and he was missing part of an ear, but his strange orange eyes were keen. He and Tom stared at each other, sizing up the contingencies and evaluating potential stratagem. They stayed like that for some seconds, then the yellow broke its glare, turning to the others.

"Greetings," Tom said formally. "May all be well with you."

The yellow brought his gaze back to Tom. "And you, stranger," he replied tonelessly.

"I apologize for entering your zone without invitation, but we're on a mission. I assure you, we're not looking for any trouble with you...or your clan." He added the last as he saw two more felines, a female and a young male, peeking out of the box shelter.

The yellow sat on his haunches, a gesture of tolerance, but he made sure his seat was at a higher elevation than the newcomers. "A mission?" he mused. "And what sort of mission would that be on the Culmination of Tri-Night at the gates of the realm of the beast?"

Tom settled too, politely remaining low. Choosing to ignore the sarcasm, he said, "You seem familiar with our cause."

"Who among us is not? We salute you. Here, meet a few of my family—come on out, you two." He motioned to the pair behind him. They each took a step closer to the strangers but that was all. "This is Frea and Kelvin. And I am Polaris Elonius, master of this tract from the river to the under-bridge, and from the sky-colored can to out past the old crone's hovel. Welcome, confederates."

Lise relaxed a little at the big cat's friendly manner. Tom remained alert though he breathed a sigh of relief as he introduced his own legion.

"I'm sorry to rush, but we must find the beast as soon as possible," Tom said after the requisite moment of polite intermingling. "I'm not familiar with this place. Maybe you can help us."

"Of course," said Polaris. "What is it you need?"

"The portal to the Cursed Realm. Are we very near?"

Polaris gave Tom an ambiguous look, his tangelo eyes gleaming. "The portal—yes. It's something we don't usually speak of, but for you, I'll make an exception. After all, we are on the same side..." He laughed. "Are we not?"

Polaris began to give Tom directions, cat style, with many embellishments and flourishes.

"From here you go toward the scent of the hills, turning ocean-wise when you reach the venerable tank..."

The instructions droned on with trenchant dips and scurrilous hillocks, but Lise had stopped listening. Something about the yellow cat didn't seem right. She stared at the massive male but could find nothing to back up her doubt. Still, there it was, like a thorn in the paw, an overwhelming sense of evil.

A jab of prescience hit Lise full on, along with the dimensional shift that she had come to associate with her insights. As if the sea had parted, she knew now what was nagging at her. With no further thought, she moved toward Polaris and without apology, stepped between him and Tom.

Tom began a hiss of reprimand for Lise's rudeness, but she interrupted him.

"No, look," she commanded.

Tom shot her an angry glance before comprehension dawned. He scanned Polaris closer and then he saw it too: the seething hateful fire in his eyes. Tom would have kicked himself for not noticing sooner but there was no time. The skirmish was on.

Polaris jumped for Tom, his orange eyes made crimson by the searing inner flame. Kelvin ran at Malovar and Percy. Percy went one way and Malovar, the other, both slipping easily away. Frea started toward Lise, but Lise had been ready even before the others. With one good swipe across the female's chops, she too, was off to safety. Tom rolled from Polaris's grasp and dashed after.

The traitorous creatures chased them for a short time but soon lost interest, content with yelling oaths: "Power to Seh and his Minions... You're all going to die!"

When they could no longer hear the taunts, Tom turned to Lise. "Thank the Originator that you saw what I did not," he said profoundly. "How did you know?"

"I'm not sure what tipped me off," she replied. "Something didn't feel right. Horace told me to watch for ones not like us— ones with fire in their eyes. The moment I saw it—the little blaze that burned like a torch behind their pupils, I panicked."

"Who's Horace?" Tom asked.

"Someone I met when I was lost after the battle with the squirrels. He helped me. I didn't mean to make such a scene."

"You did the right thing," said Percy.

"It's always hard to believe that our own would turn on us," Tom brooded, a dark fire of his own smoldering within his golden gaze. "I should never have been so credulous. Seh's minions come in all forms. I must remember."

"What would they have done to us?" asked Ferrin anxiously.

"Oh, I think they were just trying to put us on the wrong path," Tom replied. "Trying to delay us. They probably figured if we wasted enough time looking for the portal, we would fail to find Seh by the close of Culmination. I thought those directions seemed a little off. I suppose we'll have to locate the way on our own."

"Evermore," Percy said quietly. "Put worry aside for now. You will find the path."

"We'd best be going," Tom sighed. "We can't afford any more distractions, or Polaris will get his wish after all."

The five began to move, Tom at the lead sniffing out a new track. They traveled quickly, keeping keen eyes on their surroundings for any sign of those who might mean them harm. Lise hoped they wouldn't run into any more servants of Seh, disguised or not. As they passed without incident, she began to feel more at ease.

Suddenly, a hand shot from the hulk of a burned-out car and grabbed Malovar by the scruff.

"Gotcha, you little devil!" a gravelly voice proclaimed. "You'll be comin' with me."

Lise whipped around in time to see Malovar dangling helplessly from the meatball fist of a man the size of a grizzly bear. Malovar squirmed in the big man's grasp but to no avail. In fact, the man seemed to find the young cat's yowls of protest enormously amusing.

"You ain't goin' nowhere," Bear-man spat with a cuff to Malovar's right ear. "'Cept into my cooking pot. Martha said she had a yen for stew. And guess what, little critter? You're it." With that, he gave a laugh that sounded more like regurgitation than an expression of joy and struck out in heavy strides through the maze of wreckage.

Either he hadn't seen the others or he didn't care. Ferrin

unsheathed her claws, and with a scream of rage, leapt after her brother.

"No," cried Tom, bounding behind her. He caught her and brought her down. "No, Ferrin," he repeated. "Not this way, or you too will become part of the soup."

Ferrin writhed and spit and then went still. "Malovar," she moaned. "Tom, we can't let him get cooked."

"And we won't." Tom rose off the kitten and gave his shoulder fur a nervous lick. "But we can't just walk up to the man and ask for him back, either."

"What, then?" Percy asked.

Tom thought for a moment, then beckoned them nearer. "Here's what we're going to do."

The group huddled close as Tom gave commands. A few seconds was all it took for them to prepare. In perfect sync, they turned and slunk like a single shadow in the wake of the bearman, Tom's plan of attack clear in their heads.

It didn't take them long to catch up with him as he wove his way through the garbage as if it were a parkway garden. A right turn at an old wood stove, a left between a pair of paint buckets, overtop a soggy pink mound of insulation. He was fast for such a giant but no match for cats.

They were on his every move until he rimmed a hill of scrap lumber. Cautiously the clowder followed, but when they gazed over the mound, the man had disappeared.

Percy cast a green eye across the empty landscape. "Where did they go?"

His query was met with silence. No one else knew any more than he.

"Listen," Ferrin whispered. "I hear something."

She bounded down the sack of boards, then moved more cautiously toward what looked like an ancient rust-covered diving bell.

"I hear it too," Tom breathed as he joined her at the bell. "He must have ducked inside."

Without a sound, Tom scampered up a precarious puzzle of discarded girders and peered in through a filthy porthole near the top. "They're here, alright," he mouthed back at the companions, "and I don't like the look of this at all."

Ferrin scampered to Tom's side. As they peeked helplessly through the bars and heavy glass, their hearts stopped. Bear-man had tossed the little cat into a lidded basket. He was lighting a camp stove and pouring murky water from a plastic jug into an aluminum pot, his fat gray lips curled in anticipation.

"What do we do now?" asked Lise who had silently joined the duo.

Tom said nothing though his mind was racing.

"We've got to get him out!" Ferrin cried in panic. She was back on the ground, dancing in anxious circles, barely containing her dread.

Percy came beside her and smoothed his sideburn against hers. "First, we need to find a way in." Percy's tone was even and calm, conveying a little of those emotions to those around him.

"Right," said Tom. "Anyone care to make a guess?"

The four cats surveyed the metal sphere and gaped through the dirty portholes, but from every angle, the shell seemed smooth and uncut.

"The man got in, so we can too," Lise reasoned, "but for the life of me, I don't know how."

"Look!" Ferrin exclaimed. She firmed her muscles and threw herself up the smooth side of the bell, only to slip back down again when her claws found no purchase. "Up there," she cried, going for a second try.

Lise saw what she was aiming for. "I see it. At the top. There's a door."

Sure enough, at what would have been top center if the bell had been sitting straight was the hatch. It was a circular opening hardly big enough for the bear-man to fit through but a breeze for a cat. Unfortunately, it seemed impossible to get to as Ferrin confirmed, sliding back down the slick surface for a second time.

"The sides are like glass," she pronounced, collapsing in dismay.

"What now?" Lise asked Tom, but he wasn't paying attention. Instead, he was staring through the porthole window, transfixed by something inside. The hackles on his back were beginning to rise.

"We're about to have company," he bellowed, springing off the scaffold and ducking behind a worn-out tire just in time to avoid being hit by an old running shoe.

"He must have heard us," Percy said as he, too, dove for cover.

"Scatter!" cried Tom.

By the time Bear-man climbed laboriously out, there was no sign of cats. Satisfied the shoe had done the trick, he turned back to the bell and his dinner preparations.

"No way, jerk-face!" yelled Ferrin as she charged.

"Ferrin, no—" Tom managed, but it was too late. Ferrin had already latched onto the big man's beefy leg where she stuck, claws firmly planted in his thick calf.

"You're not going to eat my brother!" she cried before sinking her teeth in for a bite.

With a strangled cry, the bear-man dropped and rolled in the filth to dislodge the little cat. Ferrin was holding her own but Tom knew it couldn't last long. Without thought, he burst from his hiding place and attacked from the other side.

Lise was poised to follow when Percy held her back. "Let's get Malovar," he said, "while the human is distracted."

She nodded and the pair darted for the diving bell instead.

"How do we get to the hatch?" Lise asked. They were back to the dilemma of how to scale the mirror-smooth sides.

"I do not know, but we must find a way."

"Maybe it's better from the other direction."

"Whatever we do, we need to act fast," Percy said, glancing back at the skirmish. Tom and Ferrin were battling valiantly, but the sheer bulk of the man was a danger in itself. Hopefully they could hold out a little longer. With a final worried glance, Percy and Lise stole behind the sphere.

There was a moment of promise when they saw a succession of metal hand-holds leading up the face—probably what the bear-man used for access—but the rungs were too far apart for little paws as they soon found out.

"What now?" Lise began.

Percy didn't answer. He was looking through a porthole to the inside.

"I don't see him anymore," the old cat scowled.

"The man put him in the basket. He closed the lid."

"The lid is open now. And Malovar is not inside."

"Could he— I mean... Already?" The two stared with horror at the cook-pot simmering away on the camp stove.

"Malovar," Lise whispered, shedding a sudden tear.

"No, look," Percy exclaimed. "There he is."

Lise followed Percy's gaze to the top of the bell where Malovar's coal black head was just poking up from the hatch. In a split second, the kitten was out and safe on the ground, followed by a black shadow four times his size.

"Horace?" Lise shrieked in surprise.

"Why, if it isn't my little one," Horace returned, touching noses.

"Boy, am I glad to see you," she cried. "And you, you little rascal." She turned her gaze on Malovar. "We thought for a minute... Well, never mind what we thought. You're back, and that's all that matters."

The young cat purred with the thrill of release, and Lise would have been content to stay like that forever, but Percy broke through her reverie. "Quick, we must help the others. We need to let them know Malovar is safe."

Skirting the bell again, he yowled for Ferrin and Tom. Bear-man was just about to bring down a malicious blow on Ferrin's vulnerable backbone when she heard Percy's call and caught sight of her brother. Like a flash, she and Tom were out of there and the fist came down onto bear-man's own shin with a bone-cracking smack. His cry of pain was so terrible that folks shuddered in their hovels for blocks around.

The group of five plus their newest member listened to the wail dwindle as they made fast tracks from that ghoulish place. Soon as they were away, Tom stopped and sank into a crouch. For a moment, he panted, then he gathered himself into a sphinx-like repose, his golden eyes closed and his breath even and slow. The others followed suit, a moment's rest after their ordeal.

"Who's your friend, Lise?" Tom asked of the newcomer.

"This is Horace, the one I was telling you about, who helped me last night."

"R. Horace Alanos—best feline ratter in alley-town," the big cat boasted amicably.

"Glad to meet you, Horace. Your appearance was timely, to say the least."

"How did you get up the sides of that metal thing?" piped up Ferrin. "I tried twice but couldn't do it."

"Well, you see—" Horace began.

"I think the tales must wait," Tom intervened. "Right now we have work to do." He looked intently at Malovar. "And we're late, as it is."

"What's up?" asked Horace, excited to suddenly find himself at the center of the action.

"Apparently, we're in search of Seh," Lise explained to her ally-cat friend.

"Got room for one more?"

Tom gave him a penetrating look. "You were brave to rescue our friend, but I'm afraid the next battle will require more than fortitude."

"The little one enlightened me. That's why I came. I'd like to tag along, if you don't have any objections."

"No one has ever confronted Seh in its lair," Tom warned. "We have no idea what we'll be facing, aside from evil beyond belief. I would understand if you declined."

"Decline a fight with Seh? Not going to happen!" Horace attested. "You can count me in."

After a moment, Tom nodded solemnly. Lise made swift introductions all around. Horace's braggadocio and the daring rescue of Malovar had bolstered the companions. With spirits high, they advanced to meet their foe.

• • •

The clouds had settled low in the sky, bloated and yellow with smog. Lise felt the temperature drop as they crossed the slums toward the heart of Old Town. With splatters the size of bird-droppings, the rain began. More like January than July, the steely pellets hit the ground like bullets, exploding into slimy puddles that soon spread into rivers across the cobblestone streets.

The elation hadn't lasted. The group was silent now, each lost in their own concerns. Most of them were wondering if they would still be alive tomorrow, and if so, what would tomorrow bring? Even Horace had dropped a little of his grandiosity. Drenched to the skin, fur hanging in limp shanks from the long-haired ones, they plodded toward the unknown.

Tom paused on a lonely street corner. He sniffed the turgid air, then stared into the gutter where the rain water surged in oily torrents down the vortex of the iron grate.

"The portal," he pronounced grimly. "This is where we begin our search for Seh."

"Down there?" Lise asked in shock.

"I'm afraid it's the only way."

Lise turned to Percy who nodded in solemn agreement.

"But..." Lise stammered, watching the whirlpool gulp leaves

and debris down its insatiable maw. "It doesn't look safe. We'll be of no help if we die trying."

"You won't die," Tom replied flatly.

"But it looks so cold, so foreboding. Besides..." She paused. "...I don't like water."

No one spoke, but on looking around her, Lise saw five faces filled with the same dread; five others who didn't want to go down there; five who hated water as much or more even than she. Suddenly, she knew she was not alone.

"Lise is right to be afraid," said Tom. "This will be a formidable journey. I can't guarantee we will all come out of it alive. If any of you intend to turn back, now would be the time. No one will think less of you for feeling what we all feel here today."

The kittens, Ferrin and Malovar, cowered under the gargoyle eves of an old store front, their hesitance clear in their demeanor. Horace was inspecting a nearby fire hydrant as if it were the most important thing in the world. Percy stuck close to Lise in hopes that proximity might shelter them both. Tom looked at his army and sighed.

"Tonight may well be the death of our species as we know it, but it also may be the birth of a World without Seh. Each of you must decide for yourself how best to serve, but decide quickly—time is running out."

With a courageous leap, Tom threw himself into the watery maelstrom and dove in between the bars of the grate. With a rush of sludge, he was gone. To where, only those with the fortitude to join him would ever know.

Horace was first. His brave cry of "Freedom!" turned into a muted gurgle as he, too, was flushed into the drain.

Next, Ferrin and Malovar rushed to the edge together. Ferrin hung back at the last minute, but Malovar swept her along with him. They were swallowed without a trace.

"Time to go, Cohabitor," Percy whispered softly.

"Is it the only way?"

Lise's question was answered by Percy's nod.

"Okay," she said with a boldness she didn't feel. "Let's do it."

She leapt, following on the tail of her old friend. As the water closed over her head, her claustrophobic terror crescendoed until she felt she would explode. Then, suddenly, it was gone, replaced by a new strength as immense and organic as an oak tree.

I will survive this! she found herself thinking confidently. *And our World will survive, as well.*

10. Loss and Change

Lise scrambled out of the deluge and joined the others on a narrow shelf at the edge of the sewer. Beneath them raced a river Styx of city scum. The sound was deafening as it crashed against the round brick sides of the tunnel and gushed its deadly overflows into the echoing gloom. If Lise hadn't been so agile, if she had miscalculated her steps, if she had made the tiniest slip she would have been in big trouble.

Peering through the darkness, she saw her companions, shadows against the slime-covered wall. As her eyes adjusted to the low light, she realized with shock they didn't seem glad to see her. Uncomprehending, she looked around once more, face to face to face. Comprehension drove, jagged-edged, into her heart. She now knew what was wrong. Only four shapes huddled in the cold rising mist; only four pairs of sorrowing eyes returned her gaze.

"What happened?" she breathed as Malovar let out a bone-chilling wail. "Who—"

"Ferrin," Percy told her bleakly. "She did not make it onto the ledge."

Lise stared at the churning turbulence below. "Ferrin fell in? Quick, we've got to help her!"

Percy lowered his eyes. "It is too late. She is already lost."

"We can't just leave her alone in the cold and dark," Lise exclaimed, unwilling to accept what her unbelieving eyes knew to be true.

"To follow would be suicide. She has crossed Beyond and is with the Originator now—her soul is free."

"But her death will mean nothing if we shirk our task," said Tom. "We must go on."

"Smaller for the loss of her," said Percy.

"Yes," Tom grieved.

"I don't understand," said Lise. "Why didn't she shift to the Alter-tier like cats do when they are close to death? What about her nine lives?"

"The ability to shift is cultivated over time. I'm afraid she was simply too young."

"But—" Lise began, then faltered. Her heart cried for her little friend, but she knew she had to accept what was done.

"I'm so sorry, Malovar," she said, moving close and smoothing his water-soaked fur.

"I will fight for her!" he howled.

"We will all fight for her," Tom pledged. "For Ferrin!"

"For Ferrin!" the group returned.

The echo of their voices died quickly, as if plucked from the cavern and cast down the black river in pursuit of their fallen friend. They gave a few moments of silence, then Tom rose and slipped decisively through a crack in the bricks. His small but dedicated army trailed solemnly. Nose to tail, they slunk with singular determination downward through the earth and away from the site of their first terrible tragedy.

The going was hard and took all their concentration. Stunted roots grabbed from above like netting; jagged, razor-sharp rocks gouged their sides. Apart from their beating hearts, the hollow throb of water on stone was the only sound that pursued them as they plunged farther and farther from everything they knew.

After a long decent and some turns and twists that challenged even a feline's contortive abilities, the path opened into a small subterranean cave. Cold and black as a void, at its dark center was a single slab of stone jutting from the mud floor like a grave-head. Without a word, the cats encircled it.

The cavern was shallow and the stone nearly touched the low granite ceiling. It was a barren, oppressive place, and Lise shivered as she took her stand in the ring. She hated this cramped sodden hole, but she kept her feelings to herself. With a deep breath of stagnant air, she waited.

Minutes passed but nothing happened. Lise glanced at her companions but each sat stiff and rigid as the standing stone itself. Four ghostly cat-paths swirled about their feet like auras, glowing dully in the darkness. The wet surface of the slab reflected their unearthly shine.

Time stretched out into infinity, but just when Lise thought she could take no more of the monotony, she began to note a shift in her perception. The stone seemed wider, blacker, smooth like onyx. The cave was larger than she had first imagined it. In fact, the cave was immense, and so was the stone! It towered above her like a cliff face. She didn't understand how it could have been so until she felt a shimmer of prescience and recognized the subtle signature of the Alter-tier. The cats were shifting in space and time, and she had been traveling along with them.

The cavern was tremendous now, and not a natural cave at all but a huge marble-walled chamber. Great iron candelabrum shed a harsh glimmer from above. The central stone was now an ebony pillar as thick as a redwood trunk climbing into the shadows.

The change in Lise's surroundings was unnerving, but more so was the startling transition of her friends. In place of the small cat-bodies, fearsome human shapes were beginning to form. Robed in diaphanous color, the four rose, lofty and threatening, in sudden supernatural splendor.

Instead of a big orange tabby, Evermore Tom was a man and by the look of him, one of great power. He was tall and muscular with deep amber curls cascading across his brawny shoulders like a lion's mane. His strange golden gaze seemed to pierce the darkness. At his side hung a broadsword and around his neck dangled a large ruby pendant. The blood-red jewel reflected nothing, instead radiating an eerie light of its own.

In awe, Lise took a step backward. Tom gave her a reassuring and very human smile before he returned his attention to the pillar.

"Do not be afraid," a nearby voice whispered.

She turned to find herself face to face with another human stranger, but as she looked more closely, she realized that the old man with the long white hair and flowing beard wasn't unknown to her after all. In fact, she knew him with every breath in her body.

"Percy!" she exclaimed.

His deeply wrinkled eyes smiled on her with love. The intense green color had not diminished with the shift, nor had the emotions behind them. Lise touched him cautiously, as if he might disappear. His furless skin was warm and real.

She looked with curiosity at Horace and Malovar. Horace had taken the shape of a robust, dark-skinned soldier outfitted in shimmering armor. Raven coils stood out from his sleek head, and his copper eyes smoldered like coal. His clean-shaven jaw was set with determination. He nodded to Lise, but his soul was set for battle.

Malovar, the youngest, stood a little back from the others. The anguish of the loss of his sister was etched on his youthful human face. His emerald eyes were grim with grief and hate. Long slender fingers played nervously with a lock of his straight black hair. He looked as if he was primed to go off at any moment.

Suddenly, Lise got a fresh whiff of lily of the valley. She looked around and then down at herself and found a corsage of tiny blossoms pinned at her human breast. She, too, had transmuted, but not into anything like her usual form. Her long, lithe body was garbed in a close-fitting robe of a color that transcended the limits of the rainbow. Over her long, crimson tresses hung a lace veil and from her neck dangled a little key on a golden thread. She had no idea of their significance, but she sensed that when the time came, they would show their worth.

Taking one more glance around, she realized the group had been joined by one other, a handsome mid-aged man with flowing, silver hair. His electric blue eyes were turned on her, filling with warmth and mirth.

"Dominic!" she cried, running to him and throwing her arms around his neck. She didn't understand how he had come to be there; she was just glad he was.

Malovar turned in embarrassment from Lise's brazenness while Tom cleared his throat self-consciously.

"Master, I apologize. She doesn't know—" he began.

"It's alright, Evermore," Dominic interjected in his resonant human voice. "This one saved my life. The least I owe her is a simple touch of friendship." To Lise, aside so the others would not see, he winked.

Lise disentangled herself. She could never forget what had passed between them underneath the orange tree in the Altertier, but it needed to remain their secret. She smiled conspiratorially into his ocean eyes and politely resumed her place.

After assuring himself Dominic wouldn't be subjected to any more inappropriate acts, Tom announced, "We are here, Master."

Dominic studied those around him and his face grew grave. When he came to Malovar, he sighed. "Not all, I see."

Malovar's muscles tautened and his eyes snapped shut. Dominic bowed his head in respect.

"Let us begin."

"Let us begin," repeated the others.

Tom moved forward until he was an arm's length from the ebony pillar, then he took the peculiar ruby in his hand and touched it to the stone. With an eye-searing flash, the chamber exploded in a hailstorm of blood-red light. The air became charged as tiny cerulean bolts shot from above, striking the startled companions with small shocks. Still, everyone held their place.

The pillar was expanding now, spinning outward like a Chinese lotus toy. It enveloped the group like a tornado; faster and faster, it held them in its cyclone dance. Lise's stomach flipped. For a moment she thought she would be sick, but just as she could endure no more, the motion stopped, dropping them like seeds into vacuum.

There was an audible pop and a scene began to materialize around them. Lise surveyed the terrain, but what she saw seemed more like something out of a surrealistic painting than any earthly place. A mat-black sky hung like a backdrop for a play: no dimension, no horizon. Rolling wheat fields stretched for a little way into the distance, then stopped as if that was all the set painter had bothered to put up. A stunted breeze passed through the dry grass with the rattle of insect wings. It seemed to recall a dream.

A dirt path meandered randomly through the mock-up meadow. Dominic began down it, and in single file, the others followed with Malovar bringing up the rear. No one spoke, no one voiced the questions that burned in Lise's mind: *Where are we? Why are we here?*

Suddenly, there came a cry from behind. A pack of monstrous dogs had sprung from the tall grass and set upon Malovar. Three of the largest mongrels Lise had ever seen were giving the young man the fight of his life, but he had his sword out and was bravely fending them off. Their dead-red eyes marked them as the minions of Seh.

Strangely enough, the brutes took no notice of anyone but Malovar. Horace saw his advantage and began to Malovar's aid, but a strong hand stopped him.

"This is his fight," Dominic said solemnly.

The soldier, quivering with the hunger to avenge, stared back at the master with incredulity. "But I can help him. After Ferrin, we cannot lose the bother, too."

"No, Horace," Dominic insisted. "Your time will come. Leave Malovar to his."

With that, the master turned his straight back on the growling of the hounds and the grunting of the valiant young man and began to lead on down the path, sweeping Lise along beside him. Uttering something between a sigh and a growl, Horace gave in.

Lise trusted Dominic implicitly, but she, too, was concerned. "We're just going to walk away?" she whispered discreetly, so no one else would hear her question the master.

"Our charge lies elsewhere," he replied enigmatically. "We will meet him again, I promise."

Giving a last glance back at the conflict, she saw that one dog was already down and another was flagging. She also noted the look of triumph in Malovar's emerald eyes. There was something else there, too—an aura of healing. For the first time since the loss of his sister, Malovar had a smile on his face.

The five walked on silently; the grassland scene never altered. It was as if they were traveling the same lifeless ground over and over again. Lise began to feel like she was acting out the nightmare where one goes and goes but never gets anywhere.

Just when Lise was wondering if they would walk this strange plane forever, she began to hear something new. Above the haunting wind that moaned through the dry wheat stalks, a sound like a far-away siren cycled on the edge of the high frequencies. As it intensified, Lise began to pick out separate pitches, as if not just one thing was creating this motor whine but many things working together.

There was a shudder in the playhouse sky, a ribbon of dark rising up from the flat horizon. The sound rose too, sheering into the silence like a skilsaw. In an instant, the air was gorged with a mass of dung-brown wings, blotting out the light and bringing with them a stench that made the companions gag.

"Cockroaches!" Lise cried in horror as clouds of hard-shelled insects began to zoom in on them as if they were targets.

"We're nearing Seh," Dominic coughed. "The beast must be troubled if it sends its forces to stop us. These pests are sordid but they cannot hurt us. Whatever happens, we must remain calm."

Then, the infestation was upon them. Lise batted the flying pests from her hair. *Remain calm?* she thought, as they clung to her dress and crawled on her body. *And just how does he expect that to happen?* Even knowing they were harmless, she felt she would jump out of her skin.

Horace leapt forward. "This one's mine!" he announced, shooting a brief glance at the master.

Dominic nodded.

The swarthy soldier raised his sword high above his head and reached into his coat of mail, pulling out a fist-sized globe that glowed cold blue from deep inside its icy surface. With a battle cry, he strode into the midst of the swarm and was instantly consumed by the brown buzzing maelstrom.

"Go!" called Tom. "Run! Hurry!"

No one had to be told twice, even though the flying roaches didn't seem to follow. As Lise glanced behind her, she could see a pale blue radiance begin to blossom from within the insect cloud.

He will prevail, she promised herself as she hastened away with her ever-diminishing companions.

When they could no longer see the cockroach swarm nor hear its space-ship drone, Dominic slowed the pace but continued purposefully along the path. Once again, they returned to the tedious task of traversing the never-ending field. It was monotonous going. Lise felt more like a mouse on a treadmill than a hero out to save the world.

She was beginning to wonder if they were stuck in some space-shift time loop when an ear-popping explosion sent her hurtling backward with its percussive force. Ahead of them appeared a roiling black wall of smoke.

This is hard on the psyche, she silently charged when her heart began to recover from the adrenaline. *One minute, boredom; terror, the next. It's enough to drive a sane girl mad!*

The smoke which stunk like burning meat and stung her eyes was clearing, leaving a net of sooty wisps through which a gigantic shape began to materialize. It was a tree, although to call it a tree seemed a stretch of the imagination. It might have been alive once, but now, the interwoven branches were gray and brittle, and the massive crocodile trunk was pitted and sloughing away. Its decaying limbs reached out threateningly, as if it were angered by its lack of life. Its menacing shadow fell directly across their path like a black hole.

"Only a dead tree," Lise exclaimed with relief. "I thought it might be another contingent of Seh's minions."

Dominic eyed her dubiously. "It may seem innocent, but it is of Seh—no good can come of it." He scrutinized the mammoth carcass. "However, the path is set. We have no choice but to pass."

"We must remain alert," Tom cautioned. "This thing may be dangerous in some way we can't perceive. We'll proceed one at a time—I will go first."

He stepped forward and disappeared into the abysmal shadow. Lise felt a shiver of foreboding as he vanished into impenetrable dark, but after a few moments, he reappeared unharmed on the other side. He turned and nodded to Dominic that it seemed safe enough.

Cautiously, the master went next. He, too, crossed without incident. Apparently, the tree was as dead as it looked.

It was Lise's turn. A second shudder played between her shoulder blades, but she moved stoically ahead. As the cold shade slid across her skin like oily ice, her throat tightened but in another instant, she was through and back in the pseudo-sunlight, none the worse for her journey.

Lise was considering the possibility that they had been wrong about the tree when she heard a scream. Percy! As she turned to look, she saw a gush of mange-gray bodies frothing from the hollow trunk. The foul unkempt fur and lifeless red eyes marked them as Seh's demon squirrels. A steady stream was pouring forth like blood from a gaping wound. One after the other, they surged up the old man's robes, clawing and biting as they went.

"No!" Lise cried, leaping toward the foray. Strong arms caught her mid-jump and held her like a harness.

"No!" she wailed. "Let me go! You don't understand!"

Dominic's hold was steady, the powerful arms unrelenting.

"But you don't understand. He hates squirrels! He hates them..."

"Lise, stop," Dominic crooned in her ear. "I cannot let you go. I will not."

Finally, Lise surrendered, sobbing against the master's sturdy chest. He still held her, but now his embrace was soft with solace.

Turning her away from the grisly scene, he guided her on down the path. Tom followed closely, but kept an eye on the trials of his comrade. Percy had gone down under the first wave but had managed to get himself up again. With a thrill of pride, Tom saw an increasing number of squirrel bodies piled on the ground around the old man and a decreasing number of reinforcements spouting out of the dead tree. For an instant, he caught Percy's ice-green eye. Tom thought he detected a wink of pure triumph. He smiled to himself and continued on the path.

"He's going to be alright," Tom told Lise softly. "He's strong, and this fight has been long in coming."

Lise knew a little of her cohabitor's blood feud with the squirrels, but it didn't seem fair he should have to face them alone. Her heart was breaking. Of all those they had lost, this was by far the harshest for her to bear.

Lise was sick of bouncing between fear, grief, and tedium. She craved release. Whatever pestilence Seh set upon them next, she would take on herself. No matter what Dominic said about trials or the time being right, she could no longer stand idly by as her friends were brought down.

As if the master sensed her thoughts, he turned. "What you do is your choice, but know this: all is proceeding as it should. This war will soon be over."

Over, yes; but who will prevail? Lise wondered. Grimly, she fell into step between her two remaining confederates, Dominic and Evermore Tom.

They hadn't traveled long when another high pressure discharge burst through the drear. This one was of such magnitude that its impact made Lise wince with pain.

What now? Lise swore, belatedly snapping her eyes shut and covering her ears. When she opened them a moment later, a carbon bank of smog churned ominously up ahead. She held her breath as she waited for the smoky curtain to scatter, trying to imagine what horror this cloud might hold.

The fog dissipated, leaving behind a stark concrete edifice that hadn't been there before. The barren block building seemed small in relation to the endless fields surrounding it, and not until the three reached it and stood staring up at enormous glass doors did they realize how immense the manifestation really was. Its significance, none of them could guess.

The fabrication was so out of place in the theatrical tundra that Lise almost expected it to be fake, a false front like a set in a Hollywood western. Cautiously, she reached out and touched a python-sized door handle, but the cold brass was solid. She gave a little push and the glass panel yielded, revealing a crack of darkness. Letting it slide soundlessly back into place, she turned to her companions.

"Now what? Do we go in?"

"It appeared in our path—there must be a reason for it," Dominic replied, but he sounded unsure.

"But what if it's filled with rabid stoats or some equally obnoxious minion of Seh?" Lise countered.

The master was ambiguous. "I somehow doubt that's the case this time."

"You don't seem very certain, for a master," Lise whispered so only Dominic could hear.

Looking at Lise, his face lightened a bit. "You must be patient with me, dear—it's not as if anyone has ever done this before."

She smiled at his candidness. "I see what you mean."

Dominic turned to Tom. "What do you think, Evermore?"

The brawny human thought for a moment, then gave a nod. "I say we go. What else have we got to do—other than trudge across this interminable prairie, of course?" Without waiting for an answer, he pushed his way through the mirror-black door and disappeared into obscurity.

Dominic took hold of the smooth handle and, slightly more cautiously, pulled the door wide. Nothing but shadowy gloom greeted them through the orifice.

"After you," he said politely, then looked dubious. "Or on second thought, maybe I had better go first..."

"Nonsense," Lise replied, taking a deep breath. She grabbed the master's hand and in they went, Dominic comfortably close behind her.

The pair emerged in a dim featureless hallway. Tom stood poised a little way inside. The only other being in the room was a wolverine.

Lise blinked in the dusk. By the dim glow of the ornate fixtures high above, she could make out a long narrow chamber with patterned wallpaper and plush carpeting running its length like a maroon roadway. Another door squatted in the middle of the wall like a cartoon mouse-hole. To the side skulked the wolverine, its red eyes glaring vacantly, and its teeth bared in a vicious grin.

"Tickets," it hissed in fuzzy but understandable language.

The three looked at each other blankly.

"Tickets!" it repeated loudly. A glint of saliva appeared on a pointed yellow fang.

"We have no tickets," Tom said defensively. Lise noticed his hand traveling discreetly toward the pommel of his broadsword.

"No tickets?" sang the wolverine. "Ooo, that's bad."

With a cackle, the animal charged, scrambling toward Tom with such naked aggression that the tall man jumped backward. He was about to draw his weapon, but the wolverine stopped just out of Tom's reach and smiled. With a flick of a razor-like claw, it held up a pair of finely engraved notes.

"But no problem, you see," it snarled. "I have your tickets right here. You may enter whenever you wish. The show will be starting soon."

"Show?" Tom pressed, but the creature merely gestured toward the small door.

Tom reached for the slips, but before he could touch the smooth vellum, the wolverine lashed out and bit him on the wrist. Jerking back his ravaged hand, Tom yanked his sword partway from his belt, but the wolverine had gone quiet again, staring at the warrior with inert eyes.

Sensing that aggression would get him nowhere with this unnatural creature, Tom moved toward the little door. One step, two, but when the animal growled menacingly, he shrugged his shoulders and withdrew, nursing his bleeding bite-wound.

"I don't understand, creature. You tell us to go in, but then you don't allow us to pass."

"Not you, curly. Just them," the wolverine snapped, waving the tickets toward Lise and Dominic.

"And what am I supposed to do while they're at the show?"

The animal cackled with brutish laughter. "I'm sure I'll think of something."

With a leap, it was upon him, snarling and nipping viciously at his head. Tom went for his broadsword in earnest this time.

"Go on!" he shouted to Lise and the master. "This battle seems to be mine." He tore the ruby pendant from his neck and flung it to Dominic. "Prevail!" he shouted as he turned on the raging brute.

Dominic caught the chain and quickly pulled the amulet over his head. The two tickets had slipped the wolverine's grasp and were floating to the carpet near the master's feet. With a last heartfelt glance at his comrade, he swept them up in his long fingers, pushed open the tiny door, and thrust Lise into the room ahead of him.

"Good luck, old friend," he called back as he followed her inside.

11. The Theater

There seemed to be no one to take the infamous tickets. The theater was dark except for an eerie green exit light near the stage. Lise could see no other door, only a velvet drape that wound all the way around the curved walls. Like an old-fashioned movie house, rows of seats were set to face a blank white screen covered by a thin curtain, also white. She could almost smell the hot oil scent of popcorn hanging in the dead air.

Lise looked at Dominic who raised an eyebrow, as surprised as she by their strange surroundings. Maybe more so. Big tabby cats probably didn't go to movie theaters much. In this case she had become the expert.

"What do we do now?" Dominic whispered.

"I don't know," she replied. "The wolverine said something about a show. Maybe we're supposed to sit and wait for it to begin, like in a normal theater."

Lise walked down the aisle and slipped into a row toward the center front. After a moment, the master followed. He settled himself stiffly, arranging his robes around him, and stared at the radiant wall of whiteness.

"I've never seen a place like this before. It's like a great barren basement but without the damp prey smells."

"Don't worry, Dominic. I've been in theaters many times. Though never one quite like this," she added, glancing around once more to make sure there were no surprises lurking in the shadows. "It's for viewing movies. Sort of like television—you must have come across television in your travels."

"Ah, the box of light images that aren't really there," he replied knowingly.

"Yes, that's it, only bigger. Big as that whole white screen." She paused, thinking. "I wonder who's running the projector—if there is a projector, and if so, what do they intend to show us?"

As if on cue, a burst of tinny music blared from the speakers. The curtain parted, gliding gently to the sides. The house lights went down, leaving only a blue flicker in the control room behind them, and the show was on.

The first gray footage was so scratched and garbled that it was hard to make out its content. Vehicles of some kind, moving slowly along a crowded street. Mobs were yelling and throwing streamers. A quick cut of a laughing child extending his hand in a mock salute. "Heil Hitler!" he soundlessly mouthed. Lise realized that the vehicles were tanks.

"What is this?" Dominic hissed.

"It must be from World War Two," Lise told the master. "More than half-a-century ago. It was a terrible war that ended up involving many nations before it was over. Millions of people died."

Dominic gave her an uncomprehending look that tore her heart with its innocence. "Why?" he asked bleakly.

She almost smiled. *How do you explain war to someone who doesn't feel hatred?*

"The quick version? A small group of selfish people wanted to take over the world. They killed anyone who looked or thought differently than they did. It took the whole rest of the globe to stop one tiny country."

Dominic sighed. "Evil claims many victims, and not just the ones who cross Beyond."

"We won in the end," Lise put out defensively.

Dominic gave her a cryptic look but didn't pursue it. "We remember this period," he said instead. "The presence of Seh was pandemic. Everything was infected."

Lise thought about it. "I guess I'm not surprised. I suppose that's why we're being shown these clips now."

The scene had shifted to some of the more gruesome images of carnage: bombs erupting, soldiers dying, bodies tossed in piles like trash. Though Lise had seen much of the footage before, this time was different. She had always thought of war as a horrible but unavoidable act of human nature, but now she wasn't so sure. Knowing of Seh's evil influence on human mind changed everything.

The subject flipped to a different sort of torture, a starving child, each bone sculpted in relief under his taut skin. His tiny hand reached out imploringly. Huge brown eyes stared vacantly from his fly-dotted face. Lise found with a start that she recognized those eyes. Although they weren't blood red in color, they were the eyes of the slaves of Seh.

Again, the image transformed. People, dirty and poor, pulsed across the screen. The camera flew as if possessed through crowded cities and overloaded homeless camps. Sullen, defiant, needy, weak, humanity by the billions, swelling to the farthest shores.

The scene zoomed out, high above the earth, and the city sprawl coalesced into dead gray splotches among the living green and blue. Lise remembered this view from a half-waking dream. She had thought it looked like a moldy orange. She wrinkled her nose in disgust even though there was no smell.

"I recognize this," said Dominic. "It's what your species is doing to our World."

"From this angle, it looks like fungus."

"Yes, and is as toxic to its host." He frowned though Lise

could barely see in the flickering dark.

She sighed. "You'd think we would know better."

"To grow and thrive is basic to nature," Dominic remarked. "It is Seh who has turned instinct into compulsion."

"But why can't people see the obvious? We do have wills of our own, you know."

"Overpopulation is one of Seh's most powerful tools. The beast knows if a species propagates without consideration, a waterfall of malevolence and suffering will ensue. Meanness and insanity, ignorance, want, sickness, and perversion—all Seh's favored afflictions."

He paused, watching an especially repugnant scene of a crowded inner-city slum. "Seh has lulled them into a false sense of security. Thinking is discouraged and hedonism is fostered in its absence. The result is a type of mass hysteria. As with the rats."

"Rats?" asked Lise.

"It's a simple premise. When population exceeds its resources, a new breed of survivor must emerge. In humans, the crazy, amoral, and psychotic tendencies surface. With rats, they just start eating each other."

The film moved on to the dark and bloated features of disease, the Black Plague, the pox, scarlet fever. Tumors, Ebola, the open sores of radiation poisoning. Cancer, hepatitis, Alzheimer's, AIDS, and a hundred more, each crushing their victim with painful and merciless torment.

Just as Lise thought she might be sick herself, the picture switched again. She relaxed a bit as she studied the faces that appeared now. They seemed common enough—no great tragedies here, she thought. But when monochrome flashes of gruesome slaughters and blood-drenched murder cut through the banality, Lise realized just who these harmless-looking men were. Fish, Bundy, Manson, Dahmer, Jack the Ripper, along with their unfortunate prey, illustrating in graphic detail the depths of man's madness. With every atrocity, Lise sensed Seh's presence growing stronger.

The images were intensely disturbing, injecting their filth deep into her soul. Lise felt a new wave of nausea building. She leapt to her feet in rage.

"Damn you, Seh!" she shouted. "I've seen enough. I already know what you signify. You don't have to convince me of your cruelty."

For a moment, nothing happened; then, the big screen went blank and the music moaned out like a dying balloon. Lise turned to Dominic, her face naked with fright.

"What have I done?" she gasped.

Dominic hesitated. "All I can tell you is that things are proceeding as they should be."

She stared blankly at the master. Realizing that he was as uncertain as she, fear flooded her veins with ice. "I can't do this alone," she said.

"But you can. You are She Who— You must find your way. The skill is there—everything you need is within you. Trust yourself. I know you will prevail."

Dominic gazed at her with unshakable calm. He was right— she *did* know what to do.

Taking a deep breath and summoning her energy, she formed her dread into a small hard cube and cast it away as she had when Seh's servant invaded her mind. The power within her pounded like a heartbeat. That she had felt such strength once before was reassuring, but would it be enough to take on the devil himself?

As if in answer to her challenge, a cyclone of horror opened up above her. Like a child slamming a cup down over an insect, a malicious presence seized the room. The proximity of evil was suffocating. Seh was close at hand.

"You sense our nearness," came an unearthly metallic voice. "That is good, Aliselotte Humankind. Soon you will be with us. You must get to know us better."

The machine-gun clatter that echoed through the amphitheater could only be interpreted as laughter. It was the coldest sound Lise had ever heard.

The profane mirth cut off abruptly. With a tremor that shook the air itself, a maelstrom appeared, black and deadly as the maw of hell. From this vortex issued a figure. The form was human, but as it slowly descended into the room, Lise knew it was no man.

Tall and lean, attractive even, if not for the hateful sneer slashed across its face, its sand-colored hair fell in careless locks over its shoulders. Its dress was casual, jeans and dark-colored sandals. Lise could make out an earth-from-space screen print on the front of its black tee shirt.

It was impossible to pinpoint the age. One moment it seemed young—a teenager—and the next, it could have passed for fifty. It grinned widely, showing straight white teeth. It resembled a person in every way except the eyes.

If eyes were the mirror of the soul, then this thing had none. Those orbs were as vacant as a void. With one brief glance, Lise knew they could drown her in their emptiness. She looked away, but not before she felt the biting thrust of its icy tentacles reaching hungrily for her living soul.

It stopped at the head of the aisle. "You are designated. You will submit," it announced. Malice pulsed in every vicious word.

The body of the beast may have been transmuted, but the harsh inhuman voice remained. Lise had no doubt this incarnation also retained all Seh's demonic skills and would not hesitate to use them.

Lise felt a warm touch, and a burst of prescience shot

through her, revealing for a millisecond a future bright with harmony. She glanced at Dominic standing beside her, brave and serene as ever.

He smiled. Heat radiated from his being, charging her with regenerating power. Silencing her doubt, she began to cleanse her mind of everything but the mighty need to vanquish this monarch of woe.

Lise moved from the row and came down into the aisle, stepping onto the maroon carpet with the lightest of treads. Within her pulsed a force that she had barely begun to fathom. As she started toward the figure, she felt as if she were floating on a breeze from a better place.

"I will never submit to you. And I will not stay here to be brainwashed by your propaganda, either. I've read history—I know there's a lot of bad in the world. I used to think there was nothing I could do about it. But I was wrong."

With a mocking grin, the nuts-and-bolts clatter broke again. "You think you can vanquish us?" it charged. "You think that anything you could do would have the least effect on us—abomination incarnate?"

"I can, and I will," Lise said with quiet resolution.

Keeping an eye on Seh, she motioned to Dominic. He moved up close to her. Standing together, fingertips gently linked, they began to unite their minds, wrapping a wreath of protection around themselves as they prepared to shift.

"I'm not sure I can do this," Lise whispered under her breath, hoping the man-beast wouldn't sense her misgivings.

"I have faith," Dominic replied quietly.

"But I don't really know how to space-shift. I did it that once, but..."

"We're in a shift now, remember? That will give you power. You will succeed. And I'll help you for as long as I am able. I am somewhat of an expert, so they tell me."

She smiled, then grew pensive again. "But what if..."

She searched his eyes for the answer. It was there, telling her confidently that she must have faith, too.

She closed her eyes, and together, they began to alter time and space.

12. Escape and Ensnare

It began only as a tender vine springing from the plush covered floor and winding its soft but determined stem up the edges of the velvet drapes, but soon it was joined by another, then another. With each floral infiltration, the aura of Seh's evil faltered slightly.

Lise was heartened by this small achievement.

"Don't fool yourself, girl," Seh growled as if it were reading her mind. "You will be with us soon. You will become what you most despise, and we will be laughing."

Lise made no reply as she continued to weave the sweet-smelling bower into every corner.

"The nature of the universe will not be changed by a few pretty plants," it scoffed. "You are foolhardy if you think it could be that simple." The beast was still smiling, but Lise thought she saw the ghost of a tic play at the edge of its human mouth.

Again, she ignored it; the hardest thing she had ever done.

Seh found her composure enraging. It stepped closer, crushing the fragile vines beneath its shoes. All sign of the smile was gone now.

"I suppose, like most humans, you require proof." The vacant eyes locked on Lise's, and this time, she couldn't look away.

A bolt of blue fire arced between them, hitting her full on and she staggered, struggling to breathe. Panicking, she fought against the invisible hand that gripped her, but her power was submersed in fear.

Suddenly, the fear evaporated and, like sun through a storm, she realized that she could do this. She couldn't combat the potent and debilitating energy—it was far too dynamic—but she could dismantle it, defuse it as if it were a bomb. She had known all along—she just hadn't known she'd known.

With her mind, she seized the unseen force that held her prisoner, breaking it down, piece by piece, molecule by molecule, until it was no more potent than smoke. Steadying herself, she then reached out her will.

A shudder ran through the substructure of the building. The walls exploded outward like a burst melon. The ceiling flew into the air like the lid of a boiling pot. Nails screamed as they tore from the boards; debris rained down like snow. The timbers began to sprout leaves. Within seconds, the hall had grown fresh and green with Lise's garden.

For a fraction of a moment, she felt no emanations at all from Seh, but the respite was short. Like an infectious disease, Seh's corruption resurged. The foliage turned yellow and became blighted. Leaves fell dead from the stalks while the beast laughed and laughed.

"Trouble with your greenery?" it mocked.

"No," snapped Lise, turning her back on its presence and stretching her fortitude past all boundaries of human thought.

The luxuriant jungle slowly, painfully rematerialized. Like a healing wound, the demolished theater was replaced by the loveliness of living plants. Lise heard a raw grating sound and knew it to be Seh's ire.

"You are fighting a hopeless battle!" it roared as Lise and Dominic continued their shift.

"You will never win! Our essence is fused into the very core of your species, mingled with the helix strands of genetic code. You can no more change human nature than you can destroy us!"

Lise noticed the mechanical voice was becoming muffled.

"You are designated! You will..."

"You will..." it tried to reiterate, but the sound diminished. The voice was gone.

Lise didn't let up but pushed even harder. With a final press and with Dominic's help, the lush forest of the Alter-tier enfolded them. Not a scrap of Seh's presence oozed into its serenity.

They stood in an arbor at the edge of a meadow bright with wildflowers and lavender orchids, a perfect breeze playing through the leaves. Lise allowed herself to collapse into Dominic's strong arms. Laying her head on the master's shoulder, she gulped the perfumed air, trying to rid her lungs of the evil. She knew this peace was passing, that soon enough Seh would find her, and then it would begin all over again. She needed to gather strength while she could.

They began to stroll across the cool grass. "How can I change what already is, Dominic?" she asked the wise man.

"I don't know, but you will achieve it somehow. Evermore chose you for a reason."

A bird cried overhead, and Lise looked up thoughtfully. "But what if Tom was mistaken?"

"I don't think he was."

She smiled, but only for a moment. "You heard what the beast said—depravity is programmed into us. Even if I manage to disperse Seh's influence, will it make any difference, or will we just re-invent evil somewhere else?"

"Seh is the binding force that turns instinct into corruption—without Seh, the flaws of human nature will be benign."

"But the seed will still be there. How can I change DNA?"

"Perhaps when the evil is absent, humanity's blueprint will alter itself."

She took a step backward and stared into his electric blue eyes. "So there may be a chance after all?"

"There is always a chance, Lise. Hope is a condition that even Seh cannot corrupt." Dominic smoothed back a lock of her auburn hair, briefly touching the lace veil she still wore upon her head.

A new frown shadowed Lise's face. "I wish I knew what Seh thinks I'm designated for," she said pensively. "I swear I'll never submit to anything that fiend has to offer. The idea gives me the creeps."

Dominic sighed. "We will know soon. Even though the two of us are moving through time and space, the hours of Culmination are ticking away back home. Time grows short. The end will come before we expect it."

Lise stared back in shock. "The end? But I'm not ready! We haven't done anything yet except wander around in a make-believe wheat field and watch some disgusting movies. We managed to escape Seh, but we certainly haven't come anywhere near to defeating it."

"Not so far, maybe," said Dominic. "But that will change soon enough."

"What's going to happen to me?" she asked in an anxious whisper.

Dominic studied her brave but doubtful stare. "I don't know," he answered bluntly. "You are the instrument that will bring about the conclusion of a long and vicious war. There will be much adversity in the hours to come." Suddenly, he began to smile. "But you shouldn't have to face it alone. I think it's time to gather reinforcements."

He grasped the ruby pendant with his left hand and moved the other in a swift circle. Accompanied by a dry snapping sound, a vague form appeared at the edge of the woods.

Lise's adrenaline surged when she saw the shape of Seh standing among the tree shadows. It dusted off its robe and inspected a torn sleeve, then strode casually toward them. When Lise realized who it really was, she couldn't believe her eyes.

"Tom!" she cried with delight. "Is that you?"

"It's me," the tall man replied. "And all in one piece, too. But I'll offer some good advice to you— never pick a fight with a wolverine. As a feline of great instinct, I should have known better."

"Did you have a choice, Evermore?" Dominic asked.

"I suppose not, Master."

"I'm just glad you're alright," Lise said gently.

She couldn't tear her eyes away from his amber curls and dancing golden eyes until she heard a rustle in the bushes behind her. When she turned, another of her companions was stepping through. This time, she didn't even question her joy as she ran to the advancing entity. Throwing her arms around him, she purred with gratitude for his safety.

"Parsifal!" Tom exclaimed. "You survived the squirrels, I see."

"Yes, indeed," the old man replied. "It was the fight of my life, but I prevailed." He was grinning proudly, and his human skin held a healthy glow. "That contest was long overdue."

"I know you hate squirrels," Lise said reflectively, "but why? Was it something that happened? Something terrible?"

Percy looked at her deeply, letting his ice-green eyes reach down into her soul. "It is a sad story and hard for me to speak," he finally replied, "but you have been faithful all my life, Cohabitor, and if you wish it, I will tell."

Lise said nothing, letting Percy go at his own pace.

"When I was a kitten, before I had come to live with you, I wandered from home and became lost. Without realizing, I entered a place where Seh's minions gathered. I did not know the danger, but I soon found out."

He paused to gulp a few breaths.

"The minions do not usually attack the young. The possums, starlings—even the rats let me be. But the squirrels were another matter. Before I knew what was happening, they were upon me—squirming, biting, trying to drag me into their hole."

"What did you do?"

"I will never know what awful plans they had for me because my mother came to my rescue."

Lise sighed with relief, then saw the woeful look on Percy's face.

"She diverted them from the hole," he went on, "teasing them until they chased her and I could creep away in shame. But there were too many of them and they were too quick. They got her. The last sound I ever heard from my mother was her final dying scream."

Percy hung his head. "I have carried the weight of that tragedy all my life, and I have always been terrified of squirrels, even those that do not belong to Seh. But this fight has freed me. I have now faced my fear and triumphed. Nothing will bring my mother back, but by helping you as she once helped me, I am no longer afraid. Those kind will never torment me again."

Lise held the old man close, stroking his long silky hair. "I'm sorry," she said, knowing her words were insufficient.

"Thank you, my dear. I consider that a blessing."

The two were silent as Tom and Dominic looked on.

"Why so somber?" came a cheerful voice from behind them. "This is supposed to be a celebration."

Lise broke away and whirled toward the meadow. "You've come back!" she cried as Horace and Malovar walked up to join the group. "Thank God. I didn't think I'd ever see you again."

Their presence quickly restored the triumphant mood. Lise gave them both hugs of greeting, then turned and scanned the trees once more.

Dominic touched her shoulder lightly. "That is all," he said solemnly.

She looked up into the expanse of his clear blue eyes, hers misting slightly. "I guess, what with the others, I thought maybe..." She let the words drift.

Dominic shook his head. "Ferrin has crossed. Even in this magical place, we don't own the power to return her to us."

Lise bowed her head. "I had hoped."

She moved off into the meadow. It was hard to accept that her little friend was gone. Dead. Crossed Beyond, as the felines called it. Everyone else had survived their ordeals. Why couldn't she have come back, too?

As Lise stared out across the field of flowers, she began to notice a strange effect to the air. It was similar to gazing through antique glass—not quite distorted, yet not quite true. She was about to remark on it when she felt a tremor beneath her feet. Her ears rang with pressure. It was time again.

The companions were already mobilizing. Back to back, they stood in a circle. All weapons were raised as they watched for the enemy to appear. None could guess what form it might take this time.

"Lise!" called Dominic. "Here. Quickly."

She hurried to him. He grabbed her arm, none too gently and pulled her into the center of the ring.

"We'll do what we can, Aliselotte, but I'm afraid we're no match for the army of Seh," Tom confessed.

"You must shift again, Lise," Dominic commanded. "Somewhere secure. And, Lise?"

"Yes?"

"Remember the key. Remember..."

She never quite heard what he said next because at that moment the thunder began. Within the onset of the raging din, talk was out of the question.

She began to sense a change in the lush grass around them. A foul smell rose from beneath the green fronds as they withered and decayed even as she watched. Up from the blackened soil, huge bubbles of sludge were sprouting, growing like boils until what had been a meadow was now a primordial sea of scum. The slimy domes swelled until their distended skin was nothing more than a thin film. Through the film, she could see the abominations inside.

"Servants!" cried Lise as she recognized the prenatal form of the monsters of Seh. No one could hear her over the deafening peals, but they knew just the same.

One by one, the bubbles burst in a sickening gush of bile-green fluid. The larvae-like forms uncoiled until their immense bulk towered above the little band. Slowly, as if rising to consciousness, each opened its single seeping eye.

Nothing was left of Lise's jungle forest except for the small grassy patch on which the warriors took their stand. All else had turned rotten, caustic, and gray. Lise tried to rematerialize some of the vegetation, but it didn't work this time. Not even a sprout grew out of the foul muck. She was powerless against the advancing hoard.

In desperation, she tried again, but her second attempt fared no better than the first. Something was blocking her. She could no more change the scene than make cats fly.

The slug-like atrocities had begun to move in on the circle of defenders. The group fought bravely, managing to hold them at bay, but they couldn't last. The servants had the advantage of being dumb senseless lumps of flesh that didn't care if they were poked with a sword or pummeled with a cudgel. The men, on the other hand, suffered each torment inflicted upon them. Soon, they would weaken; then the advance would be complete.

The ring of safety was growing smaller and smaller. The time for contemplation was over—Lise had to act.

Since there seemed to be no avenue of retreat, that left only one option—attack, but not with the body. With the mind. If she turned the tables and became the aggressor, maybe she could surprise Seh. Maybe, like Percy's brave mother, it would switch its attention to her.

Summoning her will, she reached out to the servants of evil. Their resistance broke easily, and she entered their senseless brains. Although communing with their slow ulcerous thoughts was disgusting, she didn't withdraw, instead pushing even further, extending her mind right through the servants and beyond, into their ruler's realm. That was her goal, to use their link with their lord to summon Seh.

At first as she probed, she detected nothing but the maggot-squirm of the fiends' witless minds, then as sudden as an injection, she felt another presence. A monumental force lifted her up like a fish on a line, only to drop her moments later into vacuum. After the turmoil of the battlefield, the sensory deprivation physically hurt.

"We are here!" roared the presence she had come to know as Seh. With every word, a shower of static hit the air like shearing metal. "You have sought us out, Aliselotte Humankind. Does that mean you are ready to submit?"

She slammed her mind closed before she could betray herself. "It's possible," she replied ambivalently, hoping she could sound convincing. "Let my friends go. If it pleases me, I will hear your case."

"You will be with us. You are designated." Lise felt a slippery sensation crawl over her skin like eel-slime and realized that the thing was smiling. "But we would prefer that you come of your own accord. It would be more... pleasurable that way."

Lise cringed. She still didn't know what the beast wanted of her, but she had a bad feeling it was something that she really wouldn't like.

What sort of obscenity did the devil find pleasurable? She wondered to herself. Before she could stop them, images of filth and corruption had flooded into her mind.

Though she tried, she couldn't contain her revulsion. At once, Seh perceived her betrayal, and with a shockwave, she was cast into space.

• • •

Lise dropped onto the wooden deck of a sailing ship. The sea pitched and rolled like manic roller coaster, and the gale shrieked through the rigging. She grabbed the rail, nearly tossed over the side.

She wasn't alone. Rough-looking men raced to and fro across

the slippery deck. Their faces were unreadable, but their eyes were glazed with fear.

"Where am I? " she cried into the storm.

For a moment there was no answer, and Lise thought maybe Seh had brought her there to die. Then, she felt the presence, colder than the gale itself.

"We are everywhere!" boomed the metallic voice in her mind.

"Throughout your history and across your world," it continued, but this time the words came from close at hand.

Lise turned to see Seh in its man-guise leaning carelessly against the mast as if they were on a cruise ship. A smile played across the chiseled facade. Something about its arrogance drove her from fear to anger.

"Why have you brought me here?" Lise shouted into the blustery night, her voice eaten by the storm.

"You must experience the magnitude of our power," the beast replied.

"Power?" she challenged, salt water streaming into her eyes and mouth. "All I see is a storm. As terrible as that may be, it's natural. Or are you claiming to control the weather?"

A look of annoyance darkened its brow. "We do not need to command nature to provoke terror in the hearts of the men who will die here today. In the wink of an eye, we can drop them into hell where they will lament for all eternity." With a harsh chuckle, it stuck its face close to Lisa's. "Would you like to see?"

Behind the soulless eyes, hatred crouched like a predator. Slowly, determinedly, it winked.

There was a great crack of thunder, and lightning struck the afterdeck of the ship, tearing away the rudder and shattering the frame. Within seconds, the sea was raging through the damaged hull. The captain was ordering the pumps sounded, but the men were fleeing in fright. They were doomed. Lise had seen that much in Seh's vacant eyes.

Did Seh want her to go down with the rest? Did it want her to die? And what would death be like on the Alter-tier? There were so many unknowns. *Why didn't I question Dominic more carefully when I the chance?* she lamented.

Tidal waves came crashing across the bow, bodies in the breakers. The heavy ship heaved like a leaf in a stream. Lise wasn't sure how much longer she could hold on.

Seh surveyed its handiwork. "We are anywhere there is terror!" it proclaimed.

Suddenly, a huge wall of ocean hit the side of the ship, and Lise was submerged. She thrashed helplessly toward what she thought might be up, but it was no use. The water was so cold she was paralyzed. For a teasing split second, her head bobbed above the waves. Then the sea closed around her for the final time.

She held her breath although she knew that soon her body would betray her, and she would of her own accord invite death into her lungs. Just as she was about to give in, she felt the familiar tug of shifting space.

Just in time! she gasped in thanks—until she forced her eyes open and saw where she was.

• • •

Lise had never liked riding in airplanes at the best of times, and she had a bad feeling about this one. For the moment, it seemed to be holding its place in the sky but it was an instrument of Seh. She settled back in her first-class seat and waited for the axe to fall.

"Ladies and Gentlemen," a woman's voice came across the loud speaker. "We will be landing at John F. Kennedy International Airport. The temperature in New York City is seventy-eight degrees and the weather is fair. On behalf of the captain and crew, thank you for flying with us today."

Lise felt the plane prepare for landing—the downward approach followed by the familiar clunk of the extending wheels.

There were only a few more minutes left to this flight. She prayed they would pass uneventfully, but she doubted that would happen. What would be Seh's point?

An explosion erupted from the rear. Before anyone could react, the cabin pressure was sucked away as if the plane had exhaled. Anything that wasn't strapped down flew for the tail section like nails to a magnet. Papers, magazines, drink cups, blankets, pillows, all a snow storm of objects— flotsam in the sky.

"Our presence is everywhere," said the man in the seat next to Lise. She spun around to find in place of the elderly businessman who had been there only a moment ago, her nemesis. The beast smiled smugly in its expensive Brandini suit.

"Feel the fear! Feel it throb as it takes on a life of its own. Don't you find it compelling?"

"Compelling? These people are going to die! But then you know that—that's what it's all about, isn't it? Pain and suffering?"

"It," Seh intoned, "is about power.

"We are anywhere there is power!" came the booming affirmation.

Lise clamped her hands over her ears although she knew it would take a lot more than that to evade Seh's violent decree.

Soon it will be over, and I won't have to listen anymore, she thought briefly before all her awareness was given over to the instinct to survive.

She grabbed the cup-shaped oxygen mask that had popped out above her and strapped it to her face. Fighting the pressure that crushed her into her chair like a clamp, she saw they were heading for the sea. In a burst of static, the captain came on the loud speaker with what might have been a prayer.

For a moment, the plane seemed to level off and the pressure lessened. Then it dove once more, and this time, even the hand of God could not have stopped it. Lise's cheeks throbbed; her flesh felt as if it were being torn from the bone. The force was too much for her frail human lungs and she tasted blood. The old couple opposite her had passed out. She knew she would be next.

"If you kill me, Seh," she hissed with her last breath, "I will never submit. I will never fulfill my designation, whatever that may be."

She felt a sudden swell of uncertainty from her opponent before she lost consciousness in a shower of star-shaped sparks.

13. Hell

Lise awoke on the banks of a meandering river. The sun, still low on the horizon, was hot on her face in spite of the early hour, and the sky was royal blue. Loquat and flowering plum trees dotted the shoreline. A stone bridge crossed the sparkling waterway up ahead.

She noticed streetcars, old-style automobiles, and carts being pulled by men is short dark robes. Asia, she mused as she peered around. Sure enough, in front of the shops, long banners displayed flowing kanji characters. The air was full of exotic scents and buzzed with city sounds.

What now? she thought to herself. Although this seemed pleasant enough, she was losing patience with Seh's disaster tour. Would it confront her with another deadly incident, then shift her out at the last minute? Or would it tire of the game and let her die? She decided not to wait to find out.

"Seh," she called, watching a snowy-plumed crane circle and dive for its breakfast. "Enough of this. Tell me what you want and how I can help my companions. That's all I care about."

There was no reply; she was talking to herself. A woman in a kimono looked at her like she was crazy.

"These displays are beginning to bore me," she muttered sullenly.

"Is boredom such a bad thing?" came a voice from nearby.

When Lise turned, there was Seh in the saffron robes of a Buddhist monk, a hank of shaggy hair pulled up in a ponytail at the top of its head. She could barely keep from laughing at the irony of the guise.

"I suppose boredom is preferable to violent death," she returned as they began to walk the stone path beside the stream. "But I'm beginning to wonder—why don't you just kill me? Soon the war will be over and things can go back to the way they were, with you making a mess of our World."

Again, she felt the wave of misgiving from her adversary.

"You are no use to us dead," it said finally. The blunt reply surprised her.

So Seh wanted her alive. For what, she still didn't know. But if the demon was reluctant to do her in, she had an edge. What would happen if she pushed further? It didn't seem as scary now that she knew her life might not be at stake.

"Tell me, the ship, the plane—is there a purpose to these parlor tricks," Lise goaded, "or are you just amusing yourself because you're incapable of anything better?"

The pseudo-monk glowered at her with dead eyes. "You should be careful what you say."

"I mean," she went on, sneaking a furtive glance at the figure beside her, "you keep showing me your scrap book of ugly deeds, but so far, they've just been commonplace disasters. I see things worse than that on TV every day. Don't you have any real atrocities, real achievements in evil?"

Seh bristled with rage, and a ripple of brutish tension exploded outward. A passing group of school children began yelling and scrapping for no reason before continuing on their way.

"You are glib with your tongue, Aliselotte Humankind," Seh snarled. "You wish to see something more convincing? How can we refuse such a request? And this time, we promise that you will not be disappointed." With that, it laughed like a mad man.

A sound began to insinuate itself on the peaceful scene, the drone of an aircraft. Lise looked up in time to see a cumbersome plane moving across the sky at low altitude. Something about the circumstance played in her mind. Nauseatingly familiar. She ought to know...

The bumblebee buzz disappeared, and an eerie silence descended over the city. Even the winding stream seemed to hold its flow. Then, all hell broke loose.

With cries that slit the stillness like a knife through flesh, birds rose from the trees, streaming into the cloudless blue like smoke. Dogs took up howling—not just one, but all of them, their primal wail louder than a factory. Still, the tumult wasn't enough to drown out the other sound, a low deep thunder that boiled up from the bowels of earth.

The thermal flash was brilliant orange then white—brighter than a solar flare. The shock wave hit with the fury of a tornado, and a multi-colored cloud began to rise out of itself like a phoenix. Within moments, the sun had vanished, a poisonous, gray-green mushroom consuming the sky.

"We are anywhere there is war," Seh pronounced. The voice was soft, yet brutal as pain.

The buildings around the park had begun to tremble and collapse. The deafening explosion went on and on. People ran in chaos, trying to beat the blast, but it overtook them easily. They fell, blackened and burned, skin peeling away from their bodies like wisps of rag.

Lise was measuring in microseconds now. She knew exactly where she was—Hiroshima, Japan, eight-fifteen a.m., August sixth, nineteen-forty-five. She had asked for a real abomination, and Seh had given it to her. The destruction of a city by a weapon so potent it could obliterate all life in the blink of an eye—the atomic bomb.

Lise had no doubt now that Seh's influence had inspired the conception of the catastrophic warhead. A perverted form of the survival instinct, she supposed. Seh was steering humanity down the road to its own annihilation. She couldn't let that happen, not again.

Summoning all the power within her, she reached out with her mind and stopped time. For a split second, there was no effect, then the world came to a halt mid-motion, frozen like a photograph. The fearful, dying people; the devastating explosion; the whirling maelstrom of glass, metal, and stone—even the mushroom cloud was brought to a complete standstill.

"I'm not going to play this game anymore!" she shouted.

The Buddha-Seh beside her winked out like a television unplugged, and her avowal was greeted with silence.

Lise peered into the suspended maelstrom. "Don't run out on me now, Seh you bastard. I'm not done with you yet!"

A ripple in the atmosphere exposed the evil presence.

"Face me," she cried, "or I will release time and allow myself to die."

With an implosive hiss, the Hiroshima street dissolved like so much steam, and Lise was back in the matte-gray stillness of the void. Shades of nothingness coagulated around her. A putrid well of hate skulked somewhere out on the fringe—Seh was still close at hand.

Suddenly, she tasted evil. It pushed at her, mauled her, beat at all her barriers, straining to get in. She tried to hold it back but it was like stopping the tide with tissue. After all she had come through, she was still outmatched.

Instantly, the power of Seh took hold of her and squeezed like a boa constrictor. Maybe she had miscalculated its reluctance to kill her. Maybe she was expendable after all.

Just when she thought she was dead, the pressure slackened. "We, too, tire of these ramblings," the voice slammed from out of the nothingness. "It is time to get down to business."

"What...business?" she coughed, shaking off Seh's throbbing hold.

"This is Culmination, as your friends must have told you. But did they inform you of your place in the plan?"

"They said I would know what to do when the time came," she retorted, wishing her defense didn't sound quite so feeble.

Seh laughed. The metallic cackle was loud as gunfire.

Lise was kicking herself for not demanding more answers from the very beginning. It was too late now. She was alone, facing a monster whom no one else in the world even dared approach.

The demonic clatter finally died away, and the pressure let up a bit more. "Your feline comrades told you that you are here to quell our mighty influence," Seh continued.

"And what if I am?" She realized that she sounded more like an ill-tempered child than a warrior.

"Do you truly believe you can prevail?"

Lise hesitated. That was a tough one. It was against all odds that she could save their World, but those who had enlisted her believed in her abilities. She must focus on that.

"I will do what I can," she asserted as forcefully as she could muster.

Seh laughed again. "Unlike your so-called friends, we have nothing to hide. We will leave you in suspense no longer. You are here for one reason and one only: Because we summoned you!"

Lise gasped. "That's not true."

"We have demanded your presence."

Lise shrank from the booming voice, the terrible proclamation. "I don't believe you!"

"Believe what you will. You still do not seem to appreciate the extent of our power. But that will change. Soon there will be no turning back."

"What do you mean, no turning back?"

Seh's clanging voice lighted for a moment. "Tonight, we will finally achieve our greatest goal. But for you to understand fully, you must know the true significance of Tri-Night. Do you? We doubt that you do."

Lise didn't answer because she could not. The beast was right—all she knew was that, somehow, she was supposed to defeat Seh before the time was up.

"Tri-Night," Seh began as if it were tutoring a very stupid child, "is the time when all living beings may transcend their natural boundaries and become more than they are."

Lise was confused. "More? In what way?"

The beast laughed at her ignorance. "Did you never wonder why your felines could suddenly communicate with you?" it sneered. "Even an ignorant thing like you must have realized that is not normal behavior."

Lise said nothing. She had wondered, certainly, but had accepted what the cats told her. Then when they began their dangerous journey, she questioned it no more.

"This particular Tri-Night," it continued, "the Honored Three falls on the virgin moon. It is called the Centenium and comes only once in eons, bringing with it great and terrible force. The last Centenium heralded an end to the time you may know as the Equilibrium. It is through the Centenium that we will finally fulfill the prophecy."

"What prophecy?" Lise asked, but through her own prescience, she already knew.

"It has been foretold that on the Culmination of Centenium, the greatest instrument of destruction ever known will be born into this world. In a few short hours, we will become unstoppable."

"You give yourself too much credit, Seh," Lise charged into the fog, suddenly sounding very small. "You'll never crush the human spirit. Even with all your so-called power, you can't stop free will."

"You are correct," the disembodied voice growled. "We do not have the capacity to create—we can only influence your species to do our bidding. But that will change tonight. Our prodigy will not be bound by such limitations."

This announcement caught Lise off guard. "Your prodigy?"

"Yes. Are you surprised? You, of all creatures, should know the significance of reproduction."

"But..." Lise began, her voice uncertain. "You just said you don't have the capacity to create. How would you beget an offspring? And even if you could, how would it be any different than you?"

"Ah, that is the question," it said enigmatically. "And we have the answer, but we do not think you will like it.

"That which you see as Seh," the beast explained, "is purely a cohesion of unwholesomeness, not an entity in itself. We can inspire hatred, avarice, lust. We can motivate genocide and sin. We can even manipulate humans to turn upon each other, but we cannot force them to go against their will. Only another human has that power."

The voice paused, then continued with its ominous prophecy.

"Our child will be human, like yourself. Born of woman, he will be man. As a man, he will lead our followers into a new age."

Of all Seh's prattle, only one thing stood out, blatant as a billboard, in Lise's mind: *born of woman*. The instrument of humanity's great destruction was to be a human child!

Oh, God! Could that be why I'm here?

"You understand your presence at long last," Seh crooned. "You are designated. You will be Mother."

"No!" Lise moaned. Coming from the beast, the title, so revered and comforting, sounded like a curse.

"It is sad that you will not survive to see your progeny, but we assure you, our son will do us proud."

The words hit her like asteroids, and she staggered under the weight of her aversion. To let this thing anywhere near her was unthinkable. To bear its child was nothing short of evil. She would rather die than become evil's surrogate. She had to escape—now!

Summoning all her will, she struggled once more to shift space. She didn't care where she ended up—even back in the atomic blast would be preferable to this abomination—but her power was gone. She was helpless, completely and utterly human.

The air began to shimmer, and there before her stood a tremendous dragon with greenish-black scales that glistened like an oil slick. Thorny spikes jutted from its bulk like urchin quills, and putrid smoke roiled from its cavernous nostrils. Only the eyes were familiar. Although huge and square-pupiled like that of a demon goat, they held the red well of emptiness as all of Seh's forms.

"You will submit!" it breathed in fiery declaration.

"I don't think so," Lise shouted at the top of her lungs, but she barely heard herself over the worm's ferocious roar. She scoured her brain for anything she could use to her advantage, but her mind was a desert.

"You are She!" the thing echoed, its voice harsh as a blast furnace. "You will submit straightway!"

The creature rose up on its haunches and sprung with amazing agility toward the defenseless girl. Instinctively, she picked up her skirts and ran.

Lise was used to running. She had done it for years as exercise. She had speed and she had stamina, and if Seh didn't space-shift her onto a rocky mountaintop or drop her into a pit of snakes, she would run till she dropped. She was out of options.

Taking a quick glance back at her adversary, she was surprised to see that the beast made no move to stop her. Thankful for small favors, she pressed even harder without destination or plan.

As Lise bolted through the sameness of the void, she attained a rhythm that carried her forward, step after step, without thought. Her mind became an even ribbon of movement. She no longer dwelt on what was behind or what was to come. For this small moment of time, she was free.

Suddenly, she caught the scent of lily of the valley and

glanced down at the corsage pinned to her robe. It had long-since wilted, but now it was fresh again, as if the tiny white blooms had just been picked. A flash of warmth shot through her, accompanied by a familiar sensation, the touch of a loving hand. She was not alone; she carried with her the hearts of her friends.

In spite of her revelation, she was beginning to tire. Her soul may have been renewed, but her body was lagging, and she had a stitch in her side. As she stumbled to a painful halt, she prayed the distance she had put between her and the monster would be enough.

Looking around, she saw why the beast hadn't bothered to pursue. In spite of her arduous run, she was back where she had started. Seh, the master manipulator, loomed over her as close as ever.

"There is nowhere to go!" The monster screamed with laughter as Lise gazed impotently across the emptiness. Seh was correct—there was no place to go because they were in the midst of nothing. But if she could find a way to change that...

She was filled with doubt, but quashed it as if weakness were a second enemy. Centering on Dominic and his gentle strength, she concentrated her will. Slowly, as if being dragged from the depths of her soul, the gray was replaced by four walls. Beneath her slippered feet she felt the hardness of floor.

Turning in disbelief, she found herself in a large, airy room overlooking the ocean. The wood-sash windows were open to the warm breeze and the gauzy curtains billowed inward like a mass of dandelion fluff. Vases of fresh sweet peas and tiger lilies dressed the sideboard and table. The old-fashioned furnishings filled her with delight.

This was a place she had been as a child. She didn't know why her mind had chosen it, but she was pleased. Just to be sure of herself, she concentrated once more. A dark ebony piano appeared in the corner as if it had always been there. She moved to it, running a finger across the ivory keys.

A rush of delight coursed through her veins as she noted the worm and all his evil presence had been left behind. She wasn't sure what she had done—not a space-shift since the things in the room came from memory, not metaphor—but whatever it was, it worked.

"Just try to get your dragon-bulk in here, Seh," she taunted with a laugh. Picturing the monster crammed under the low ceiling made her laugh some more.

The air crackled and she was joined by her nemesis, back in the form of a man.

"This is perfect!" it exclaimed, looking around the charming chamber. "We did not know you were such a romantic. Just one thing, though..." It turned its dead eyes on the ebony piano, and the great instrument transformed into a four-poster bed, laid out with ecru linens and lace pillowcases. "That is better," it announced, turning on the girl with a carnal leer.

Lise's laughter died in her throat, replaced by adrenaline surge.

"No," she cried as her fears grabbed hold of her. This was not what she had in mind.

That single slip of will was all it took; Seh was on her like a hawk on prey, crushing her toward the beautiful horrible bed. She fought against its crab-claw grip, but she was no match for its superior strength. The beast toyed with her as if she were a doll and she was powerless to stop it.

Her mind in turmoil, it was impossible to manipulate the scene into something else. Every time she tried, the beast would maul her with those rough inhuman hands, and her thread would be lost in utter panic.

It shoved her onto the mattress and howled with triumph, an ugly piercing sound like an animal in pain. Strings of saliva drooled from its grinning mouth and fell in slimy threads onto her velvet bodice.

As it slithered its preponderance on top of her, Lise smelled the last dying perfume of lily of the valley crushed under the terrible weight. Her hand shot to her breast. It was far too late to save the flowers, but as she touched them, she felt something else—something metal.

Remember the key, came the soft voice in her mind. Dominic's last, insightful words—how could she have forgotten? A wisp of hope brought her resolve back to life.

Seh hadn't noticed her change. As it continued to paw at her clothing, she grasped the little key and pulled, breaking the golden thread easily. She held it in her fist as she gathered her will like an army.

Seh was all over her, its face only inches from her own. Swiftly, Lise jammed the key toward the humanoid forehead. As the gold hit the pseudo-flesh, it sunk to its hilt like a knife through cheese. Quickly and without thought, she twisted.

14. The Seven

With a grinding crunch and the stench of burning meat, the beast ripped away from her, roaring in anger and pain. It towered above her, arms flailing. In its forehead was a deep bleeding puncture. The wound was shaped like a key hole.

Lise leapt up and fled across the room, as far from the raging monster as she could get; she didn't want to be caught near that bed again if she could help it. The little key was still in her hand. It hadn't burnt her, although she had felt it swell when she touched it to Seh's skin.

Seh continued to rail as if it had been stabbed in the heart. The key-shaped mark oozed viscous red-black blood that dripped into its soulless eyes and down across its mouth, which was grinning no longer. Where the slurry spilled onto the floor, the boards charred, sending up curls of toxic smoke.

The seaside room vanished as if a door had closed, and Lise found herself in a surrealistic place, like a painting from the dark ages. The four elements were present—earth, air, fire and water—but in an arrangement she had never seen before. A profusion of unrelated objects—a clock, a bowl, a curtain, a book, a box—drifted in their own undefinable paths, as if gravity did not apply here. The only thing even vaguely familiar, besides her own self, was Seh in its human guise, writhing like a madman before her.

"What have you done?" it shrieked. "For this, we will see you suffer!"

Lightning cracked in the undulating atmosphere. A bolt hit a free-floating globule of water and vaporized it. Lise began to fear she had gone too far. She had wounded the beast. Would she now pay with her life?

Something was happening. As she stared at Seh's tortured form, a startling transformation was taking place. Underneath Seh's skin, foul swellings rose squirming like eels in a bag. The handsome face rippled grotesquely, subdermal worms coursing across it in distended waves. The torso was inflating like a cow about to give birth. The head blew up like a bladder, dead red eyes popping from their sockets, translucent as salmon eggs.

With a scream that echoed on and on long after it had left Seh's bloated lips, the loathsome shape ruptured in two, beginning at the point where the key had penetrated the skull. The red-black blood was everywhere. Lise could barely breathe for the putrid murk.

At first, the two halves lay dormant, dead lumps of oozing flesh, then Lise thought she saw the slightest quiver. As she hoped against hope it had been her imagination, the movement repeated, a jelly-like shudder that ran from head to toe. She watched in horror as the mounds grew and changed. The pieces were reforming!

There were two bodies now, though neither resembled the man-form Seh in any way. One was small and compact like a troll. It was naked, white and sexless. Lise gasped with revulsion when she saw the bulbous head had no face. The other was no less abhorrent. Though humanoid, it was so emaciated as to be no more than a membrane stretched over a deformed skeleton. The sunken eyes gaped from hollow sockets, and the lipless mouth grimaced like a skull.

The ghastly pair hovered in the alien atmosphere, oblivious to the elements drifting around them. Their attention was focused on one thing only—Lise.

"Who are you?" she gasped.

"Don't you recognize us?" replied the one with the mouth. "We are... how would you say? Seh's bad boys." The reedy voice was as flippant as a delinquent juvenile. "I'm called Vanta, which in the Old Tongue means 'Want'. You know—privation, deficiency, lack? This is my brother, Ignorare." He pointed a bony claw. "You can reason that one for yourself. We," he boasted, giving a lifeless cackle that rattled like bones, as dry as a desert whisper, "are the primary principles of evil. From us, all sins are born."

"But where did you come from?" Lise whispered. "And what happened to Seh? Did I kill it? Is the beast...dead?"

"You can't kill what was never alive," the thing shrugged. "You must understand that Seh, supreme deity of all that is profane, was merely an amalgam, made up of separate but related parts. My brother and I are foremost of those parts. Watch and see."

The atmosphere began to crackle. Against the swirling backdrop of limbo, Lise saw a beautiful ball of green.

"Long ago," the faceless one conveyed through no instrument of speaking, "the world was a raw orb of organic matter. There was life on that ball—your early ancestors, undeveloped and primitive. They had no understanding of even the most basic occurrences: the setting of the sun; the movements of the stars; the long vulnerable darkness when the creatures attacked and the nightmares prevailed. They attributed these natural events to a divine being. The old ones tormented themselves with doubts and horrors. To ease their fears, they fashioned ritual, sacrifice, and prayer. Greed, anger, envy, prejudice, lust—all you know as sin—were birthed from these self-serving devotions. Over the millennia, your unwavering zeal has united the evils, manifesting the Great Beast, Seh, in your image."

As the soundless narration unfolded, the green ball began to turn gray and toxic. Finally, the dying world exploded in a flash of a thousand colors and was gone, but the overwhelming presence of corruption lingered, even in null space.

"As the world became crowded and resources grew precious," it continued, "our disciples increased. Thanks to your ever-growing veneration, we are stronger now than ever before."

Lise had turned her whole attention on the troll-like form and his illusive voice. *Was it a voice at all? Maybe it was thought, some kind of telepathy.* The more she concentrated, the less certain she could be. But the content of the message was clear beyond doubt: It wasn't the devil who created the sin of humanity, but humanity who had created the devil.

Seh had told Lise that the penchant for evil was woven into human DNA. Maybe that was true in the beginning, but Lise found it hard to believe that evil commanded such power now as it had in primitive times. Humanity had come a long way since the caveman days. Six million years of evolution must count for something.

She was pulled from her contemplation by a squishing sucking sound. It was happening again. The two deformed creatures, senseless Ignorance and emaciated Want, were bloating like grisly balloons while their skin crawled and twisted. Within moments, there were no longer two forms hovering in the dimensionless haze but seven.

The dismembered parts were coalescing into freakish gargoyles. The instant each creature was complete, it took off, darting around Lise like moths crazed by flame.

What now? her mind screamed as she batted aside their leather wings. *More manifestations of evil? Was the entity, Seh, being broken down into all its loathsome components?*

At first, the creatures with their gnarled and blistered hides and knife-point horns, dripping fangs, savage brows, and again, the dead, red eyes of Seh seemed exactly alike, but then Lise began to notice subtle differences. Where one was bile green, another was the irritated red of an open sore. One was collecting anything it could grab from the fluctuating atmosphere where another fluttered to the ground and fell asleep. Lise noticed with shock that one sported a huge erection, reminding her of Aubrey Beardsley's early-century erotic drawings. A particularity fat one had gone off on its own and was now devouring a chicken-like creature that had drifted into its scopes. The largest one of all hovered directly in front of Lise, ruffling its spines and puffing out its chest like a pigeon. Arrogance rolled off its lurid bulk like bad perfume.

The horde reminded Lise of something, but she couldn't quite think what. She ran it through her mind over and over until suddenly, she had it. They were the principles of evil, the incarnations of old religion's mortal sins.

"Why have you severed us?" the big one demanded of Lise.

Warily, she eyed the gargoyle she dubbed Pride.

"Why did you do this, girl?" it repeated. "Don't you know we can't give you what you want unless we're bonded? Quick! Reincorporate us." It eyed her with disdain. "Do it!"

Lise jumped at the harsh demand. "I don't know what you mean," she shot back. "I don't want anything from you."

"Of course you do," the demon retaliated, rippling its spines until they stuck straight out like a porcupine. "All humans want something. Power, riches, fame. If it weren't for your insatiable desires, we would never have been devised in the first place."

"I couldn't put you back together if I wanted to," Lise returned. "I don't know how. And besides, I don't want to. I may not have divided you on purpose, but it's for the best. Now you and your brothers can't exploit us anymore."

"Exploit? You must be joking! It is you who have exploited us. Always begging for more. More control, more money, better sex.

You wouldn't begin to know how to enjoy yourselves without our service."

"That's not true. I know lots of people who live good, positive lives."

"Well, you may be ready to give up sin, but believe me, most are not. Give up living like sovereigns while others suffer underfoot? Give up stuffing yourselves with burgers and giant sugar muffins? Give up reality TV?" It zeroed its bloodshot eye at Lise. "Give up war?" The thing exploded with laughter. "You probably think civilized people abhor violence, but have you ever asked yourself why, if that be the case, there has always been so much of it?"

"It's natural to hunt and defend," she retorted. "It was Seh who perverted our instincts into something evil and ugly. Once people are free of you, they'll find their own balance. Without greed and want and fear, there won't be any reason to go to war."

"You think?" A ripple of uneasiness coursed down its spiny back. "Here's what I think. As long as there are humans, there will be sin. Even if you succeed with today's dismemberment, soon enough, humanity will merge us back together with their adoration, and Seh will arise once more. You wait and see."

Lise was about to reply when she realized what was happening. While Pride was engaging her in a philosophical debate, the other six had been slipping farther and farther into the confusion of dimensionless space. Lise knew instinctively that if they got away, she could never recapture them. If they got away, depravity would still run free.

They must be confined. Pride had said it—people will embrace sin if tempted. As long as the demons were loose, nothing would change.

Lise couldn't let that happen. She closed her eyes to block the distracting images and focused on the golden key which she still clasped in her hand. Bringing her will to the forefront of her mind, she pushed, sending it beyond all previous limits.

First, she envisioned the key, then a lock, then the key in the lock. The lock in a gate, the gate to an iron fence. She built the fence, bar by bar, until she believed in it with all her being.

When she opened her eyes, it was there. On the other side of the fence, howling with fury, were the demons.

Before Lise could give in to fear, she launched her next attack. She focused once more and the iron bars began to wrap around the swarm. In a split second, the fence had completed its circle and fused into a single sturdy cage. The top crashed into place.

Razor talons jabbed toward Lise as she jumped for the lock, the tiny key still in her hand. Dodging the claws, she jammed the key in the slot. Quickly, she twisted and pulled away before they had a chance to slice her. The mortal sins were secure.

If the pack had been angry before, now they were livid. The fiends went berserk, throwing themselves against the barrier, beating their leather wings on the bars. Lise had once seen a caged squirrel so desperate for escape it flayed its own skin trying to push through the mesh. She had thought that was appalling, but this was worse.

The demons were killing themselves. Dark blood dripped from a gash in one's cheek where it had hit the iron with a crushing blow. Another had lost a horn, leaving the whiteness of bone where it had ripped away. Two more fluttered helplessly at the bottom of the cage, their wings mangled. The sight was unbearable.

A voice swelled in Lise's head, *Stop this savagery. It's not like you to inflict such cold-blooded torture!*

She spun around to find the speaker, but aside from the gargoyles and the objects floating in space, she was alone.

Can't you feel their misery? It came again in soft rolling tones, the voice of Dominic, her mentor. *They are dying horrible painful deaths and you are at fault.*

Could that be true? Was Dominic telling her she was doing the wrong thing? When she materialized the cage, she had never expected such barbarous results. She'd wanted to confine the menaces, not kill them. She hated seeing living creatures in such agony—even demons.

To continue is murder, Dominic accused.

Murder! This wasn't what she'd signed on for. Cautiously, she took a step toward the gate.

That's right, the voice encouraged. *Now, slip the lock.*

Lise took another small step, then paused.

Something was wrong. She hadn't challenged evil just to let it get away at the last minute. She'd been entrusted with the key and the knowledge to use it. Confining the demons of sin had to have been the correct move. It made no sense to do otherwise.

Unlock the gate, said Dominic, a note of irritation creeping into his usual serenity.

Lise resisted, although she was torn. She desperately wanted Dominic to take her burden from her, to tell her what to do, but this didn't feel right. Why would the master tell her to loose the sins back onto a vulnerable world?

He wouldn't, came the only answer possible.

"Who are you?" Lise asked the voice suspiciously. "I'm not doing anything until I know."

There was a pause. Thunder rumbled somewhere in the distance. *We are your friend,* the unseen vocalist finally replied.

The tone had been gentle as sheep's wool, but Lise recoiled as if stung. It had called itself *we*. She knew of only one entity that spoke of itself in the plural.

Instantly, Lise was on full alert. If it had been Seh and not Dominic trying to convince her to free its brood, she was still in danger. The fight wasn't over, her work to defend the world, not done.

Lise grasped the small key once more. As she concentrated,

the cage began to constrict. At first, the change was negligible—the objects seemed to be floating a little less randomly as if moving toward a central point, but nothing more. Even that might be an illusion, Lise had to concede—but no, the movement had indeed shifted. The flotsam was being drawn by an unknown force.

The stress increased. A pinpoint hole, darker than black, opened up in the center of the enclosure. The objects were being drawn toward it and so were the gargoyles. The phenomenon wasn't limited to the cage, Lise realized, but resonated everywhere. Space was imploding, collapsing on them all.

The demons were in a frenzy. With renewed vengeance, those still hale enough charged the shrinking bars. Lise, too, was being pulled inward, and a scythe-like talon slashed her arm from wrist to elbow before she could wedge a drifting table between herself and her attacker.

A howl of mechanical rage blasted through her head, dizzying her with pain. Her instincts were correct—it had been Seh all along—but the beast was out of luck now. The cage was holding fast; soon the principles of evil would be locked away for good. Even though she would also die in the collapsing matrix, Lise felt her heart swell.

The cage continued to constrict until its bars had solidified into a wall of thick seamless metal. It was now a box—Pandora's box, Lise thought wryly to herself. She wondered distractedly, as people do in their final moments, if that was how the myth had begun. Percy said the servants of Seh began to appear at the end of the Equilibrium. Had her foremother found a little golden key and fit it innocently in some forbidden latch?

Lise didn't have much time for theology though as she too was being pressed into a smaller and smaller space. She would be crushed soon if she didn't stop it, but she knew she must let it run its course.

She thought of Dominic and Percy and the others. Her three-night adventure flashed through her mind from beginning to end. If she had made a difference in the sprawl of man's wrongdoing across the overcrowded planet, it was worth it. Still, she wished with all her heart she could see her companions once more.

Then she felt herself falling, tumbling through a tunnel of darkness and light. Her stomach lurched but the fall continued. At this rate they would be cleaning up pulp wherever she was to land.

There was a flash, and she entered a place of complete darkness. Slowly, the velvet dark became indigo, then azure, then a pale serene blue. The earth with all its green and brown and white, hovered below her. It was beautiful—no gray virus encroaching on its natural splendor. The blight Seh had repeatedly shown her was one of its own making. This meant there was still hope for the World.

She was passing through clouds now; the cool vapor tickled as she fell. Below her stretched a lovely patch of verdant heath, and she was heading straight for it.

The ground was coming up fast. Lise braced for impact, though she knew no amount of bracing would change the deadly conclusion of her fall. Somehow, she wasn't worried. The falling itself was pleasurable, and her release from evil generated its own euphoria. If she had to die, she much preferred it be among the sweet-scented trees than in the dungeon nether-world, clawed by gargoyles or crushed within a collapsing universe.

She was nearly there now. Below her lay the ancient apple orchard with its circle of standing stones, the place where she had left Dominic what seemed like a lifetime ago. Impact was imminent. She snapped her eyes shut and waited for the crash.

One second, two, three and still no a bone-shattering splat. She cautiously opened her eyes. Although she was still dropping, her decent had slowed profoundly. As her body closed on the lush green turf, she felt herself glide to a near-stop. She floated the remaining few feet, then tumbled onto the soft lawn as lightly as if she had tripped.

Lise sat up and measured the damage. She was alive and uncrushed. She was home, not on some bizarre Alter-tier. She peered around for any sign of demons but the air was clear. As she took a deep revitalizing breath, she smelled roses.

She had made it! She had come through hell and out the other side. She was a mess, her clothes torn and her arm cut and bloody, but she had never felt better in her life.

Before she had a chance to explore her new rapture, however, she heard a sound, a sort of a whoosh like wind through a pipe. She looked up just in time to see a small furry body pop out of the sky and land softly on its feet nearby. Within moments, a second body touched down, then a third and fourth. Lise couldn't believe her eyes.

"Percy!" she cried in astonishment. The tuxedo cat shook out his long fur, straightened his kinked tail as far as it would go and strode leisurely over to Lise as if nothing had happened. She scooped him into her arms and hugged him. After a momentary show of catly indifference, he settled in her lap with a rumbling purr.

Lise gazed around at the others—Tom, Horace, Malovar—all returned to their ordinary feline states. She looked down at herself to see she was still wearing the velvet robe. It seemed an outlandish costume now, especially in such an unfortunate condition, but she didn't care. She was just happy to see everyone well and whole.

The companions were joyful, as well. Big, black Horace rubbed up against her legs affectionately and pranced back and forth as if he couldn't stay still. Evermore Tom hopped onto one of the standing stones, wrapped his stripped tail around him, and gazed at Lise with proud respect. Little Malovar seemed stunned from his descent; he stared around with wide green eyes, then raced away to jump up the side of an apple tree, claws clicking in the soft bark. He didn't stop till he was as far as he could go. All Lise could see were two bright emeralds peeking out from between the leaves. She laughed, but only to herself, careful not to insult his kitten pride.

Suddenly, she thought of Ferrin, Malovar's lost sister. And then she thought of...

"Dominic!" Lise exclaimed.

She let Percy go and moved quickly to the place where she had left the silver longhair what seemed like ages before. He was still there, lying on the grass as if peacefully asleep.

"Dominic?" She touched his silken fur but there was no response.

Lise turned back to the companions, but they seemed as helpless as she. After all they had been through, all they had endured, were they still destined to lose the master cat?

Lise's eye fell to a white shape on the ground, her lace veil. It must have come off in the fall, she thought, surprised it lasted that long. She'd never understood its purpose. Now, she wondered.

Everything else she'd been given had meant something—the lily of the valley, the golden key. Why should this piece be any different?

She leaned to pick it up. Strangely, even though her other clothing was torn and filthy, this delicate bit of lace was perfectly intact. What's more, it was clean and pear-blossom white as if just come from the wash.

Lise carried the veil to where Dominic lay and draped it across the cat's unmoving body. Sure enough, even as it settled, there came a twitch from underneath. A little kick rippled the fabric. A nose appeared, then long luxurious whiskers. Then, there was a whole cat, awake and alive. Dominic blinked a few times, as if his electric blue eyes weren't accustomed to the bright summer sunshine, then he sat quietly and gave Lise a look of gratitude. She answered his unwavering gaze, wishing for an instant that he were still a man.

Lise felt dizzy. A wave of nausea hit her like a fist in the gut and she fell to her knees. The impact of her ordeal was finally catching up with her. She squinted her eyes, trying to focus and failing. Her muscles dissolved into water, and her body slid all the way down. The grass was cool against her cheek. A moist nose touched her own, and there were the beautiful blue eyes again, this time only a breath away. She smiled, and so did Dominic. Then her eyes closed, and she saw no more.

15. Hope

Sparrows were chirping in the cedar tree outside Lise's window when she woke. The sun was already casting elongated shadows on the patterned rug which meant it was well after nine o'clock. She didn't usually sleep so long, but she'd been tired. A lot going on at work. All week it had been one thing after another. Today was Saturday; no harm in sleeping late, just this once.

She sat up in bed and kicked her legs over the side. As her feet touched the floor, she was tickled by a fleeting memory—a strange dream. About cats.

She rubbed the sand from her eyes. She felt a little dozy, but that was to be expected considering how long she had slept. Her muscles were stiff from lying in one position, and her head was filled with cotton. That would go away as soon as she had her coffee.

Grabbing her robe and pulling the silk sash tight, she scrunched into her slippers. The air was already summer-hot, but as she gazed out the window, she felt the sensation of undulating plants, the soft breath of cool winds. Then it was gone, the temperature resurging, all a trick of the mind.

She slogged to the kitchen and filled the coffeemaker, measuring the grounds into the brown cloth filter. Lise liked to be earth-friendly even though she had her doubts one lone person could make much of a difference in the scheme to things. For some reason, however, when she tucked the unbleached bag into its barrel this morning, it didn't seem quite so futile.

Once the coffee was gurgling away, Lise headed for her other morning compulsion, the newspaper, which would be on or near the front porch—wherever the kid had tossed it. As she passed through the living room, she paused, recalling something in the night. There was a cat, a big orange tom with hypnotic golden eyes. More of that weird, convoluted dream?

Putting it aside, she opened the front door and reached for the paper that was conveniently lying on the mat this time. As she bent to pick it up, she noticed a twinge in her arm and briefly wondered where that had come from.

Back in the kitchen, the coffeemaker was playing the finale of its percussion solo. As she took the pot to pour herself a cup, the last few drops exploded onto the element in a crescendo of steam. She had chosen her favorite mug, the one with the picture of a black and white cat that looked a lot like Percy. As she raised it to her lips, she faltered. She hadn't seen the old boy this morning. He wasn't on the couch when she passed by. It was strange for him to be absent, but it was late. He must have tired of waiting and gone off on his own. She wasn't worried.

Lise pulled a wooden tray from the cupboard. On it she arranged coffee, newspaper, and a cinnamon roll from a crisp white bakery bag. Still in her robe and slippers, she went out onto the back porch. The morning was glorious, the sky a perfect blue with just the hint of a breeze to soften the July heat. Placing the tray on the wrought-iron table, she collapsed into a cushioned lawn chair with a sigh. She didn't know how she could still be tired after ten hours of sleep, but she was.

Lise sipped her coffee and stared out over the garden. It was beautiful in spite of the lawn needing a mow and the beds awash with weeds springing up wherever they could take hold. She really should do some yard work, but somehow the imperfections didn't bother her today. The unruly space was like a jungle—lush, green, and lovely, just as it was.

Again, she sensed the ghosts of tangled leaves above her, of soft grass beneath her bare feet. The image was accompanied by a sense of tranquility, a peace she had not known since...well, since forever. She closed her eyes and let the feeling flow.

Without warning, Percy sprang onto her lap. She opened her eyes to see his face only inches from her own. The white whiskers, the shell-pink nose, so beautiful and familiar. He looked at her squarely. His eyes were so green, the green of ancient glaciers. She stared back at him, and for a moment, it was as if she were falling...

With a flood of sensation, Lise remembered everything. Percy was there, and so were his companions, a big orange one, a big black one. A huge silver one that must have been a Maine coon. Two kittens, black and white, brother and sister. She recalled their escapades through the neighborhood and up into the hill park. And another place, an ancient orchard with a ring of stones. What a dream! she thought to herself. It seemed so real! She could almost smell lily of the valley...

But there had been something else—a darkness, blacker than evil itself. This memory rolled around the edges of her mind like dirty oil. Wickedness, hatred, profanity—it was all returning now. The dream had not been so pleasant after all. In fact, parts were pure nightmare. She had confronted a terrible beast. Did she win? She must have wakened before the story was done.

That was the enigmatic nature of dreams, she thought to herself. They would start in one place and end somewhere entirely different. She should count herself lucky it hadn't turned into a work dream. At least it had been interesting. Maybe a bit *too* interesting, she thought as she stared into Percy's unwavering eyes.

"I dreamt about you last night, Percy," she said, smoothing down his back to crooked tail.

With a *prrumph*, he dropped to the ground and padded off

across the lawn into the rhododendrons. For the fleetest second, Lise thought she saw a wispy trail of neon gliding in his wake. She shook her head, scolding herself for sleeping so long she was still half-lost in fantasy.

Enough of this, Lise thought as she picked up the newspaper. She would force her senses back to reality, even if it took war and politics to do it!

As Lise was about to unfold the front page, she heard a screen slam next door and her neighbor Mrs. Biggs waddled out onto her back porch holding something in her arms. She looked the other way, wondering if she still had time to slip back into the house unseen. She liked the nonagenarian well enough but today, she wasn't in the mood. The elderly widow rarely wore her hearing aid, so it was always a one-sided conversation. If only she could sneak away—but it was already too late. The old woman had scoped her out and was hobbling toward the fence for a chat.

"Hi, Mrs. Biggs," Lise called, resigned to her fate.

"Lise!" Mrs. Biggs yelled back as if everyone shared her affliction. "Bet you'll never guess what I got here." She held out the thing she was carrying. It looked like a heap of rags.

Lise put down the unopened paper and rose from her chair. She knew what was expected of her; she must go see whatever-it-was and react accordingly. This happened routinely and usually turned out to be nothing that interested her in the least — a home shopping network purchase or a piece of mail—but now as Mrs. Biggs approached with her armload, Lise felt a stir of excitement.

"Look!" Mrs. Biggs repeated, staring lovingly at the bundle. "Look who I found on my back steps this morning."

As Lise came close and peered into the wrappings, she saw a tiny white cat, its silky fur matted with mud. The animal stared up at her with all-knowing eyes.

Lise froze in her tracks. "Ferrin..." she said so softly as to be nothing. The kitten mewed soundlessly in response.

"She's a lucky kitty—a poor, lucky kitty," Mrs. Biggs crooned. "Aren't you, my sweetie? Yes."

"What happened to her?" Lise asked while her mind did tailspins in an attempt to reconcile this reality with her dreamscape images.

"Eh?" Mrs. Biggs grunted, eyeing Lise without comprehension.

"What. Happened. To. Her?" Lise enunciated. "She looks like she's half-drowned."

"That's right," Mrs. Biggs nodded violently. "She's been gone near two days now. Thought I'd lost her. Her poor brother was right out of his mind. Weren't you, baby?"

Lise looked to see a small black cat staring up at the bundle with concern. Aside from color, he was identical to his bedraggled sister. Such a coincidence the pair so resembled the kittens from her dream.

Lise realized that Mrs. Biggs was still talking. "...must have fallen down the rain drain," she was saying. "I called the fire department and the water company, but they told me she was a goner. I was so tore up, I can't tell you. And then from out of the blue, what do I see but this poor thing trying to drag herself up my steps, half-dead! I'm taking her to the kitty doctor as soon as my son gets over to drive me. She seems alright, but I want to make sure."

Lise reached out and touched the soggy fur. The cat rubbed her cheek against Lise's fingers, her vibrant purr audible. Lise smiled. She didn't know why, but she was suddenly very happy.

"Her name's Fairy 'cause she's such a mischievous sprite," Mrs. Biggs hollered louder than usual. The little cat jumped, and her black brother darted under a lawn chair at the sudden clamor.

"Oh!" Mrs. Biggs tittered. "I guess I don't know my own voice. Got to put in my ears, you know. Better do it before Bob gets here. Bye, Lise. Wish us luck." She turned and ambled back to her house.

"Mrs. Biggs, Mrs. Biggs?" Lise shouted after the old woman. Mrs. Biggs turned and looked back. "What is it, dearie?"

"Well, I was just wondering. What is the black one's name?"

"Oh, him?" Mrs. Biggs asked as she gazed lovingly at Fairy's brother. "Why, that's Mallow, like the marshmallow. I don't know why I picked that name 'cause he's dark as coal, not like any marshmallow I've ever seen, except the burnt-up ones." She chuckled. "It just seemed right at the time."

She turned and went into her house with Mallow trotting behind. Fairy stared at Lise over Mrs. Biggs's shoulder until she passed out of view.

For a moment, Lise stood stunned, wondering what had just happened. Finally, she shook her head and returned to her chair. Taking a good pull off of her coffee and a revitalizing bite of gooey cinnamon roll, she stared off toward the fence post where Percy perched like a statue. Fairy and Mallow—Ferrin and Malovar. Lise must have dreamed about the brother and sister kittens after seeing them in her neighbor's yard. But as hard as she tried, she couldn't remember when that might have been. It didn't matter. She was just thankful the little white cat was okay.

Lise contemplated this turn of events. In the dream, something terrible had happened. Ferrin had fallen into a sewer and been swept away. Dominic had said she had crossed Beyond to the final death because she was too young to space-shift to the Alter-tier, but he must have been wrong. Ferrin was alive!

Lise checked herself. What was she thinking? That stupid dream had got her all muddled. Final deaths? Space-shifting? And a talking cat named Dominic? It was like something out of a fantasy. Nice to know she still had an imagination, but none of it was real. It couldn't have been real.

Girls do not turn into cats to fight a devil, she told herself sternly. Things were the same today as they had been yesterday and for a millennium before. And as much as she might like to change the world into a better place, it would never happen. The human propensity for evil was far too great.

For an instant, she felt a blanket of serenity settle around her and heard a quiet voice whisper, *When the evil is absent, humanity will change itself.* Then, it was gone, and she was once again alone.

Now she was hearing things as well as seeing personae from her dreams. Determinedly she picked up the newspaper and slapped it open to the front page. She forced her eyes onto the headline and froze.

Lise's heart began to thump like a highland drum. Her breath came in shallow pants. She felt as if she had been transported into an alternate universe. Maybe she had, because this headline could never happen in the world she knew.

Yet, there it was in bold forty-eight point type.

Her mind ate up the unimaginable words. If what they said were true, it would be the greatest transformation society had seen since the industrial revolution. As impossible as it seemed, it would mean the very thing her dream had embraced—change.

"PLANNING FOR THE FUTURE..." Lise read, trying to take in the magnitude of those four small words. She could not, so she read it again.

"PLANNING FOR THE FUTURE— Geneva, Switzerland," it read. "Yesterday in an unprecedented show of solidarity, the leaders of all UN countries met to discuss the future of our world. A unanimous vote was cast to move ahead on several strategies to curb the many crises we face today. All countries agreed to implement the plans immediately. Analysts claim this will change life as we know it."

Aghast, Lise jumped to the next article. This one was a local reaction to a rigid proposal a majority of countries—including the stubborn United States—had agreed to put in place. Nearly as fantastic as the plan itself was the widespread response of acceptance. People from all sides were coming together in support of this global development.

Changes like this don't just happen overnight, Lise thought in stunned surprise. *Why haven't I heard about it before?* But she didn't care why. She was just thankful it had come before it was too late.

Her eyes darted across the pages. Headline after headline involved major transformation. Nuclear security, world health, inequity, and climate change. A strategy for education, a universal healthcare, a creed of acceptance, and a condemnation of abuse. There was even a full-page pledge to uphold the rights of earth's animals with particular care awarded to replenishing the vanishing species endangered by human greed.

It was impossible. There was no way this could be happening so fast.

There was no way this could be happening at all!

Maybe Lise was still dreaming, still in a fantasy world. She would wake up any minute, back in the cruel, materialistic, unfair world she called home.

Or maybe not.

Lise gazed into the distance, catching the glint of ice-green eyes among the leafy arbor of the fig tree.

In spite of her confusion, she smiled.

CAT SUMMER

Part 2

1. 100 Years Later

Lise sat on the plex-wood bench in the moonlit courtyard garden of her co-housing domicile contemplating her death. She had led a long and fulfilling life, but now she was old, even for twenty-second century standards. In spite of the electroceutical neuron blockers, she was always in pain, and if it weren't for her life support implants, she would be gone within minutes.

But it wasn't her pain nor her age nor her frailty that turned her mind to gloom; it was the world. Her wonderful, perfect world without evil that she had helped to create.

One hundred years ago this summer, she thought to herself. It had been a full century since the Tri-Night of the virgin moon when the demon, Seh, was cast out and evil no longer held a place in humanity's heart.

It had taken time for the human spirit to grasp in fullness that it was finally free of those longings, temptations, and fears, but eventually a Reawakening had come about. With a concerted effort, the overwhelming population had dropped off in a sensible manner, putting an end to poverty, want, and ignorance which in turn eliminated war, prejudice, hatred, and many of the debilitating diseases. The world was a far better place.

Or was it?

Something was missing, gone along with the evil. The art produced in the last century was mediocre at best. No "greats" had sprung up; in fact, just the opposite. As time went by, there seemed to be less and less creativity and inspiration. Now, the arts were little more than amusement and decoration, designs to fashion a pleasant habitat for the masters of the new peaceful globe.

Science had suffered as well. The will to achieve, to learn, to discover had been put aside for the pursuit of a harmonious lifestyle. People were happy, prosperous, comfortable, but something was absent. The old ones remembered. The young ones never knew such a muse had existed at all.

Most of those who grasped the loss were content with the trade-off; life was better than it had ever been back in the old days. No one in their right mind would want to return to that suffering, even if it meant there would be no van Goghs or Mozarts in humanity's future. After all, digital holograms of the originals were readily available through the libraries and communal centers. Who could ask for more?

Lise stared at the cat-faced globe of the moon as it hung close above her like a living breathing thing. Once, men had journeyed there, but now space travel was passé. People no longer had the drive to leave their cozy planet. Of course, anyone interested in history could read about John Glenn, the shuttle missions, or the old International Space Station in the archives. As Lise pondered the celestial orb, somehow that didn't seem enough.

She looked away with a sigh. It was late. Laurelhurst Community was still, the warm air soft as silk. A transplanted nightingale sang in a magnolia tree nearby. The scent of honeysuckle and mock-orange drifted on the breeze, almost tangible in their sensuous pleasure, but they held little charm for Lise. She had experienced decades of summers, thousands of lovely evenings, multitudes of birds singing in trees. She had seen it all, many times over. That was why the thought of her passing seemed all the more apt. For some time, she'd procrastinated, hoping to come across a reason to continue, but nothing had popped up. She was obsolete. Her end was imminent and unlamented, except...

Some unseen spirit whispered that it was not over yet.

Who would miss me? she argued. *I've outlived my children, my husband, my friends. Would anyone even know I was gone?* The fact that there was no one to whom she could voice her fears seemed a point in itself.

Lise felt a shift in the calm night air, and a soft weight dropped onto the bench beside her. As if in answer to her query, a pair of glass-green eyes stared at her from out of the darkness, dancing with independent love.

"Graywood," she said, reaching out arthritic fingers to smooth the cat's velvet fur. "Don't worry, dear. I won't abandon you. Your food bowl will always be full, I promise."

The stocky storm-gray feline rubbed his sideburns against the familiar hand and purred acknowledgment. For a time, the two sat side by side, watching the stars cross the heavens.

Finally, Lise rose, adjusting her Personal Mobile Transport suit so it would hold her in an upright position. "Let's go home," she told her ward.

She gave a final glance into the green-upon-black shadows of the arboretum, then slowly began to propel down the plex-brick walkway toward her compartment. Sensing something amiss, she stopped and looked back—Graywood had not moved.

She eyed the big cat. "Come on, Gray. There's nothing for us here." Usually, the gregarious animal was eager to be near her, but this time, he sat like a stone icon, his unblinking eyes locked on her ancient ones.

Lise frowned. Suddenly, she felt light-headed. *I've seen that look before,* she thought to herself, scrutinizing the cat. *Years ago, but...*

Warily, she returned to the bench. "Graywood?" she began, as if requiring him to explain, but now his attentions were elsewhere. His complete concentration had refocused outward, to the huckleberry, the bay, the wild jasmine that surrounded them. Lise followed his gaze, but saw only darkness among the satin leaves.

Then out of the murk, a shape began to form, a wisp of darkness that grew and coalesced into the figure of another cat. As it stepped into the moonlight, its coat shone like molten snow, its long fur lustrous and ever-changing. Padding down the path with soft determination, it stopped directly in front of Lise. Like the cat-gods of ancient Egypt, it sat erect, eyes like disks of mirror shining up at her, pulling her in.

Lise was feeling giddy and dream-like. A strange combination of excitement and peace washed over her, smoothing away her pain as it took root. Her mind opened like a channel to a different time and place, and she remembered.

"The way has been cleared and all is in order," came the command.

Lise couldn't be certain if it was real speech or telepathy, those clear quiet tones resounding gently in her head. Then, the silver cat skewered her with its compelling stare.

"Person, it is time. Will you follow us again?"

2. A Wisp of Imagination

"Dominic!" Lise exclaimed, her heart filled with joy and confusion.

"I regret, no."

Her hopes dove. "No, of course not. What was I thinking? But for a moment I could swear..."

"I am called Raphael," the stranger interjected. "Dominic was my illustrious forefather, and I'm honored to remind you of such a one." The silver rose and smoothed his fur along Lise's legs. Without hesitation, she reached down to touch his soft cheek.

"How wonderful! But am I dreaming again?" She shook her head, unsure if this wasn't just one of her whims or fancies. They had been coming more often lately, moments when she would suddenly find herself among her feline friends, cruising the endless summer night. Dominic, Tom, and her own dear one, Percy whom they called Parsifal. The beloved black-and-white had passed on long since—crossed Beyond, as he would have called it—taking a piece of her heart with him. He was only the first of many. What a shame they hadn't devised a way for cats' lives to parallel their cohabitors'.

But even though Lise vividly remembered bits and pieces of her strange long-ago adventure, she had never quite convinced herself it was real, even when afterward the world had changed so drastically. Natural evolution, she had told herself sternly. After all, cats do not speak.

At least, no cat had spoken to her since.

Until tonight.

A feeling of dread began to form in the pit of her stomach. If this were real and not just a wisp of an old woman's imagination, why was Raphael here? Why would he need her? What could she possibly do for anyone now?

In the last crusade a century ago, she had nearly lost her life. Lise visualized the great beast, Seh, and shuddered. She'd been young then, and even so it was a great trial. Now she was old and feeble, barely capable of performing the most basic functions without assistance. She would never survive another quest, let alone aid in its accomplishment.

"I see your concern," said Raphael, sensing Lise's turmoil. "And it's justified. But please hear me out." When she didn't respond, he added, "In my ancestor's name, I implore you."

Lise hesitated a moment longer, but something in the cat's stalwart demeanor had forged an instant trust. There was a nobility about him, a rare dignity.

"It's been a long time since I've had the privilege of speaking with a cat." she answered, reseating herself on the bench. "Please, go on."

Oddly, she was feeling better…better than she had for a long time. The dizziness had become a pleasant floating sensation, and her pain had softened in a way to which no drug could ever aspire. Lise suddenly felt strong and sharp as crystal instead of weak and slow and tired. She didn't question the miracle, but reveled in it.

Raphael sniffed the air as if he'd caught a scent, but he made no comment. Instead, he began his tale, speaking to Lise as if she were the only person in the world.

"Tonight marks the Commencement of Tri-Night," he began. "As you know from your sojourn with my ancestor, this is the time when we transcend our natural limitations and become more than we are. The results are different for every species. Among other things, we felines gain the ability to communicate with your kind."

"I remember Tri-Night," Lise said softly, recalling that first strange time she heard a cat talk.

"That's good. It's important." He hopped up onto the bench beside her, blue eyes blazing with intensity. "Long ago, our predecessors had an evil to overcome," Raphael went on, "and with your help, Aliselotte Humankind, it was done. But a century has passed, and a new task has come into being. We're here to ask your service again."

"I don't remember being asked on the first occasion."

"Admittedly not," Raphael confessed. "The fact that I'm here means you have been chosen, that you are already part of the plan. But we hoped you would come of your own heart." He peered up at the elderly human with such a pleading look on his furry face that she had to laugh.

"Alright, I'll listen. But first you need to answer a few questions for me. I'm no longer young and easily led. I refuse to budge until I'm convinced that an old lady such as myself could be of any use to your cause."

Raphael looked at Graywood, but the dusky cat just blinked innocently. "Alright, fair enough. We'll tell you what we can. What would you like to know?"

Lise thought. "Well, first of all, who exactly is 'we'?"

As if it were a summons, cats began to emerge from all over the arboretum; down from the trees and out from the shrubbery they materialized like specters. Most sat quietly erect or lay in casual but guarded poses. A few made their way to Raphael's side.

Lise hadn't seen so many cats in one place since the party at the standing stones. She'd learned then that it took a grave situation to bring such a number of independent felines into one another's presence.

Rafael greeted his colleagues with a blink and a flick of his luxurious tail, then turned back to Lise. "I'll introduce my associates, if I may."

Lise nodded.

A slim pure-white cat was the first to approach, his movement as graceful as a saint. When Lise looked down at the newcomer, she saw that one of his limpid, knowing eyes was emerald green and the other bright and blue as a glacial stream.

"This is Prospero," said Raphael.

Lise waited for him to continue with a long string of cat names. When he didn't, she raised a sparse eyebrow. "Just Prospero?"

Raphael gave her a questioning look and then smiled. "We can forgo the lengthy designations of our forebears. It may have been appropriate for them at the time, but we of the modern age prefer not to encumber ourselves with such formalities."

"That's too bad," she sighed. "I rather liked the formalities. They seemed so…feline."

"Prospero is a discerner," Raphael continued. "There's really no true correlation in your society—the closest I can come would be a seeker or possibly a priest, without all the fancy trappings."

As Lise looked at Prospero, the strange-eyed feline's penetrating gaze pulled her toward a well of pure abstract thought. She sensed a speed-of-light awareness, the perception of all things comingled. For a moment, she felt that in those endless depths, one actually might see God.

Lise bowed her head in respect. "Hello."

The discerner paid her no mind.

"Make sure to speak toward his face," Raphael told her. "Ones like him tend toward deafness."

"Oh, of course." Lise turned full front. "Hello, Prospero," she offered once more.

"Greetings, Aliselotte Humankind," the discerner replied, his voice high and clear as mountain air. Lise felt his words wash through her with the peace of a hymn.

Next, Raphael turned to a small brown female seated

demurely at his other side. "This is Winnick. She is our weaver."

"Weaver?"

"Yes. She takes all the threads of our task and ties them together in a way that all can follow."

"Like a coordinator? That's a good idea. On my last adventure with your kind, we just plowed our way through to the end, space-shifting to an Alter-tier whenever things got rough—which seemed to be all the time in fact. I never knew what was going on. I don't think any of us did, including Dominic, even though he was our leader."

"Your observation is accurate," Winnick said in a reedy multi-toned voice akin to a melodic meow, "but this time things will be different, I promise."

"How so?"

"Hum," Winnick mused, considering how to best answer. "The way history tells it, in the past challenge you were set to vanquish an enemy. Correct?"

"Yes, basically."

"Well, there you have it! Fighting is an action, one that requires courage, strength, and ingenuity but very little thought. With this challenge, the enemy lies within. The only way we can prevail is by executing a plan so precise it must be synchronous with our entire World. We must get it right the first time," the weaver forewarned. "Tri-Night is short; there will be no second chance."

"It sounds complicated." Lise looked at the silver cat, suddenly alarmed.

"Don't scare her, Winnick," Raphael cut in. "That's why we have a weaver," he gently explained. "To take care of such things."

So like his forefather, Lise thought to herself, smoothing over the perils of their task so his companions wouldn't worry.

"And the last of our clowder is Ton-e," he resumed, quick to change the subject.

Lise looked around but no one stood out. Raphael cast an eye about the dark parkland, then imperturbably flicked a silver-tufted ear.

"She'll be with us when she's ready." That seemed to be that for the absent cat.

"Who are the others?" Lise asked of the silent watchers scattered throughout the grounds.

"Helpful souls, all, but only Winnick, Prospero, and Ton-e will accompany us on our journey."

"Journey? As in on-the-road?" Lise cut in, all the circles of thought suddenly clicking into place. "I don't mean to be rude, but I don't think so. If you haven't already noticed, I'm extremely old. I don't travel well—in fact, I don't travel at all. Haven't for years."

Winnick looked at Raphael in alarm, then settled her gaze back on Lise. "You must come. Your thread is the central to the tapestry."

Winnick's sense of urgency was compelling, but Lise stood her ground. Even though she was feeling relatively well at the moment, she knew she was still in no shape to go chasing around the countryside. Her medic would have kittens if she even considered it.

"I need to know more about this elaborate task before I make any commitments," she said with the pragmatism of her age. "I have to be sure it won't kill me."

Raphael turned his piercing blue gaze upon her. "How ironic to hear such concern for yourself, when just moments ago you were considering the most difficult journey of all," he reminded her sternly.

Lise recoiled as if touched by something cold. In the excitement, she had forgotten all about her morose contemplations. Now, the idea of self-slaughter seemed alien. In only minutes, this strange encounter had done for her what nothing else could—given her a reason to live. Suddenly, she realized she must follow Raphael to the end. The alternative was far more grim than death.

The silver male seemed to sense her decision. "We must be moving. We can talk as we go." At his words, the clowder merged back into the landscape, leaving only Raphael and his companions among a swirling mist of cat paths.

Raphael swung around and began to saunter down the winding trail, tail high, with no more outward concern than if he were going to his food bowl. As one, the others followed across the gardens.

Graywood rose and stretched, first his front part, then his back, right down to his perfectly pointed tail. Jumping from the bench, he nudged Lise to also get under way. It was slow going in her PMT suit, but Graywood stayed close, prancing in small circles, six steps to her every one.

"I suppose you can speak too, Gray," Lise said matter-of-factly as she half-hovered, half-rolled along.

"Yes, Cohabitor," the muscular cat stated simply, never much of a talker, even in feline dialectal.

"Then maybe you can explain where we're going. I hope you can tell me more than the mysterious Raphael."

"What's the crisis this time...?" she inquired.

"What's the plan...?" she asked.

"Anything at all...?" she finally demanded in elderly frustration.

Graywood paused and looked up at her, his night eyes shining like globes of mercury. "We need you. That's all I know."

"But for what, Gray? What can I do..." she motioned to her PMT, "...like this?"

Graywood blinked. His look was serene, neither worried nor afraid of the quest ahead. "Firstly," he answered in his cryptic, quiet tone, "you can open the gates."

This time, it was Lise who hesitated, staring at Graywood with disbelief. The dusky cat twitched a sleek eyebrow but seemed otherwise unperturbed.

"The gates to the Interchange," he clarified. "Only a human can release the latches."

"The Interchange? Gray, No! You can't be serious." The idea was absurd. Not only was it against the law for non-humans to wander the Interchange; it was downright dangerous.

Things had changed since Lise's day. Aesthetics were as important as convenience—the chateau-like design of the communities reflected that—but the trade routes, power conduits, and monorails for the private and public pods had to go somewhere. Like a moat around a castle, those unsightly essentials were moved outside the community proper. The super-heated trenches were safe enough if you were inside one of the transportation pods but lethal everywhere else.

Because of the hazards, companion animals were required to stay within the beautifully manicured enclosures. They had the run of the complex, the courtyard gardens, and the vast arboretums, but no cat, dog, or degu could pass those massive safety doors to the outside.

Lise thought she saw a flicker of doubt cross Graywood's glass-green eyes, but all he said as he turned to catch up with the others was, "It is what it is."

Lise hesitated but decided to wait and see what happened before jumping to any conclusions. Maybe Graywood had got it wrong. Maybe there was some magical cat way around the Interchange that he knew nothing about.

The little group traversed the grounds as silently as night, the only sound, the oscillating hum of Lise's PMT. She wondered if anyone was watching from the balconies above. What a strange sight that would be—an ancient human following a trail of wandering cats. But it was late, most lights were off, and the chance of being observed was minimal.

The first gate loomed between the cream and sage stucco lodgings. When Raphael saw it, he turned aside and seated himself with all the formality of a cat in waiting. Lise caught up and floated to a stop.

"Graywood tells me you intend to enter the Interchange," she said uneasily. "That can't be true."

"It's true. We must go that way. Would you please release the latch?"

Fear rose like bile in Lise's throat. "But you could be killed out there. Electrical cables and darting pods—you won't survive!"

Raphael was silent, unmoved and unrelenting.

"And once I let you out," she argued, "what then? If you're lucky enough to reach the next community in one piece, who's going to let you in again?"

"We'll manage," Raphael told her quietly, "if you'll just open the gates. But first you must take off our micro-links. Soon our cohabitors will realize we're gone, and they're bound to come looking. It wouldn't do to have them drag us back home before our work has even begun."

Lise sighed, studying the silver feline. There would be no dissuading him, as there had been no dissuading Dominic, even in the face of mortal danger. Bending her PMT and reaching down, she unclasped the identifying bands each animal wore around their necks. "What will your people think when they find the empty collars?" she asked.

"Remove the gray one's as well, in case someone becomes curious or concerned." Raphael charged. He turned toward a decorative copper urn flanking the path. "Put them in there. The red metal should inhibit the signal. If all goes well, we'll be back for them before the Culmination of Tri-Night."

"Three days," Lise reflected.

"Our cohabitors will only know we are absent. They can always blame faulty links."

Lise dropped the four collars into the urn and heard the hollow clang as they struck bottom. Moving to the touch-panel set into the stucco beside the gate, she looked at Raphael once more, but his determination was palpable.

With a quick gesture, or as quick as can be made by a PMT glove, Lise pressed her first two fingers to the plate. The gate slipped silently back, and together they entered a stone-paved courtyard. To either side, glass sliders led into living quarters. Opposite was a second gate, this one large enough to accommodate the mobile corridors that connected to the pods, the storage containers on the monorail, and anything else that came in and out of the community.

Beyond this shown the shifting darkness of another garden, but Lise knew it to be, in fact, a mirror image, a reflection in the impenetrable plex lining. As the company neared, their likenesses merged among the bowing branches, growing into eight cats and two very old women standing before the gate.

Again, the cats waited. This was it. Beyond the mimicking door lurked not more parklands but the urban jungle of the Interchange.

Lise hung back. Opening that door was tantamount to murder. Everyone knew that an animal on the outside was no better than meat.

"You won't be held responsible," Raphael interjected. "Go on. You must."

She took a breath and touched the pad. The smoothness of its face belied the treachery she felt in her heart.

The big doors shuddered, then slid aside. As they opened, a hiss of hot, stale air whisked in. There was no corridor connector at the moment, so the access opened directly onto the flow of traffic and exchange. The noise was terrible: the clash of metal; the roar of a thousand moving parts as they whizzed by on their way to elsewhere. Lise's ears ached, and the sensitive felines were in agony.

Raphael was the first to regain his composure and move out onto the concrete landing. With the courage of their larger ancestors, the others joined him, standing by.

"Farewell, dear friends," Lise called over the hubbub. "I wish you luck." She was feeling a great emptiness as she stepped back into the courtyard. Soon, they would be gone; even her Graywood. Just another dream? Would she ever know?

If it is a dream, Lise quietly prayed, *please let it last a little longer.*

As if in answer, Raphael turned. "This is far from farewell, Aliselotte Humankind. You must come, too."

"If only I could," Lise blurted, "but I wouldn't make it five meters in this suit. Oh, it gets me around the compound without falling on my face, but it isn't made for hiking." She surveyed the block hills and craters of this mechanized outer world. Even a fit person would have a hard time traversing the hazardous planes without transport. Unless someone had procured a pod they'd omitted to mention, she was going nowhere.

Raphael eyed her enigmatically. Suddenly, she could almost feel his essence burning within.

Something was happening. Lise watched in wonder as her PMT suit unlinked and fell away from her ancient body. For a brief moment, she began to crumple as the support was withdrawn, then something miraculous clicked in. She continued to go down, but it was different now. She was no longer falling, instead crouching onto four legs. Strong and powerful legs. Legs that responded instantly to her every command.

Her physical functions had been managed by machine for so long she'd forgotten what it was like to be in control. It was exhilarating, completely glorious! She was whole again and as healthy as a mature feline could ever wish to be.

"I don't understand..." she began, but already she could barely remember—the suit, the pain, how it felt to be too old to live. Old age was different for this species—felines never gave up, neither mind nor body. From the smallest kitten to the most venerable tom, through illness or affliction, they persisted, strong and stalwart, until the day they died.

"Now will you come, Lise?" Raphael put forth.

"Yes! Yes! I'm ready," she cried, jumping in amongst them.

Without Lise's human touch on the pad, the heavy doors slammed shut behind them, but it didn't frighten her.

Nothing frightened her any more.

Together, they advanced upon the Interchange.

3. An Impossible Purpose

"I think we're being followed," Lise whispered, glancing anxiously down from the scaffolding high above the Interchange. She saw nothing in the eerie green light of the conduits aside from the speeding machines—certainly no sign of life—but in spite of the absence of evidence, she knew she wasn't wrong. Someone was out there, someone very interested in her movements and those of her friends.

The companions had traveled a long way from Laurelhurst Community. They made good time once they decided to take the skyway instead of hiking the treacherous trenches below. Always practical, Winnick had come upon the idea when she noticed the skeleton-like structure that held the guideway for the monorail. The struts ran in fluent avenues high above the thoroughfares. Shinnying up the plex poles to reach them hadn't been easy, but once there, the road was free and clear. The platform was narrow, but they were cats and had no difficulty maneuvering the tightrope way.

Lise still had no idea where they were going or why, but it didn't seem to matter as much now. More important was putting one paw in front of the other as they moved ever closer to their destiny. It was imperative that nothing stand in their way which was why the thought of a stalker disturbed her so.

Lise hiked along the moon-lit bar in silence, wishing the bad feeling would go away, but instead it intensified, as if she could feel strange hot breath on her tail. The others didn't seem to notice, or maybe they were simply less concerned than she.

Again, she stopped and peered around. There! To the side of the monorail track below, she saw something. A blur of black against the electrically-lighted night. She watched as it moved, echoing their actions like a doppler.

"I see him!" Lise cried, only to have the thing disappear as easily as air.

This time, Raphael responded with a low purr. Balancing gracefully on the strut, he turned and sniffed the breeze. A wide smile crossed his silver face.

"You're right, Lise," he announced. "Someone has been following us. You have better instincts than I gave you credit for. But this isn't an enemy, nor, as a matter of fact, is it a 'he'."

"Ton-e!" exclaimed Winnick, as she, too, tasted the night.

"Yes, Ton-e," replied Raphael with a sigh. "One never knows when she'll show up. Or where." His expression filled with excitement. "You had best come out before our new friend succumbs to her curiosity."

Lise sensed more than felt the large black female land lithely on the bar behind them. How that much bulk could arrive without a single vibration amazed her. Not a tremor had passed along the slim viaduct; she was stealth-incarnate.

Ton-e stalked up to Raphael, and the two touched noses. Her movements were as elegant as an athlete's.

"Greetings, brother," she uttered, her voice soft as sparrow down.

Raphael nodded and she fell into place. Silently, the crusade started up again, cruising the wide star-filled night.

• • •

As Lise watched an ember-red fissure slice the onyx sky, she realized why poets referred to sunrise as "the crack of dawn". The zig-zag slash seemed to cleave the darkness the same way molten lava ruptures the cold black layers of rock that strive to enclose it—moving, changing, growing until all the mountainside is a glowing current of flame.

It was nearly morning, and the companions had followed many tracks and crossed over many communities on their way toward their destination. Everyone was tired, paws dragging as they silently paced ahead. Lise was more fatigued than she had been in fifty years, and it felt wonderful. That her body was mobile enough to tire at all was stimulating in itself.

The band had cut across the wide expanse of the river and was nearing another community, a great circular patch of parkland darkness in between the neon causeways of the Interchange. As they rounded a turn and came to one of the crow's nest turrets used for servicing the monorail line, Raphael stepped inside.

"We'll rest here," he announced, seating himself abruptly.

No one argued, and for a time, the group sat in quietude. The chirp of pre-dawn robins rising from the trees below caused a few tails to twitch but little more.

Lise studied her surroundings, gazing down at the tops of the dark-leafed elms, then back to the small space where they huddled. "Where's Ton-e?" she exclaimed. The black feline had faded away as inconspicuously as she had come.

"She's here," Raphael said cryptically. "Always here."

"Oh, I see." Lise frowned. She really didn't see at all, and it was not just Ton-e's unsettling comings and goings that confused her. It was everything. The long walk after so many years of confinement; the miraculous strangeness of Tri-Night. Lise had never felt so elated—nor so bewildered—as she did in that moment.

She looked at Graywood. Of the group, he was the only one she really knew. As he returned her pleading gaze, his glass-green eyes filled with love.

"What now?" Lise whispered.

Graywood didn't answer but turned his eyes to Raphael where they remained, drilling like lasers, as if by sheer force of will, he could induce the leader to assuage his cohabitor's fears.

Raphael returned the stare for a moment, then settled into a tight bundle, paws tucked underneath his plushy breast. "You require an explanation," he said matter-of-factly. "You might as well get comfortable. This may take a while."

As if she hadn't had enough of balancing precariously above the ground, Winnick hopped onto the sheer edge of the turret and made herself at home. Prospero took a stance Lise had come to recognize, somewhere between sitting and lying down, his front part erect and his hindquarters sprawled to the side. Lise thought it an undignified pose for a cat, though she would never say as much to the respected discerner. Ton-e had re-materialized, and took her place next to her silver male. When everyone was arranged, Raphael turned to Lise.

"I'll tell you of our task, but I think you already know most of what I'm about to say."

The statement caught Lise off guard. "What do you mean?"

"You have lived while generations of our kind have come and gone. In that time, you must have gained a great insight of the plight that has befallen our World."

Lise stared at the leader as if he were speaking another language. "Plight? What plight?"

"You knew our World as it was before the decomposition of Seh, when evil ruled the human heart," he went on, ignoring her question.

Lise nodded.

"And you have seen the aftermath which they call the Reawakening. The two are very disparate, I imagine." He blinked at her expectantly.

"Yes, of course," she stuttered, unsure of what he wanted from her.

"Maybe you could explain it for those of us who haven't witnessed the transformation first-hand."

"Well, alright," she said, not getting it. Still, there was no harm in playing along.

She thought back. Way back.

"When I was young," she began, "a very long time ago, the world was a different place—you wouldn't have recognized it. Bad things happened all the time—murders, crime, prejudice, even war. We were accustomed to it, figured it was just the way things had to be. But then I met Dominic and Tom, and they showed me that evil wasn't inherent in human condition as I'd always presumed, but the influence of a demon called Seh."

"Go on," Raphael urged when she hesitated.

"But you know the rest. You must."

"Indulge me."

Once more, Lise stared down at the filigree of trees. There had been rain sometime in the night and the leaves were flecked with a thousand droplets of rainbow. "I don't really understand it all myself. Somehow, we got rid of Seh, and after that, everything changed. Things began to improve—slowly, at first, but consistently; a cascade effect. To begin with, we stopped hurting each other, then we made a concerted effort to stop damaging the earth—after all it is our only home. We became more conscious of things like overpopulation and pollution. I suppose we let go of our self-centered belief that those things didn't matter.

"We dragged the planet back from the brink of destruction. Once the population was no longer growing out of hand, it became possible to accommodate us. People learned to share and take responsibility for their actions. Everyone is much better off now."

"In what way?"

Lise looked at Raphael as if he were demented. "Why, in every way. Now everyone has a home and food and an education. There are no more wars because there's nothing for anyone to fight over. And people are kinder, more tolerant of each other. Bias is obsolete, as are hatred and jealousy. We're all finally happy."

"So humans don't fight any more?"

Lise knew Raphael was baiting her, but to what end she couldn't guess. "Of course we still argue sometimes. We're individuals, after all," she added defensively.

Raphael skewered her with his electric-blue gaze. "Are you?"

His question brought Lise to a complete halt.

"It seems to me," Raphael expanded, his ears flicking back and forth, "that after Seh was banished, your species actually lost your individuality. Your remarkable ability to think creatively has certainly gone by the wayside." Lise began to comment but Raphael put up a paw. "Oh, you may like the blue decor in your domicile where your neighbor may prefer the green, but in the ways that count, you've become a race of sheep—no insult intended to our bovid brothers," he added.

Lise weighed what Raphael was saying. Even though she felt the need to defend her species, those very thoughts had crossed her own mind. Her new world was peaceful and prosperous but that was all. True uniqueness—artists, musicians, philosophers—there were none of them in the comfortable present day.

"Alright," she conceded. "I think I know what you're getting at. But it's a tradeoff—we gave up some of our individuality for the good of all."

"Then that would assume individuality is linked with evil," Raphael broke in incredulously.

"I've never thought of it that way," she contemplated. "History is full of remarkable people with tortured souls."

"We cats feel differently. We believe the spark that moves the human spirit to be the greatest honor the Originator could bestow. To reject this gift is to reject the Originator itself."

"What do you mean?" Lise asked doubtfully. This was more than a moral debate; he was touching on something important.

Raphael paused and looked up at the heavens where all but the brightest planets had been eaten by the oncoming dawn.

"We believe," he said somberly, "that something has gone

wrong with humanity, something that reflects back to the ousting of Seh." He stopped to run his flat pink tongue across his lips. "And we also hold that something must be done about it, before it's too late."

Lise was shocked. Although she had oftentimes reflected on the mediocrity of *novi hominem*, she had never considered it to be a malady. It was unfortunate that the young people of today didn't have the ambition to shape their world much beyond making a cozy nest for themselves, but what could be done about it now, short of...

"You can't want to bring back Seh!" she blurted. "To revert us to what we were. All that misery and hardship? You weren't there, but I was. For millions of people, it was a living hell."

"Seh must not return," Raphael boomed, then his voice softened into sadness. "But the beast's downfall was never meant to engender this stagnated existence your people have embraced," Raphael pronounced. "Safe and coordinated, pleasant and comfortable as it may be, don't you see it's the spark of inspiration that brings the human spirit to its full potential?"

Lise rose and stalked a small way from the others. Her mind spun between Raphael's words and her own thoughts only a few hours before. Could it be true? Had she and that brave feline band taken a wrong turn when they vanquished the amalgam of evil one hundred years ago?

"Alright, Raphael. Say I accept that humanity has lost this spark. What can we do to get it back?"

"It will not be easy," Prospero volunteered.

"I could figure that much. But can it even be done?"

Prospero was silent. Lise turned back to the silver cat, but he had let his blue eyes drift closed as if a nap were in order. Winnick took up the torch, rising to balance on the narrow rail, one paw in front of the other, her long slim tail whipping against the wind.

Winnick the weaver was deceptively small, her short fur dappled with brown tabby markings. She was barely noticeable against most natural backgrounds—until she opened her eyes. Those moss-green globes blazed like two separate satellites, gold-flecked and intense. She trained those twin orbs on Lise as if she were the only life on earth.

"It can be done," she began hesitantly. "Generations have been preparing for this reconstruction. You see, it didn't take long for our ancestors to realize their Tri-Night accomplishments were incomplete. The evil was gone, but so was the thing that made human life worth living."

Lise felt a shiver of *deja vu* shoot through her. One hundred years ago, she had been chosen by a group of sentient felines to save the world—their World, as they called it. One hundred years ago she had been young, impressionable, and easily led, but that was no longer the case. She had questions for these would-be saviors of her species, beginning with: "Why is the fate of humankind is so important to you?"

Winnick's answer was decisive. "As long as you are incomplete, our World cannot function as it should, either."

"You mean we're responsible for everything else on the planet? I can't quite see how."

Winnick and Prospero looked at each other. "You're the discerner," tossed Winnick. "You explain it." She lay back down on her ten-centimeter bed and gazed off in another direction.

Prospero gave Winnick an unfathomable look, then turned purposefully to Lise.

"All life is intrinsically connected," he began, speaking slowly, as if Lise were a child. "And all things in the universe have life, each in its own way. Take Seh, for example. Seh was not a flesh and blood being, but an amalgam of evil. Yet, you of all people know that it did live, separate and apart from the sins of which it was composed."

Prospero began washing a paw, an action Lise knew cats to do when they felt restless. "The Originator is another case in point. All living beings know that God embodies love, but love is an emotion, not a being. Therefore, is God merely a wisp of emotion? Most will agree It is much more.

"Of course, not everything is quite so logical." He held the paw outstretched as if forgotten, then resettled it on the turret floor. "Creativity, inspiration, the muse as it is often called—these are not just words but living powers, spirits if you like, capable of positive motivation." Suddenly, he frowned. "Contrarily, the spirits of indifference, apathy, and disregard work negatively, binding humanity in their stagnant cocoon. But that is another story, and we are veering away from your first question—what is it we must do to make your species whole?"

Lise didn't like the hint of fear in Prospero's tone when he mentioned the untoward spirits, but she was too stunned to pursue it. "Alright, what?"

Winnick gazed toward the horizon where the sun would be full up soon. "We've commiserated with both those of our kind and others, and the best of us—the Eldered—have laid out a plan to reconstruct what was lost."

"And what is that?"

"We call it the Spark of the Human Spirit. The trick will be to bring together all the necessary elements."

"I'm afraid to ask," Lise commented.

"One is common," said Winnick. "We should have no trouble locating the first of the three. The second will prove more difficult, but Raphael knows what must be done, and I have no doubt he'll be able to get things in order before Culmination. It's the third that gives us pause. We know the essence of our requirement but not how it will manifest itself in usable form." Winnick regarded Lise solemnly. "We were hoping you would help us with this third."

"I'll do what I can," Lise vowed, "but you're going to have to be a lot more specific. What are these three ingredients? What is it I'm supposed to be looking for?"

No one answered, their attention suddenly focused elsewhere. In the distance Lise made out the wail of the monorail's train-like whistle. The others had heard too and with every passing moment, their inborn fear was mounting.

The scaffolding began to shake as the noise rose in volume to a deafening scream. The companions cringed in terror, their quest momentarily forgotten. Underneath them, far too close for comfort, a sleek chrome pod zoomed by like a one-twenty KPH earthquake. Then as quickly, it was gone, running down another track.

Raphael opened his eyes and scanned the scenery. During their ordeal, the sun had broken over the eastern mountains, its red rays swarming across the land like wildfire. He deemed the noisy monster gone and breathed deeply. Standing, he stretched as if this morning were no different from any other.

"What's to eat?" he asked, giving his fur a perfunctory lick.

Lise stared at the leader in disbelief. She couldn't grasp how he could be so aloof, impartial to the scary monorail, indifferent to the significant work ahead of them. "But what about the three elements?" she pressed.

With a swish of his great tail, he motioned to the landscaped circle of the community below. "We've reached our destination," he announced, his eyes touching Lise's. "Soon, all your questions will be answered."

"No matter how silly they are," added Ton-e. The implication was humbling, but the mood was friendly. "It's okay, Lise," she added softly. "We all have concerns about the mission. But think of it this way: By this time two days hence, they will have been resolved—one way or another." She giggled, then moved to Raphael's side as he once again began the trek.

4. The Dream

It was a perfect summer's morning. Honeybees buzzed in the flowering treetops, and songbirds warbled to each other as they streaked through the cerulean sky. The diamond-faceted lake lapped a hypnotic chant on the grassy shore. In spite of the early hour, there were a few morning strollers on the promenade, reminding Lise of an impressionist painting.

But not. The scene lacked the vibrant color of Monet or Renoir's diversity of style. She had never noticed before how monochromatic her society had become, as if someone had dressed them all to match. And their minds... but she did not want to get into that.

Change might be good, she thought to herself. A good shaking up. But what would actually happen? No one had told her what this new New World would be like.

Raphael and his followers had landed on Central Lake Community soil in the first few minutes of the new day. Entering the secured enclave hadn't been nearly as difficult as Lise had imagined, but it wasn't exactly effortless either. From the turret they utilized a tall redwood to shinny down to the park below. Grown high past the rooflines, the old tree's languid branches rested against the monorail platform, and all it took was an exhilarating jump into its cradle of greenery. The band had done so without mishap. No one would ever know that Central Lake's population of cats had just increased by six.

Central Lake Community had been built in a perfect circle, the stucco facades of the domiciles, like all communities, facing inward, away from the unsightly Interchange. Within the habitat ring was a huge arboretum, some areas landscaped with both local and exotic flora and others left as natural forest. In the center, logically enough, was Central Lake, a clear blue disk reflecting a clear blue sky. When Lise first spied its perfect symmetry from above, she couldn't believe it was real.

There had been no more discussion of tasks or elements, sparks or the human species; it was morning-time and breakfast was in order. The companions, so intimate in their night's adventure, had suddenly broken into a sextet of individuals, each taking their own path in search of food.

Graywood and Lise stuck together. Whether the storm-gray cat sensed Lise's need or was answering a need of his own to be near her, the result was the same.

Graywood's first and favorite pastime, Lise knew from their four years together, was sleeping, but only slightly beneath that was his compulsion to eat. He was a connoisseur of cat food and it didn't take him long to sniff out a small bait shack on the docks of the lake. There would be good eats there, but they had to be careful not to get caught without their collars; stray animals just didn't happen anymore. If their providers couldn't be located, the community council would assign new ones. New collars would be issued, and it would take until next Tri-Night for them to get back to Laurelhurst Community, their home.

"Wait here," Graywood told Lise as he slunk down the floating pier to the rear of the shack. The shadows were still long and dark against the growing radiance of the day. Thankfully, the big cat would seem no more than a ghost to anyone watching.

As soon as he reached the shed, he turned and nodded. Lise streaked across the open space as if chased by demons. For a moment, the two of them huddled in the cover of the outbuilding as Lise caught her breath.

The next step, getting in to where the fish was located, looked to be more difficult. Leaving Lise on her own for a second time, Graywood rounded the corner to the water side.

Lise heard his sigh of relief. "Come," he called, and she obeyed, just in time to see him leap onto the sill of a small window some eight meters up the wall.

"Careful," she whispered, somewhat after the fact. She wasn't used to excitement, if one excluded the occasional win at solitaire, and she found the furtiveness nerve-racking.

"Don't worry. No humans. Our breakfast awaits. Can you make the jump?"

Lise looked at the wooden sill high above her. In any species, she would no longer be considered young, but she had to try. Gathering her strength and tightening her muscles, she prepared.

She sprung into the air, her sinewy legs launching her higher than she ever thought possible, but it wasn't enough. Briefly, she clung to the sill, her back claws scrambling on the shingles as she tried to push herself the rest of the way, but it was no use. Frustrated, she dropped back to the ground.

"Try again," the gray cat encouraged.

"I don't think so. You must remember, Gray, that I'm over a hundred years old. What do you suppose that would be to a cat?"

Graywood had no use for mathematics and shook his round head. "Never mind, I'll bring you something." Not stopping for a reply, his stocky form disappeared from view.

Lise slipped back into the shadows and sat down to wait. The air was sweet as it tickled the water, and she thought how lucky she was to be there—not just in an important historical moment of time, but there, on the dock, tranquilly sniffing the cool clear breeze.

Her feline senses were so keen it was hard not to be distracted by every little thing. Her sharp nose picked up a symphony of river smells: fish, rotting wood, black tar, algae. Less intense came the overtones of things farther off: a whiff of newly mown grass, a suggestion of roses.

Her hearing was also acute, and she could pick out insects gnawing inside the log mooring, a dragonfly lazily skimming the water's edge. A pair of human voices, deep in discussion, floated up from the far end of the pier.

Lise tensed. The voices were coming closer.

"Graywood, hurry!" she hissed toward the black hole where she had seen him last, but there was no response.

Anxiously, Lise pranced underneath the window. The pair was near enough now that she could make out their dialogue.

"...and that's what Duggan told me," declared the male. "We've got to be on the watch for the next coupla days."

"Duggan's nuts," replied the female. "Things like that only happened in the old days, before everybody mellowed out."

"I know that, Irenei, but I got a bad feeling. Something's coming. I'm just saying we should be ready for a fight."

The voices intensified, and now Lise could feel their approaching steps reverberate through the planks. In a gesture of distress, she reached up the wall as far as she could, stretching toward the high window. The feel of the warm wood against her body did nothing to assuage her fears.

"Graywood," she said in a cautious whisper. "Graywood, you've got to get out here right now."

"Fight? I've never seen a fight in my life," the female named Irenei was proclaiming. Even the near-deaf Prospero would have been able to hear her clamor.

"Would you rather watch everything we've worked for go down the drain?"

"No, of course not. But what can a pack of cats do? That's ridiculous!"

Lise shrunk to the ground and took a peek around the corner. Sure enough, two people, casually dressed in pastel shorts and tops, were heading for the front of the shack. Who knew what they would do if they found the stray Graywood there? She wasn't worried they would hurt him—people didn't do that anymore—but they would surely take him away. Lise couldn't bear the thought of her beloved boy being reassigned to someone else.

"Gray-wood, Gray-wood, Gray-wood..." she chanted softly as she paced. She could hear the whine of the press lock as it processed Irenei's fingerprint. It was already clicking assent.

As the old door squeaked open, a figure soundlessly hit the windowsill and then the ground beside her. Graywood beamed around two fat sardines clasped tightly in his jaw. He dropped them at Lise's feet. "Breakfast," he announced proudly.

Lise stared at him aghast. "You nearly scared me to death, Gray. Some people went in the front just as you came out—did you know that? Had you been a moment longer, they would have caught you. And they were talking about cats. Cats, and having to fight them. What does it mean?"

Graywood frowned, then tucked into his fish. The silence stretched out for a very long time.

Hunger was getting the better of Lise, and natural instinct took over her thought process. She accepted his muteness with a sigh, and keeping an ear tuned for any more threats, set to her own tasty treat.

The pair was quiet now, content with their slurping and crunching. Lise was beginning to pick out working sounds from the still morning: a knife being sharpened, freezer doors being opened and shut. Nothing out of the ordinary. Nothing that threatened.

Graywood sat back to meticulously wash the fish oil of his polished velvet face. "I really wasn't in any danger, Cohabitor," he said innocently.

Lise gave him a black look but continued her meal.

"You underestimate me. I'm well equipped to take care of myself. I heard those people coming. My actions were perfectly timed."

Lise had to give him that one—he had been as quick as a computer when it came to calculating his escape. Her brow knit as she thought of the other thing. "Did you hear their conversation?"

"Not the words. Too busy."

"They said something about cats and how cats were jeopardizing everything they'd been working for. The man told the woman they had to watch out for the next couple of days. The next couple of days, Graywood! That just happens to be the time frame for Tri-Night. Maybe I'm paranoid, but is it a coincidence, or could they be talking about us?"

Graywood looked perturbed. "I don't know."

Lise lowered her already soft voice. "And what about the 'fighting' part?"

"Don't know that either. We should tell Raphael when we get back."

"When will that be?"

Graywood yawned, exposing sizable teeth and fangs. "After a nap, I should think."

He rose, stretched, and began to trot down the pier toward the string of sleek water craft moored there. "Are you coming?" he called over his shoulder.

Lise started to object, but hesitated. A languidness had flooded her body at the word, nap, and the worry drained from her mind, replaced by an exquisite torpor. She was nearly asleep on her feet, she realized with a shock that woke her up again though not for long.

Can't argue with heredity, Lise thought to herself. It had been a hard night and she could see the wisdom of facing whatever was to come in a rested state.

Peaceful now, she moved off into the boat silhouettes after her friend.

• • •

When Lise snapped awake, alert and fully refreshed, the light had already moved to the other end of the spectrum. The copper disk of the sun hovered over the western hills. Night would soon fall, and with the night, the quest would continue. She couldn't wait!

She and Graywood had found a nicely deserted pleasure boat with its cabin door left ajar. Graywood curled up on a checkered sleeper in the Captain's bunk. Lise was not so bold and chose to stay topside where she could see what was coming. A pile of soft old canvas tarps was as good as any other bed, she figured.

She had slept well. Better than...well, better than she could recall. At times, her somnolence had been nearer to a nap state, floating just below consciousness on the wake of silent meditation. Others, she was so far into the realm of slumber that she was oblivious to all. Now she was done, every fiber of her being rested. Now she wanted to be active, and was more than ready to go.

She listened for Graywood, but there was no sound from below. For a fearful moment, she wondered if he'd abandoned her, and she rushed headlong to the captain's cabin, but he was still there fast asleep. She laughed to herself. She should have known; after all, sleep was his favorite pastime.

Pouncing onto the mat beside him, she prodded him with her paw. "Time to get up, Gray."

He opened one glass-green eye and gave her a dirty look, but that just made her prod harder. Soon, the second eye joined the first in the land of the living. With ultimate elegance, he arose onto all fours and arched his back, curling his tail into a perfect treble clef. After a wide yawn, he settled down and began to groom.

"Can't you do that later?" Lise asked impatiently. "I want to move."

"Beauty is a gift," he replied emphatically. "Those of us born to it have an obligation, even in times of adversity."

He was, indeed, beautiful. Lise sat back to wait, watching his rhythmic licks smooth each of his silken hairs into perfect symmetry.

As she relaxed into the plush of the sleeper, she suddenly remembered dreaming, strange mosaics of events and emotions taking her down paths she had never imagined in her human life. *A dream within a dream*, she thought to herself, because in spite of what her greatly-improved senses told her, how could the phenomena of the past twenty hours be anything other than a convoluted fancy?

Still, whether fantasy or whimsical reality, her dreams had been decidedly strange. There was something...something important in that fleeting collage of thought. If she could only grasp the undulating tendrils, maybe she could remember.

A face, human and arrogant. And beyond the face was a shadow, a living wraith that writhed and whorled yet remained as still as a rock. The shadow seemed to control the face like a mask on a stick. It was turning the helpless visage this way and that as if searching. Then it stopped, angry eyes trained straight ahead. As the scene zoomed outward, Lise saw its objective. She felt no surprise; she had already known on whom the cruel gaze would land.

In the blackness of her dream state, six souls blazed like neutron stars. She was among them. The shadow pressed the face nearer, then swept from the living countenance to engulf her little group in suffocating dust. When the dust cleared, her companions were gone, leaving only the shadow and the face in the onyx dark. The face was laughing.

Lise gasped as she recalled the intensity of the vision.

"What is it, Cohabitor?" asked Graywood, suspending his bath.

"It's...nothing...really..." she stuttered, still chilled. *Just a dream, just a dream*, she repeated to herself unconvincingly.

Graywood blinked enigmatically. "There is no such thing as 'nothing'."

"It was a dream, that's all. I guess it was a continuation of that conversation I overheard this morning. But it felt so real, so portentous. There was a face, and a shadow..."

"Stop!" Graywood cried suddenly. "Don't name it."

Lise was baffled. "Name what? Why?"

The gray cat peered around the small cabin as if it were haunted. "Because by your thoughts, you could summon it here."

"What? What would I summon?" Lise asked confusedly. After all, it was only a dream—*her* dream, not his.

"I don't know for certain, but not all forces of nature support us. Not everyone agrees with what we plan to do."

"You mean restoring the Spark of the Human Spirit? Someone wants to stop us?" This was a new turn. No one had mentioned any enemies they might have to avoid or overcome.

"Not some*one*—some*thing*."

"Oh, no!" exclaimed Lise, dread like fingers of ice gripping her soul. "Not Seh and his minions again?"

"No, that one has been eliminated. But other negative influences have invaded our World."

"Like what?" Lise was growing more anxious by the moment.

"You need to ask Prospero about those things. He's much more knowledgeable than I am."

"Prospero isn't here, Gray," Lise retaliated.

Graywood seemed disturbed. He sniffed the air and went to the cabin door. "We must be moving now."

Without waiting for a reply—or any more questions—he slipped through the small space, scampered across the deck, and hopped to the pier. Looking back to make sure Lise was coming, he said, "Ask Prospero, Cohabitor. We'll see him soon, I promise."

Lise had little choice but to accept this compromise and scuttle after the retreating cat. Like the wind, they flew toward their destination as if there were not a moment to lose.

5. Mid-Eve

The evening was clear and still as Lise and Graywood met up with the others in the wooded area near the lake. Here, tall Douglas firs and fragrant pines had been allowed to grow wild, their underbrush of huckleberry and sword fern intercrossed with hard plex pathways where people could safely walk, roll, or hover beneath the peaceful canopy of forest. The companions crouched behind this leafy screen, well-hidden from passersby. No human suspected they were strolling within centimeters of those small creatures who might soon be the answer to a lifetime of mediocrity.

Lise and her cohabitor had been the last to arrive with the exception of Ton-e who was undoubtedly around but out of sight. Lise had wanted to tell Prospero of her dream first thing but Graywood stopped her.

"Let's see what Raphael does first," he said. "There will be time for counsel later."

It seemed she would have to hang on to her dubious news. As soon as Raphael saw all were present, he turned like a dark illusion and moved off into the thickening bush.

"Come," he called over undulating shoulder blades, and there was no choice but to follow like echo behind him.

The group traveled quickly, furtively, burrowing deeper into the natural thicket of the forest park. Soon the track diminished without a trace, not even the iridescent cat paths showing with wisps of color where another feline had passed. Vines tugged at their feet and wild briars clawed at their sides, but they paid them no mind. Not even the alluring scent of wild rodents slowed their progress.

As they drove on through the interwoven wilderness, they began to lose sight of one another. That Lise could still hear their footfalls did little to assuage the fright she felt bubbling up inside her. Where will this lead? she fretted. Last time she'd been steered into battle against forces beyond her imagination, she nearly died. Attacked by demon squirrels, pursued by slug-like incubi, crushed within collapsing space—she wasn't sure she could face that sort of terror ever again.

A twig-snap resounded through the wood like a firecracker, and then silence. Suddenly, Lise realized all sounds had ceased and she was alone.

Where are they? Where have they gone? Are they alright? Have they been taken?

In panic, she plunged ahead, pushing herself harder through the net-like undergrowth. Just as her adrenaline spiked and raw instinct threatened to drive her to frenzy, she broke through into a tiny clearing, and there she found her answer.

In the murk of the glade were her companions. They had stopped, and like statues of Bast, now sat in mute anticipation.

"Please be seated," Raphael said as Lise hurried to join them. "We haven't got much time."

Lise obeyed, adding her silhouette to the others just as the last hint of daylight surrendered its life's blood to the oncoming night.

"We have reached the Mid-Eve of Tri-Night," announced Raphael in a somber tone, as if beginning a ritual prayer. "Tonight, we gather what we need. Tonight will tell us if our plan to restore the Spark of the Human Spirit can be realized."

Lise fidgeted. She was as eager as she was fearful. How could the others keep so still? Even Graywood, who was naturally prone nerviness, sat straight as the pine trees above him, his attention resting solely on the leader.

"Tonight," Raphael continued, "we'll locate and obtain the three essential elements. Each of us must work single-mindedly to this end. In order to reconstruct what was lost, we must be ready to integrate the three by tomorrow—Culmination. Our weaver will tell us the plan. Winnick?"

The tabby's lanky tail twitched uneasily, and Lise thought how unlikely a candidate the little cat seemed for her job. After all, this project was huge, and Winnick was very small. But appearances were deceptive; already Winnick had shown a keen mind and great understanding of the significant undertaking before them.

The weaver blinked moss-green eyes. "There are two parts to our agenda," she began thoughtfully. "Locating the things we need, and then combining them together as instructed by the Eldered. Here's what we're going to do..."

True to form, Ton-e had slipped in when Lise wasn't looking. "I'd rather hear why than what," the black cat interrupted. "Why bother doing anything? The humans provide for our needs quite satisfactorily without this Spark." She slumped down to chew at a claw, apparently exempt from the rigid, statue-like pose of the others.

Winnick frowned at the dissenter. "Not all of us look on our cohabitors as servants, Ton-e. We have a responsibility to them as well. And according to the forces that guide our hand in this task—forces beyond our comprehension," she added with exacting gravity, "their species requires the Spark of the Human Spirit to reach their full potential. It fuels creativity and motivates the sentient mind to move outward from itself, just as the universe does and has done since the beginning of time. Without it, the human psyche tends toward lethargy. Unless the Spark is reinstated, the humans will become indolent, which can be as deadly as evil. Everything will suffer—including us."

"They'll quit filling your food bowl," Raphael translated.

"Then what, dear Ton-e?"

With a small hiss, Ton-e glanced away to watch the fruit bats sail across the matte-black sky.

Winnick moved around the circle until she came in front of the malcontent. "Whether we succeed or fail, things will not remain the same—change is a cosmic law." She set her green gaze on Ton-e. "You must do your part. A plan has been devised that may save the humans from their own inertia. But in order to carry it to its fullest, we must believe with all our minds, souls, and hearts."

Returning her attention to the gathering, Winnick went on. "First, we must assemble the elements which are as follows: the Heart of Humanity, the Seed of Life, and the Wellspring of the Universe. I realize these designations tell little of the magnitude of the articles themselves, but we've been assured they do exist and can be found within the time allotted."

"This Heart of Humanity," Lise asked. "What is it?"

"Let's skip the Heart for the moment and move to second element, the Seed of Life. The Seed of Life is in fact that initial mixture which stimulated matter to become self-empowered millennia ago. Strangely enough, of the three, this element will be the simplest to find. Life is everywhere. All we need is a living example of its most basic form."

"Great," purred Ton-e. "And what about the next one, the Wellspring of the Universe? Do we pluck a star from the sky," she mocked, "or gather a bit of moondust?"

"The third ingredient will prove more difficult," Winnick admitted. "It requires the recreation of the diabolical conditions which brought our universe from nothingness billions of years ago. This regeneration is beyond human skill today, but that wasn't always the case. Before the Reawakening, when people still strived to resolve the conundrums of the cosmos, there were great machines which did just that—produced a proto-universe. This proto-universe will be our wellspring."

Her announcement was met by mixed reaction. Graywood shook his head and sank into a reclining position as if to say, it's all too much for me. Ton-e melted back into the foliage like a hallucination. Lise's thoughts raced as she tried to dredge up what she knew about the Big Bang machines that Winnick was referring to. It was a long time ago, but she seemed to recall some fuss over a group of nuclear physicists who wanted to simulate the conditions of the universe in the moments after its birth. It was thought at the time that their experiments would tear space into sub-atomic shreds. She didn't remember the outcome, but obviously space was still intact.

"How do we make this proto-universe without the machine?" Lise asked.

Winnick smiled coyly. "We have the machine. It's right here."

Lise looked around her. Those sort of things tended to be large, if she remembered correctly. For as far as she could see, there were only forest, trees, and sky. "Where?"

Winnick's smile broadened. "Beneath us. We are sitting on the site of the largest apparatus ever built."

Suddenly, the images slipped into place: the circular layout of the community; the disk-shaped lake at dead center. Central Lake Community had been built on top the huge particle accelerator. But even so, the fact that the capacity to jump-start a universe was within their grasp seemed to raise more questions than it solved.

"Does anyone know how to run it anymore? It must be very complicated." She hadn't meant to be brusque, but her anxiety was rising. This was dangerous stuff, even for the scientists who created it. How could a handful of stray cats hope to fathom its arcane and ancient intricacies?

A scary thought struck her. They couldn't expect, as a human, that she...

"Raphael will arrange for the Wellspring, Lise," Winnick said confidently. "It's the first element on which you must focus."

Relieved, Lise thought back. "The Heart of Humanity."

"Yes, but unfortunately we have no idea what that even means. Do you?"

Lise looked at her blankly. "Is that heart as in 'center', or heart as in 'love and emotion'? Or are we looking for a great beating organ?" Was she supposed to have the answer? Because if that were the case, they were out of luck.

The circle was quiet. Winnick, hopeful at first, soon realized their human as clueless as the rest of them.

The small weaver sighed. "Don't worry. The solution will come."

Returning to the subject at hand, she said, "We'll go in teams. Prospero, Ton-e, and I will make up one team, and Raphael, Lise, and Graywood, the other. We'll begin with the two elements we're certain of and hope the third makes itself known in the meantime."

Lise rearranged herself in the long cool grass. "I have one question," she said, knowing that to be an understatement of grand proportions.

"Yes?"

"When we get all the elements—the life forms and the proto-universe and whatever the heart thing turns out to be—what then?"

"Then we pray," answered a high clear voice. It was Prospero, his moon-white face shimmering against the curtain of dark.

Lise thought how much the discerner's cryptic pronouncement sounded like something a human clergyman would say. But Prospero wasn't clergy, and he didn't leave his listeners suspended in symbology as his human counterparts were so often known to do.

"Are you familiar with the Alter-tier?" he asked Lise.

"Yes, I've been there—wherever 'there' is."

"Good. We will be space-shifting to the Alter-tier as soon as the elements are gathered. The metaphoric nature of the farther dimensions will provide the power to fuse the three components into one. In the moments when the Heart, the Seed, and the Wellspring bond, a new order will unfold, one which includes inspiration and initiative for its sentient dwellers as well as the peace and well-being they enjoy today."

"That's where the praying comes in, you see," Raphael said with a wink.

Lise smiled. She did see. In spite of all his outward confidence, there was no guarantee their plan would work. If they couldn't find all three elements... If the elements acted differently than expected... If the ominous Big Bang machine got out of hand... But she refused to think about what might happen then.

Raphael rose and addressed them one last time. "Now we must go. I, for one, have a lot to do in very little time. Keep your minds open for a glimpse of the Heart. The Eldered assured us we would find it."

He paused. "We have many silent partners in our World, but be wary—for every action, there is reaction. There may be influences who wish us to fail because our success would bring an end to their favor."

With a cold contraction in her heart, Lise thought of the people at the fishing shack.

And then she remembered her dream.

Graywood was looking at her sharply. Did he think she should tell them? Suddenly, she felt silly; after all, she couldn't be certain the couple's dialogue had anything to do with the mission. Their reference to cats may have been a coincidence. And as for the dream—well, dreams weren't real.

Then again...

"Lise heard something," Graywood volunteered, making the decision for her. Five pairs of mirror eyes turned her way and there was nothing to do but begin.

As factually as possible Lise told them about the conversation at the pier. Then she laid out the essence of her dream, trying not to sound too melodramatic when she described the face and the shadow. Everyone listened with rapt interest. She could see they were taking her tale seriously, though she wasn't sure if that made her feel better or worse about it. "Graywood said that Prospero would know what it meant," Lise offered, "and why I shouldn't say the shadow's name—not that I know the name anyway." Her voice fell to a whisper. "Do we have an enemy out there?"

The moon was topping the points of the evergreens, casting long inky imprints across the luminescent pearl. Crickets sang from the gloom, an eerie mechanical whine that rose up to meet the sky like a summoning. The breeze was warm, softly rustling Raphael's luxuriant fur. How could this summer night hold anything harmful? The look of alarm that swelled in Prospero's odd-colored eyes proved it did.

"Gray of the Woods was correct to have you tell us this," the discerner declared, "and correct to keep you from speaking the name. We had hoped to avoid confrontation, but it seems we may have failed."

"The null powers have already converged against us!" Ton-e cried balefully from an overhanging branch. "It's worse than we thought."

Raphael shot her a dour look. "This changes nothing. We must persist."

"Yes, exactly," Winnick quickly agreed.

"Now more than ever, we cannot let our momentum slacken," Prospero added, his manner dead serious.

Ton-e hopped down onto the soft grass and fidgeted impatiently. "Well, let's get on with it then."

Raphael looked at Prospero and nodded. "Alright, you and Winnick are with the dauntless Ton-e." Moving to her side, he gently touched her nose with his.

"Luck to you, brother," she said softly, smoothing his sideburn with hers.

"And you, my love," replied Raphael before turning back to his team.

He eyed Graywood and Lise. "Set?"

Graywood rose and took a brief stretch. Lise was already up and dancing between anticipation and fear. With one poignant look back at Ton-e, Raphael and his team moved off into the underbrush.

6. A Glimpse of an Enemy

Again, Lise found herself streaking through the green-black thicket, but this time instead of becoming denser, the way was beginning to clear. First, the scrub resolved into shaggy grass, then box bushes and trim rhododendrons dotted the forest floor. They were crossing more pathways too, and Raphael kept a keen lookout for travelers even though it was well past midnight and most folks were home in bed.

When he came to a broad plex-brick walkway where white petunias glowed like celestial trumpets in the moonlight, the silver cat paused. Ducking behind the flowers, he sniffed for scent, assured himself they were alone, and turned onto the open road toward the habitation ring. Lise sensed Raphael's intensity. He raced ahead, slowing only to check direction. She and Graywood tried to keep up, but his single-minded passion drove him like a spur.

"Where are we going?" Lise asked Graywood as they followed the petunia path. She was more curious than ever, and the not-knowing was beginning to wear on her. Theirs seemed an impossible task, and sometimes she felt as Ton-e—Why bother? But then her excitement would click in again, and she would see that impossible was merely a state of mind.

Even so, she was tiring. In spite of his lethargic lifestyle, Graywood was strong and muscular—he had no trouble with the pace, but Lise was feeling her age. With a silent sigh, she wished they would get there, wherever there might be this time.

"Raphael seems determined, doesn't he?" she said, hoping that conversation would distract her from the fatigue. "Maybe even a little obsessed?"

"He's very ardent. It's his lineage. All his ancestors were important statesmen or mentors. Raphael must uphold tradition."

Lise thought of Dominic, Raphael's great and great grandfather. Although the two were different in many ways—Dominic tending more to the spiritual and Raphael very much the soldier—she remembered that the master had been obsessed as well.

"What's the thing between him and Ton-e?" asked Lise. "Is he really her brother? They don't look like each other."

"Not brother, as in 'kit of the mother.' It's brother, as in 'soul mate,' a part of oneself. Raphael and Ton-e have been together many seasons."

Lise hesitated. "I didn't think felines mated for life."

"Oh, we don't," Graywood replied, giving her a funny look. "But we bond on occasions. It's not for reproduction but much deeper to the core. Haven't you ever felt love for someone without the instinct to bed them?"

"Of course," Lise laughed. "But for the most part, deep relationships outside of family include sex."

"That's because your species is in perpetual heat. It's all mixed up in everything you do. Felis only becomes carnal at certain times. That leaves the other times open to a completely different way."

Lise remembered when blatant sex was everywhere—television, movies, advertising, sports. After the Reawakening, attitudes improved, partially because without greed, advertising became obsolete. But Graywood was right—sex still managed to be at the forefront of the human mind.

Lise noted their tempo was slowing. She shook herself from her contemplations to see Raphael trotting down the center of a poplar-lined lane. The shovel-shaped leaves shimmered like tinsel in the night breeze, and beyond their tracery rose the outlines of houses.

They were back in a residential district, but this one was totally unlike the stucco-faced domiciles Lise had become accustomed to. Instead of modern compartment habitats, these were single-family dwellings, and what was more, they were ancient. Although in pristine condition, she recognized some styles that dated back to the nineteenth century. Homes like this were hard to come by. In Laurelhurst, only a few had been preserved as museums, but here was a whole neighborhood of the stately patriarchs. It had been decades since Lise had seen anything to compare, and she was filled with nostalgia.

"This reminds me of where I grew up," she said, turning in excited circles, "except in my day…" She motioned to the twelve-meter strip of grassy parkway that curved around the old homes. "…all this would have been pavement."

Raphael was peering closely at each house. Their black windows stared back at him, and their wide porches smiled beckoningly. "Then maybe you can help me find the one we want. I know we're close, but all these dwellings look the same to me."

Lise was surprised. To her educated eye, each was unique. Here a Gothic; there a Queen Anne. An early twentieth century bungalow was flanked by a box-like Federal and a strange geometric high rise that might have been designed by Frank Lloyd Wright. All were now museum pieces, a part of lost history.

Lise glanced from one beautiful house to the next. "What are we looking for?"

"It's supposed to be a small one, like a domicile only all by itself."

She glanced up and down the row, but several could fit that description. "Do you know anything more about it?"

"It has grass and flowers in front."

No help—all but the Frank Lloyd Wright had gardens. "What

else?"

"It's supposed to have a koop-a-la," Raphael said, peering back and forth in frustration, "but I don't know what that is."

"A cupola is a little decoration that sticks up from the roof. Sometimes it can be a small room in the attic."

"What is an attic?"

"Oh, dear. Well, never mind. Cupolas are easily recognizable if you know what to look for. We should find it in no time."

Engrossed in their search, they didn't notice the shimmer of lights rebounding off the trees behind them until they were suddenly caught by the bright Halide headlamp of a trolley. With instant cat reactions, they dove for the cover of a quince hedge, hiding before the beam could give them away. There was little chance of being seen within the obscurity, but still Lise felt the hair on her spine begin to rise.

The trolley inched along like a green enamel tortoise. As it approached, bursts of conversation rose over the electric hum though Lise couldn't make out the words. The trolley's occupants also seemed to be checking out the historical street. At each house, they paused and looked before starting up again.

As they came nearer, Lise could see the riders in the pink glow of the streetlamps. It was a collection of men and women with nothing particularly distinctive about them until she noted the couple in the front seat.

Lise barely stifled a gasp—the pair from the bait shack! To come across them twice in such a large community seemed more than coincidence, but that wasn't what had given her the start. It was the big man who stood like a captain at the prow of his ship. She recognized his face, too—it was the man she had seen in her dream.

"I know them," Lise whispered soundlessly to her companions.

Ears flat against his head, Raphael nodded but gave her a sign of silence. There would be time for discussion after the danger had passed.

The trolley was humming along once more, and in spite of its crawling pace, it was closing on the quince hedge and the fugitives concealed there. When it pulled parallel, it stopped. This time, Lise could hear every word said.

"...a waste of time," the woman was complaining to her associate.

"Yeah, Irenei, but just think about what'll happen if we let them get away with it. Things won't be the same. Everything'll change. Hell, you might not even be you anymore."

Irenei seemed to take this to heart and sat back in contemplative silence.

The brawny man—Lise's dream-face—paid no attention to his colleagues' chatter. Instead, he turned his vengeful brooding stare toward the house. His eyes grazed the cats' leafy hideout, and for a chilling moment Lise feared they had been marked. Then his cold scrutiny slipped away again, attaching itself to the dwelling like an octopus to its prey.

"No," he said brusquely. His voice was dry as gravel.

"Come on, Duggan. Let's go home," someone whined from the back of the bus. "It's late and I have to work in the morning."

Duggan ignored him. "Next," he grunted as the trolley snapped to life and again moved down the line.

"Maybe they're not here," said the small woman who clung to Duggan's arm.

"They're here," Duggan growled. "I have it on good authority they're in one of these houses. Those six evil cats connive to bring back their overlord," he grumbled, "but we'll find them. They'll get theirs. Right?"

There were a few weak echoes of, "Right. Right you are."

Duggan spun and faced on his comrades. "This is a threat to the world, boys and girls. Let's hear a little more enthusiasm." He raised a fist in the air. "Eliminate them, whatever it takes!"

Eliminate! came the voice of the crowd, a little stronger this time.

"The last remnants of Seh, wiped out forever!"
Forever!

"Forever!" Duggan repeated, then the booming voice faded as the trolley continued down the parkway.

When the conveyance was out of sight, Raphael cautiously stepped from the bush. After a moment, Lise and Graywood followed. They looked at one another, trying to make sense of what they had just heard.

"The six evil cats," Graywood intoned. "Is that us?"

Raphael nodded. "I fear so."

"But how do they know?" Lise asked. "And what did they mean, 'the last remnants of Seh?'" The thought that her arch enemy might still be on the loose scared her stupid.

"I believe they must have discovered something of our plans for reconstruction—the big one referred to changes about to be made, changes that will affect our World."

"Yes, but it sounded like they think the changes will be bad," Lise frowned.

"If they believe Seh to be the designer of the change, then they have every reason to be afraid. They may consider us the beast's minions. They may even think we intend to restore Seh's power as it was before the Reawakening."

"That makes sense," said Graywood. "It would take something unimaginable like that to motivate good people to such blatant hatred."

"So Seh isn't really back?" Lise asked again, just to be sure.

"No, Lise. I don't think that's possible. There has to be another power motivating this warring band."

"Who?" she shuddered.

"We'll talk about it later," Raphael declared. "Right now, we need to find the house before they do." He turned, tail swinging level with the ground, to resume the search.

"But, who?" Lise repeated.

"I'm not certain," Graywood told her. "Someone who wants to stop the reconstruction I'd say."

"But why? Why? Recreating the Spark of the Human Spirit is a good thing, isn't it? I don't see how anybody could object to art and inspiration in their lives. Unless there's something about this plan Raphael hasn't told me..."

Graywood looked at Lise like she was crazy to question their leader, and she lowered her eyes. "I don't mean to doubt him. I just want to know what's going on, that's all."

"As Raphael said, for every action there is a reaction. It seems only natural not everyone would agree with our mission."

"But that was more than a disagreement." Lise motioned toward where the trolley and its malicious occupants had disappeared into the night. "Did you hear that man? He said he'll stop us no matter what. That sounds like a threat of violence. Who would use force in this day and age?"

"It might not be a who," Graywood said ominously.

"What do you mean?"

"You saw it yourself in your dream—the human was driven by something else, the..." Graywood glanced around warily, as if he were being watched. "The Shadow," he finally mumbled.

Lise cringed. So there was an enemy after all.

Raphael was still making his way down the block from place to place as the trolley had done, but in the opposite direction. He looked back at the two who lingered by the quince bush.

"Come on," he yowled as he disappeared around a corner.

Lise sighed, knowing speculation wouldn't accomplish anything. Running to catch up with the silver-furred leader, she zipped around the bend and nearly fell on her face.

"Are you alright?" Graywood asked, coming up at a more moderate pace.

Lise just stared in shocked silence.

"Lise, what's wrong?" he pressed. "You look strange."

"There's our cupola," she announced with satisfaction. "And our little house with the garden." She turned to Raphael. "What do you think? Could that be it?"

Raphael raised his nose and tasted the air. His ears swiveled to pick out the smallest of sounds. He froze into a furry moon-lit statue, then when he had deemed it safe, relaxed again. Sauntering up the walk, he came to the red paneled door. In the bottom panel was a cat flap. Without hesitation, he squeezed through, disappearing into the unknown.

Lise and Graywood eyed each other skeptically. "After you," said Graywood, masking his trepidation with chivalry.

"No, I insist," countered Lise, nursing her own fears.

In the end it was Graywood who went first, cautiously sticking his head in for a quick look before committing himself. He must have felt alright about what he saw because his body soon followed. Closing her eyes, Lise pushed across behind him, half expecting an ax or a shoe or some other metaphor for catastrophe to fall.

Instead of the pits of hell, she was relieved to find herself in a nice plush entryway. The living room beyond was done up in true historical decor, and Lise gasped with emotion at the remembrance it invoked in her. The walls dripped with moldings and the ceilings arched at the corners, setting off the five-globed light fixture hanging nobly at the center. The south side of the room was lined with bookshelves made of what appeared to be real wood. There was a stone and tile fireplace in one corner, unlit though it looked functional; in winter whoever lived here might burn pellets, for the ambiance. A brown velvet sofa crouched upon a huge deep pile Oriental rug. On the sofa lay a cat.

Still as the antique furniture around it, the huge wheat-gold Persian trained her yellow eyes directly on Lise. Beside her perched Raphael. Graywood was already settling onto a divan nearby. It all seemed harmless enough, yet why did her hair prickle so?

7. The Doctor

"My cohabitor will be with you shortly," said the voluminous Persian.

"We will wait," replied Raphael.

"As you wish." The Persian closed her eyes indifferently. The massive cat seemed to consider herself above polite amenities.

Raphael, who was not to be outdone in coolness, squeezed his eyes shut as well, and the two of them posed motionless as monks at prayer.

Graywood hadn't had a chance to preen for the last few hours so he used the opportunity to catch up, beginning with his shapely feet and needle-sharp claws and moving methodically up his brawny torso until every storm-gray hair was in place and his coat shone, sleek and polished, in the lamp light.

Lise wondered briefly whom they were meeting at this hour of night, but between the exercise, the excitement, and the constant edge of fear, she was too exhausted to care. Within seconds of curling up on a cross-stitched piano bench, she found herself nodding. The nagging voice of reason told her it was unwise to nap in the viper's lair, but the cushions were soft, the fresh air, cool, and the repose so compelling she couldn't help but give in. Keeping one eye slit for the viper, she let her dreams unfold against the brocade backdrop of somnolence.

She knew she was dreaming because of the glow. It was the old fashioned living room, yet here, wherever she looked—the chair, the table, the lamp—a soft starlight luminescence shown from within, as if each thing had a soul of its own. The others were there—Raphael, Gray, the Persian. Their auras burned flame-like, adding brilliance upon brilliance until Lise's eyes stung with their glory.

Someone was with them, a man, tall and regal. He, too, blazed with inner luster, his handsome face and deep brown eyes radiating both splendor and calm. When he smiled at her, it was as if the sun came out, blinding her.

Lise blinked and the scene vanished. It reminded her of something, a *deja vu* from long ago when she first met Dominic, Raphael's ancestor, on the Alter-tier. That too had been a brief but emotional meeting, swept away by the blink of an eye.

The Alter-tier—was that where she was now? Was that where she had seen the prepossessing man? But he was gone without a trace, and with him, the comfortable glimmering room.

Lise found herself somewhere completely new, a non-space, without substance, nebulous and gray as a vacuum. She too was vapor, less than the air she had breathed only a moment ago. Shock shot through her, materializing as hot cobalt fire against the gloom. She could see it arcing into the nothingness, reassuring her that her nonexistence was only temporary.

Something was happening. Wherever the fire bolts touched down, shapes were emerging, points were crystalizing, objects were coalescing into solidity. The world was building itself around her as she watched.

Gazing out over the emerald fields and sapphire skies of her own making, she felt their endless beauty. She saw within the ambient waves of grass a deeper, hidden life. Each stalk was imbued with its own unique potential. Each seed held the infinite diversity of God.

As she reached out to touch the wealth of possibilities, she felt a presence at her back. Swiftly, she spun around, but no one was there.

She scanned the landscape, realizing that in that instant her perception had changed. The scene remained—blue sky, green grass—but instead of uniqueness, Lise saw only repetition in the billowing shafts. She found it hypnotic, the way they echoed each other's movements, fused into a single common design. It was an ordered place—no diversity here, but that was alright. Clearly, nothing could escape the pattern from which it was cast. How could she have ever thought otherwise?

Diversity was a myth. Only in similitude could life be at peace. Why were her cohorts so bent on stirring up trouble? She would have to talk to Raphael, make him see that the Reconstruction Project was all a big mistake.

But that could wait; all she wanted now was sleep. Hadn't that been her intent? Yes, sleep—dreamless sleep. For a few short minutes, the world could go on without her.

She plopped down in the soft grass, letting the breeze wash over her in soporific ripples. Her eyes were closing...her lids, so heavy...they had to fall...

The moment her eyelids touched, she found herself back in the null gray, but this time it was different. Something was in there with her—something horrible. An abomination inside her own skin.

Her fatigue vanished, replaced by terror as she breathed the acrid smell of dust. Before her, an outline was beginning to coalesce. It was a face.

Lise instantly recognized the scowling visage of the man, Duggan, but it wasn't the hate-filled frown or the cruel eyes that made her want to scream and hide. It was the thing behind the face, a shadow so dense no amount of light could bleed through.

Suddenly, she knew it had been the shadow just now, whispering words of weakness and resignation into her mind. She would fight it—she must! If only she weren't frozen with fright.

The mouth of the face was moving. Through it, the shadow was attempting to speak:

In-Ars, it hissed, its non-voice thrusting through the human lips into her shock-filled consciousness. *You will call me In-Ars.*

• • •

Lise jumped awake. Her heart beat wildly. Her mind was jumbled. She couldn't remember where she was until her eyes lit on her companion, Graywood. He was sitting nearby, staring intently at something just beyond her shoulder.

The high-pitched whine of a fine-tuned motor broke the silence, and Lise whipped her head around to see a wizened old man moving about the room with the aid of a PMT suit, the same as she had worn for so many years. Her heart instantly went out to the old boy; those contraptions made it possible for the aged and frail to lead some kind of life beyond a hospital bed, but they were neither comfortable—that was where the neuron blockers came in—nor were they user-friendly. Even though the anti-grav and power assist mechanisms allowed the infirm to control the suit themselves, Lise had always felt like a clumsy cavalier in full iron body armor.

The old man glided across the plush carpet, making for his pet Persian when suddenly he noticed the other cats. Pulling up short, he peered at them one by one. Lise was ready to bolt out the cat flap if he turned hostile, but he didn't seem aggressive. In fact, he was giving them a broad and friendly smile.

"Well, Ti, I see you've brought your friends home again," he said to the Persian.

It was hard for Lise to imagine that the prissy female had any friends, but the old man was another story. In spite of her trepidation, she sensed only warmhearted kindness from him. "You might as well introduce us," he went on as if he were used to talking to cats, though Lise doubted he expected any more than a meow or a purr in return. She laughed, thinking he was in for a surprise.

Ti rose and rubbed her tawny cheek against his proffered hand, then began to move between the newcomers. "Raphael,"

Ti announced of the silver. Her voice was a rich but detached contralto. "Gray of the Woods," she drawled, passing the dusky boy. With a shrug, she turned to Lise. "Aliselotte Humankind. A human like yourself," she added, flopping onto the floor to worry an itch.

The old man didn't move a muscle as he stared with unbelieving eyes at the literate cat. Lise wondered if she had looked as stupid the first time she heard cats speak. Probably so, she realized, watching the funny way the old man's face crinkled with wonder. It was almost cute.

He was still for so long Lise was afraid his suit had seized up, but finally he cocked his head to one side and said in a soft voice, "Could you repeat that, Ti?"

The Persian was done with congenialities and merely jumped onto the velvet sofa, arranging herself like an art form among the chintz. The old man waited patiently, but when Ti began to nod, he turned his incredulous gaze to Lise.

"You," he said rather smoothly for someone who had just had his reality rattled. "You're...human? Well, you don't look it, but then, what do I know? Maybe you can help me out here."

Again, he waited for a reply, but Lise hadn't heard a word he said. She was staring into his eyes—brown eyes as deep as the earth itself, filled with love and hope and something akin to inspiration. She had seen those eyes before although not in this face, not in this dimension. He was the man on the Alter-tier. There was little left in the time-ravaged body—only the eyes—but they were more than enough to be sure.

The man bent down to touch Lise gently on the cheek, and she responded with an inadvertent purr. "Say something, or I'll think I am finally going senile."

Lise hesitated, then mumbled a vaguely-articulate, "Hello."

The old man sighed in satisfaction. "That's better. You know, I always suspected cats could communicate far more than they ever bothered to. And now I'm proven right—I can die happy." With a cyborg burr, he folded himself into an overstuffed chair, a wide grin playing across his wrinkled features.

"We can't always do it," Graywood volunteered unexpectedly. "This is a special time when all things can be more than they are."

The man's pensive gaze snapped to the gray cat sitting prettily on the chair. "Even we poor humans?" he asked wryly.

"I'm not sure... I've never thought about that before." Graywood lapsed back into his normal silence, but Lise took it as a great commendation that he had spoken to the stranger at all.

"Well, my talking felines, now that you're here, what shall we do?" the man asked judiciously. "Play a game? Take a nap? Expound on the philosophy of life? It's your call."

Raphael, who had been mute until now, blinked surreptitiously. "Dr. Brin Templar?"

"You know my name? But then, why not?" The doctor shrugged, seemingly accepting what was put before him as if he greeted strange circumstances on a regular basis.

"We need your help."

This took the old man by surprise. "How in the world could I be of help to you lovely creatures?"

Raphael rose, hopped from the couch, and stepped carefully up to the doctor. "Are you comfortable, Dr. Templar? Because I have a long story to tell you in a very short time, and I must be assured of your full attention."

The doctor hunched down in his chair and switched off the humming motivators of his PMT. The suit went slack, but because of its bulk, it made little difference to his stance. He touched a screen on his arm band that intensified his proximate hearing and subdued all other noises that might intrude from outside.

"Lay it on me," he replied with zeal.

• • •

For the second time since the beginning of her journey, Lise watched the sun rise, its blazing tendrils stealing through the small east window to alight like puddles of gold on the Oriental carpet. It had been quite a night, but she was no longer tired. Great things had been accomplished even though they had never left the cozy pleasant room.

Raphael had begun with a little history. Lise was able to offer some details of the revolt against Seh as one who had seen it firsthand. Dr. Templar, also a centenarian, remembered that time. When she described the vanquishing of evil and the subsequent Reawakening, he nodded profoundly. "That answers questions I didn't know I had until now," was all he said.

Once they were up to date, Dr. Templar remaining surprisingly calm despite the strangeness of the situation, Raphael explained their present dilemma and what they hoped to do about it. Finally, he touched upon the actual plan for the reconstruction. When he came to the part about the Heart, the Seed, and the Wellspring, the doctor raised a weathered hand.

"Stop there a minute. It's late, I'm old, and I need some tea." Reinitiating the PMT, he moved to a walnut wall cupboard and pulled open the finely-tooled doors to reveal a modern snack machine. Touching the 'green tea' icon on the face of the snacker, it was only milliseconds before a plex china cup descended and began to fill with the steaming beverage. He carefully removed the brimming cup and placed it on a small table. "Anything for the rest of you while I'm at it?" he asked, the perfect host.

As one, Raphael, Lise, Graywood, and Ti came toward him, tails in the air.

"I guess some things never change, even with the onset of sentience," he chuckled as he touched the icons for feline supplement, sashimi tuna, and crab cakes. There was a short time-out while man and cats shared a quiet moment enjoying the necessities of life.

When they were finished and Dr. Templar had returned the

dishes to be recycled by the snacker, he reseated himself. "I understand your theory," he said. "I've read of one similar that deals with life, matter, and thought. But I'm not convinced that it can be taken quite so literally—no offence to your intellectual elite. It's an abstraction, and to expect such a precise outcome..." He shook his head contemplatively. "Well, you had better tell me the rest of it. Everything. Then we'll see if this bird can fly."

Immediately, Raphael began to describe the particulars. He sorely wished Winnick were there, being more versed in the technicalities than he. Though he understood the essence, he was a doer, not a thinker. Still, in her absence, there was nothing for it but to forge ahead, so he did.

When he finished, there was a profound silence. Everyone knew that Dr. Templar's response could make or break their plan.

The old man paused to ruminate, a far-away smile forming of his gaunt lips. "I can imagine a world where people strive for new discoveries and take pleasure in understanding the mysteries of life. It was so once, before the Reawakening, but all that's left now are shelves of dusty rag books and a few old codgers like me. Yes, that world would be a good place. I will do what I can."

Lise sighed with relief, realizing only then that she had been holding her breath. She noted that everyone else, including the outwardly-disinterested Ti, had a similar response.

"But the idea of recreating the Big Bang," he went on. "You realize that no one has fired up the machine for nearly a century. I doubt anyone knows how to do it anymore."

"*You* know, Doctor," Raphael replied.

"In theory. Only in theory. Studying the heavy ion collider experiments is just a hobby, something to pass the time. Oh, I've read a few antiquated volumes, visited the ring once or twice with a tour, for curiosity's sake..."

"You are a doctor of physics, aren't you?"

"Yes, but all I do is teach postulation to a handful of bibliophiles who find scientific history vaguely intriguing. There haven't been any experimental physicists since I don't know when. No one cares any more. I'm afraid postulation is a far cry from what you ask, even if the machine were up and in running order, which I'm quite sure it's not."

"We may be able to compensate," Raphael stated solemnly, "on the Alter-tier."

"Alter-tier?" Dr. Templar demanded. "What is the Alter-tier?"

"It's another level of consciousness—a place we felines can go to, well, for various reasons."

"Never heard of it."

"Of course, you wouldn't have. But we must be moving now. It's already morning, and there is much to prepare." Raphael looked intently at the old doctor. "If you truly intend to help us restore the lost Spark of the Human Spirit, then you need to trust us."

Ti jumped into Dr. Templar's lap, circled and lay down in perfect round, her yellow eyes fixed on her cohabitor. Templar reached a hand into the plush fur and kneaded distractedly. "What do you think, Ti? No one's asked your opinion here."

Ti yawned. "They're telling you the truth, as they know it," she finally replied. "But whether we should be meddling with these sorts of affairs, I can't say. There are many hazards. What if the plan doesn't work and they destroy the world or bring back the evil? We're happy now. I don't quite see why—"

"Yes, there are others who think as you do, Ti," Raphael interrupted hotly. "And, yes, we could leave things as they are. The humans would continue their comfortable existence—for a time. But without the Spark of the Human Spirit, that comfort will eventually slip into complacency, and then even the drive to produce and interact will wane. For a reason not even our wisest can discern, lethargy has become more than a state of being throughout the past century—it has taken on a life of its own. Don't you feel it, Ti?" he charged, but Ti was drifting in the doctor's lap.

Pleadingly, Raphael met Templar' eyes, but the old man was silent.

Lise had stopped listening. When Raphael spoke of lethargy, of it having a life of its own, it had triggered a memory, and a fear.

"In-Ars!" she exclaimed, urgently drawn back to her vivid nightmare.

"How do you know that name?" Raphael hissed, his face filled with dread.

"I had another dream just now. That shadow-thing was back, hiding behind the face of the man we saw on the trolley. It said its name was..." She paused, sheepishly remembering she was not supposed to speak the name out loud. "I mean, it told me what to call it."

"In-Ars," declared Dr. Templar, as all frightened eyes spun toward him. "The root words for 'inert', as in inertia. In Old Latin, the words meant 'not art'. How apt a designation for an embodiment of lethargy."

"But how can lethargy be dangerous?" Lise asked. "Isn't it just being lazy, lacking energy?"

"Ask the Greeks who sailed on Lethe, the River of Forgetfulness. In Hades," he added for clarification.

"Pardon?"

"The river Lethe flowed through the cave of Hypnos, god of sleep, where its murmuring would induce drowsiness. The shades of the dead drank its waters to forget their earthly life. Lethe was also the name of the goddess personification of forgetfulness and oblivion. Need I continue? This idea goes back a long way."

"But that's myth..." Lise began.

Dr. Templar smiled knowingly.

"It's not a myth?"

He gave a motorized shrug. "What you're asking me to believe here and now is as wild as most classical mythology."

"Myths are based on something," Raphael declared. "And to answer your question—lethargy is dangerous because no one is immune. No species, no breed, not one living thing."

"All matter tends toward inertia," Dr. Templar interposed. "It's a physical law."

"That's right," Raphael agreed. "If lethargy is taken to its extreme, everything will come to a halt. Plants will stop growing; animals will not pursue reproduction; humans will stop caring for themselves—let alone, us! Ultimately even the cells within our bodies will cease to thrive. If that happens, it will be the end of all life."

Lise glanced at Dr. Templar and noticed a strange smile playing over his face. He seemed to be envisioning the inertia conundrum as some complex equation, taking its bizarreness at face value. What was more, he looked like he was thoroughly enjoying himself.

"You have convinced me!" he exclaimed, leaping from his chair in a flurry of motorized motion and turning the slumbering Ti out onto the floor. "It certainly is a puzzle—science meets the astral plane in order to change an innocuous condition that could destroy the human race? It's like an old sci-fi movie. I still have some of them, you know. From before the interactive venues, back when passive entertainment was still the style. The classic, 'Star Wars'! Ah, that was a story. And 'Blade Runner'—the original, mind you..."

Dr. Templar continued his happy tirade, but Raphael understood none of it except that the man had agreed to help.

And not a moment too soon.

"Doctor," he put in. "I thank you for embracing our quest, but now we must move quickly."

The old man fell silent as the visions of space ships and furry aliens faded back into his memory. "I'm afraid speed is not my strong suit," he sighed. "We must find a pod. The projection chamber is outside the community, you know." He looked down at his rumpled night coat. "But I think I should change. They'll put me in the elder-garten if I go running around like this."

With an electric whir, his suit revved up and propelled him through the bedroom door. Raphael looked at Lise and Graywood.

"We must hope the good doctor has learned enough from his pastimes to do what we need him to do."

"And we must also hope we don't run into you-know-what any time soon," added Graywood, pointedly not mentioning the name Lise had disclosed.

And I must hope and pray I don't have any more dreams, Lise thought to herself.

As if summoned, she smelled dust. The murky shadow of In-Ars rose in her mind and grinned.

8. The Parting of Ways

Before leaving the house, the doctor pulled down a half-dozen dusty tomes and flipped through a catalog of virt files to find all he could on the old physics research facility where the Big Bang machine was housed. Built over a period of decades in the late twentieth century, the ion collider had been state-of-the-art, but at the onset of the Reawakening, people's interests had veered elsewhere. The buildings were still intact and were opened occasionally for historical tours, a popular hobby with the new generation, but the machine itself hadn't been activated for nearly one hundred years.

Templar leafed through a leather-bound book, "Advanced Physics for the New Age", until a little slip of paper fell out. "We're in luck," he announced as he retrieved it. "No tours this month. We should have the place to ourselves. Just let me find my pod card and we'll be on our way."

He stopped with his hand half-way into his pocket. "Something occurs to me," he mused. "How are you three expected to ride in the pod?"

Raphael, Graywood, and Lise looked at each other. There was no way three collarless cats could hide on a public travel pod.

"I have an idea," said Dr. Templar. "I can take one of you in Ti's carrier. You won't mind, will you Ti?"

The Persian turned away unconcerned. "As long as it's not me," she clipped.

"No, I think it had better be someone more familiar with this innovative plan." He looked at Lise. "I, for one, have no idea what's supposed to happen after we have the machine up and running...if we make it that far."

Lise felt a tug at her heart. How she wished she could go with him, but she knew it should be Raphael. He was the leader, and he knew more about the project than anyone else there.

"I will go," Raphael announced, making the decision for her.

"Alright, you're it," said the doctor, and Lise thought she heard just a trace of disappointment in his sonorous voice. "Step right up." He motioned to a hexagonal Plex carrier in the corner of the room. "Once you're in, no one can see you don't have your tags."

"I don't really care for being enclosed," Raphael commented just before he stoically ducked inside. "Be careful, will you? I wouldn't like a bumpy ride."

"Finicky, isn't he?" Dr. Templar bantered, then said aside to Lise, "I had rather hoped you would accompany me, though I understand the choice."

Lise felt the blood rise beneath her fur. "Maybe we'll meet again," she mumbled, knowing her small words couldn't convey how much she wished it to be so.

"Since I'm going off to shape the future, perhaps I'll write in a program stipulating that we must."

"I don't think it works that way," she replied with smiles in her eyes, "but it couldn't hurt to try."

"The two of you, take care," Raphael said from inside the opaque box.

"Wait! Raphael!" Lise blurted. "You haven't told Gray and me what we're supposed to do while you get the machine working." Suddenly, Lise feared she had outlived her usefulness and would now be returned to her dull and painful human life. Her resistance to that idea surprised and scared her.

"The other team is rounding up the second element," came Raphael's voice through the grill. "Dr. Templar and I will, with luck, take care of the third. That leaves only the first element, and that is up to you."

Right! She had forgotten all about the Heart of Humanity—her task. At least they still needed her, but that brought a different worry. "I have no idea where to start."

"Graywood will help. Won't you, Gray?"

"Um, I'll try," Graywood sputtered, looking at Lise in dismay, as much at a loss as she.

"See you on the Alter-tier," Raphael declared before the doctor latched the screen; once the grill snapped shut, the only sound from the carrier was a short feline growl of discontent.

The doctor, ignoring Raphael's primal protests, levitated the carrier with the controls on his suit and began to guide it out the front door. "This should be fun!" the old scientist exclaimed. He winked at Lise and followed the case outside. The smart-door swung shut behind him.

"The Alter-tier?" Lise repeated, staring dumbly at the blank facade of the closing door.

• • •

"The Alter-tier..."

Something about the strange other-plane had started Lise thinking, but her thoughts kept drifting away from her before she could catch the gist of them. Her brain felt sluggish and torpid, as if she had forgotten something that she knew she knew.

"Gracious!" she hissed. "I just can't remember."

Graywood peered at her from behind his fairy screen of fuchsia blossoms, but there was nothing he could do. Lise would have to work through her thought-strings on her own.

Lise and Graywood had remained a little longer in Dr. Templar's comfortable living room. They both felt a little lost, wondering what to do next, but it was so beautiful outside— poignantly lovely as only those last full days of summer can be— that next thing they knew, they were bidding farewell to Ti who preferred to remain on her velvet sofa, and trotting out the cat flap into the sunshine.

For a while they wandered, savoring the grand out-of-doors. They knew nothing of this community and had no particular place to go so they just gave over to fortune and cruised. It had been joyous, the breeze caressing them with cool fingers even as the heat lavished down on their sleek coats from above. Lise had been caught by a strange sensation, as if time had slowed or perhaps stopped, waiting. The flowers seemed poised under the flat blue sky and the trees stood motionless. Even the birds in the branches hung back as if holding their breath. It reminded her of those moments before a thunderstorm when the pressure builds to palpable proportions, but the heavens were clear. Something else was causing this glitch.

When Lise and Graywood were thoroughly lost amongst the twining parkways of Brin Templar's historical district, they had picked out a convenient garden and settled down for a rest. Lise needed to think. Something was nagging at her. Maybe it was merely the fact that she'd been given the impossible task of finding an unknown element before nightfall, but she felt there was more to it than that.

Lise recalled how afraid she had been at the idea of going home, back to her lonely domicile. But home, the confining PMT, and her frail and aging body were an inevitability. Actually, she hadn't completely convinced herself this languid cat-world was anything more than a fantastical dream. If that were the case, her crashing return to reality could come at any time.

Don't worry about that now, she chided herself. She had more important things for her brain to do. She had to find the Heart of Humanity. Everyone was counting on her. If she didn't figure out what it was and how to get it, all their work will have been for naught.

She had needed to meditate, and Graywood wanted a nap, so they chose a waterfall of mammoth fuchsias to tuck in under. The shade was cool and softly scented. Honeybees droned from bloom to blazing bloom, and an occasional hummingbird gleamed green among the pink and purple. If she couldn't get her thoughts in line in this peaceful placid place, she'd be plain out of luck.

The Alter-tier... Why did her reflections keep slipping back to that? Was she anxious about returning into those divergent dimensions? She didn't think so. Her last trips, so long ago, were remarkable in their range of experiences, but what she remembered most was the sense of well-being and confidence, her abilities no longer limited by physical law. No, if anything, she was looking forward to it. Besides, it wasn't fear that was making her crazy but something far more elusive.

"Graywood," she said thoughtfully. The dusky cat opened a glass-green slit and trained it at her. "Gray," she went on, oblivious of his displeasure at being disturbed. "Tell me about the Alter-tier. Have you ever been there?"

"Yes, once," he replied through a large yawn.

"What happened?"

His eyes came open the rest of the way. "Do you remember the cold season when I was gone for a long time?"

"Of course I do," replied Lise, recalling her dread at his twenty-hour disappearance. "I was worried sick."

"But I survived."

"Yes, and you were fine, if a little hungry. I was so thankful—that was a bad freeze." She looked into his eyes and realized what he was driving at. "You mean..."

He nodded. "If I hadn't space-shifted to the Alter-tier, I wouldn't have made it." Gray paused and Lise reached out to touch his paw.

"I was caught in the storm, that night when everything froze under sheets of ice. I remember being tired, so tired I had to stop for a nap, even knowing that no one in their right mind would sleep in such deadly temperatures. But I wasn't in my right mind—I was already beginning to cross Beyond. Before I knew it, I'd begun to slip away. I could feel myself approach the bridge to the Other Side."

Graywood shivered slightly at the memory. "Then, something took me over, an inner strength I never knew I possessed. In another instant, I found myself in a summer garden. I was warm again. Everything was warm, in fact. Even the cushions of the porch swing were heated. My fur was dry—it was exquisite. I stayed there for a while, then something told me it was time to go. Before I'd finished the thought, I was back in the ice, but this time I was clear-headed and barely chilled at all. I ran home, and the rest you know."

"Oh, Gray, poor you!" Lise crooned, momentarily reliving that horrible night.

"It would have been 'poor me' if I hadn't shifted to the Alter-Tier."

Lise was quiet a moment. "So you shifted because your life was in peril. Does it always have to be that way—a matter of life or death? Because long ago, I knew someone who shifted just for his own pleasure. He said it was like taking a trip."

"I suppose one could," Graywood considered. "After all, it's a different plane of existence and has very few rules or boundaries. I imagine if you didn't mind being in such a weird state of flux, it could be fun."

"But what exactly is the Alter-tier? Is it really a place at all?"

"No, not like here—something more on the level of a dream. But it's not a dream either, because what goes on there is real and has real consequences."

"So what makes it work the way it does?"

Graywood fidgeted. He was not especially knowledgeable about—nor interested in—transcendental phenomena. He would rather have his dreams unburdened with questions of why.

Lise sensed his plight. "Okay, for example, say you're in danger and you space-shift to the Alter-tier—how do you decide whether it's a garden or a building or a graveyard for that matter you'll be shifting into? Or do you do decide at all?"

"It's symbolic projection, a metaphor brought to life."

"Yes, but how? The metaphor must come from somewhere."

"Hum," Graywood began, longing to answer his cohabitor's question intelligently even though he knew it was beyond his range. "I must have shifted to somewhere warm because I was freezing, but it wasn't just anywhere—it was a special place I made up from my own individual need. I guess it has to do with what you're feeling at your true core."

"Feeling..." Lise contemplated. "True core..."

She leapt to her feet and started pacing back and forth like a panther. "The heart!" she exclaimed. "I don't know about cats, but for humans, the heart is considered to be our true core. Maybe the Heart of Humanity is an Alter-tier metaphor. Maybe it will reveal itself when we shift."

She stood poised for a moment, then sank back to the ground and sighed. "But what if I'm wrong? Some would argue that the mind is the true core, and the mind and the heart rarely agree. If the Alter-tier shows us what's in our minds instead of our hearts, it won't be anything near the same."

Graywood pushed close to her, nosing a fuchsia sprig aside to touch her gently. "I know how you're feeling, Cohabitor. All this science is beyond me. The only reason they brought me along is for you, though what good I'm doing you I'm not certain."

Graywood spread out beside her, and for a time they were quiet, Lise berating herself for her lack of insight and the gray cat sliding toward slumber, guilelessly disconnected in spite of his best intentions to care.

Eyes shut, he began to purr. "I think your idea about the Alter-tier isn't half bad."

"Really? I don't know." She suddenly felt so frustrated her mind blanked. "I don't know anything at all!"

"Don't worry so much. Raphael brought you here. That

means you'll do what you must when the time is right."

She gave her friend a look of utter sorrow. She was so afraid she would let them down, afraid that in spite of her new shape, she was no better than the old useless carcass she had left behind.

"You will do it," Graywood reiterated before he drifted into dream, leaving Lise to brood on her own.

"He is right, you know," came a soft voice from a nearby bush.

Lise jumped up as Prospero came out into the open to sit like an alabaster statue, staring at her with his strange blue and green eyes.

"Prospero!" she gasped, irked at being startled but extremely glad he was there—she could use all the help she could get.

"We have procured the second element, the Seed of Life," he announced proudly, "and Winnick and Ton-e are already on the Alter-tier. At least I think Ton-e is there—you can never tell with that one."

Hearing the voices, Graywood opened his eyes a crack.

"Greetings, Gray of the Woods," said Prospero. "I hope you have rested well because now it is time to go. I have come to guide you to the shifting place."

"We can't do it here?" Lise asked.

"We could. A shift may originate anywhere, but we would be better off to start in a more secluded spot. We do not want anyone happening upon our unprotected bodies while we are gone from them."

Lise nodded. The thought of Duggan's gang finding her, prone and helpless, gave her the creeps.

Graywood rose wordlessly, completely awake now and eager to be on the move again, but as Prospero was about to step into the parkway, the gray cat butted him back.

"Wait!" Graywood hissed, swiveling his ears and sniffing warily at the breeze.

"What is it—" Lise began, then she heard it too, the sound of heavy footfalls reverberating on the plex pathway. The footfalls were coming closer.

Thank goodness for Graywood and his sensitive ears, Lise thought to herself. The wind was in the wrong direction for scent, and the near-deaf discerner would have walked right in front of them had it not been for the warning of the dusky cat.

Shrinking back under cover, Lise, Graywood, and Prospero peered down the lane. There, moving along at almost a march, was Lise's fears come to life: Duggan and his followers. This time, they were armed with motion seekers and nets. Lise couldn't remember seeing such a mobilization since before the Reawakening, and it made her think of things she would rather have left forgotten.

She kept reminding herself that these people were not the storm troopers of the old days. They were civilized intelligent men and women. But those nets said something else about them. Although they'd been born into a world of peace and consideration, the instinct to fear the unknown was stronger than training.

"Don't move," Prospero mouthed, but he need not have. Lise and Graywood were as still as the earth, knowing that the slightest twitch would set off the seekers' sensitive alarms.

The group spread out as they moved closer, taking up the whole parkway with their bizarre maneuvers. As they came even with the fuchsia, one of the men, a stout middle-aged laborer, stopped directly in front of it to scrutinize its filigree shelter.

"What?" Duggan grunted, also slowing his pace.

"Thought I saw something, but I guess it was just a bird." The man made a sound like a punctured tire. "We'll never find these stupid animals!"

"Quit your complaining," spat the woman by his side. "Think of this as a stroll in the park. And by the looks of it, you could use one, Jonah!" She laughed, nodding toward his ample girth.

"I get plenty of exercise," the big man protested. "It's my genes. My great-grandfather was a sumo wrestler."

"And what was your grandmother, then?" a wiry man chuckled from behind.

"Shut up!" said Duggan, shooting a dirty look over his shoulder. "We don't have time for jokes. Pay attention to what you're doing, or you might miss something. And you all know what that means." His words were like an ice bath, and in a heartbeat, the troop fell back into line.

Duggan gazed at his seeker and then up at the sky. "We will find them," he said coldly. "No one rests until we do." He flipped the device shut, vehemently adding, "if it takes all night." With that, he moved on down the walk, his followers in tow. The sound of boots abated, leaving the cats alone once more.

"Quick," said Prospero, bounding off in the direction of the lake. "There is no time to waste."

9. The Old Room

Lise, Graywood, and Prospero plunged into a particularly wild section of the forest just as the blazing orb of the sun slipped behind the alders and pines. There was something almost malevolent about its crimson flare. A slight haze had gathered, and the pressure was mounting. They all could feel it now, thrusting against their sensitive ear drums like a migraine. The air was metallic, so highly charged that their fur stood on end. Every step brought small electric shocks to the pads of their feet.

Through the tangle of trees, the lake flashed like molten lava, reflecting the blood of the sky. As Lise approached the roiling waters, she had the distinct feeling that the cosmos was hanging by a thread. With the smallest shock, that thread could be severed and the universe as life had ever known it would be swept away in the blink of God's eye.

Prospero had stopped in a knot of saplings just short of the sandy lakeside. His piercing gaze swept the deserted shore. Across the water were the boat docks and public marinas, but this side had been left native, no trampling feet allowed off its infrequent pathways to endanger the ecosystem. It was part of the tiny arboretum and wildlife sanctuary that every community kept up with pride. Birds, both native and exotic, noisily crowded the trees. Marmot, vole, mouse, and frog scuttled through the underbrush. With the thrill of discovery, the cats could smell them on the air. The scent made mouths salivate and teeth yearn for the crunch of living flesh. But that must wait.

"Here," Prospero signaled.

Lise pushed through the underbrush to stand next to him, gazing out onto the beach. It was certainly secluded enough for their purposes, but there was something more, a tingle to the atmosphere that hinted the presence of power.

"Where are we?" she asked carefully.

"The water-meets-land place," he replied enigmatically.

Lise frowned. "Yes, I can see that, but there's more to it, something else about this precise spot."

Prospero blinked innocently, but she stared him down.

"You are correct," he finally relented. "This place is special. We have come to the edge of the Rift."

"Rift?" She gazed around but saw nothing remotely fissure-like in the flat landscape.

"This isn't a geological rift but an intersection between ourselves and the other levels. It will be within the Rift that we meld the elements. You will know it once we reach the Altertier."

She nodded and hoped that to be true. Everyone else had so much confidence in her. Why didn't she feel it too?

"It is time. Close your eyes and find the place inside yourself where there is only your soul. No feelings, no physicalities. No sound, not even the sound of my voice..."

Lise clamped her eyes shut and tried to center beyond Prospero's hypnotic tones but she was a century out of practice. She was too hyper, her mind buzzing with thoughts of their quest and the difficult assignment ahead. Her traitorous body distracted her, the tension making her skin itch with pin-points of fire.

I'll never be able to shift like this, she chided herself. *All I can think about is...*

There was a split-second sense of distortion, then gone were the forest and lake. Instead of sky, she found herself staring up at the stone ceiling of a dark chamber. Oil lamps hung in the gloom, their sickly light barely illuminating the space around them. Gothic columns wound with creeping fungus vanished upward. The air was smoky from the lamps and stung her eyes as she strained to see through the haze.

She tried to sit up and felt the bite of leather straps holding her back. Her terror rose—nothing good came from being tied up in a mediaeval dungeon, and it didn't take a wizard to see that. Instinctively she thrashed against her restraints, but it only made the straps grow tighter. She worked to corral her fears and was relieved to feel them loosen again.

This is absurd! she thought to herself. She didn't even know where she was—or why. She had the very strong feeling that she shouldn't have been there at all.

She had to get free. Escape was a prisoner's first duty, she recalled from one of the old spy novels she enjoyed as a girl. To do that, she needed more information though. Struggling to slow her ragged breathing, she began to take inventory.

She was in a room or a cell—her restricted vision had told her that much. The air was so strongly tainted with the harsh oil smoke and the skank of decay that she couldn't smell anything else, if in fact there was anything else to smell. From somewhere off in the cavernous dim, she heard the hollow drip of water on stone meaning it might even be a cave.

Where are Prospero and Graywood? she wondered briefly, but the question was moot.

Stretching her cramped muscles, she began to inspect the pallet upon which she lay. It was made of something hard and cold and...

Her heart froze. She checked again but her senses weren't deceiving her. She was laid out on a smooth stone slab fit with ropes and pulleys that attached to the cuffs at her wrists and ankles. She knew this contraption only from ancient chronicles, but she instantly recognized it as one of the most fearsome implements in the history of man, a torture rack. Her panic returned and she began to writhe and scream. The screaming went on and on, echoing through the dim until it rolled back on her like a chorus from hell.

When, finally, her hysteria dwindled into silent throat-searing dread, she began to register a new sound. *So I'm not alone after all!* she flashed with a wisp of hope. Maybe it was some benevolent soul come to set her free. Of course, it was equally possible that it was not.

She jerked her head around as far as it would go, and out of the corner of her eye, she glimpsed a small green demon standing with a grizzled hand on the wheel of the rack. It eyed her with its bloodshot gaze, then letting out a raucous cackle, began to turn.

Imploding with fear, Lise braced for wrenching pain, but the pain did not come. Instead, tiny bird-like creatures fluttered up and down her torso beating barb-tipped wings along her naked skin. Though the sensation was more of a tickle than a stab and certainly preferable to being drawn and quartered, it was awful just the same. She reminded herself this was only a space-shift composite, a metaphor for something in her mind, but that didn't help. The unrelenting scratchings were so annoying she couldn't concentrate, and unless she concentrated, she was incapable of shifting anywhere else.

I...have...to...focus! she was ordering herself when, like a soap bubble pop, Prospero appeared beside her.

"Come," he said, taking her hand. Before Lise knew it, the dank grotto was gone.

In the new place, there were no walls or confinements, no features except an unending ethereal blue. Lise basked in the shimmering luminescence and thought it must be like being inside the sky. A small knot of humans talked softly nearby, but once Lise determined they weren't a threat, she paid them no mind.

"What happened?" she sputtered, gulping breaths of the clean sweet air to expunge the smell of rot.

"You mis-shifted. Your concentration must have fluked. But

you are with us now. I will make sure it does not happen again."

Lise remembered what she had been thinking right before she found herself in the gothic cavern—that interminable itch! As she recalled the bird-creatures with their pricking tickling feathers, she realized that was probably what set it off.

No accounting for the ramblings of the mind, she told herself now that she was safe. She would have to be more careful in the future. No telling where she might end up if she let her thoughts run away with her.

Ironically, the stupid itch was still there. Reaching up to scratch it, she started in surprise—she had taken on a new form.

Lise was human again, but not in the shape she had come to think of as her own, that an old woman, stiff, slow, and useless. This body was young and strong, imbued with wild energy that fed every cell of her being. Even in her youth, she had never felt so alive.

But there had been once...

Yes, of course! she realized. On the Alter-tier! That time, she had also taken a dream-shape. She, along with her company, had assumed various human forms and guises. Dominic told her they were metaphor.

Quickly she glanced at Prospero and saw he was no longer a small white cat but a tall lithe human male. His age was unfathomable, anywhere from fourteen to forty. His blue and green eyes shown with the same luminosity even though the pupils had transformed from slits to circles. His face was sober as he watched Lise work through her revelations.

She remembered the other people, two women and a man, she had noted when she first arrived in the blue. She was beginning to catch on now, and it was not hard to recognize the shy muscular youth with his adoring smile and striking close-cropped head of dusky-gray hair as her friend and companion, Graywood. The sleek dark brunette with the bearing of a princess and golden eyes that left nothing unseen had to be Ton-e. Winnick was the young child-like blonde with the serious face. She was carrying a beaker in which blazed an ember of pure blue light.

"Is that what I think it is?" Lise asked, instantly in awe of the shining mote.

"The Seed of Life," Winnick replied proudly, holding up the vile so its brilliance threw diamond refractions across the cerulean space.

"How beautiful!"

"This is only as it appears in this place," Prospero qualified.

"What is it really?"

"Amino acids, mostly. The building blocks of life."

"It looks like life," Lise commented, watching the flashes dance around her. There was something divine about it, though she knew those who considered animate existence merely a chemical inevitability might disagree.

Prospero interrupted Lise's musing. "We must go now. The others are waiting."

"The others?" She looked up in dismay. Raphael and the doctor. How could she have forgotten? Her mind seemed to work differently in this alter-existence. Each perception was acute, but she could only seem to hold one thought at a time. It was nothing like the overcharged buzz of half-finished cogitations common to her daily life. This singlemindedness was a relief, but she would have to be careful—it was disconcerting to think she hadn't remembered her friends.

"Yes. It is time we join them," Prospero was saying. "If you will follow me."

He turned and set off in a seemingly arbitrary direction since to Lise, the blue firmament looked the same for as far as she could see. Prospero must have discerned the correct path— it was his function, she reminded herself. Without question, she followed behind Winnick, the man Graywood falling in by her side.

As they moved along, things began to change. The colors fanned the spectrum until the blue had slipped through magenta and red-orange and was melting into a clear sunshine yellow. Sometimes it felt as if they were walking, and others, Lise could swear their bodies were still, the light merely rainbowing around them. But before she could decide, the environment would mutate again. It took all of Lise's attention to keep up.

At some point they moved into a virtual world where shapes rose out of the dimensionless plane only to crumble and fall back down a moment later. A tree, a lake, a mountain, a universe. If there was some symbology to the images, Lise had no clue of what it was.

Graywood stalked beside her, alert with trepidation. Ton-e took up the rear, and when Lise glanced around, she saw the dark princess circling warily, recoiling as each new scene broke the placid surface. Only Winnick and Prospero seemed undisturbed by the constantly-shifting surroundings. Winnick, although as diminutive in her new form as she had been in her old, walked guilelessly as a child. Prospero strove ahead, and Lise had the feeling that even under the most grievous conditions, his stalwart facade would never waver.

The manifestations were coming faster now. It was all Lise could do to follow their ever-changing impressions. Trying to assimilate the flashing patterns was making her dizzy. She was beginning to wonder how much more she could stand when, thankfully, Prospero stopped.

As if some stagehand had killed the lights, the world went black as space. Lise grabbed Graywood's arm, but a new realm was already building from the darkness. This one seemed stable, growing more and more solid until it appeared completely real.

The five were in a huge room. It was difficult to tell by the minimalist furnishings, but the place seemed extremely old. Vast painted walls cast off delicate chips of soft mauve and gold to accumulate like moth wings on the dusty hardwood beneath. Deep pile carpets, distilled to a resplendent specter of their former beauty, lay scattered across the floor. Somber wooden moldings bordered the high ceiling, encircling its veins of cracked plaster like a Rococo picture frame.

At each end of the room was a large pocket door, one shut and the other standing open a notch, leading into obscurity. A bank of tall windows spread across one wall, and opposite, a mural had been painted in the style of the romance artists, but that had been centuries ago. All Lise could recognize now was a dim pastoral landscape veiled with layers of feathery dust.

Even though it looked as if no one had been in the room for eons, Lise felt a distinct sense of well-being. The air was sweet and not the least bit stuffy, and the muted light filtering through gauze curtains cast long patterns on the floor, reminding her of something she had seen in childhood or maybe in a dream. But dream or real, she knew this place, knew it like her own heart. She had been there before—and what was more, she had loved it.

Turning to take in each familiar detail, Lise realized that her companions' clothing had changed. Actually, now that she thought about it, she couldn't remember what they had worn when she first saw them on the blue plane. It must have been something innocuous for her to forget so quickly, but she was sure they had not been naked—that, she would have noticed.

Graywood now wore soft faded jeans and a sparkling white tee shirt, its cotton old and smooth as a lily petal. Resting unobtrusively against the door jam, he reminded Lise of the boys from her long-ago youth.

In contrast, Ton-e was clothed like exotic royalty in a sheath of sheerest blue-green silk. Her long fingernails were painted blood red and her kohl-lined eyes flashed as violently as the thick golden choker she wore upon her slender neck.

Compared to Ton-e, Cleopatra would have seemed drab, but poor little Winnick had taken it a step farther. Her costume was quite up-to-date and modern—for a twenty-second century businessman. Lise supposed it made sense considering Winnick's position as weaver. The suit was efficient and practical, but this was the Alter-tier—why had she not come up with something a little more adventurous than the mole-brown jumper?

Lise's eyes moved to Prospero. His dress made perfect sense, a simple floor-length robe of natural linen. His only other adornment was a ring on his left hand, set with a large stone resembling a diamond. *If that's real,* Lise speculated, *it would be worth as much as a small planet.*

Lastly, she studied her own garb. For the life of her, she couldn't remember what she'd had on before, but she was almost certain it wasn't this beautiful gray dress. Made of some soft and supple material, the bodice conformed to her every move as if she were wearing mist. The long straight skirt, instead of being heavy and cumbersome as she would have expected, felt as light as a flower. She took a few steps and turned quickly to gauge its reactions, but in spite of the way it swirled like fog around her legs, she felt as if she were wearing nothing at all.

Prospero and Winnick had their heads together, deep in discussion at a small café table in a corner of the room. Graywood was still reposing against the wall. Ton-e had disappeared, though Lise had no idea when she had gone.

"What now?" she asked of no one in particular. Her voice echoed in the great empty chamber. The two in conference ignored her, and Graywood smiled sympathetically. Lise sighed, then turned to tour the large room for lack of anything better to do.

As she approached the open doorway, she began to pick up a sound coming from beyond. Graywood heard it too and straightened warily. It was a repetitive clicking-tapping that bounced off the naked walls like a ping-pong ball. There was no rhythm to it, slowing and speeding up at a whim. Sometimes it stopped altogether and then took off again like some demented woodpecker. It seemed familiar, not threatening, but Lise couldn't think what it might be.

She knew she'd heard this sound many times before. She took a few puzzled steps closer and then stopped, remembering.

"A keyboard!" she exclaimed. "Someone's working at a keyboard! I haven't heard one of those since personal interfacers became a thing." She looked eagerly at Prospero who seemed unconcerned. "Is it Raphael and the doctor working on their project?"

"It is."

"Do you think they've collected the Wellspring of the Universe yet?" Lise cried excitedly. "Can I see them?"

Without waiting for an answer, she dived through the doorway and into the murk, following the clicks and taps as if they were a lifeline.

10. A Disturbing Reunion

Lise ran through the next room and more after that. The house, if it was a house, seemed to be one long sequence of chambers, all joined by cavernous double doors giving the impression of a neglected cathedral. Some rooms were lit, others pitch black, but always those inevitable doorways leading her on.

The tapping sound grew louder, then began to dull again, and Lise realized she had missed her mark. She scanned her surroundings, a small salon hung with swarthy lengths of lavender brocade, and spied an old-fashioned panel door in a dim corner. It stood ajar, beckoning, though its frosted window was a square of obscurity and the open crack showed nothing of what was inside.

Without thought, Lise slipped through. From the glow that seeped in from behind her, she saw a flight of stairs, the worn wooden steps descending into inky gloom, disappearing beneath her as if an artist had erased them from the page. There was no telling how far down they went, or if they went anywhere at all. She had no idea why Raphael and Dr. Templar would be holed up in the darkness, but her ears told her she was in the right place.

Lise inched down the staircase, holding the time-polished railing and feeling along with her toes. The sightlessness was disconcerting, but after a dozen treads, she hit bottom: not a pit of writhing snakes but the smooth safety of a plain plank floor. She could now sense geometric shapes that must have been furniture, and beyond, solid walls. The place reminded her of something long past like an old-fashioned school room or an office space.

She hesitated, still gripping the handrail. Though she felt no imminent danger, the thought of navigating her way across the oblivion scared her. Like flying blind, maybe she would make it, but maybe...

Without warning, a shape materialized in the umbra. Lise started, but only for a moment. Even in his new guise, that of a tall silver-haired man in mediaeval dress complete with chain-mail shirt and chausses, she couldn't mistake the self-assured bearing.

"Raphael, you startled me. But thank goodness!" Her eyes skimmed the dusk. "Where's Dr. Templar?"

Raphael tossed his snowy mane toward an electric glow at the far end of the room. She hadn't noticed it before, though now the radiance was as clear as the northern lights. Within the neon borealis was a lean silhouette hunched over an antiquated keyboard—Brin Templar.

Lise quietly approached the busy doctor. His appearance had changed, too, but this time she was not surprised. She had seen this attractive young man before, in her dream. The sandy brown hair, the virile physique, the penetrating eyes gently wrinkled with humor instead of age were all hauntingly familiar.

"Hi, there," she said softly as she walked up behind him.

The doctor whipped his molded plastic chair around to face her, excitement raw in his eyes. "Why, hello, Lise. Don't you look beautiful. And please, call me Brin."

"Thanks," she stammered. "You're not so bad yourself," she added, grateful for the dark that did not betray the blush his compliment had evoked.

"This is wonderful. Look!" He clicked on a small table lamp and jumped from his chair to do a little dance. "Have you any idea how long it's been since I could accomplish such a feat on my own?"

She smiled. "More than you might think."

He re-seated his graceful body, giving the chair a spin. "This place is amazing! Is it a dream? I asked Raphael, but he just told me it's the way things work in this Alter-tier place. He looks quite nice in his mail and surcoat, don't you think? Quite magnificent—such imagination! I still can't believe it's real."

Brin Templar was babbling like an overstimulated child, but Lise let him continue; after all, she knew from her own experience what he was feeling. The adrenaline flow, the heightened senses, the wonderful young body, nearly impossible to keep still.

"It's probably just the upshot of something I ate before bed," he was saying. "Onions or tuna, cilantro maybe. I knew I shouldn't have had that valerian martini. But everything feels so...so solid! So natural! Every part of me feels youthful and healthy. My dreams were never this good, even at the best of times."

Lise seated herself in a second chair, arranging her long light skirt around her. "Oh, it's real enough, or at least it's some form of reality. But I know what you mean—I could never quite grasp the whole thing, either."

He pursed his lips. His deep brown eyes gleamed like onyx as they stared unabashedly into hers. "But you're at an advantage—it sounds like you've done this before."

"I suppose that should matter, but it doesn't seem to. It's different every time and so fantastic, I don't think I could ever get used to it." She paused, musing on the past. "If you want to know the truth, up until now, I wasn't actually sure the Alter-tier existed. When you get back to the other world—the one we spend our lifetimes in—this part fades just like a daydream. If it weren't for all the things that happened afterward—unmistakable results—I would have considered myself a nutcase long ago."

"No one can deny the changes, Lise. I was there, and I know. Although I had no concept of the true story until you told me tonight," he added. "Was that only tonight? It seems like ages, doesn't it?"

She nodded.

"But I do remember," he went on solemnly. "It was as if the world had a sudden and acute attack of empathy. People began to accept each other's differences. You felt a sense of compassion, even from strangers on the street."

"Sometimes where you least expected it," Lise commented.

"Yes," Brin snickered. "Lawyers and government officials—now there was a turn-around. The face of government was never the same."

"Acceptance was the trend of the day," said Lise. "Even the bureaucrats couldn't swim against the tide."

"I remember people falling head over heels to help each other. That was all it took. Amazing how one small step can change everything."

"The beginning of the Reawakening."

"There was a similar point in twentieth century history—I think it was called the hip movement—when an entire generation decided to pursue pacifism against the precepts of their culture."

"The hippies," Lise recalled. Her mother had been one of the peace-minded clan. "People have always preached about a better world, but not nearly as many practice their preachings."

"Brotherhood, good will towards men. Peace on earth...just not today," Brin quipped mockingly. "Always some excuse or another.

"But then it happened—a complete turn-around in attitude. At first, it seemed odd—out of character for us savage humans. But we're a short-sighted race—soon enough nobody thought anymore about it."

"I know what you mean. Even after everything I'd been through, I never really questioned how it came about." Brin flicked some nonexistent dust off his console. "I assumed it was evolution. The possibility that we could mature into an altruistic society was no surprise to me—as a devotee of science, I've always held that the progression of the human species toward a more civilized state was inevitable. I just never thought I'd see it in my lifetime."

Lise sat forward. "Yes, Brin, that's exactly it," she exclaimed. "The change happened too fast. We were way too far gone down the path of self-destruction for some sort of grand epiphany. No, as much as I appreciate the evolution theory, I don't buy it in this case. I choose to believe that one special night a hundred years ago, an evil entity was banished from our World. I also choose to believe," she went on, "something just as magical and important is happening right now. Even if I don't understand what we're doing or how we're doing it." She ran her fingers through her hair, the shock-blue glow of the control console glittering like sparks amid the tresses.

"It would be an incredible thing to restore human creativity— the artists, the scientists..." Brin gazed wistfully into the haze. "For too long, I've only considered them in the past tense."

"And now we have a chance to change all that."

"If it's not all a dream," he chuckled.

"Dream or reality, we might as well give it our best shot. Raphael is convinced, and the efforts of his ancestor Dominic worked in the past."

"Someday you must tell me about your first adventure in Wonderland, Lise," Brin said as he swung his chair back to face the multi-colored console with its tell-tale keyboard. "But I'm afraid it will have to wait. They want me to get this machine up and running as soon as possible."

He struck a succession of keys. Lise studied his fingertips as they lightly touched the board. Almost a caress, she thought to herself.

"Will it work?"

"I have no idea. I don't actually understand how my actions

in this alter-world affect the real one. Can they? Do they?"

He gazed at his hands, turning them over as if assessing their solidity.

"Obviously, I am here, at least to some extent. I can see, feel. But is there another part of me working this panel on the real machine at home as well? Another me? Or a facet of me? Are the dimensions interconnected? You know—here, there, and everywhere?" He hummed a few bars of the old Beatles song.

Lise smiled sympathetically. "I'm sorry, I just don't have the answer."

He sighed and turned back to the console. "This archaic board is nothing like the collider's actual controls, and yet," he considered as he pecked at various icons and typed in a string of commands, "in an abstract way, they're the same. I seem to know just what to do."

"Believe in it. You're doing better that I am."

He looked up in surprise. "You haven't found your element yet?"

"The Heart of Humanity?" Lise slumped, resting her head in her hands and massaging her scalp as if the rhythmic pressure could force the ideas to form. "I don't even know where to start."

"You'll figure it out." It was a compassionate remark, if not a helpful one. "What have you got so far?"

"Nothing, really. Maybe a few threads, but how they tie together—if they tie together—is anyone's guess."

"Tell me about it. Maybe it will help."

She shrugged. "Can't hurt, but I hope it sounds more rational that I think it does." Lise settled in her chair, noting how comfortably the old-fashioned plastic fit the contours of her shape.

"I got the idea when I asked Graywood about space-shifting. I don't really understand the concept of finding myself in another guise, another place, another...everything," She gestured to the metaphoric scene around her. "To my mind, it's somewhere on the level of 'Scotty, beam me up', but I figured there had to be an explanation that didn't involve mythical characters utilizing yet-to-be-invented technology."

"Ah, yes, the star journey chronicles. Wasn't Scotty the doctor who could cure anyone and anything with a hand-held thinga-majiggy?"

"No, Scotty was the engineer. I thought all scientists followed the chronicles."

"I subscribed to them when I was in school, even went to a few concerts. It's been a long time. But I interrupted you."

"That's alright," she gave him. "In a place like this, it's easy to become distracted."

"Yes, my dear, it is. This time, I promise to give you my full attention."

Lise sighed, wondering where to start since she had yet to figure it out for herself. "As I said, it had to do with space-shifting. I especially wanted to learn about shift-logic, how it chooses where you land when you shift. I understand that it involves what you're thinking and feeling, but even so, how does it decide whether a longing for peace translates into a Caribbean cruise or the stillness of the grave?"

"Did the cat...I mean, Graywood—I assume like Raphael, he's not a cat anymore, at least not here. Or is he usually human? I've forgotten. Oh, bother! Did Graywood tell you what you wanted to know?"

"Partially. Apparently where you go is guided by something he called the true core. That's what got me thinking. Gray wasn't sure what true core correlates to physically. He described it as a sense of self, a soul, even. But what if...what if the true core is really about the heart?"

Lise looked hopefully at Brin, and he found himself nodding in agreement even though he didn't wholly get what she was driving at.

Taking that as answer enough, she pressed on. "Okay, consider for a minute. Say the heart does happen to be this true core, and the true core is what guides a space-shift, then it seems only reasonable that—I mean maybe, just maybe—well, I thought we might find the answer here on the Alter-tier. It's kind of a reach," she admitted, "and I haven't worked out where the 'humanity' part comes in, aside from me being human, that is."

"It's logical," Brin allowed, "but I take it you've had no luck so far."

Lise sighed. "Not a bit. How about you?"

Brin shook his head and flicked a switch that brought two more default-blue screens online. "I'm afraid I'm not doing much better. I'm trying my best to produce a proto-universe using an Alter-tier mockup of a century-old relativistic heavy ion collider. I can visualize the massive installation in my mind—I've seen and studied it many times. I know in theory what will happen when the gold ions reach optimum speed and slam together slightly askew—for a split second, primordial matter will form as it was in the instant after the Big Bang, creating a tiny cosmos unto itself."

"The Wellspring of the Universe," said Lise.

"We hope so, but even if it works, which is certainly not a given, how does it merge in that one split second with the other obscure elements? I must find…"

His gaze returned to his labor, this time with single-minded intensity. A mask of concentration settled over his face, and Lise knew he was off in his own world again, just as surely as if he'd shifted to another part of the Alter-tier.

While Lise and Brin were talking, their three colleagues had found their way to the control room, though Lise hadn't noticed them come in. Raphael and Ton-e parked by the far wall, Ton-e draped on the silver-haired man, leaving no doubt that their relationship was beyond one of siblings. Prospero had seated himself at a desk and was quietly watching the data on the screens. Winnick sat beside him, her attention riveted on the sparkling Seed of Life which floated in a hover-can ten centimeters above the table. Graywood hung nearby in case Lise should need him. She blinked affectionately at the young man and he beamed his reply, inching a little closer to his cohabitor.

Ton-e disentangled her slender body from her soulmate and slunk toward the diligent doctor, her sleek black hair falling like a silk curtain across her face.

"Is this your famous physicist?" she asked, gazing back at Raphael.

Raphael smiled indulgently. "Dr. Templar, meet the rest of our companions, Ton-e, Winnick, and Prospero."

Brin looked up, wide-eyed, as if coming out of a trance, and nodded to the newcomers. "Welcome," he said politely before bending back to his work.

Ton-e moved closer to the console. She ran a critical eye over the equations.

"When?" she purred.

"Dr. Templar," Raphael urged, "it must be soon." Though it was a statement and not a threat, the effect was very close to the same.

"I can't tell you when," the doctor retorted. His hands were now moving like lightning across the keyboard and touch panels. "I'm working as fast as I can."

"Maybe it would be more exciting if we could all see," Ton-e announced. She made a hand gesture and the entire back wall suddenly burst into fluorescence. Lise didn't know how she'd done it but a highly enlarged depiction of the glyphs on Brin's main monitor reflected onto the flat surface. For a few minutes, Ton-e's gaze followed the numbers, letters, and runes as they climbed like insects up the huge panel, then she turned away with a shrug.

"This bores me," she proclaimed, stalking to the opposite corner of the room and arranging herself languidly on a pillowed bench.

Lise was surprised by Ton-e's candor. Granted, the repetitive data was monotonous, especially not knowing what any of it meant, but the success of the Reconstruction Project hinged on the completion of this work. To call it boring? To say it out loud? It seemed almost like a betrayal.

Lise looked at Brin who was scowling at Ton-e. The exotic female closed her eyes indifferently, seeming more like a sulky silent movie star than a compatriot in an historic venture.

"Ton-e!" Raphael blazed. One golden eye opened but only a slit. "I expect better from you. You would do well to remember we're all collaborators here. This may seem tiresome to you, but if our doctor doesn't get it right, boredom will be the least of our concerns."

"I know that," Ton-e drawled, "but I just don't seem to care." She snuggled farther into the plush of the bench, the eye slipping shut once more. "All I want to do is relax awhile—is that so much to ask?" She yawned, mouth wide, teeth bared like a cat, then was instantly asleep.

Raphael raised a dark eyebrow and shook his silver mane but said no more. Lise could see in his burning gaze the struggle between his allegiance to the project and his deep emotional feelings for Ton-e.

"She has a point," Winnick commented unexpectedly.

The diminutive weaver rose and moved torpidly to the flight of steps. She lingered for a moment staring up at the paneled doorway, then dragged herself to the top as if hypnotized. Heaving a great sigh, she pushed the door wide.

Lise was puzzled. Ton-e's dissatisfaction was to be expected since the black cat had been unpredictable from the start. But Winnick? Up until that moment, the Reconstruction Project had been her priority. It was totally out of character for her to say or do anything the least bit counterproductive.

"Winnick!" Raphael spat as he whirled to face her. It was obvious that he, too, didn't get this sudden conversion.

"No, really," she went on from the doorway. "For once, I can totally agree with Ton-e. We're being ridiculous. This rag-tag bunch of sentients change our World? Whatever were we thinking?"

Raphael was shocked silent.

"We have done it before," Lise intervened. Like a tiger protecting its kit, she felt the need to defend their quest.

Winnick turned to confront her, her mud-colored eyes blank with ennui. "So you say, human. But how do I know you're not making the whole thing up? I certainly wasn't around to see it."

"Well, I was," Brin said pointedly. He had stopped work and was staring incredulously at the weaver. "Take my word for it, things were bad. Then suddenly, they got better. I think I knew even then that something extraordinary had a hand in, though I never imagined it was a clowder of cats. The driving force behind the Reawakening was probably nothing more than…what did you call us? A rag-tag bunch? And they got the job done anyway."

Lise nodded. "And now we have a chance to do it again."

"Twenty-four hours ago," Brin went on, "I knew nothing of this, but now I believe in it absolutely. It just makes so much sense."

"But who cares?" came a man's voice from behind Lise.

She swung around to find the incongruous words proceeding from Prospero's lips. He was tipped back in his chair with his feet propped on the console. His white robes fell haphazardly around him, their solemnity contradicted by the apathetic sneer on his face.

"Suit yourself," said the doctor. "I, for one, am going to try to make this happen. If you'll excuse me, I'll be in the projection chamber." With a rough movement, he pushed back his seat and stalked into a cubicle at the end of the room, sliding the door shut with a bang.

Raphael, his rage and confusion burning in his chiseled features, stepped up to the insolent discerner and knocked his feet off the delicate web of controls with an angry swipe.

"What do you think you're doing, Prospero? This isn't the kind of thing I'd expect from you. You, of all of us, know how important this plan is, and how difficult. We'll never pull it off with internal discord."

Prospero stood, unfurling his slender body until he was face to face with Raphael.

"You think so, old man?" With an unexpected and violent movement, he shoved the leader up against the wall and held him there. "I think we should quit wasting our time. I think we should leave well enough alone. Who are we, Raphael, to make these kinds of decisions for everyone else?"

Prospero was stronger than he looked, and Raphael fought for breath. "I...thought...you...were...with us," Raphael panted and instantly felt the pressure increase.

"I suppose I was, for a while. But I've come to my senses."

"Let.. me… go..!"

Raphael jammed his fingers underneath the rough hold, but the grip continued to tighten. Suddenly, Prospero gave the neck a swift jerk. The leader's eyes rolled up in his head and he slid to the floor, his armor clanking like scrap metal.

Lise gasped, paralyzed with fright, trying to make sense of what had happened. Had Prospero killed Raphael? Why had he attacked him? Why was everyone fighting? Why had no one stopped the violence?

One glance answered her question. Brin was still in the cubicle and most likely had not heard a thing, but Ton-e lay pale as a corpse on the bench and Winnick was nowhere to be seen. Lise searched for Graywood and discovered him curled up in the corner, fast asleep. She and Prospero were the only ones in the room left conscious.

"What have you done?" she cried.

"He's fine. It's just a little nerve pinch we learn in monastic training. There are advantages to being of the ministry, you know." Prospero grinned. The unaccustomed expression seemed more like a grimace on his normally-somber face. "Now you can go home and leave us alone."

Lise was at a loss. She felt as if she were unraveling along with the project that had become her purpose in life. "I don't understand!" she blurted. "You came to find me, remember? I thought we were all working for a better future."

"It is simple, human!" Prospero spat in her face. "We do not want your change."

"My change? You're beginning to sound like..."

The discerner bristled. "Whom do I sound like?"

She was about to say he sounded a lot like Duggan and his vigilante band, but she stopped herself. Silence seemed safer since she had no desire to end up on the floor alongside Raphael.

Prospero soon tired of waiting for her answer and fell back into his chair, assuming his former feet-up position as if nothing had happened. Crossing his arms over his chest, he closed his blue and green eyes.

"Tiresome," he said. "All too tiresome."

Lise watched him closely, primed to flee in case he had another outburst but within seconds, his angry breathing slowed, and he too was dead to the world.

As Lise surveyed the unconscious four, trying to wrestle from her dumbfounded mind an inkling as to what she should do next, the door of the cubicle slipped open. Brin stopped mid-stride as his eyes took in the bizarre scene.

"What's going on?"

"I have no idea," Lise wailed, moving to his side and putting out a shaky hand. "Everyone's gone crazy. Prospero and Raphael argued, then Prospero did something to make Raphael pass out. After that, he just sat down and nodded off. Graywood's sleeping too—everyone's asleep except Winnick who up and left. We're the only ones..."

Brin frowned, distractedly accepting her hand in his. "Well,

I'll be damned," he said softly. "What do we do now?"

Lise gripped his palm tightly. "Without the others, we don't have a prayer of completing the project."

"And we're so close. How can we stop when the hope of a better world is finally within our grasp?" He gently disentangled her fingers and moved to the prostrate Raphael, checking his pulse and lifting an eyelid to make sure he was merely slumbering. Satisfied that the leader was not in peril, he turned sad dark eyes to Lise. "Do we just give up and go home?"

She took a breath and was about to tell him of course not, but she stopped mid-word. Suddenly, she felt completely drained. A wave of exhaustion washed over her, a tsunami of fatigue so profound she staggered under its pressure.

Where did that come from? she wondered in alarm. She hadn't caught much rest since her cat-nap at Brin's domicile, but until that moment, she'd felt fine. Now, she was nearly senseless, the slightest movement more than she could bear.

"I..." she began, then faltered. The extreme lassitude had spread to her mind, and she couldn't even hold a simple thought.

Suddenly through the fog came a revelation. All at once she understood why the others—Prospero, Winnick, Graywood, and Ton-e—had ceded the Reconstruction Project. The answer was plain as day.

Way too much work...

Could never pull it off...

A stupid idea...

Bottom line—who cared? Changing the world just wasn't worth the bother.

"Lise! Lise, hold on!" she heard Brin cry as she sank to the floor in a stupor.

11. The Shadow

Lise came awake inside the feline body she had left by the lake shore. Muddled and drowsy, she attempted to stand but immediately fell back among the cool ferns. Her head was spinning; there was a reason for that, but she couldn't remember what it might be at the moment. Taking a deep breath, she tried again. This time, she made it to her feet, where, with supreme effort, she remained, breathing hard and staring dazedly into the forest.

Though nighttime now, all else was just as it was when she and her companions had shifted to the Alter-Tier. Graywood and Prospero lay nearby, quiet, as if peacefully asleep.

Lise called out but the pair didn't stir. Struggling against the intense fatigue that beleaguered her still, she staggered to them, pushing, prodding, and yowling their names. Did they linger on the Alter-tier, or had they returned to these forms incapacitated? Nothing in their silent demeanor gave the slightest indication.

Lise sank to the grass in frustration. It was all coming back to her. The Alter-tier; Prospero's outburst; Ton-e and Winnick's rebellion. Raphael lying unconscious on the floor. Lise, too, had been overcome by a great lethargy— *There's that word again*, she thought to herself. A sliver of dread pierced through her, though why she should fear such a passive tendency she couldn't grasp.

But maybe it wasn't so passive after all. Lise remembered how tired she had become, so tired it had been physically impossible for her to continue, or to care. The project, the future, even her companions meant nothing in the face of that boundless torpor.

Presumably, she had passed out, only to wake up where she began. Now, recalling the drug-like emptiness of that indifference, she felt sickened.

That strange detachment was still there, threatening to escalate into full-blown apathy. A null voice in her head kept whispering that nothing mattered. The monotone drone was familiar—she had heard it before in the dreams. But she wasn't dreaming, now. How had it got into her consciousness?

Lise didn't understand the meaning of this externally-induced sleep, but she knew it to be the enemy. She also knew all the speculation in the world wasn't going to conquer it. Something had to be done. Gray and Prospero were still out cold, and that was bad. Winnick and Ton-e should be somewhere nearby; maybe they had fared better. Making sure her companions were comfortable and well-concealed, Lise sniffed for scent and set off to find the others.

In a small clearing, two wooden picnic tables overlooked the obsidian blackness of the lake. One was occupied, and instinctively, Lise ducked back out of sight, afraid it might be Duggan and his crew. Peeking from the cover of a huckleberry bush, she watched the four silhouettes. They didn't look dangerous. In fact...

Something was wrong. Creeping closer to the family, she saw they were fast asleep. But no ordinary sleep, Lise recognized with a start. The man had his cheek in a plate of wakame salad and his wife was snoring softly between cup of flat cola and a piece of starfruit pie. The two kids had their heads together, keeping each other from falling into a large plex bowl of soy dogs. Judging by the musty state of the food, they had been that way for some time.

Silently, Lise slunk past them into the underbrush. Once away, she pricked her ears for any sign of her fellows but there was nothing.

Not a single thing, she realized with a jolt. Not a night bird, not a cricket chirp, not the voices that should have wafted across the water from the marina on the other side—absolutely nothing. It was as if she were in vacuum, as if all life had ceased to be. Lise glanced back toward the sleeping people and thought about her own brush with inertia. Could everyone in the world be asleep? A mass-slumber? The thought made her shudder. Her mind jumped to the outcome of such a condition, more devastating than a plague.

As she stepped up the search for Winnick and Ton-e's cached bodies, she came upon more inert humans—a businessman slumped against a lamplight pole; a runner snoring softly by the side of his foot path; two women lying in the grass like moon-bathers, their fedora-like hats askew on their resting heads. Others peppered the landscape like lost dolls. They confirmed Lise's suspicion that not only her friends but everyone, everywhere, had somehow been made senseless.

Lise finally found Winnick and Ton-e securely hidden in a scotch broom thicket. She tried to wake them, but as with Prospero and Graywood, it was no use. They were alive—she could feel their strong and regular heartbeats—but as if their consciousness had been sucked out of them, their bodies seemed little more than empty husks.

For a time, Lise sat in the dew-damp grass, listening to the eerie quiet and wondering what to do next. She felt as lost as cosmic dust hurtling through endless space, but deeper than her own personal anguish was the awareness that the reconstruction of the Spark of the Human Spirit was receding into impossibility with every passing moment.

Why should I care? Nobody else seems to...

Quickly, she pushed the debilitating thought aside. She now knew it came from beyond her—maybe even from the enigmatic In-Ars, itself—to undermine her hope. But what hope was there? What could she do, alone in a timeless spellbound world?

Not quite by herself, she realized, as a wavering light suddenly filtered through the trees. The glow was accompanied by voices, and her spirits leapt as she envisioned Brin or Raphael coming to the rescue. She started toward the sounds, then stopped cold, her joy draining. The voices were too loud, too unruly. These people were angry, shouting. She knew instantly who she would find on the other end of those flickering beams.

Duggan and his cronies plunged nearer. The glare of their high-powered searchlights jabbed between the trees like lightning flares as they made a sweep of the park. Was it coincidence that, aside from Lise, the only others in the world unaffected by the sleep-tide were this pack of vigilantes? Lise knew better.

These people were possessed, there was no doubt of it. They stomped through the protected park, unmindful of the rare foliage though they would have known their rampage was a punishable crime. In their voices rang the granite edge of hatred, a fury Lise hadn't encountered since the demise of Seh. Were they so intent upon stopping the Reconstruction Project they would throw away a hundred years of peace for it? Why?

It all revolved back to the Shadow, the thing whose power manipulated their leader, Duggan, like a puppet. The thing strong enough to pull the plug on the whole world. In-Ars.

Lise wished she knew how it all fit together, but she couldn't think about that. Duggan and his associates, driven by the Shadow's manifest control, were closing fast.

"Here's one!" someone yelled, his raucous tone grating against the silence of the woods.

"I have another, over here," someone else called back, a cat-cry slicing the stillness like a claw through flesh. The rabid pack was looking for them. For her! It was just as before, except now they had upped the stakes.

"Bring the gas gun, will ya, Monroe?" came the first voice again. "Cripes, this stuff stinks! Are you sure it won't hurt me?"

"No, Dana, it's nucleic-based," replied the other man. "Only effects felines. It's the same stuff the D.V.M.'s use when they knock 'em out for surgery, only this is the condensed version.

When this stuff knocks 'em out, they never wake up."

"Okay, but I still don't see why we've got to kill 'em," Dana whined. "I kind of like cats."

"Everybody likes cats, but these aren't really cats at all—they're minions of Seh."

"Come on, Monroe, you don't believe in that stuff, do you? There's no such thing as minions of Seh. It's just a fairytale to scare little kids."

"No, there's minions, alright," broke in a third speaker, a boy barely past his teens Lise gauged from his oscillating speech. "I saw one once—thought it was a pig-dog until it started kicking and biting. You should have seen its eyes—crazy red, like bloodstones!"

"Aw, pig-dogs are always like that, kid. They should never have engineered that breed in the first place."

"The minions are real," a rough voice cut in. Lise recognized it as Duggan's. "Believe me. Don't you watch history? And if we don't stop them tonight, nothing will ever be the same. Who knows what evil they'll unleash if given half a chance? I, for one, don't want to find out. Here, toss that gun over to me."

Lise heard a hissing sound and smelled the acrid scent of the nucleic gas. She quailed as she thought of the innocent lives being sacrificed out of blind fear, but there was no time to mourn—she had to get away or she would be one of them.

The death squad was close enough now for Lise to see their looming umbra. There were at least twenty of them, walking a line, shoulder to shoulder, scoping every meter of the lakeside for signs of life. Soon they would be upon her and her sleeping cohorts. She might be able to run for it, but unless she could get Winnick and Ton-e moving, the two sleepers would be caught for sure.

She cringed as another howl went up, accompanied by a snake-hiss of gas. This time, she saw the whole thing. It was a large calico, not one of her friends, and maybe not even sentient, but alive just the same. A brawny man had raised the unconscious animal high in the air in front of him, aimed the deadly nozzle at her face, and without hesitation or remorse, pulled the trigger. For a moment, the frightened cat had come to, the adrenaline of near-death shocking her from her pseudo-sleep. She struggled bravely in the man's grip, but with another spurt of gas, she succumbed. Uttering one last scream, her body contorted wildly and went limp. The man tossed the carcass aside and moved on.

Lise was in shock. She was barely breathing, as if her heart had stopped. She stayed that way, locked and frozen, until another cat was lifted to its peril. As abhorrence reanimated her body, her racing heartbeat made up for lost time.

"Winnick!" she whispered sharply as she pawed at the prostrate form. "Winnick, wake up! We've got to run. They're coming!"

After what seemed like an eternity, Winnick stirred. She pried open a moss-green eye, laboring as if a great weight held down the lid. "Lise..." she mumbled. Little breath accompanied the mouthing of the word.

"Winnick," Lise hissed, continuing to knead at the slack shoulders. "That's it. You've got to get up. Those men are coming, and they're killing all the cats. They have some kind of poison." Lise tried to urge her upright but it was like moving a bag of cement.

Winnick raised a weak paw. "Lise, wait. Listen."

"Not now," Lise pressed, panting with fright. "We have to get Ton-e. And Prospero and Gray are just on the other side of those trees..."

A sharp set of claws clutched Lise's flank. The grasp was feeble but painful enough to get her attention.

"Wait!" charged the small weaver, her voice commanding if not strong. "I must tell you something first."

"Well, alright." Lise unhinged the needle claws from her

thigh. "But hurry. We don't have much time."

Winnick took a tortured gasp and forced her eyes open all the way. Lise could see it took every bit of her will to keep from succumbing again.

"It's the Shadow, the one from your dream, that is doing this," she began.

"I think so, too, but why? I don't get it."

Winnick lapsed momentarily, but Lise shook her hard. Again, the hazel eyes struggled open.

"The spirit of lethargy has become so widespread, it has taken a life of its own. Right now, it's enjoying its power, but it will lose that power if the Spark of the Human Spirit is restored—there will be no place for indolence in the new creative intelligent World we hope to generate. It knows it must stop us now, any way it can."

The weaver paused. Against all sense, Lise waited for her to resume.

"We were afraid of something like this," Winnick continued, "though until you began having the nightmares, we didn't know what form it would take. Now we see that the Shadow has chosen human emissaries to do its bidding."

"Duggan and the vigilantes."

"Yes. The Shadow—I dare not call it by name—has deceived them into thinking we are the fabled minions of Seh come to bring back evil so they would hate and fear us. They're not bad people, just misdirected. But we're in great peril. As long as the Shadow has the power to exploit its human army, to say nothing of casting its spells of inertia, no one is safe."

Winnick fell quiet, and Lise was afraid she had faded again when the weaver whispered, "Lise, you must go back. Back to the Alter-tier."

Lise was shocked. "I can't leave you here to die. And what about the others? The danger is here, now."

"The danger is everywhere, all times. You're our only hope."

"But I don't know how to go back. I couldn't even if I wanted to."

"You can," Winnick contradicted sternly. Slits of moss appeared between her kohl-lined lids. "You must. If you go back, you can change all this. We need you—our World needs for you and the doctor to complete the reconstruction. If you fail, it will all have been for naught..."

Her voice faltered and expired like the final note of a bird's evensong. Her head sank back, the third eyelid rolling white before the others had a chance to slip closed. In a painful revelation, Lise knew there was nothing more she could do.

Go back? she fretted as her gaze traced the lovely tabby lines of the sleeping weaver. Lise was alone and in danger, strung between two dimensions, fate hanging over her head. Strangely, she found the feeling familiar, like a stroll through a Hiroshima park when the bomb dropped on that historical day. She had been on an alternative plane of existence then, but the intensity would remain with her forever just the same.

Now she would face death again if she couldn't remember— and remember quickly—how to shift. Could she do it on her own as she had long ago? Winnick had sounded so sure, Lise must believe her.

She took a deep breath and was just about to close her eyes when a huge man came crashing through the bush. He lurched toward her, but before his searchlight could catch the blur of her motion, she scurried under a blackberry tangle. The thorns raked her fur, but she barely felt them. She was safe among the prickles; the man wouldn't follow. In her spiny bower, she began again.

Lise felt more than heard Winnick's terror. Her eyes burst open, already knowing what she would see within the bobbing blaze of light, the little weaver dangling helplessly from the man's mighty paw, screaming and twisting in his grasp.

"You're not going anywhere," he grumbled, bringing the gas gun to bear.

With a lightning movement, Winnick reached up and flayed the man's cheek in long parallel slashes of red. He bellowed and staggered backward, nearly dropping his charge. Lise's heart jumped. Maybe there was hope for Winnick yet!

Even as Lise braced to join the attack, it was too late. With a guttural oath, Winnick disappeared in a merciless cloud of poison gas. When the fog cleared, her body hung limp and lifeless.

Lise's heart was so filled with grief and hatred there was no room for fear. She erupted from her shelter and hurled herself on the man, dagger claws sinking to bone. He sent up a shriek, rough fingers prizing Lise's body to dislodge her clasp but she held tight. The gas gun tumbled to the ground where it lay flashing, at the ready.

Suddenly, Lise felt a vise clench on her back, and with a painful twist, a powerful hand wrenched her free. The man screamed a third time as she tore away skin where she detached. Tendering the new gouges, then pulling his bloody hands back when the contact with the raw muscle hurt all the more, he staggered and fell in a stupor next to the gun.

Lise writhed in the deadly clutch but the digits tightened. Up came the searchlight, bruising her eyes with its white-hot blaze. For a moment she froze, staring at her captor as he held her face to face. She was not surprised to see Duggan's hateful glare.

The two stayed like that for an indeterminable time, though in reality, it could have been measured in seconds. Then with one last full-body squirm, Lise broke free, dropped to the ground and bolted. With a curse, Duggan streamed his light across the forest floor, but she was gone.

Lise heard his roar of frustration as she secured herself once more in the safety of the briar thicket where she huddled behind a fallen log. Eyes like full moons, she watched the hunters' assault and tried to control her sobs.

Go back, Lise, came a voice in her head, this one sweet and clear, a balm for Lise's raw grief. *The way is set. This is my last wish.*

Lise no longer had a choice but to fulfill Winnick's plea.

• • •

Fixing her eyes shut tighter than ever, Lise concentrated as Prospero had instructed her. She made certain not to allow any superfluous thoughts to influence her shift—she had no desire to land in a chamber of itchy tortures again, and this time there was no one to pull her out if something went wrong. She visualized the scene on the Alter-tier: the rambling house; the rooms after rooms; the control chamber. And somewhere waiting for her, the only one who could help her now, Dr. Brin Templar.

Instantly, Lise began to feel the electric tinges of prescience that accompanied a space-shift. Then came the giddiness, only for an instant but enough to make her jerk her eyes wide.

At first, there was only blackness.

Then, the blackness coalesced, and she was staring up into the doctor's deep brown gaze.

12. Physics

"What happened?" Brin demanded as soon as he saw Lise was awake. "Are you alright?"

She was back on the floor of the control room, the doctor holding her gently in his arms. For a moment, she felt utterly content. Then, the contentment vanished in a burst of anxiety.

She struggled to sit up. Her head was fuzzy from the transition between realities, but one thing she remembered clearly.

"Sabotage!" she cried before collapsing back into his secure grasp.

His umber eyebrows curving into a frown. "Sabotage? Here?"

"Yes," she gasped. "Someone doesn't like us very much."

"The Shadow?" Brin was astute in his quick take of the situation, but then she expected nothing less from the canny scientist.

"The Shadow," she repeated, "and its disgusting gang of followers."

This time, Lise made it into a sitting position, her anger reviving her strength. "I was back in my body—my other body, the one I left in Central Lake Forest when we shifted—and Duggan and his people were there. They were the only ones conscious besides me. Everyone else had been put into some unnatural sleep."

"It can do that? I mean, manipulate people in the real world? I thought those things only happened on the Alter-tier."

"Who knows what it can do. It wants to stop the reconstruction—it's managed to make Duggan's bunch think we're the minions of Seh come to revive the evil of old. They're doing whatever it takes...

"Oh, no," she gulped and clutched Brin's arm as the details came crowding back to her. "They were making a sweep of the forest park trying to get us. They're gassing anything that looks even remotely feline."

"You mean, putting them to sleep?"

"No, poisoning them. Using fatal doses. It was terrible." Lise's eyes grew dark with pain. "Winnick!" she moaned in woe.

"They got Winnick?" he gulped.

Lise nodded. A tear on her cheek sparked blue in the console's cerulean glow. "But before...before it happened, Winnick told me if I came back here and we completed the project, everything would be set right. My God, I hope it's true!"

Brin stared at her, then he smiled. "That's quite a tale, Lise, but I'm afraid you must have been dreaming. You were out for less than a minute. I didn't even have time to go for aid—that's assuming there's anyone left awake in this place." He gave a skeptical look around.

"Everyone's still..." She turned to see Gray, Raphael, Prospero, and Ton-e right where she had left them, sleeping like worn-out kittens. Could it have all been a terrible dream?

With Brin's help, she pulled herself up off the floor and into a chair where she dropped heavily. For an instant, she felt clumsy and trapped in her human body, then it passed and along with it, all remnants of her fatigue.

Lise brushed the long hair out of her eyes as she studied her companion. His concern for her showed naked in his handsome, chiseled face, and his strong hand held hers like a lifeline. For an exquisite moment, her tensions ebbed in a tropical waterfall of emotion. She hadn't experienced such intimacy for decades, and found herself basking in it, wishing she could keep it with her, wrapped in velvet like a precious jewel, for the lonely hours to come.

It was not to be. A raucous burst, an alarm bell tore into her daydream with sharp staccato beeps. *No time for romance,* she chided herself as she returned her attention to the situation at hand. *Besides,* she thought sadly, *it's far too late for that.*

Brin spun back to the console and flicked a red toggle key on the central controls. The sound cut off, leaving a pulsing echo in its wake.

"A reminder warning," he explained. "We should be ready to begin the first phase soon."

Lise banished those last wispy reflections, both the gruesome horror of the parkland death sweep and the sweet longing for the young man who sat so nearby, and concentrated on the endless flow of glyphs that raced up and down the wall screen like pods on the Interchange. "How are you coming? I kind of lost track there at the last."

"I'm still working these commands. I'm running this thing blind, you know. I think I'm getting somewhere, but we're not going to be sure until it happens. Or doesn't happen, as the case may be." Brin shook his head. "I was doing fine until everybody began to go strange. I didn't know whether to help them or keep working—I was at a place where stopping meant I might lose everything I'd done. But then you passed out and there was no choice." He gave her an ardent look before turning back to the console. "Now I guess I'm a little behind."

"Why didn't you fall asleep like the rest of us?"

Brin shrugged. "Too obsessed to know when to quit?"

"Maybe so," she replied unconvinced.

"But this is it now," Brin continued, his eyes dancing with delight. "Well, here goes."

Lise contemplated the maze of flickering lights. "Can I help? I'm not a pro, but I can push buttons with the best of them."

"I'll take you up on that. Get on the other board." He signaled to the work station next to his. Instantly, she was there. "Now watch the screen for a series of prime numbers—you know what prime numbers are, don't you?"

"Yes, of course. The ones that can't be divided—like one and three and so on."

A smile played over the young doctor's sensual lips. "That's basically it, although these will be a bit larger. Anyway, I'll be here if you have any questions. When you see them, begin depressing the green bars on the board, one at a time. I'll be plugging in the directives. If I'm right, this should bring the tandem generator online."

Lise studied the board, located the green bars—now dark—then looked back at Brin. "What will that do?"

"The generator is the launch pad for the heavy ions, the first step toward recreating the conditions of our universe's birth. That's where the electrons are stripped from the atoms. For what we're doing, the electrons would only get in the way."

He stopped to type in a few more lines, then continued his science lesson. "Each ion contains quarks, one of the smallest subcomponents of matter we know of. These quarks are bound together by gluons. Quarks and gluons—the two prime ingredients for our proto-universe."

Lise nodded attentively though his tutorial wasn't doing much to improve her flimsy grasp of physics.

"We're going to shoot the ions into a huge ring where they'll spin in opposite directions until they reach near-light speed. This will hyperexcite the quarks. Then when we slam the rocketing ions together, the gluons will come unstuck. For an instant, the quarks can roam free. This quark-gluon plasma is as close as anyone's ever come to the type of matter that existed at the very onset of the Big Bang." Brin paused, suddenly noticing the bemused look on Lise's face. "The Big Bang was the outburst from which we believe the universe to have been born."

"I know that part—that's about the only part I do know, but I'm not the specialist—you are. The thing is, how does it translate into our element, the Wellspring of the Universe?"

"Some fifteen billion years ago when the cosmos was only a fraction of a second old," he began to explain, "this plasma-matter was everywhere, but almost immediately it went through a phase transition, condensing into protons and neutrons as they are today. The theory is that if we expand them back out again, we can recreate those primordial conditions. Ergo our proto-universe. At least, that's how it was supposed to work a hundred years ago," he said with a sigh.

Lise thought for a moment. "If we create a proto-universe, what happens to the universe we're in now?"

"Good question. The old experiments were on such an infinitesimal scale, the conditions lasting for such a short time, there was never any effect. But here on the Alter-tier... Well, isn't that the whole point—tweaking our universe a little?"

Lise shook her head. "I hope Raphael knows what he's doing. I remember people thinking this machine could tear space into subatomic shreds or create a black hole that would eat our planet."

"Strangelets," Brin replied thoughtfully. "Strange matter that can overload the nucleus of normal matter producing an infinite loop of destruction."

"Something like that. Could it happen?"

"Improbable. A strangelet with a positive charge would most likely transmute into a harmless isotope."

"Whatever an isotope is, I hope that's what happens."

Brin smiled. "It will be okay, I promise."

In the radiance of his certainty, Lise couldn't hold her doubts for long.

"This is all very interesting," Lise remarked, "But shouldn't we get on with it? I don't know what time it is in the real world, but I'm sure Culmination's ticking away."

"Ah, yes. I keep forgetting we have a deadline. As both a theoretical physicist and a very old man, I'm used to death being my only time restriction. Are you ready?" He looked at her, his excitement burning like a supernova.

"I think so." A jolt of adrenaline reminded her that she better not mess up. If she failed, the world would succumb to lethargy, and closer to her own heart, her friends back in Central Lake would remain dead forever.

"Go!" he announced with no such qualms.

Brin's hands flew over the controls, eyes flitting between the board and the wall. Lise stared at the screen and closed her mind to everything but the patterns of numerical flow. A stream of numbers insinuated itself overtop the ongoing rows of signs and symbols. It was hard to follow, but Lise didn't think these were the prime numbers she was watching for.

Suddenly, like a lull in a storm, Brin stopped, motionless and waiting. Lise paused as well. To her, it was like being balanced on the brink of the precipice, praying she could fly while dubiously anticipating the inevitable fall at the same time.

"Now—the bars!" Brin shouted. "Press them in sequence and hold them down a bit, just to make sure. We can't afford a mishap."

A row of zeros glided across her vision, mutating quickly into long numeric strings. Lise clamped her hand over the set of slim green rods and pushed in order. One by one, they disappeared into the console board. The prime numbers were multiplying until it took the whole display for a single figure. She was glad Brin had cued her; she would never have been able to follow these darting sums.

Brin's hands were idle now, knotted into white-knuckled fists. His eyes devoured every cypher. "Yes," he was saying, more to himself than to Lise. "Yes, that's it. Keep going. Okay—yes yes yes!"

He turned a radiant face to his companion. "Looks like we've done it. The generator's been engaged. According to my calculations, we have a few minutes before the next phase." He slumped in his chair and gave a great groan of relief. "We can relax a little while."

"Where is the machine?" Lise asked as she too sat back with relief.

"In this dimension—who knows? Is there even a 'where' to the Alter-tier?"

Lise chuckled. "Good point." She smiled, feeling for the first time since she began this strange journey that they were getting somewhere. She still hadn't found her element, the Heart of Humanity, but somehow, she wasn't as concerned as before. It was beginning to look like they would at least have two out of three. Maybe that would be enough. And she still might figure it out, somehow...

A concussive implosion banished her reflections, shaking the walls and crushing her eardrums. Both she and Brin whirled to see a roiling typhoon erupting in an arc of ultraviolet light, illuminating the windowless room in sharp purple detail.

That was fast, Lise thought to herself. Brin had given the impression there were still several steps to go before the proto-universe would emerge. A mote of doubt flashed through her mind. But if this were the Wellspring, what was it doing here?

Suddenly a huge man stumbled out from the twisting chaos. As the electric lightning-play fizzled back into semi-gloom, Lise saw to her horror this phenomenon had nothing at all to do with the Wellspring.

"What is this place?" demanded Duggan, his dark eyes wild with terror. He stared around the room until his confused gape settled on Lise. "You!" he swore. "You brought me here, you little..."

Diving for a fire quencher that hung on a nearby wall, he brandished the hefty cylinder like a club. "Don't come anywhere near me, demon or I'll brain you!"

Lise caught hint of despair in his cry. The big man was acting more like a trapped animal than the stolid leader she had confronted in the park. Suddenly, the pieces fell together. The panic, the desperation? This trip to the Alter-tier hadn't been Duggan's idea. He must think he'd been captured by Seh's minions, or worse—the beast itself. No wonder the poor man was afraid.

"Please try to be calm," Lise said as evenly as possible. "We're not demons—we're people, just like you."

"Yeah, and my mother's a clone," he spat back. "You're the one, alright. I recognize you from before." His glare deepened with bewilderment. "You look different, though. What'd you do, change your hair?"

Lise thought that an understatement, since the last time they met, she'd been covered with fur.

"Where's the rest of your devils?" he persisted, peering around fretfully. "Waiting to claw out my eyeballs as soon as I let down my guard?"

"No one's going to hurt you; I—" Lise began, but Duggan was deaf with fear. He lunged at her, holding the quencher tight and high, leaving no doubts about what he intended to do with it.

Lise froze as Duggan bore down fast. Her brain raced, but she couldn't move. From out of her web of terror came a mewling sound like a kitten in pain. *Someone help it, please!* she thought, then realized the sound was of her own making.

Duggan was almost upon her. Lise screwed her eyes shut and put up her arms, expecting the blow. She could have sworn she felt the heat of his breath; next would come the cold, hard edge of the quencher...

"Duggan Georgenson, is that you?" said a quiet voice from out of the dim.

For those last, long seconds, she'd forgotten she wasn't alone. "Brin!" she cried with relief. Her numbness gone, she wasted no time ducking behind a desk.

"Duggan Georgenson," Brin repeated. His tone was smooth and firm.

The big man stopped mid-stride and eyed him suspiciously. "Dr. Templar?" he murmured. The quencher dipped slightly as he peered at the young man, then it lowered, slowly but inevitably as a drawbridge coming to rest.

Brin rose and approached Duggan with self-assurance, as if they'd run into each other on the street. "Yes, it's me. Don't be afraid. This is my friend, Lise." He gestured to the apprehensive girl. "She's not going to do anything to you, Duggan, and I assure you, she's no more a demon than I am."

Duggan squeezed his eyes into suspicious slits, debating the new possibility that Dr. Templar might be a devil as well, then decided against it. A smile broke across his broad face, transforming the brawny features from a mask of evil to the visage of an ordinary man.

"Gosh, Doc, am I ever glad to see you. Where the hell am I anyway? I was...somewhere, outside—it's all kind of blurry now." He glanced around at the shaded walls, the shifting screens, and the blinking neon of the console. "But I know for a fact it wasn't here."

"Don't be scared. You're...someplace safe," Brin said, choosing not to explain the intricacies of the Alter-tier to this simple traveler.

"Okay, if you say so, Doc. I know I can trust you." Duggan gave a doubtful glance toward Lise. "But I'd still like to know what in blue blazes I'm doing here. This place is strange. I'm feeling kind of..."

Suddenly, the big man staggered, catching his balance only in time to keep from falling over.

"What was that?" he clamored, once again on guard.

Brin frowned. "I'm not sure. What did it feel like?"

"Like trying to stand up in a turbo-train when it switches tracks. Kind of dizzy-making."

"Here, sit down." Brin motioned to a wooden armchair next to the sleeping Prospero.

Duggan looked doubtful but acquiesced, tumbling into the sturdy chair like a toppling tree. Lise noted that he really didn't look well. Even in the reflected light, she could see how pale he was, like a giant ice-blue ghost. His eyelids were beginning to flutter and droop. Might his lethargy-inducing ally be turning against him?

"I gotta shut my eyes," he mumbled, slumping forward in the chair. "Just for a second, Doc..."

Brin moved close to him, helping him into a more comfortable position. "Go ahead and rest."

"Just for a second..." the big man repeated before his head fell back and his mouth opened into a quiet snore.

Brin turned astonished eyes to Lise as she cautiously emerged from her sanctuary, her gaze fixed on the recumbent giant.

When she was sure he was down for the count, she looked at the doctor. "Thanks. You were amazing. You have a way with crazy people."

"He's a neighbor. We're not exactly friends, but we know one another to speak."

"He recognized you in spite of your age-change."

Brin shrugged. "Who knows what he sees. He recognized you too, and your change is much more profound than mine. But how did he get here? I didn't think just anybody could do this...space-shifting. I know I could never have managed it without Raphael's help."

"Maybe you couldn't and maybe you could," Lise said cryptically. She was beginning to suspect there was more to Dr. Brin Templar than anyone, except possibly Raphael, had ever suspected. "But as for him," she nodded toward Duggan's slumbering form, "I wish I knew."

The two fell silent, listening to the soft sleeping noises of everyone else in the room—Ton-e, Raphael, Prospero, Graywood, and now, Duggan.

"What say we leave the mysteries to philosophers and dreamers and get back to work?"

Lise pulled herself around. *Work. Why not?* she thought. At least that way she could pretend for a while longer that things might still be alright in spite of the setbacks, the fighting, the deaths.

She was about to ask Brin what to do next when she caught the smell of dust and felt a corpse-cold presence at her back. Swinging around, she was confronted with absolute terror for a second time.

13. The Wellspring of the Universe

Something was happening to Duggan, something grotesque. His lips, nose, and eyes had begun to spew a foul dense smog. Opaque and dark as silt, the tendrils wormed into the air around his head like Medusa's snakes. What Lise could still see of his face behind the malignant curtain was contorted, muscles seized into a grimace of woe.

"Brin, look!" she cried.

The doctor turned and stared, riveted by the hideous transfiguration. "What is it?" he asked with shameless curiosity.

Lise shot him a harsh glance—this was no time to play scientist.

"Do you think we should do something?" he posed, pushing up from his chair and starting toward the afflicted man.

Lise grabbed his arm. "Don't touch it!"

"But maybe I can help..."

"You can't," she blurted.

"How do you know?"

She let go of him. "I just know, that's all."

Though conflicted, the doctor held back. The fog was curling closer to them, sending a cloying scent of musty filth into the air.

"We need to get away from here," Lise moaned. "Now!"

"No, we can't." Brin's eyes flashed from Duggan to the console. "If I disengage the generator, it will be too late to restart it again. Come on, Lise, we're on the Alter-tier, remember? It's probably not dangerous, just a metaphoric manifestation like everything else around here."

Lise stared at Duggan's thrashing body. "I don't think so. Not this time." She could sense malevolence in the noxious fog as it unfurled like an attacking squid. The fog was separate from the unfortunate man, with a life—and powers—of its own. "Brin, please," she whimpered. "We can't afford to take any chances."

She sprung from her chair and snatched up the vial that contained the Seed of Life, ready to run. Brin vacillated, torn between his important work and the serpent-tongue of unwholesomeness slithering toward him.

"Please!" Lise repeated. She grasped his hand and pulled as if he were a wayward child; like a wayward child, he held back.

"Wait," he exclaimed. "I have a thought"

Lise paused though she never took her eyes from the advancing haze. It was filling the room now, consuming everything it contacted with leaden nothingness.

"Hurry, Brin. It's almost upon us." Somehow, she knew that if that cold colorless effluvium touched even the smallest part of her, she would turn to stone, disappear, or something else as terribly final. She also knew that if she died on the Alter-tier, her body back home would die, as well.

"I have an idea," he reiterated, centering his attention on his work station. "And if I'm right..."

He was taking deep calm breaths and staring intently at the complex computers, totally disregarding the danger creeping up behind him. Lise could almost feel his mind reaching out, commanding...

With a burst of blue-green light, the array was gone—control panel, screens, everything. Lise blinked in surprise, gazing around her as if the massive mechanisms might have jumped to a different part of the room. Her scan came up empty. Everything to do with the Wellspring of the Universe had disappeared as suddenly and completely as a mirage.

She looked at Brin, trying to figure out what had just happened and found him smiling broadly. In his hand lay a small computer pad. He held it out to her, as proud as a boy with a pet rat. To her disbelief, there lay a tiny precisely detailed simulacrum of the control board, its diminutive screen flickering blue with all the appropriate glyphs and numbers.

"What did you do?"

"I'll tell you later." This time, it was the doctor who took her hand and began to retreat up the short staircase. She did not resist.

Giving one last glance at the fog that now filled half the room with its impenetrable void, she turned and raced ahead. The magic show she had just witnessed—and anything else, save running for their lives—would have to be put on hold.

• • •

Lise and Brin made a single-minded dash through three of the long, sequential rooms before slowing to a jog. As the pressure eased, Lise began to take note of her surroundings and the cathedral-like house that seemed to sprawl randomly and unendingly on. Each room was so unlike the next that every doorway could have been a portal to a different kingdom. The first few had been domestic: a small old-fashioned study; a salon, barren except for a steamer trunk covered with fine white dust; a depression-era kitchen with a green enamel gas stove and a white gate-leg table. The once-glossy wall paint was chipping away in deep lightning-bolt crevices, and the linoleum floor curled like cinnamon bark at its aged seams. Tattered gauze curtains billowed from the open window, but when Lise took a quick peek outside, she saw only a diffused brilliance, a shimmering imitation of sunlight, impressive but not quite real.

They came to the room where Lise and her friends had first landed, the one with the impressionist mural and that wonderful feeling of home. As they passed through, Lise tried to figure out what made this space so special. It was more than just the muted colors and the faded opulence. She wished she could linger, breathing the scented air, but that was impossible now.

After the pleasant room came a series of small offices, then a bedroom in the style of Louis XIV, then other compartments, both interesting and mundane. After a time, Lise lost track of how many or what they held. The variety no longer enthralled her as it had at first, becoming like trees along a freeway an inconsequential blur as she rushed toward somewhere else.

The persistent pace was wearing on her. She wasn't exactly tired—they had toned the jog down to a brisk walk—but being in a constant state of retreat made her feel like a mouse on a treadmill, going nowhere fast. Would the parade of vacant rooms go on forever? Or would she and Brin eventually come full circle and run smack-dab into the fog they were trying to escape? On the Alter-tier, who could tell? So far, they hadn't seen another soul.

Then, just when Lise was giving up all hope of the course ever ending, there they were. It was a lovely place, a bright terra cotta courtyard with a wide domed ceiling painted aquamarine. A water fountain trilled in the center and parrots flew through vines overhead, but for the first time since they had arrived at the strange long house, there were no double doors—no doors at all save for the one they had come through. This was the end of the line.

"Where to now?" Brin asked, pulling up short, the little computer pad still clutched tightly in his hand.

Lise stared around at the opulent greenery. Huge-leafed philodendrons adorned the ceiling; palms and ferns blanketed the lower walls. In one especially thick bower, the luxuriant fronds gave a slight flutter against the tile.

She pointed to the spot. "Look! Over there."

Brin paced to the cascade of ferns. Pushing the foliage aside, he ducked behind it and disappeared. Lise gave a start, then bending low, she followed him into blackness.

She found herself in a cramped hallway, dark except for the blue pulse of the Seed of Life and a far-away diamond of light which was presumably the other end. Brin was already making for it, feeling his way along damp plank-wood walls as she hurried to catch up. The ceiling hung claustrophobically low, only a few centimeters above their heads, but the tunnel was short. They soon reached the threshold and stepped into another world.

Lise stared with awe. They'd finally made it outside the strange house and onto a rooftop balcony overlooking a measureless valley of light. The softly-moving air was crisp and clear, and above them sailed a cloudless tempera-blue sky, but it was the valley itself that commanded every bit of her focus. Though Lise had glimpsed it through the window of the old kitchen, nothing could have prepared her for the awesome magnificence of the radiant canyon that stretched before her for as far as the eye could see.

"The Rift!" Lise whispered.

"The what?"

"The Rift. Prospero told me of it. It's where the dimensional planes intersect, whatever that means. He said I would know it when I saw it. And I do."

Brin gazed at the burning ether, enthralled by its luminosity. "It feels...powerful."

"Yes, I think so, too. Look at the Seed—how it flashes." For a moment, they watched the little ember zap and arc, reaching with blue-white charges toward the valley of light. "It's interacting with the Rift! Maybe we were meant to come here all along."

Brin surveyed the wide, even scenery, then shot a glance back the way they had come.

"Well, looks like we eluded our pursuer at least." He frowned, an expression Lise was beginning to recognize as intense cogitation. "A peculiar phenomenon, vapor exuding from the body like that. I wonder what could have caused it."

"I know what caused it," she told him firmly. "The Shadow,

In-Ars—the personification of lethargy itself."

"Personification?" he commented. "It wasn't altogether person-like—"

"But an entity, all the same. I could sense its presence. Couldn't you? It must have infected Duggan so it could manipulate him onto the Alter-tier. Maybe it couldn't get here by itself."

Brin said nothing. As a man of science, he had witnessed many phenomena both wondrous and strange, but never in his experience had he come across anything like Duggan's disuniting. Lise's explanation, though as good as any on the Alter-tier, had little basis in what he considered fact. Still, he trusted her; moreover, he knew she was right.

"It must have been controlling him for a long time, poor man," Lise said.

"He seemed to be coming around when I was talking to him," said Brin. "Back to himself."

"The Shadow must have decided he was of no further use and pulled out. None too gently," Lise added with a shudder. "Do you think he'll be alright?"

Brin shrugged strong shoulders. "You're the expert on the Alter-tier."

Lise hung her head. "Maybe I shouldn't have panicked like I did. Maybe we should have tried to help."

"We can go back," Brin posed, "but I think we're better off staying well away. I doubt there's anything we can do for him—this place has rules of its own. Hopefully, he'll wake up wherever he left his body and go off about his own business."

"Free of the Shadow."

Brin nodded. "Yes, free—a luxury we have not yet accomplished."

"Lethargy, apathy, sloth—who'd have thought such passive tendencies could do so much damage?" Lise mused.

"Nature favors situations which expend the least energy for the greatest return."

"But how could our society let it get so far out of hand?"

"It's a physical law," Brin shrugged.

"Well, that law's about to be broken," Lise avowed. "Once the Spark of the Human Spirit is restored, all that will change."

A troubled look came into her companion's eye.

"What is it?" she asked, then her face fell. "Oh."

Walking to the of the edge of the parapet, she gently set the Seed of Life on the wide stone rail where it flickered like blue fire. "It's not going to happen now, is it? We've only got the one element, and time's nearly up."

Brin's expression altered, his firm jaw setting in determination. "It'll never happen if we give up." Joining her at the rail, he seated himself cross-legged and stared intently at the tiny pad in his hand. "We may still have a chance, Lise. In theory, this little gizmo should do everything the console could. I'm going to start trying to kick in the accelerators."

Lise stood by him as he worked. She couldn't take her eyes off the intricate computer board, its maze of controls as complex and delicate as lace.

"Where did that come from, Brin?" she asked softly. "Did you make it?"

"My little experiment in thought projection on the Alter-tier?" He smiled and shook his head. "I would have to say yes, considering the results, but I really don't know." He stared out toward the mock-horizon, but his mind was back in the control room. "I remember thinking how regrettable it would be if we had to give up everything we've worked for. I was wishing I could just pick up the whole business and take it with me. Then all of a sudden— I can't explain it—I knew it could be done. Next thing, this pad was in my hand, poof! It has something to do with transmuting matter, but how it works is completely beyond my comprehension. I'm sure it requires the particular properties of this dimension. If this little thing functions like its counterpart, we have the Alter-tier to thank."

Lise thought of her last adventure on the Alter-tier. She too had found the ability to manipulate the world around her. It had come to her as naturally as it seemed to have come to Brin, although in her case, the needs were more basic. Shifting space and conjuring simple objects were parlor tricks compared with what the doctor had done.

She looked at this exceptional man. He was already back at work, operating the tiny keys with a diamond-point stylus. The odd honeyed light painted his tanned features with an ethereal glow. How beautiful he was in his intensity, Lise thought to herself—severe, and yet, altogether compelling.

For an instant, Lise thought of the young men she had known when she had bloomed with youth. It seemed like—and was—so long ago. At the time, she had thought it would last forever. It did not. Her looks faded with age. The young men grew old and died, leaving Lise alone for a very long time.

But here she was with something most people never get, a second chance. Maybe not for love—this was hardly the moment—but at least to feel her heart race, her throat tighten, her face color with the warmth of a blush. She allowed her fingers to run lightly through Brin's sandy hair. He glanced up at her and smiled before returning to his figures. His welcoming look filled her like luscious, liquid gold.

• • •

"Okay, I've got it!" Brin exclaimed with a decisive jab. "Don't lose hope yet."

Instantly, Lise's fantasies dissipated, replaced by real here-and-now elation. It was one thing to watch this incredible man and dream of what might be, but even better was the undeniable reality. He gazed at her with such joy that she found it easy to believe he felt the connection too. For a burning moment, it buzzed between them like an electric tide, then once again his eyes returned to his pursuit.

"Check this out," he said with the confidence of a child. The screen was flashing with colored numbers; Lise watched over his shoulder as they morphed through the spectrum like pulsing droplets of rainbow. She had no idea what they meant, but the inadvertent patterns were fascinating in themselves. She followed their ebb and flow like one hypnotized.

Suddenly, the screen went blank. "What happened?" Lise sputtered.

Brin was still smiling. "We should know in a minute, although I can't tell you how the results will manifest themselves on this plane." He set the pad down on the wall next to the Seed, its job finished for now.

Keeping an eye on its darkened face, his gaze swept the scape around them. He was looking for something, and Lise followed his expectant stare, but all she saw was the matte-blue sky and the one-dimensional brilliance of the Rift. If he was expecting a change, it wasn't happening. Even the slightest variance would have been notable, but the valley of light and the azure firmament lay like a twin-stripped ribbon from east to west and back again.

Suddenly, something flashed past, streaking like a comet, following the gradual contour of the Rift. It was so small and fast that at first Lise wondered if she had been seeing things, but when she turned to Brin, she knew the truth. He was sitting on the rail in mute ecstasy, looking as if he were about to cry with joy.

When the words finally came, they poured forth like a waterfall: I can't believe it! and Will you look at that! There was a lot of technical jargon about antiprotons, the heavy ion transfer line, and increased beam energies, but by far the most wonderful words to Lise's mind were the ones he spoke over and over like a mantra: We did it! We did it! It's a success!

Lise laughed with relief. "I take it everything's working correctly?"

Brin paused, regarding her with surprise, then he laughed, too. "I must sound like a crazy man— Yes! I believe it will work. The booster's come online, and what we're seeing—there it goes again!" he cried, pointing to the fleeting dot of light as it flew past. "What we just saw there has to be the ion beam. It's so beautiful. I had no idea what it would be like. In our world, this would all have occurred in the subterranean confines of the machine. The only thing we'd actually see would be a string of raw data on a computer screen."

Brin's elation was contagious, or maybe it was a side effect of the beam itself. The tiny golden shooting star—an iota of sunlight hurtling boldly through naked space—was like nothing Lise had ever seen before.

She watched the beam rocket by again. "This is good?"

"Oh, this is very good," Brin attested. "Very!"

"Now what happens?"

"When the beam reaches speed, it will split into two streams that will meet and collide. That should be the beginning of our proto-universe. My God, how do you think that will appear?"

Lise couldn't answer his question, nor did she even try. She had questions of her own. "Brin, how are we seeing this? I mean, aren't ions incredibly small? It seems like this should be impossible to detect with the human eye."

"It is." Brin smiled even wider. "But don't you get it? The whole thing's impossible, Lise. The literate cats, the Alter-tier, these fantastic new bodies." He looked down at himself and then at Lise with an intensity that made her flush. "Don't tell me you're beginning to lose faith now?"

Lise laughed at herself. He was right; this was no time for skepticism. Nothing about this experience could be found in a reference book.

The beam was moving at such a rate now that it had smoothed itself into a staccato dash and then an even thread of gold. Once again, Brin took up his pad.

"I have to bring the boosters online." He punched a rapid succession of glyphs with the stylus. "Now, we engage the linear accelerator, then the particle accelerator—this will get the beam up to relativistic speed, as close as we can come to the speed of light."

He was wrapped up in his project, energized and enthusiastic as a scholar, but Lise was no longer paying attention. Her sight took in only one thing—the tiny strand of lightning, so thin yet so bright it made her eyes water. Spun sunshine, it flared across her sight like a wire of forged flame. One thought reverberated through her mind: *We might just make it yet!*

With a staggering sense of loss, she wished Raphael, Graywood, and the others who had worked so hard to make this happen could witness its final success. As far as she knew, they were still trapped in that dark room with the perilous Shadow, or worse, entombed within their true bodies and like Winnick, ravaged in Central Lake Park. Raphael had made it clear that he would give his life for his cause, but Lise was certain that wouldn't be his first choice. And Graywood...little Graywood who had been the one bright sparkle in her old age—if any harm came to him...

Like a revelation, she remembered Winnick's last words: If you go back, you can change all this. Did that include the torture her friends might be enduring at that very moment? The death? She had to believe it did.

With conviction, Lise's resolve to triumph doubled. She turned to Brin. He was busy but still smiling. She took that as a good sign.

14. The New Bang

Before anything else, she smelled it, the dry stagnant odor of a long-closed room. It sucked the fresh air from around them, replacing it with the cloying stench of dust. In her excitement, she had forgotten their assailant, but with the persistence of a virus, the Shadow had not been so careless as to forget them.

Brin sensed it, too. "No!" he hissed. "Not yet! Not yet!"

The Shadow paid him no mind. A tentacle of darkness uncoiled through the small doorway. It paused as if seeking, then reached with greedy fingers to snatch Lise and Brin into its grasp.

Lise grabbed the precious Seed of Life. "Time to go," she hissed, pulling at Brin, her fearful grip claw-like.

"Not yet," he repeated, but this time he rose as he said it. He knew, as well as she did, they couldn't stay. If they were caught, all chance to complete the Wellspring of the Universe would be gone for good. Brin grimaced. Whether he liked it or not, they had to move.

While he put his computer pad on suspend, Lise cast about for an escape route. To her dismay, she didn't see one. The small balcony seemed to be floating on air, nothing above or below, and beyond, only the vastness of the Rift. It was either jump off the rail into mystery or go back the way they came, past the Shadow—or through it, since In-Ars's vaporous form had now completely filled the outlet.

The rail! The wide stone rail that ran along the edge of the balcony was broad enough to walk upon, and it looked as if it kept going past the high stone wall that marked the end of the parapet. Lise didn't like the feeling in her stomach as she hopped up and peered into the bright unknown, but the alternative was far worse.

"This way," she told Brin, and in spite of his protests, he followed.

In a few strides, they had skirted the corner of the balcony and were on the other side, staring across an expanse of sprawling rooftops, vast flat tracts of slate and tar that rose and dove like hills and valleys into the far distance. The roofs were dotted with chimneys and smokestacks, some spouting gray-white fumes, others abandoned for eons, crows and martins nesting in their crumbling bowls, but they barely noticed. Instead, they scanned the surreal landscape for something they understood, something they could use in their flight.

They continued along the precarious rail until they came to a set of ornate turrets where navigating the stony embellishments took all their attention. The last turret ended in a set of stone risers, each as large as a table—a staircase for giants, rising toward the sky like an Aztec temple. Uttering a quick prayer for her strong young body to hold out, Lise hefted her way up its chiseled slope. In her normal state, she would have dropped dead within the first few steps, but it was little more than an athletic challenge for her now. Even so, they could move only slowly. The Shadow, creeping after them like smoky death, was never far away.

Brin glanced at Lise as they scaled the angular hillside. "If I don't bring up the final transfer line," he said between huffs, "the beam will just keep circling till it dissipates. We've got to find a place to break, and soon."

Lise looked over her shoulder at the Shadow as it lazily, balefully dogged their every move. "You don't ask much, do you?" She felt a flash of anger, but it originated from fear and frustration. She knew he was right—the running had to stop.

They made it to the top of the pyramid where the four sides came together in a carpet-sized landing. Lise paused to take a breath and gauge where to go from there. Behind them the steps were already consumed in fog, but down the opposite side stretched a wide terrace, a bleak field of coal-black slate. Her hopes rose. On the level surface, they could put on some real distance. They might be able to ditch their stalker yet.

"Look, over there," she said, pointing across the plane.

Brin saw it immediately. In the distance, a colony of stone walls rose like huge geometric mountains, monoliths of zebra-striped granite stacked one upon the next like dominos. It looked to be a maze, difficult territory to navigate and notoriously easy to get lost in, but the only cover visible on the chess-board span. Lise and Brin nodded to each other and bounded toward it.

Once on the flat, they sprinted full-speed, their footsteps echoing like timpani on the slate parquet. They were making time, and miraculously In-Ars seemed to be lagging.

When they reached the entrance, the Shadow was nowhere in sight. Even so, they ran on, unmindful and uncaring of direction. A right turn here, two lefts there; they could never have kept track even if they'd wanted to. Always above them was the bright strip of azure sky. Nothing moved, nothing changed aside from their own interminable running.

Just when Lise thought they might be lost forever, they burst through a small cleft onto another balcony. Brin pulled Lise to a halt before she shot herself right over the edge. She crumpled to the ground, and he sank down beside her, breathing hard.

"Let's stop here. I need to start working on the final implementations. Shadow or no Shadow, if I don't do it now—"

"Go for it." Lise tucked the Seed of Life into a safe niche, and in spite of her fatigue, hefted herself to her feet.

Without waiting for further encouragement, Brin took out his pad and hunched over it protectively while he brought the computer out of suspend mode.

"I'll take watch," she said, assuming a place between Brin and the door. She had no idea what she would do if In-Ars did come. Its amorphous form was impossible to fight, but she shoved that part out of her mind. She had to protect her charges, the heavenly thread that wound around the horizon like a jet stream in full sun, and the man—so like a sun, himself—who was pulling the strings.

Secure for the moment, Lise began to take in her surroundings—the heavy stone balcony with its wide block rail, the sky, the Rift, the beam. It was an exact twin to the place they had left behind, and she wondered briefly if they had somehow retraced their steps without knowing it. But it made no difference. All that mattered was that they were there, and In-Ars was not.

Brin tapped away at his little machine like a honky-tonk piano, then every so often, he would glance expectantly at the transcendent beam. Lise followed his gaze, watching the sky until her eyes burned, but whatever was supposed to happen wasn't. At least, not yet.

Brin was becoming anxious; the glaze of perspiration that painted his face had nothing to do with the gauntlet they had just run. Finally, he gave a huge and mournful sigh. Tossing the pad down by the Seed, he stared off beyond the gold horizon.

"Can I help?" Lise asked.

For a moment, Brin was silent, then he looked up at her. "Where are you from, Lise?" he asked quietly.

This sudden personal question was the last thing she expected. If he'd told her the world was about to end, she would have been less surprised. But his interest was genuine if poorly timed—she could see it in his eyes.

"Laurelhurst," she answered finally. "It's north of Central Lake. I live in a studio domicile."

"Alone?"

"With my cat."

"Graywood?"

"Yes." She turned aside, her heart aching for her absent companion. How far away that life seemed right now. Would she ever live it again? If not for Graywood, would she want to?

Brin rose slowly, placing his strong hands on her shoulders. His grip was warm. He smelled of maleness and soap.

"I was wondering... Do you think I could see you when we get back?" His tone was soft, and if Lise didn't know she was talking to a man who had witnessed a century of life, she would say it was almost bashful. "Assuming we get back," he added, echoing Lise's own tremulous thoughts.

This touch of ordinariness in the face of their bizarre circumstances caught Lise off guard. Much to her horror, she began to giggle. Confused by her laughter, Brin pulled back. Like any man asking for a date, he hadn't known what to expect, but he certainly wasn't anticipating mirth.

"No, wait... I'm sorry," Lise tittered, unable to control herself and embarrassed by it. "It's just that... Well, this isn't the real me, what you see in front of you, I mean. If we got together back home... If you saw me as I really am...you might not be so keen." She looked him square in his deep brown eyes, her laughter draining. "I'm old, Brin," she said bluntly. "I'm older, as you are."

"I know that," he countered. "You were a young woman when the Reawakening began. I can do the math." He skewered her with a somber gaze. "As you noted, I'm not exactly a spring chicken myself."

Lise was kicking herself. Here was the first man to notice her in decades, and she had shrugged him off. What was worse, she had done it rudely. But the most devastating part was the simple fact that she had wanted so desperately to say yes. And now, it was too late.

She looked up at him. "I've been ungracious. Please accept my apology."

"And I was being presumptuous. To expect an exceptional

person such as yourself to indulge a dull old scientist..."

"Oh, no. That's not it at all," she quickly contradicted. "It's just been so long since an attractive gentleman has expressed any interest besides pity or revulsion. Well, I guess I couldn't believe you were serious."

His eyes lit. "You think I'm attractive? Now, there's a concept. But you've had the dubious privilege of seeing me in my old skin. I don't cut such a dashing figure in my PMT suit."

She smiled. "That's not true. I thought you were quite debonair."

"Yes, a veritable Cary Grant," he said with congenial sarcasm.

"Now who's being cynical?"

He took a deep breath and gave a quick glance at the beam, but it remained as static as a photograph. "Let's start over, all cynicism aside."

He took her hand, gently, hesitantly, as if for the first time. "I'd like to see you again, Lise," he began, "whether this hand be smooth or wrinkled and arthritic."

To her surprise, he bent and softly kissed her cheek. "Whether this face be flushed with youth or lined with age."

He let his fingers play through her fine red tresses, an action that sent sparks down her spine. "Whether these locks be full and luxuriant or white and thin as angel hair. Those things mean nothing to me. Beauty is transitory and extremely superficial. You are better than that. Young or old..." He smiled slyly. "Or a completely different species—you, Lise, are someone I have come to love."

For a moment, he held her gaze, then he gave an abrupt laugh, defusing the intensity. "I rather liked you as a cat. Very sweet, though I'm sure your claws were as sharp as any."

With that, she laughed, too. Taking a brazen chance, she stepped into his arms and was instantly caught up in his circle of warmth.

All things came in circles, she reflected: the circle of the earth;

of the seasons; of life itself. The circle of a solar system as it spread from its central star. The circle of the beam as it girded the Rift. Circle upon circle, she suddenly saw them all, superimposed one upon the other. And spun within their matrix, inexorably tied with everything, were wild bright circles of yellow, green, and blue—cats' eyes.

Eyes, beams, solar systems—they were all related, bound together in space, time, and love. And she was an integral part of it—not just now as she languished in the circle of this man's steadfast arms, but forever, even when she was alone.

With a flash of awareness, a thought hit her. "The Heart of Humanity! Could it be something as simple as love?"

Brin stepped back a little to look at her. His sharp mind was already working on the possibilities. "Love? Maybe so. If I had to choose one thing that humans do well when they have a mind to, it would be love." He pondered for a moment. "Do you suppose we—our feelings for each other—could be part of the element you're seeking?"

"I'm not sure." Lise frowned and fidgeted. "It makes sense..." Her frown set harder. "But Prospero said I would know, and I don't. It's not like it was with the Rift. I recognized the Rift immediately, but this is different. I'm sorry."

"That's okay. There's still time. Trust yourself—I do."

She gazed into his eyes, calm pools of burnished walnut, and hoped he was right.

All of a sudden, the screech of an alarm broke through the serenity. Lise tensed and Brin jumped for the pad, his charged fingers already grasping the stylus and punching out commands.

Pointing toward the Rift, he cried, "Look, there it goes. The beam is splitting!"

Lise followed his stare and saw that the golden thread was changing, evolving. Refracted light crackled in all directions, shooting out paper-thin shafts so brilliant she could barely look at them. With colors that transcended the spectrum, the line was dividing in opposing directions, throwing out a red so deep it was barely visible and an ultraviolet so bright as to be near-white. As these vivid filaments resonated across the dimensions, there was no mistaking the power they held. The Rift dulled to a coal-orange glow, and the matte-blue sky turned black in the presence of such luminous radiance.

"It's almost time," Brin told Lise. He was euphoric, but Lise was concerned. If all went as planned, the Wellspring was about to manifest itself. Then it would be time to join the newborn proto-universe with the other elements.

A physics experiment, some sludge in a jar, and an emotion—if in fact the Heart did turn out to be human love. It seemed an impossible task.

"Brin, I..." Lise began but stopped mid-word, her misgivings forgotten as fear clenched her to its airless bosom. Once more she smelled the stink of long-dead dust. When she looked around, darkness was stealing up on them like a tide of murk. This time, there was no place to go.

"Oh, no," she whispered.

Brin dropped the pad and jumped to her side, but she waved him back. "No," she hissed. "Finish your work. We're so close, you can't stop now. Maybe I can distract it."

Brin vacilated, then gave in. "If you can hold it off for just another few seconds," he said, vaulting for the discarded pad. "But don't take any chances. Without you, there's no point in going on."

Lise wasn't so sure that was actually true, however she had no desire to tangle with the life-sucking mist of lethargy if she could avoid it. She remembered all too well the mindless stupor it had imposed on her before, an apathy so profound it hurt. In spite of herself, she whispered, "Hurry!"

The Shadow was spreading into a seething blanket of gloom. It threatened from all sides now, looming above her and coiling around her, the blue-gray color of carcinogenic smoke. It was closing in, trapping her in its lethal cocoon. Soon there would be nothing she could do to save either of them.

Hurry! Another instant and it would be too late.

Lise felt a wind at her back. Warm and steady, it blew past her, hitting the Shadow square on. At first, the two factors reacted like oil and water—and like oil, dark and tenacious, the menace twined ever-nearer—but the balance was quick to shift. The current was intensifying, and the vaporous foe had to struggle against it. In another instant, the wind prevailed, and the Shadow was thrown back upon itself like seaweed caught in a tide.

Lise stood in awe as her nemesis began to discorporate right in front of her eyes. The foul fog was growing wispy at the edges, the groping tendrils fragmenting into shoals of tiny streamers. In a piteous show of force, the Shadow flailed them impotently in the air. Hot as a sirocco, the wind blew harder, but Lise barely noticed. For some reason, the blast didn't affect her as it did In-Ars. While she stood unflustered, the baleful vapor was being viciously shredded, ripped asunder like mist in a hurricane. Before she knew it, all that remained of the menacing cloud were a few innocuous puffs of silt and dust.

With a soundless scream, the last noxious wisps discorporated. For a moment, Lise was pummeled by an overpowering lassitude—the deep unwholesome lethargy that the Shadow innately spawned—but even as it threatened to drag her into its nothingness, the feeling lifted. All lingering skank was being flushed away by a clean pure breeze, redolent with a scent she had not savored for far too long—lily of the valley.

In a matter of moments, In-Ars, lethargy made manifest, had been stripped of the very embodiment that lent it its power. The Shadow was purged, resolved back to its essence, a human condition, no more effective or dangerous than any other state of mind.

It had happened so fast Lise couldn't believe it, but when she turned into the wind, she was faced with another surprise. There, suspended above the Rift were her companions, Raphael, Graywood, Winnick, Prospero—even Ton-e. Restored to their original cat-forms, yet not, they hovered on soft furry wings. It was the beating of those wings that had caused the air movement, though how the delicate appendages could have conjured up that tempest, Lise couldn't know. She didn't care. She was just happy to see her friends.

"Raphael! Gray!" she said, starting toward them, but at her first step, the figures began to waver like a mirage on a desert highway. With mournful fascination, she watched them fade, becoming translucent and then crystalline. In a chance blink, they disappeared completely, and the air was still, though the sweet scent of lily of the valley lingered on.

"Wait," she called softly and without any real hope of being heard. They had done their job and she was safe. Saddened but safe.

Lise walked over to Brin and touched his shoulder. "The Shadow is gone."

"Thank you," he said distractedly. "I'm glad you got it to go away." He hadn't noticed the winged cats, his whole attention fixated on the Rift and the red and purple streamers soaring there. "Your timing's perfect—the ion beams are about to collide. Now we'll see if we've actually created a proto-universe."

Rising to his feet, he gave Lise an earnest look. "Shall we go?"

Boldly, almost nonchalantly, he hopped up onto the wall, ready to accept whatever was about to happen. Lise seized the Seed of Life and climbed up beside him, her heart racing. Instinctively, they took each other's hands.

The ribbons were beginning to hum in synchronic vibration. The low drone mounted until it became the harmonic resonation of every note on the scale, an avalanche of sound that pressed in and in, until Lise thought her eardrums would explode.

Then silence.

All stop.
Everything.
Even time itself.

• • •

No longer ribbons but two tiny cusps of fire, the ions moved inevitably toward each other. Lise's rational mind knew they were traveling at thousands of kilometers per second as they closed, but somehow, she could see them as clearly as waves nearing shore. The nuclei had flattened into slim disks from the force of acceleration. The air began to tingle. Green sparks flashed as they approached the convergence. Then in a blast of energy and light, they were one.

A million points of frozen flame hailed from the collision zone in a shower of brilliance. Stretching toward infinity, the ions blew apart, and swirling out of the darkness from the central core, a tiny universe burst into existence.

Lise looked at Brin, and he at her. The Rift had vanished, and the matte-black sky had become the living onyx of space with the pinpoint motes reaching out to embrace the heavens. All sign of their previous environment—the balcony, In-Ars and the winged cats, even the Alter-tier, itself—had been erased. They were alone in the newborn place.

Lise felt Brin's muscles tense, readying for the final leap.

"No," she said, holding him back. "I know now—It isn't us. It's me. I am the Heart of Humanity."

"Are you certain?" he said doubtfully. "If the element is love, then shouldn't we both go? I'm not afraid," he furthered, brave but unconvincing.

"I'm certain," was all Lise said.

"But what am I supposed to do?" choked the young-old man. As terrified as he was of diving into the newly created cosmos, he far more feared being left alone.

"You've done your part," said Lise, her tone weighty as the

gold ions that had created the New Bang. "If the reconstruction succeeds, humanity will have back its lost spark, and you will return to a better world, just as I did one hundred years ago. It really is a wonderful feeling," she added kindly. "Like being an emissary. You will see the changes, remember how it was, and always know—even if no one else does—that you had a hand in the making."

"But what about you?" he asked softly, as if his voice might break with grief.

"I'll take the Seed of Life into the proto-universe. That is my destiny. Strange as it may sound, I think I've known it all my life."

He turned away. "Which is a polite way of telling me you won't be coming back."

Lise hesitated. "Not as I am now, no." A part of her could feel his pain; another part, a more primal part, felt only exaltation. That part was already gone. "Who can say?" she put out with gentle finality. "Energy goes on forever—as a scientist, you must know that."

"I don't want you to go," he said, his hand still gripping hers.

"I'll be with you in our New World. I promise."

Tenderly, she disentangled her fingers and lightly touched his face. Then, before anything else could be said that might make parting more painful, she clenched the vial with the bright blue ember and stepped off the ledge into eternity.

• • •

Inside the aura of the expanding universe, the precious Seed pulsed like a living sapphire, the promise of skies and seas, and somewhere, a beautiful blue-green planet filled with a diversity of life.

Within the throbbing blueness, Lise's face glowed red as blood. Her crimson hair fanned out like a nebula into the farthest expanses of space. Where the fiery strands met the cerulean bolts, the two combined, twining into a radiant double-helix: infinite possibilities, infinite potential.

Lise smiled one last time, then her features dissolved, leaving in their place only the glow of cosmic dust.

From the dust, stars began to form.

15. The Road Ahead

A soft rain fell, washing away the last grit of summer, teasing the grass to grow green again and the autumn crocus to bud up from the ground in lavender splendor. A fan of geese glided across the silver sky, their far-off cacophony a testament to the advance of the season. Dr. Brin Templar sat on his front porch and contemplated this cycle, a sequence so integral to the process of the earth that there could be no life without it.

Life is so fragile, yet so strong, he mused. *Life will out, and what's more, it will strive to improve.* The desire for betterment was built into the genome. Survival of the fittest, humankind's ever-questioning mind, all forged on the incredible instinct to thrive.

Brin thought humankind might finally be moving in that direction. It had been six years since the restoration of the Spark of the Human Spirit, and the difference was outstanding. Retaining the positive qualities they had cultivated since their passage from Seh's evil, the human species had now added curiosity, creativity, and inventiveness to their shining list of attributes. The Reconstruction Project had worked. The inspirational property that had been lost a century ago had resurged like never before.

Will there be future developments? he wondered. *And what bizarre circumstance will bring on the next leap forward?* He wished he could even imagine.

During his Tri-Night adventure with the cats, he had learned there was more to evolution than a fish growing legs. Something had aided that fish. Whether cosmic synchronicity, the intelligence of another species, or an influence from beyond human comprehension, one thing was certain: guiding hands were hard at work.

Brin had been a part of a new beginning, an instrument in a plan he had not yet begun to fathom but had sworn to unravel even if it took him the rest of his life. So far, he had made no real progress toward explaining the Alter-tier, space-shifting, or why a particular time of summer gives all living things the power to become more than they are, but he wasn't discouraged. He knew his experience had been real. All he had to do now was prove it.

"Dr. Templar," came a shout from the walkway, breaking into his deliberations and making him sit up in his chair. He peered at the figure standing there, pausing a few milliseconds while his visual accentuators digitally recreated the face in a form that his brain could recognize. Once the familiar features of his student, Juno, came online, he smiled.

"Come in, my dear," he said, his vocal chip making it possible for his ancient tones to be heard all the way to the gate.

"Thanks, Doc." The young woman approached the steps but stopped there, looking up at the doctor. She wondered, as she always did, what kept the old man alive. He was well over one hundred, and every centimeter of his original body either replaced or enhanced with a jumble of bio-aides. Yet, his face underneath the wrinkles was kind and bright, and his deep brown eyes sparkled with the vital promise that the world was a most wonderful place.

He was also the smartest and most well-versed person she had ever met. Nothing seemed to faze him. He took it all in stride, as if he had seen what lies beyond these mortal coils and did not fear it.

The two stared at each other, comfortable in their passing thoughts, then Brin finally said, "As much as I love your quiet company, I expect you're here for a reason."

That was just like him, Juno thought. He always seemed to

know her mind. "It's about the science club meeting next Tuesday. Are you going to be able to lecture?"

"Of course, I will. All those young unsullied minds? Like virgin processors, just waiting for a few definitive programs to be downloaded. How could I say no?"

"Great! Thanks, Doc." She grinned. "Then, can you give me a hint as to your topic? I'd like to put it in the news-brief if you don't mind. It always draws more people when they know what it's going to be about."

"I hadn't quite decided. I'm vacillating between 'Felines: Another sentient species?' and 'Reinventing the universe: it can be done.' Which do you think?"

Juno raised a dark eyebrow. "They both sound intriguing, Dr. Templar, but I'm partial to cats. I believe beyond all doubt that my cat knows everything I'm thinking, sometimes before I know it myself."

Brin laughed. "And don't forget their ability to put their own thoughts into your head at will."

"Yeah, like 'feed me!'"

"That and other things. 'Let's play' was a favorite of my Ti. Sometimes when I'd think about tending the garden, I'd notice Ti staring at that little place just above and between my eyes. She knew that if I gardened, I'd wave a branch for her to chase." He shook his head. "I was merely a pawn to her many whims."

"That's real!" Juno exclaimed with a knowing smile.

There was a soft thump, a whisper of displaced air as a sleek shape appeared on the newel post beside them. Whether telepathically called or just a coincidence, the cat sat licking a velvet paw.

"Graywood," said the doctor lovingly. He gathered the cat in his arms, PMT boosters allowing him to lower the heavy animal into his lap without snapping a bone or pulling a muscle. Graywood circled and settled. With a cat-sigh, he closed his eyes, enjoying the comfort of the man's gentle hand along his spine.

"That's a beautiful one," said Juno.

"Yes, he is, isn't he? His person is also quite lovely."

"You mean he's not yours? He looks so at home with you."

"I guess he's with me now, since my Ti crossed Beyond."

Juno gave a funny look at the doctor's choice of language, but even though the phraseology was unusual, the meaning was clear. She waited, but Brin chose to skip the subject of his departed companion.

"Graywood's cohabitor is a dear woman from Laurelhurst Community," he said instead. "We met...traveling."

"Where is she? What happened to her?"

Brin paused. His gaze slipped out past the girl, past the tree-lined street, past the clouded sky to things that could not be seen. "She's gone, too, I'm afraid."

"I'm sorry."

"It was her destiny. I only wish she could have known what a wondrous world she helped create."

Juno scrunched her sable brows into a frown. "I don't understand, Dr. Templar."

Brin looked at her. The clear green eyes, the long red hair reminded him...but he could never tell her that. No, he had said too much already. To Juno, the world had always been filled with artists and authors, scientists and scholars. For her, growing up meant choosing the thing she loved best and reveling in it. She would never have to know how to live without her dreams or the way it had been when the only purpose to life was one's own superficial comfort.

"I'm rambling," Brin apologized, returning his attention to the cat in his lap. He caressed the velvet fur, smoothing a spike on the storm-gray flank. "He seems to be growing his winter coat."

"Yeah, my Juliana's doing the same thing. She's got a whole new layer of wool underneath her long fur. That means we're going to have a cold winter this year."

Brin smiled. "Does it? I must add that to my sentient feline lecture: their uncanny ability to physically predict the weather."

"That's real!" Juno declared again. "Well, I have to go now. But I'll see you Tuesday." She turned and strode across the flagstones. Off to her next important task, Brin assumed. Everything was so exquisitely dire at that age.

Brin petted Graywood, glad of his comfort and company. The day was turning dark in spite of the early hour. Brin reminded himself he'd better get used to it. Summer had passed, and soon, autumn would be gone, as well. Then night would fall in the middle of the afternoon and remain until mid-morning.

On the breeze floated the musical strains of the Central Park Choir. They were doing some new works by an up-and-coming composer whose pieces suggested a Mozart-Zappa fusion. Brin could not help thinking that this simple pleasure wouldn't exist without the Spark of the Human Spirit. In the days before its restoration, one would have been lucky to hear Mozart or Zappa, even played off a wire.

But things were different now. There was music in the streets and art—murals, paintings, sculptures—everywhere one looked. A huge section of the community had been converted into a learning center and people from other communities came to pursue their interests, bringing with them the knowledge of their own home places.

Even Brin at his advanced age had prospered from the change. He was finally free to teach—and learn—his scientific studies, not only physics, but biology, chemistry, the historical sciences. His heart could finally sing with the joy of knowing.

Yes, all in all, he felt extremely lucky to have experienced the transformation. Most people never caught on; they just evolved with the coming of new ways. He alone knew the truth, the reality, and the sacrifices.

He thought of Lise, as always. Even though they had known each other only a short time, he missed her as if she were a limb blown from his body. He also felt a heated pride in her bravery.

Mostly he just felt right. It had been her destiny, as she said. Sometimes he wished he'd gone with her—but then there would be no one left to remember.

Graywood nestled in Brin's lap and looked up at the old man with his glass-green gaze.

"You remember her, too, don't you?" Brin said to the cat.

Graywood's eyes squeezed shut for a poignant moment, then the two sat in silence.

"Dr. Templar?" came a voice from the walkway.

Brin looked up. It was another of his students, come to ask him some all-important question. Inwardly, he smiled and thanked Lise one more time for the exciting world she had helped into existence.

• • •

Graywood caught the shimmer of cats in the trees, their individual scents letting him know their names. Salazar; Euphrates; Simeon. He heard their breath rise and fall. He caught their whispers. Their season had drawn to a close.

Soon would come winter, a time to linger in half-comatose repose until the soft scratchings of springtime brought them to their senses again.

Then, like the reincarnated, Caffre's sons and daughters would awaken and rise, stretch and yawn, blink eyes of green and gold and blue. They would step into the weak milky sunshine again to taste the call of summer.

The Author

Native Oregonian Mollie Hunt has always had an affinity for cats, so it was a short step for her to become a cat writer. Mollie is the author of THE CRAZY CAT LADY COZY MYSTERY SERIES, featuring Portlander Lynley Cannon, a sixty-something cat shelter volunteer who finds more trouble than a cat in catnip. The 3rd in the series, CAT'S PAW, was a finalist for the 2016 *Mystery & Mayhem Book Award*, and the 5th, CAT CAFÉ, won the *World's Best Cat Litter-ary Award* in 2019. Mollie also published a non-cat mystery, PLACID RIVER RUNS DEEP, which delves into murder, obsession, and the challenge of chronic illness in bucolic southwest Washington. Two of her short cat stories have been published in anthologies, one of which, THE DREAM SPINNER, won the prestigious *CWA Muse Medallion*. She has a little book of Cat Poems as well.

Mollie is a member of the Oregon Writers' Colony, Sisters in Crime, Willamette Writers, the Cat Writers' Association, and NIWA. She lives in Portland, Oregon with her husband and a varying number of cats. Like Lynley, she is a grateful shelter volunteer.

From magic to murder, from felines to faeries, the authors of **NINE DEADLY LIVES** spin thirteen tales featuring those sometimes aloof and occasionally dangerous but always adorable creatures we know and love as cats! Whether it's mystery, fantasy, historical, or romance, these cat tales provide plenty of entertainment and thrills!

Made in the USA
Columbia, SC
07 September 2019